MANACONDA

SOLDIER'S DIARY OF LIBIDINOUS MISSIONS

M.D. FENN

Order this book online at www.trafford.com
or email orders@trafford.com

Most Trafford titles are also available at major online book retailers.

All Characters are 18 and above.

Print information available on the last page.

ISBN: 978-1-4907-6145-9 (sc)
ISBN: 978-1-4907-6147-3 (hc)
ISBN: 978-1-4907-6146-6 (e)

Library of Congress Control Number: 2015909699

Trafford rev. 06/29/2015

PUBLISHING® www.trafford.com
North America & international
toll-free: 1 888 232 4444 (USA & Canada)
fax: 812 355 4082

CONTENTS

This book is dedicated, most wholeheartedly, to the myriad of Black men who have taken on the task of raising "one of their own" who are not biologically one of their own. Little is said and praised about the Brothers who have swallowed that task. If not for the Black men who have accepted the offspring of some other "baby daddy" into his bosom as his own, more hell would have broken loose in the Black community. Because of slavery, it's in your blood yet I thank you for my children's sakes. I love you Man!

VARIOUS VERNACULAR VARIATIONS AND INTERPRETATIONS

ah - a / are a / will / of

ain't cha - aren't you

ain't nah - aren't you

beddah - better

befoe - before

be lee - believe

bigga - bigger

bouff - both

'bout - about

burf troll- birth control

buss - bust

cah - car

cep - except

chullun - children

com' meer - come here

com' moan - come on

comp knee - company/guests

coss - cost

curr - care

dah - the

firss - first

flo - floor

'foe - for / before

geh - give

ghen - again

goh - going to

gotta - have to

haddah - had to

haf tah - have to

he ah - here

high - how

hiss - his

ho - female

huh - what?

huh(s) - her(s)

I ah - I'll

ig'nant - ignorant

I'mma - I am / I will

in - and

neh vah - never

nigh - now

nunna - none of

nuttin - nothing

outta - out of

ovah - over

'pose - suppose

prob lee - probably

rubbah - rubber

seent - seen / saw

sho - sure

skead - scared

stow - store

swole - swollen

tah - to

toll - toldruss - trust

truss - trust

try(in') - test / confront

dan/den - than / then
dare - there / their
dat - that
dees - these
dem - them / those
dey - they / their / they're
dey ah - they're
doe -door

eh vah - ever
et - ate

fah - for

fay vah - favor
fee - feel
figgah - figure
fine - find
firss - first
fittin' - getting ready
'foe - fore / for

juss - just

kant - can't
kin - can
kinda - kind of

lass - last
lease - least
lee - leave
leff - left
look did - looked

lotta - a lot of

'member - remember
mo' - more
mouff - mouth
muss - must
mustah - must have

uh huh - yes
undah - under

wanna - want to
ware - wear
whey - where
whey - where
why - while
witch - which
won
drin - wondering
wont - want / wasn't
would
nah - wouldn't

yah - you
yella - light skinned
yestiddy - yesterday
yo' - your
yo's - your's

CHAPTER 1

NAUGHTY BY NATURE

GONE WITH THE WIND

IT WAS LIKE a jail break. A bunch of us Army recruits were let loose after weeks without pussy, on a payday. After a bus ride from Fort Knox into Louisville, I crossed paths with two girls at some obscure night club. My first time off base, first time without the supervision needed for any teenager, my first libidinous mission evolved as two females rocked my carnal world.

The light-skinned one, Ruby, was not the type a coochee connoisseur would call eye candy. She had small breasts and just a noticeable bump of firm, high-sitting hips that reminded me of a bubble on postal wrap. She had tee-tee boodee. The thing that most grabbed my eye was her stance and gait in heels.

When Ruby strutted or danced her legs were spread as if somebody was fisting her. That boodee bustled under her skirt, like her pussy was primed for prickly punishment. Gapped thin thighs made it appear as if this ho was inviting dick. It made me take notice but I expected crossing that line would require begging. I wont about that, at first. Still wanting to touch whatever I could, I went over there to do the "bump" with her.

Her friend, Francis, was big-boned and I wondered how she got all that black in back stacked in her slacks. "Dey call me "Bay-bay," she told me. It was easy to mistake her cushion for curves. Her breasts were full, thighs thick, and shelfed-ass appealing. Although robust in the midsection she didn't appear to be that stank, sweaty kind of BBW. Her arms were perfectly rounded for a hug after a hurt and when she grabbed me to "slow drag" I found her ass soft.

Both girls were running game on me and being naturally inquisitive and aggressively horny I was in play. No doubt, they came as a pair, I noticed, because when I bought one a drink I had to buy for the other. Entertaining them both, needless to say, was emptying my pockets. Mama's advice was in my ear and I tried to get away but they double-teamed me with "eyes." Ruby asked me if I had enough money for a motel room.

I hadn't pounded a pussy, it seemed, since Prohibition. When "Slim" used the words "money" and "room," I interpreted the words as "pussy" and "nutt." Secure with a round- trip Trailways bus ticket back to Knox, I said, "Yeah, let's get a room."

In hindsight, it seemed those females may have worked this type of arrangement before. Once we were in the motel room they went into the bathroom to talk, like those treasonous Republicans did on Obama's first inauguration to plan how to "Just Say No!"

Slim came out ordering me around. I figured we'd get it on while big gurl stayed in the bathroom and listened. That made me more excited. I always had to sneak to get a piece. Now, somebody was going to be listening to me fuck.

My first libidinous mission order was to assume an inferior position. That went against General Patton's tactics but pussy, I figured, needed to be conquered. "Git necked in lay down," I was told. I followed that cunt's commands like the lead canine of an Iditarod sled hearing the word "mush."

Usually, mutual hand jobs were how hoes and I got started but once we were both "necked" Slim invaded my space like The White Man colonizing Africa. She swung a leg across my chest, putting her butt in my face. Between her legs was scary hairy and stopped directly in front of my nose. We had a family dog, not a cat, and I wasn't sure whether I was allergic to feline fur. This sexual formation, I learned, was called the 69. Like the Army, it was new to me but from my parents and education I had been conditioned to learn first and later challenge or accept.

I thought Slim was going to sit on my dick. Conformity would have been made easier if she had done that. She failed to slide her hips towards my waist and I thought to myself, "This girl still got her ass in my face." As Ruby brandished her butt my hands naturally went up to block her hips from getting too close. This wasn't the way I learned to fuck so I spoke up. "What are you...?" Slim cut me off. "Hush," she said. That "Hush" sounded, to a dogg like me, an order like "mush" so I did as she demanded.

I was 18 years old; young, dumb, and full of cum; a thousand of miles from home; in an unfamiliar land with two hoes; and about to receive a porno lesson from horny, uncertified teachers. I supported public education and felt fortunate to get any type of scholarship. I decided to go with the flow.

Ruby began a personal relationship with my rod. Several times, as my jacked dick got larger, she would say, "Jesus" or "Lord have mercy." When the penis was completely stretched out, she whispered, "Naw, fuck naw. Dis muthafucka too big." She had told me to "hush" so I kept quiet. As my attention returned to keeping her ass away from my face, the red bone measured my member via her hands climbing my dick. I was flabbergasted.

Slim yanked my yoke with her left hand, underhanded, like she was restricting a puppy from running into the street. Being right-handed myself I defined her left paw as perpetrating on my pulsating penis. She worked angles of stroke that my individual adolescent efforts had never achieved.

Ruby's southpaw grip did it for me. A left-handed ho was Superman's kryptonite. The iron flag just below my pelvis was stiff, signaling danger like a polecat's tail or a snake's rattle. My dick was filled like a frank and I was on a ball-busting bluff of a sexual apex of potential energy, like a bicycle pedal nearing its optimum position of "Go!"

I was "shocked!, shocked!" when Ruby used her jaws as pliers and pulled my penis with her mouth. My dick head was wrapped in warm and wet in something that grabbed. Her mouth became a competitor to pussy. The fact that this ho not only put her mouth on my dick but was sucking it blew my mind. I looked around the corner of her hips to make sure what I was feeling was what I was seeing. She looked like a chicken pecking at feed. My mission objective to stab Ruby's cunt with my cock became secondary.

As I was looking at her coochee it manifested itself like a visitor from outer space with parallel lips. I recognized it's propensity to pervert my mind and that made it distressful for a sexual retard. The alien was covered sparsely with hair which concealed any earthly vaginal features

I had seen in men's magazines. I wasn't sure if it would bite, growl, or engulf. Had it spoken and said, "I mean you no harm" or "I cum in peace" or "Boo!" I believe I would have run up outta there. In the night's light, that thing looked like a giant caterpillar from some "B" movie.

There was apprehension towards making contact with the alien yet I didn't want to act like a punk, as if I had never seen a movie monster before. I squeezed Ruby's ass, with a cheek in each hand, as protection against any possible alien sneak attack.

Slim was a pro in my book, especially in the way she mashed my balls without hurting them. She handled my heredity holders like she was fondling favorable dice. She manipulated mouth on my dick head like a SSBBW breaching a box of bon bons. It didn't occur to me that she expected me to take on the commensurate task of pleasing her punanny with the same vigor with my mouth, at first. Cunnilingus curiosity was building however. I scooted further under her ass to get more dick into the entrance of her throat and Ruby's pussy split. It made a unique unwrapping sound like the cover being taken off something new.

That prompted an investigation and I snorted that rascal. It was unlike anything I had smelled before and my taste buds reacted with salivation. Immediately, Slim leaned back and absolutely, positively pushed her pussy onto my mouth. No doubt about it, that ho intended to initiate me into commonality.

Upon the alien's contact with my mouth, somehow the first thing I thought about was my homeboys. Darville would have straight-out chastised me for "eatin' at the Y." George would have shaken his head in disbelief, even if I reported it was only a rumor that I sampled "camel toe soup." Rudy would have asked, "What it taste like?" and followed with his family's giggle. If Drew found out, I was convinced he would never hang out with me anymore.

My final thought was that I was in Kentucky and not Florida. I convinced myself no other Black man would know what I had allowed on my lips. My buddies would stay in the dark and I'd never see this girl again. Anonymity made me hypocritical.

The coochee's approach and aim was pre-conceived and taken as a desire. I loved the thought that it, she, or whatever you might call her pussy craved my mouth. I basically knew what I was supposed to do involved my tongue and lips. This would be easy, I thought. I would just pretend I was in a Fourth of July pie-eating contest.

I had to be prodded by my sense of smell to do "it" - a psychological saving grace. It's human to yield to temptation and I wanted to reciprocate Ruby's "generosity." That's why I mashed my mouth on her muffin.

All my senses lit up like Star Trek sensors. The alien mutated, right on my mouth, while its covering brushed my teeth. The coochee had the flesh consistency of meat with an aroma of protein-laden heat and sugary sauce. As I continued to lick and probe with my tongue the pussy seemed like a perpetual snack, like having my cake and eating it too. As Ruby's vagina vacillated the square footage of my face hints of piss, poot, and perspiration progressed into a taste of honey. Sweetness washed all over my tongue.

When you take on an unfamiliar function, it takes practice to become good at it. I was prepared. Basic training had brainwashed me to become the best at being belittled.

I surmised I would need much practice at cunnilingus after, to me, Ruby seemed dissatisfied with my effort. She raked her cunt from my nose to my chin, like her groin was a groundskeeper and my face was a pitcher's mound. I have no doubt she was wiping her ass hole across my mouth. Every time I see a dog dragging its butt on a carpet, it reminds me of what she did.

The pressure she wiped with seemed punishment for pubescent performance. I decided then and there to be the best cunnilinguser on the planet, so I wouldn't get hurt.

Slim wallowed her coochee on my nose and lips, forcing me into cunnilingus even though force was not necessary. She ground that thing against my grill like they do corn to make grits. That's what made me boost her butt away. I flipped her over to remove her pooter and pu-nanny to give my gums grace. I told that ho, "Slow down."

I put her on her back and began to instigate my own method of cunnilingus. The tingles on my tongue allowed me to distinguish various parts of her cunt's anatomy. I found in her bush an entourage of items - like that button at the top of her cunt. I learned it was the coochee's communicator. I kissed that curator although I was being coerced to conform. It must have known I was a novice.

Ruby, however, was relentless in requiring my face during her pleasure. After more kisses, licks, and tongue tickles she pressed more. I licked that pussy like a lion lapping at a waterhole without sympathy for that which moaned during its beforehand banquet. It was something my ancestors could to relate to and I was glad to make that connection.

Like the areas in Africa called The Great Rift Valley, The Sahel, and The Rain Forest, I realized Slim's coochee geography also required mapping. Certain areas were soft, pliable, sensitive, as well as resilient. Others had a more functional disposition.

In the military when you're given a mission you're expected to get the job done.

That's why I licked, kissed, sucked, and folded her cunt lips in my mouth greedily. As my facial facilitators worked as a team, I revisited Pavlov's study of involuntary reflexes. I better understood why bees do what they do and why General Sherman was so destructive. At one point I put my entire mouth over the entire pussy and sucked it. I sucked it like something I was more familiar with eating, like a ripe mango. When I did that, Slim quietly said, "Hmmm!"

Follow-up moves made her respond also. I would end an oral vacuum by flicking the tip of my elongated licker carefully against her clit. I pushed every inch of my tongue into pure, unadulterated pussy to capture every drop of the juice that covered my flavor sensor.

Sometimes I had my mouth closed and tongue protruding like I was blowing bubble gum and other times I ate her pu-nanny like it was a stack of potato pancakes and I was Irish.

Whenever I drilled my tongue she would say, "Shit!" or "Woo!" or "Oooh!" or "Woo, shit" or "Oooh, shit!" or "Shit, shit!" and push more pu-nanny into prominence. When I put my nose into the coochee and shook my head like I was saying "Oh, No!" Slim would tactfully moan, "Oh, yes!" After I removed my drilled nose from her cunt she growled, "Do dat ghen!," in a forceful manner. I did.

Slim succumbed yet I wanted confirmation from her that I was doing "it" right. I removed my mouth to speak and caught her at a heightened moment of passion. All of a sudden that ho slammed my head between her legs and screamed, "Eat dah pussy nigga!"

For a split second I was confused because I thought name-calling ended with the Civil Rights Bill of 1965. Being called a "nigga" sounded like a bad thing. According to a thesaurus it meant I was "threatening." I wondered, what had I done wrong?

I, however, didn't have time to size-up her speculation of me. I was too busy following her latest order. With my face deep in cunt again the other girl came out of the bathroom.

I had forgotten about her and didn't want a Black woman to see me, a Black man, chomping on clam chowder. Slim held my face against her cunt, nuttin' big time. By the time Bay-bay made it over to the bed I was only interested in trying to breathe. After grunting like a child at the end of a whipping, Ruby finally released me.

My muff diving was now public. There was now a second witness in my imagined Colored People's Court, "Brothers Do It Too" case, charging me with Caucasian-American cultural conformity, like wearing weave.

Not unlike child support court, I could expect an adversary judge. Possibly a female judge who likened me to her baby's daddy who had favored a hoodrat over her and now "don't play." Or, maybe, a White male judge whose daughter went Black and couldn't go back. Then, maybe, a judge who had a golfing appointment and "didn't want to hear it."

Judge Hatchett (with a rat-tooth stare): "You know you ate the pussy, admit it. Your shameful look here in court makes it obvious. Circumstantial evidence says your tongue was deep in the coochee. Was it? According to her testimony, you victimized her vagina when you put the entire muffin in your mouth, hogged the honey oozing out of it, and stopped when she was about to bust a nutt. Did that occur? According to your defense, you didn't know it was a crime to come off a cunt when it's about to bust a nutt. Is that true? Carnal ignorance is no excuse." (TV commercial).

Judge Hatchett (with a look of disgust): "No doubt you also slobbered on her boodee hole. That's freaky by itself. No doubt she face-sat on yo' nasty ass. You probably liked that, huh? How a ho supposed to react with your tongue languishing on her labia and your nose nuzzling against her anus? Speak up! Answer me!" (TV commercial).

Judge Hatchett (with dampened panties): "Before I make a decision I need more direct evidence. Court is adjourned for a half-hour. Bailiff, I need the defendant in my quarters NOW! Cuff him! He better not put his hands on me."

After such direct interrogation from that supreme, no man would be able to overturn a cunnilingus conviction. I could expect an added charge of contempt had I not allowed that judge to sit on my face until she nutted and was lapped clean. Hoes in the audience would rush home to their ol' man to have him do what I had "allegedly" done.

Based on a Constitution written by condoning if not actual rapists, overwhelming circumstantial evidence, credible eye witnesses, and a licked litmus I would have been convicted of conducting cunnilingus. My muff diving was impossible to cover up.

Something else I was somehow aware of were the people in the next motel room. They must have heard someone scream, "Eat dah pussy nigga!" They probably would peer through their curtains the next morning to see the "nigga" who was ordered to "Eat dah pussy." The following morning was the only time in my life I wanted to be Caucasian. I could only perjure myself by mimicking the Apostle Peter by saying, "It wasn't me Lord" and decided when and if I ever reached a bridge to admission I wouldn't reply.

Like I said, after the other girl came out of the bathroom I was forced to re-evaluate where I was and what I was doing. This evaluation happened in a matter of seconds because this soldier had LSD (long, stiff dick) to deliver.

My dick now had a "take charge" attitude. It, he, or whatever you might call my penis was throbbing. I wasn't familiar with lick-in-stick back then but my totem had tolerated being teased and was becoming impatient.

As big gurl peeled clothes off, Slim was at the end of the bed squatting and wiping pure pussy like she had just gotten out of a shower. She took noticed of my dick flopping from my knees to my navel and grabbed the hardened heathen. My body was forced to follow the direction of her pull to where my feet landed on the floor. That's where Slim kneeled and put my bulging banger back into her mouth.

Meanwhile, Francis slung a relatively huge thigh across my chest as she maneuvered into the 69 position over me. She put my upper body in lock-down with her thighs and ass but I managed to keep my arms free. Her boodee, a bodacious burro with an impressive broadway, looked the size of New York. I was bedazzled by her cheek buildings checkering a creased avenue the color of a Fifth Avenue candy bar.

Bay-bay put me in a pliant predicament which challenged my physical freedom but not my mental manhood. A Black female's ass in my face somehow seemed like home.

As opposed to Slim, there was no such thing as handfuls of ass. Baby gurl had a bountiful backside. I formed a natural inclination, need, and desire to hug that boodee. I did. I hugged that huge hunk of dark chocolate with my shoulders, biceps, triceps, forearms, and wrists. I hugged that lovely ass like a man consoles a baby mama after the "break-up to make-up" because he had been caught cheating. I did a sit-up and clutched Bay-bay's behind like it was the trophy won for a NBA Championship.

It was right there, at that point, I ascertained that the rear of a woman; where my sexual salaciousness, cultural conditioning, social substance, and hereditary harkening; was my most favored habitat. I had much fun pulling apart that big bale of boodee then letting it clap back together. I found dark-skinned women had it going on. To my personal pleasurable disgust, slavery had done some good.

While I was admiring big gurl's ass, both hoes were orally entertaining my dick as if they were competing to see which would get my rifle's ammunition down-range first.

"Look high long dis muthafucka is," Slim told her pseudo-conformity co-conspirator.

"Yeah, and it big too," Francis replied, "Let me git some of dat."

I wanted to watch the porno show going on between my legs but I also wanted to continue marveling at that bullion of butt in my face. That big, black ass was blocking my view of their sport but I could tell which ho was doing what and when. Slim was slick when she sucked the dick like my penis was a Chico stick. Big gurl would snatch the prick prize from Slim and suck the dick dastardly like it was Denzel's and she wanted him to leave his wife.

Like lionesses playing with a tortoise, I was in their control. They had occupational charge of me because of my socio-medical condition of "horniness for hope." The "White Man's" social, capitalistic, and religious lessons had taught me to expect rewards via an "investment return." It was ingrained so I acted accordingly.

In my mind I wasn't being weak, as a preacher might proscribe. I felt I was doing what I was doing because my ancestral guidance counselor had either been a confused Christian, immoderate Islamist, nasty Nazi, narrow-minded Napoleon, or a dick like Cheney; each of which wanted to fuck somebody.

Slim pulled seniority and just took over handling the dick. I hated that because the way Bay-bay lathered her tongue over my dick head made her fellatio feel more freaky.

Like a dictator, Slim would take the dick from Bay-bay for long stretches of time, refusing to let big gurl intercede. Bay-bay was remanded to sliding her big ass closer to my face because she didn't have anything else to do. It forced me into what politicians define as bloc intervention.

The only definitive "vice" in my life which has prevented me from becoming President of the United States has been lust. Until Francis put her bare big ass in my face I believed it to only be "The White Man." Bay-bay's boodee directed me, due to I believe reincarnation rationale, not to choose public office, a 401k, and a mortgage.

It's not Bay-bay's fault I chose private sex over public service. For example, she didn't know I was Pulitzer Prize caliber. She unknowingly used her tools for me to collect the text needed to gain accolades for literary brilliance. Like any ho, she was just trying to get hers.

Bay-bay's butt set a standard where I would never introduce a White girl to my mama.

Voluptuous dark hips that move culturally accordingly is the advantage real Sisters carry.

Her dark-skinned mass in my face was reflecting perfectly off the faint light peering through the curtains. With ass galore gleaming, I finally understood why only a few bodacious big butt Black females ascended to the tinted glass ceiling. Brothers have something for that before those hoes can even begin to dream.

I could have stayed with the enjoyment of mashing Bay-bay's dark chocolate in my hands while Ruby ravaged my rod. Or, I could have moved big gurl's backstop and watch Slim's head prompting a protein paroxysm. My next move was decided for me when big gurl "backed that thang up" and plastered her boodee onto my brim.

That Sister's butt concreted the thought that I, a Black man, had two enemies, therefore little control, by boldly sitting on my face's forward features. Bay-bay's boodee squirmed down my forehead, flopped over my face, and comfortably curbed itself on my mugg like I was a love seat. It was like I was scuba diving with an empty tank at The Great Barrier Reef, surrounded by spectacle while in procedure of passing.

A BBW sitting on your face is akin to being in Heaven with Lucifer at the gate. It is the ultimate position of Black female power; exciting to confirm my death was up to a higher power. Her move explained what a Black mom meant when she would say, "I brought you here and I'll ah take you out." Fortunately, when her ass hole planted itself on my nose I naturally recognized the need to relieve pressure on my lungs. Dying happy was one thing; dying was another.

At the same time Slim had me ready to "buss" a nutt. I split big gurl's ass cheeks apart, so I could inhale enough air to shoot off. When I did that, Francis farted.

It was more like a poot but what's the difference? Flowering funk and self-esteem, in that order, gave me reasons to push her rude ass away. No, no I didn't push her all the way off. Like polishing my boots everyday I had learned to live with scuff marks. I moved her just enough where oxygen was more abundant than methane.

"'Cuse me," she said, before both of them giggled and Slim said, "You so nasty."

Bay-bay responded by saying, "It a accident. I couldn't help it."

The fart; the gas; the audacity of what occurred overwhelmed me. I may have been suffering from the effects of being vaporized when I interpreted the fart sexually. In other words, I got "wind" of her ass hole's effort to get my attention.

The poot sounded informal idioms I interpreted as speech. It was as if all Black women had branded the message "It's all about me!" in my face. The audacity of the experience was how both girls put together a pleasant conversation about the fart. The gas, as breathtaking as it was, spoke for itself.

The moment that fat-ass girl farted on and in my face I became a freak. I'm positive, that's when it happened. It wasn't that I was in bed with two women that made me odd. It wasn't that I slobbered on some pussy that made me anew. It was that a Black female farted in my face and I liked it. It advanced my attitude and permissiveness about sex.

What could be a more self-realizing event than being "happy" about a Black mama farting on your face? I handled the funky flatulence like I did my military training - in stride. I realized a woman's ass hole, like a ho saying "No!", was an imminent threat that had to be dealt with one way or another. In other words, I needed to get accustomed to it.

I also recognized, like a sniper in a crow's nest, an ass hole can't be ignored.

Having a coochee and anus in close proximity, like a rapper and a red neck, may be conducive to harmony but that combination can combust into a broadside bomb.

I re-evaluated my libidinous missions planning and developed a philosophy for further inquiry, methodology for handling unexpected actions, as well as gained an understanding for the probability of misfires which, I had heard, occurred with the M-16 rifle during firefights in Vietnam. In other words, I realized habits offer recognized differences. That fart did "all dat."

I tried to reason why Bay-bay's ass hole waved wind my way. Why me? Why now? The glass half-filled optimist in me didn't believe that ho intend to fart. So, I took the "error" like a poor infielder who the ball somehow finds.

The Narcissus part of me accepted the poot profoundly. I felt I needed to thank that starburst for the "enlightenment" it shone. To me, it was like buying a ticket to a Cubs game. I deserved experiencing mediocrity if I showcased being a fan.

A turd-cutter should only be on the rim of sexual activity but Bay-bay's butt broadcast itself as being in the realm of reality TV. There are people who consider the anus as a missing link during sex or, at least, an exciting deviation. Being a future author, amateur sociologist, and now freak - that intrigued me. All of a sudden, both girls' poot shooters were viable victims for libidinous vigilance.

Because it spoke-up, Bay-bay's boodee hole became of special interest. It became a lobbyist pandering to a politician. It was a heralded rookie ball player, still trying to justify draft position or make the team. Understanding all that, I pulled big gurl's hips towards me as though they held Chaka Khan's bowel button. I gave the boodee hole a kiss. A loud purr from Bay-bay allowed me to imagine it was Chaka saying, "Ummum!"

Hearing big gurl's approval of what I had done, Slim doubled her effort sucking the dick. She worked like it was the last bone of a rib sandwich and she was still hungry. I simply thought her renewed effort was the result of her trying to make up for the rude, slightly stink interruption by her friend. Nothing about this night was easy to understand.

Slim was doing good work. Inciting a riot wasn't her thing. Instead, she would pull her head off my penis like a pro football lineman on the edge during a sweep. That ho allowed the strain of my dick's deliberation whether to nutt into her mouth get to a certain point then block its relief.

Ruby announced to the world I was enjoying her pro tongue. "Skeet comin' out!" she said excitedly, as if universal healthcare had been passed in 1972. "Let me see," Bay-bay replied. That's when I lost the awesome comfort of big gurl's butt blanketing me into delirium.

I could only squeeze Bay-bay's big, black ass while both women orally mauled my manhood like skeet was a natural resource. Slim would stroke her hand underneath ponderous prick launching cum gum drops the size of OPEC oil barrels. Big gurl would occasionally jump-line to snatch any new dew. It was competitive. Those hoes used a technique whereby Ruby gnawed on the length of my dick while Francis frenched my exposed knob.

My skeet sleet must have gushed because Ruby snapped at Francis. "Stop!" she ordered. "You gonna make him shoot off." Again, I got the feeling they had done this type of thing before. Upon Slim's latest command both girls, like the "Do Nothing Congress" definitely during Obama's first term in office, stopped or slowed performing their public services. My prick's nonpartisan practice of civility was perturbed. My boner bowed.

At that moment I wondered whether the rules of United Nations applied. After all, I was a soldier trying to correct a "cruel" world. Torture, pure and simple torture; that's what it was like. I now know why targets of drones don't condone contrived cadaverous bird droppings.

Both hoes headed towards the bathroom. "Where ya'll going?" I asked. Ruby claimed they needed to "wipe." Wipe what, I wondered; nothing had been spilled.

There I was lying in agony, my dick uncomfortable; its autonomy abandoned. I didn't know how to console it, him, or whatever it might be called. I grabbed it, him, or whatever with a familiar hand but my touch wasn't what it, him, or whatever wanted. For the first time in my life I considered that maybe my dick had mind of its own. I was either being led by ancestral guidance and/or was a cohort of meaningless copulation.

A person has to be careful in a motel room with stranger entities scheming in the bathroom. I wasn't worried about them robbing me. All I came with was LSD and copious cum and was more than willing to relinquish both.

The intermission I used to play detective and went to listen. "Hiss dick too big," Slim said before Bay-bay added, "Yeah, and it long, too. Dat nigga kin shoot pool wit' dat dick." After both laughed, Bay-bay told Slim, "You ain't gotta fuck 'em. I ah geh him some pussy. Why I eat you, I ah let him fuck me from dah back."

No doubt, their plan was to interpret, for me, what our fucking would include.

Scheming war mongers manage mediation meticulously and manipulate the masses with menacing mayhem. Their "secret" talk ended as they turned off the utilities. My dick weighed like a filled holster and my penis was peaked like Pike as I tip-toed away.

Ruby ordered me off the bed. I followed direction immediately because now I wanted to fuck her and her reluctance. Once on my feet, the mast of my wand stretched far and beyond, pointing East towards The Mother Continent with my dick head dancing.

Slim said, "Damn, dis nigga dick still hard," and then laid down and opened her legs. I moved to fuck her in the missionary position. That's when big gurl dropped her head on Ruby's pussy like it was an anchor. She hit that pond of pussy without any hesitation. All I could see was the redbone's pubic hair and Bay-bay sliding her mugg against the coochee, licking up and down that cat. Slim was watching Bay-bay and moaning loudly.

It hurt my heart to see another woman muff diving into my "office pool" like she was raiding my business, my pet project. I should have expected competition. They were both looking serious too. Slim seemed happy with Bay-bay's browser as she scrolled her mouth like a mouse arrow, invading Ruby's laptop with hacker techniques and versatility.

As for me, I hurt. My dick was kicking like Karate and stretching like Yoga as it and I witnessed, for the first time, same-sex stuff. Francis was eating Slim's pussy like she was trying to convert a convent. I felt like a free-lance journalist whose excellent editorial had been bombed by a believable blogger.

That's when I got manly, as if I was in charge. I spread Bay-bay's big ol' thighs and scouted for the portal point between her legs. Big gurl "backed that thang up," but refused to stop doing lesbian. In-turn, Slim was pulled further down the bed. Directing my sexual chauffeur, I probed Bay-bay's cunt hood to get a better idea where to install my life line. I eased my dick past the guardians of her gold into her fat pussy.

Big gurl's coochee taxied my dick. It was grabby like Uber, insisting it was best. I tried to get deeper but her boodee bordered beyond my lap. All that ass, I knew it would be difficult not to bust a nutt and had to be careful because I really wanted to cream Ruby's cat with my loin lion.

I learned, again, that a dick, sometimes, is its own being. When it gets it's own ideas a dick owner has to be as "hard headed" as the dick to control it. That's "hard."

Fortunately those girls taught me about control as they tag teamed my penis. Although it felt good humping Bay-bay's bulk of badonkadonk, it came down to which had more control, me or my dick. I held the opinion that Slim had nutt-taking responsibility for purposely pointing pussy prominently at my prestige.

My dick was so ready to bust a nutt I had to shift carefully. Holding back from nuttin' was accomplished by downshifting my strokes from fourth to second gear. I experimented with which types of thrusts were best to reduce tension while simultaneously watching Bay-bay's big, black boodee bounce whenever I expanded her gut. Also to keep from prematurely causing a testicle earthquake, I completely pulled out from time to time.

During one moment of impending quake, I exited her equator and two or three eccentric eruptions of skeet sailed to the floor. I had to flip the script or I would tsunami in this ho. So, without provocation I got on my knees, split Bay-bay's ass cheeks, and volunteered to eat some pussy.

After watching Francis perform on Slim, I realized I had been callow in my oral consumption of coochee earlier. I was determined to do better. I ran my nose down the crack of Bay-bay's butt like a roach scooting across a kitchen counter. As I surfed her backside web face-first I didn't expect the pop-up advertisement of her ass hole. I admit that I sniffed at the manhole cover of her bowels then tasted it for a morsel of who knows what. Tangy; that's what I tasted; tangy.

Another poot from the mysterious perforation between her beach ball-sized hips was desired. I craved audible feedback more loudmouthed than it gave earlier but not enough where it talked shit. Leveraging with my thumbs to expose her alimentary canal, I divided her backside like I would a peeled grapefruit. I was like a mariner in the doldrums looking for a breakwind.

As a part of my effort to get her ass hole to make a noise, I googled the boodee hole with my tongue and licked her anus. That wasn't enough to induce any audible tropical breeze. I gently kissed it over and over. The boodee hole still didn't make a sound. I picked a finger and used it to slightly enter its dark side, thinking a massage would prompt a response. Again, there was no answer.

I thought maybe it needed to clear its throat so I vacuumed the air out of that slot. Sure enough, that produced a somewhat strange response.

The ass hole sounded one syllable, like it said, "Breeze!" with emphasis on the "b" and the "z". I may have been the only one who heard the "silent but deadly" muff puff because neither girl said anything.

Getting a response from her poot poodle was like finding the perfect puppy at the pound. Now it was my pet. I kissed it like it was mines. I let it lay on the lap of my lips while I braced for another flattery of flatulence. I licked it wet; real wet.

I wanted my congress of sexual sidekicks - my mouth, tongue, and nose to continue attending to the boodee hole. My carnal gang leader, the dick, desired diving into her ass.

After a democratic decision to go oral, my rod ran radical like an extremist evangelical. It ignored a supreme court's vote that was supposed to prove some sort of "dominance domain," while referencing its Second Amendment right to screw the closest threat to historical order.

Nature took over. At that moment, my dick preferred Bacall over Bogart; Hepburn over Tracey; Lucy over Ricky; and Rogers rather than Astaire. My dick hurt in a revengeful manner just to get its way. It hurt; it hurt bad.

It was the next move that confirmed my dick was possibly partisan. I learned I had a dick capable of malevolence. I was young and had yet to realize my standard could be a palpable porno player. It, he, or whatever you call it wanted to fondle my freakiness by attacking Bay-bay's boodee hole.

My dick was determined to inflict collateral damage by going towards a previously non-expected foe, like Republicans did the Black man who became President. My hard- own, base solely on revenge, headed for Bay-bay's anus. My penis wanted to ransack that rim. Come to find out, making babies was only a by-product of my dick's diligence, not its due.

I had to therefore give my dick - it, he, or whatever you call it - a name. "Henry" is best thing I could come up with at the time. "Kunta Kinte" was already taken. Because of its point-area of responsibility, I gave my dick head the name of "Skeeter." "Fiddler" would have been too 18th and 19th Century.

Being wet from my slobbering and lax from vacuum therapy, Bay-bay's ass cavern reluctantly accepted, I could feel, half of Skeeter. Henry wanted to show who was first to get into her planet and moved forcefully to do so. Unhesitant to unfasten, at first, her anus slowly but surely opened. Unfortunately, the boodee hole was willing but Bay-bay wasn't.

Big gurl reached back, yanked Skeeter out, and put Henry into the pussy.

Slim must have been ready to bust a nutt because she wiggled away from Bay-bay's head. There I was righteously stroking pussy when big gurl began moving forward away from my loin stiletto because Slim was scooting away from her. Bay-bay was committed to clawing to have her countenance remain connected to the red bone's retreating cunt.

After a couple of times loudly slapping her thighs against big gurl's ears, Slim sounded like a runaway slave seeing the North Star after clouds cleared. "Lawd, Lawd, Oh, Jesus!" she hollered. Her quick, hard slaps of thighs on big gurl's ears signaled Slim was busting a nutt.

After a final visible tremble Ruby got up and Francis followed, causing me to lose my coupling. Slim stumbled to sit at the end of the bed in front of me and Henry. She slowly began licking and slurping the liberal lay of lubrication on him. Not to be left out, big gurl massaged my balls and braced Henry for Slim by holding him at his base.

Henry had robust rigidity when Slim turned, got on her knees with elbows on the bed, and stuck her hips up in the air. Her ass swung back and forth like waves at the beach.

"Git it like dis," she told me. I directed the dick head to do just that but Henry jumped on the redbone's boodee hole. Dammit if Bay-bay didn't yank away and insert my dick into Slim's cunt. Automatically, Henry started plowing her strawberry field like a skilled sharecropper in Slovenia.

I took an oath to serve the citizens of the United States. I took that oath very seriously. After many weeks of military physical conditioning I was duty bound and prepared to lay pipe in that ho. I drilled down directly and that pussy couldn't help but stretch.

Slim began having second thoughts. "Oooh, shit!" she repeatedly exclaimed. "Hiss dick too big! Hiss dick too big!" She moved away like a person who had just seen a shark in the water. While Slim's pussy recovered from suffocation, Bay-bay sucked my dick like a Black mama snitching on a neighbor to the police to protect her young. After enough of a break, Slim looked back at Henry and said, "Okay. Put it back in." Big gurl granted Red's request and jammed my dick back into that cushy pussy like she was filling paperwork.

Back in the day a TV commercial depicted a "Sam Breakstone" as a demanding person. Sam Breakstone was portrayed as "hard-nosed" and unwilling to settle for less- than. As Henry banged into Slim's belly he was like Sam Breakstone. He didn't bend a bit. The type of strokes I put on that pussy could best be described as determined. Henry pounded like a jack hammer, breaking barriers while bulging like a bicep before brunch and penetrating with prowess. Skeeter worked like a back hoe clearing erotic acres. Henry was fitting himself into her coochee like he was trying on a new glove.

No way can I adequately describe the feeling I had stroking Slim. She had a smaller ass which allowed a more conducive atmosphere for my sexual lightning to flare. My dick, hips, and pysche worked as a team - as on-time as news at nine. Henry deciphered angles that DiVinci, Einstein and Bruce Lee hadn't discovered.

This soldier toppled walls in that pussy with the shock and awe only the United States military is known for. Once, again, Ruby had to take a break. "Take it out! Take dat muthafucka out!" she yelled.

This time Slim turned to lay on her back, as if she was totally through. Bay-bay switched her head between pussy and dick like she was answering questions at a news conference. She ate Slim's pussy wit' attitude, scooping honey from deep within Slim's flavor factory, while occasionally slurping Henry like an alcoholic getting a needed drink.

I again noticed I had previously been rude to Ruby's pussy with my novice choice of cunnilingus chomps. If I had known Slim's cunt's name I would have called it by that and apologized for my robotic amateurism. I thought a vagina was supposed to be devoured like a pie or mango. Big gurl gnawed on Ruby's cunt like it was a neckbone.

Based on the meal methods Francis used to orally stimulate her friend, I recognized my learning curve to conduct competent cunnilingus. Just like eating anything, I learned I should refrain from wolfing coochee wantonly. Feasting on a fallopian folder should facilitate festivity. In the future I hoped to adapt to savoring a forbidden fruit's flavor; how to peel it; when to suckle it; when to deepen the tongue; and find where its "right there" spot was. I had to discern an order of devouring it.

That night, as I played two coochees like a harmonica, I was experimenting on an unfamiliar instrument. I found that the initial eating of a cunt required oral meandering and time-served is very dependent upon many things. Most importantly, I found that laps on a ho's libido is sometimes required for a ho to render rent. I wasn't near the oral level of Stevie Wonder or Jose Feliciano, two great harmonica players, but I tried.

Another thing I had to contend with was how the dogg in me wanted to fuck some ass.

After scoring a touchdown, I didn't want to go for one. I wanted to run a dive play into an "end zone." Something, however, told me Slim wouldn't let me befit her boodee with a beastly banging or allow Skeeter to scoot into her beautiful butt burrow. I figured Ruby, like Francis, hadn't been properly propagandized to perform such a ploy.

There were also consequential concerns to my visiting Ruby's forbidden planet, to crack her crack. First of all, I didn't want another rejection of my dick while it was impersonating the Statue of Liberty entering the Lincoln Tunnel. If she said "No" or "Stop" I wouldn't like that. So, I left Slim's boodee hole without trial of penetration and reverted back to my original libidinous mission objective of just getting some pussy.

I got back into the redbone's creamy cavity and tried to deposit my dick, ancestry, balls, hips, knees, and high school diploma in her bank of bang. My deep diving dorsal of LSD went all up in there.

I was Seal Team Six entering Bin Laden's compound. I was Forrest Gump saving Lieutenant Dan. I was honoring the unknown soldier from the Korean Conflict. I was Audie Murphy charging up a World War II hill. I was Sgt. York in a World War I trench defending truth, justice, and the American way. In that particular pussy at that particular time I was Voyager searching the solar system.

Maybe that's why Slim had to take breaks from the dick. She had been taking it like a paid heterosexual promoter which she wasn't. Call it professionalism or just the vibe she had but throughout the night Ruby found the appropriate time for us to take a break.

For instance, one time my dick head was lined-up with dead top-center accuracy like a hunter with a deer in his sights. Just before the squeeze of my trigger, Slim quickly moved away. It was as if her coochee felt, like the instinct of an animal, exactly which moment of opportunity for survival had been breached. My dick was left bobbing and weaving in mid air, panting like a predator which had just missed a killed.

That ho would cock her head backwards and look at me like I had blanks then move away. It was like President Bill Clinton's confession into a TV camera when he said, "I did not have sexual relations with that woman," or when President Richard Nixon said, "I'm not a crook." Moving her cunt away was her telling "True Lies."

Slim's repertoire of revolts harkened Henry, each time making him as straight-lined as the highway on I-95 near the Florida-Georgia line.

Somewhere along the genetics of freak and femme, I don't believe an experienced Ruby really wanted us to exchange body fluids in the wearisome way proper partners posture. The missionary montage was too mundane for this ho. Being a freakazoid there was little likelihood we were going to just fuck, go to sleep, and then head home.

Doing it doggy style again, I reached underneath Slim and massaged her civic center as if my nutt legacy depended upon that type of crucial contact. I was astonished to experience how such a small pact of ass could show so much buttress. It didn't have the same bounce as Bay-bay's "black stack" but it had its moments.

I was laying pipe, deep pipe, into Slim. I executed the play just like coach drew it up. I set my rifle sights just like it says in the manual. Henry marched in-line, with left-right- left-right rhythm. Skeeter was filled with pride like the chest of a combat veteran on Memorial Day marching in a parade down Main Street while his granddaughter watched.

Before Skeeter could spray Ruby's receiver and reward my resolute resilience, big gurl busted our biological blitz. Slim hollered a hurt on a down stroke and Bay-bay removed Henry on an outstroke. With her mouth, big gurl exerted more force on my dick head than I initially believed she would, could, or should.

Bay-bay tried to separate Topper from Henry. She was abusive. She locked her lips on the leverage limb of my dick head, and grabbed the point of my practice like she intended to rough it up for slamming Slim. Point-blank, Bay-bay almost sent me to the hospital with a decapitated dick head. Nature produced the force and greed generated the graft. It was unbecoming of her to clamp her thick lips on the collar of my reproduction representative and use the laws of physics to partition my penis.

Henry must have figured the best way to get her mouth off Skeeter was to nutt. So, "we" busted that nutt. No way I could have consciously counted the blasts. It was like rapid gunfire. My emotions were just as biased as a grand jury against a Black man in Mississippi. If I had to fill out a report, I'd say I emptied my barrel with a skeet, skeet, skeet, skeet; skeet; skeet, a quick break then, skeet, skeet, skeet; skeet.

How many determinable dick detonations there were I can't say. My magazine was relieved of its full compliment rapidly; that's all I know. I don't know where most of the blanks went after rushing out its chamber. Sperms were panicking all over the place, like refugees in a Syrian civil war; like America did getting out of Hanoi; like Blacks folks after the Rodney King verdict. There was a gulp and a gag from Francis before she was hit above the eye. She said "Shit!" then verbally added another four-letter word. It was something else I wasn't taught at home.

I give her credit. That ho voluntarily faced my firemen's hose. She had to realize those cascading shots of protein were uncommonly huge and strong. Only arrogance could have led her to "handle" Henry's onslaught of liquid like she did. The one thing I'm sure of is that the shots comforted the shooter.

I'd like to say that my remnants of rejoice only went onto her face after she yanked my dick out of her mouth but that wasn't the case. Some relief went on the sheets, I subsequently found. For my diary's sake, I wish I could have been absolutely able to ascertain what was happening during those stretched seconds of time. However, I was "out of it" while my dick was skinned back to its base boldly bolting bricks of biological bombs.

I was weak afterwards and collapsed, still leaking an unfortunate next generation. This wasn't the first time since paying for the room I wasn't mentally sharp. Many times that night I didn't have the capacity to conclude. Extremism requires a few minutes and counseling to cycle back to reality. I didn't take advantage of either.

Bay-bay went into the bathroom. Slim was on lying on her side and I ended my scoot next to her where my mouth was directly across from her poot chute. I split her ass cheeks and liberally licked and thoroughly lapped her flatulence fermentation fig. Slim pushed her butt back and I took that as permission to analyze her anus. I ate at that boodee hole like it was melted chocolate still on the candy wrapper. My plan was to flirt with her fire starter and afford Henry the opportunity to spelunk that cavity.

I put Skeeter on Slim's boodee hole, ready to hunch, when penis and anus were rudely interrupted. Big gurl returned and she and Ruby began kissing. Females become terrorists when they do things like that. My dick sulked from submission as we all fell asleep. Henry, hard as marble, woke me up. Bay-bay's butt was a convenient ambition. I put Skeeter against her ass hole and hunched hard. Again, Francis placed my heap in the next available parking space. I thought she was sleep. My bad.

I squeezed Bay-bay's full ass with a finger in her ass hole. Her anus wrapped around my finger like it was a band-aid and the next thing I knew her pussy was taking protein prisoners. After the nutt, Henry beached itself like a pilot whale and curled-up like fat on fry. I got up and left before those hoes did.

CHAPTER 2

THE ROAD NOT TAKEN

FIRST SUNDAY

WITHIN THEIR TOUR of duty soldiers are faced with a myriad of environments. A change in war zones requires adapting better chances of survival. That's the reason the military switched from jungle green camouflage to desert brown. Assigned to Fort Bragg, North Carolina in the summer of 1972, I tried to blend in.

My priorities were to maintain a comfortable level of skeet and stay out of jail. For better chances of survival and to acclimate myself to Bragg and the local largest city of Fayetteville and Cumberland County, I joined pussy hunting groups a bunch of us guys called Wolf Patrol.

That's how I met Annette. I was on Wolf Patrol and spotted, without binoculars, a thick red bone with hips like a hippo. Her ass crowned perfectly enough to hark Henry's hustle. Carrying the biggest boodee I had seen thus far in Carolina made her an easy target. She had a decent head of hair and beautiful brown eyes that asked me to fuck her before I could find out whether she was jail bait. Come to find out, she was a Hope Mills transplant just graduated high school.

Annette was how I learned Fayetteville. She nor I had a place to fuck when we first got together so we rode a lot. Annette didn't like home. Whenever I dropped her off there, the closer she got to the front door the slower she walked. Once she was assured that the car I was driving was mine and I was not from Fayetteville, we started to see each other regularly.

When we weren't cruising we often parked at a local pick-up restaurant called "Vick's." That's where I "messed" with her. Her breasts were her self-esteem and she liked her self-esteem caressed. They were gorgeous 18-year old titties. It became a game of mine to see how quickly I could get her inverted nipples to pop out. It didn't take long.

Once Annette's nipples announced she was hot, she had me on demand. She would say, "Take it out," and then suck my dick like a thief siphoning gas. Her only concern was what to do when it came time for me to skeet.

That girl had the nerve to hand me a napkin. "Here, put it in this," she said, as she offered an unworthy grave for my gene pool. No man will allow his nutt to be put into a napkin unless he ain't got game. Since Louisville, I had game.

While she was rubbing my dick I pretended I was thinking about what to do with the skeet. I already knew what I wanted to do with it but I had to convince her. When I confronted her about taking the nutt in her mouth, she demonstratively refused. "I ain't gonna swallow no sperms," was the way she put it. Her animation made it seem like I was asking her to join me in a suicide pact.

This girl went scientific on my ass, talking about sperms. I understood how somebody would have difficulty letting a dick shoot off in their mouth. So, I thought how to best respond. A moment later, the greatest reply popped into my head. I told her "it" (skeet) ain't nothing but protein and swallowing "it" would help her hair and fingernails grow.

I told her that swallowing "sperms" would be just like taking medicine and would "rectify" her need for false eyelashes. I think using the word "rectify" and commenting on her false eyelashes made her take notice. The scientific connection to protein was just icing on the cake. While she considered what I said, she watched my pulsating penis expand in her warm, pressing palm. When she said "Okay" I got like Sister Johnson only on first Sunday - happy.

Annette liked to deep throat my dick. It must have been the way she learned. Then again, she could have been challenging herself to see how much LSD she could drop. She selfishly slobbered all over Henry and her eyes would redden. The young thing was just being ridiculous doing it that way. After chokes, gags, and near pukes I interrupted her.

Gently lifting her chin away from my lap I introduced her to Henry and Skeeter, taking time to explain everything. "The dick name Henry and Skeeter is the dick's head. Skeeter is naturally shaped for you to suck on. Henry is designed to get to the bottom of the pussy.

Don't try to put all that in your mouth. Just suck on the dick head," I advised. Annette leaned the dick over to her lips, looked at Skeeter like it had a specific purpose, and sucked. "Like that?" she asked. "Yeah. Like that," I answered. From then on I was helpless when Annette sucked my dick - helpless.

This ho became my hero because she actually cared how she sucked my dick. Her only problem was, "I like the whole thing in my mouth," she told me. Annette, literally, wanted her chin against my balls. "You can't get all that in your mouth," I reasoned. "I kin do it," Annette answered. We compromised. I told her when she got "happy" she could see how much dick she could take. She did.

I was anxious to see how she would react, her first time, to taking her "medicine."

She tried to raised off the dick but I held her head down for her own benefit. I felt the vibration of her throat as she guzzled each injection. Afterwards, she looked up at me, with big, brown, "I love you" eyes as if I was supposed to kiss her, say "Thank you," or do something.

No way I was going to kiss her after she had just gargled skeet. Annette used that same napkin to wipe her mouth. Too weak to move anyway, once Henry calmed down I hurried to zip and moved to get her a drink to wash the sperms down. She got the message not to try and kiss me after taking a nutt in the mouth. I would hug her or said, "I love you," if it was a nutt I requested. If she was the one that asked to suck the dick (which was most of the time) I would act as if nothing happened.

Henry became Annette's pacifier and her head became mine.

We had to progress from me only fondling her tits while she forged iron with her jaws.

The cramped backseat of my two-door Javelin was too small for her big ass. We - no, I - had to find somewhere to fuck. I had buddies who lived away from the Army base (off- post) and certain ones would leave their house (trailer) door unlocked for me to bring in a Wolf Patrol patron.

The first time I saw Annette fully naked I played it cool but Henry was like a buzzard hungry enough to kill something. She was fine, just like I said. Her breasts were the basis of her self-esteem but they were just starting blocks. Her ass was the first place podium.

The titties were fool's gold; her butt was the gold mine. Her breasts were a gate; her ass was the house.

That boodee was high-yella butta without a blemish. The curvature had a crown with a slippery slope. Her hips went straight back from her waist, enough leverage for elbows, then dropped like a cell phone call. I be damn if that girl didn't have a beautiful bottom.

I wanted to mess with all the parts of her body I was unable to reach in the car - like between her big yella thighs. Had Annette been a one-night stand maybe I would have jumped directly into that pussy. But I wasn't going to let anything be short-lived and planned my explorations to last a good long time. Besides, mining pussy is like drilling for oil - there are procedures to follow.

I rubbed the cunt to get the pussy wet. Her coochee lips were just like her, thick, and the coochee was sparsely covered with "good" hair that stopped halfway down the side of her vagina. The insides of her thighs were a darker color than her complexion and the contrasting colors were a turn-on for me. Picasso couldn't have painted better. She had a peeking clit. From the size of the bump, I figured a fierce fin was hidden.

With her knees bent back towards her chest, I softly kissed her on the bottom of her pussy where the hole is. I followed that with long strokes of licks up and down the absolute middle of her body. With my nose I opened her charm's entrance, sniffing for a scent. It was odorless and that disappointed me.

A pussy is supposed to stink; not offensively stink but yet have some sort of odor. That's how a dog measures a bitch's heat.

Looking for a clue the coochee was ready to be fucked, I stuck my tongue deep between the flaps of that fat beast and hummed an "Umm." She didn't move nor moan. I wiggled my face in the cunt from side to side. She said nothing. There was no Oooh, Ahhh, or Hmmm. I put her fat coochee into my mouth and sucked. Again; no response.

I took a moment to pause and the pussy lips slowly reverted back to their original shape, covering the pink my face had found. I liked this girl and was determined to acclimate myself to this new battlefield. I closed her thighs on my ears, forming a love tunnel, and sucked a mouthful of fat red snapper. She was motionless and mute.

After another taste test, it was clear what I was working on. There was no sweetener in her cunt chemistry. The juice was severely sub. In other words, her pussy was artificially flavored and arbitrarily arid. Those hoes in Louisville had a set standard for cunt honey.

It's the honey more than the pussy itself that prompted me to put my mouth on a coochee. Annette's cunt wasn't close to being up-to-par.

Disappointed in Annette's sperm collector, I diverted my attention to her clit. I skint that bugger back and it emerged from its cover like a sailor going topside. I flicked at it with my tongue multiple times, hoping for growth. It looked like the eyes of a shark, lifeless, and useless for keeping my attention unless Annette was getting off. She seemed non-stimulated and unimpressed.

She seemed content to let me playground between her legs, I guess, because I seemed content doing it. I shouldn't have been surprised. Annette enjoyed pleasing me more than being pleased. Having realized that, I figured the best way to please her was to let her please me. The result, however, was that my sexual activity with her was reduced to how deep I could get Henry in all her holes.

She inspected everything from my balls to my pee hole, like she was a doctor or something. With room to maneuver she put a oral hurting on Skeeter unlike she had done before. She combined her desire to please me with what I taught her into giving me a perfect blowjob. I had created a monster trumpeter.

It came time for Annette to recognize my dick's fucking ability, not just how it felt in her mouth. That's why I plucked my dick out of her face and flipped her ass over to flog that pussy from her flank.

Her yella ass looked as large as Texas. She was butt-blessed, no doubt about it. I went after it like it was my favorite pillow and gave it a great big hug. I kissed all over her butt, especially the area from the crown of her hips to the crease where her thighs started. I put hickeys all over that boodee's square footage. Annette let me play with her beautiful butt all I wanted to.

I was more than merry to finally meet her boodee hole. This was not happening in the dark, like in Louisville. This mole hole was in plain view. It stared at me menacingly and gave a look like somebody yelling, "Cut off that light!" I stuck tongue in that boodee hole and her anus closed instinctively, like someone realizing their zipper was down.

The ass hole is a tempting perforation for puncture if you fantasized loving such a thing. I fantasized. I sucked that rascal and kissed it like it was a mouth. I used the tips of my lips to suction a departing and

Annette said, "Oooh!" Finally a response I thought to myself. I wanted Annette to voluntarily fart in my face and not say excuse me. I didn't get gassed and, to me, that meant the boodee hole didn't care to be bothered. She had a great looking piece of ass and a sensual dark brown, chubby boodee hole but it was a mute.

Annette's anus used sign language, winks, to communicate. Each gesture of sign it gave hardened Henry. He wanted to stop it from blinking. I told Henry he had to be patient if he wanted to unfasten the brown button between her buttocks. I told Henry we had to get the pussy first. I promised him that one day soon I would get him in the ass but this was not the right time. He wasn't happy but went along to get along.

With Henry temporarily barred from the boodee hole, I knew from Louisville that devious him might still try to get up in her ass. I made sure my aim into her cunt was true.

However, Annette's pussy disabled my dick because of her lack of lubrication. Henry got in but stopped suddenly. As a matter of fact, Henry bent. "Don't hurt me," she said.

"Take your dick baby. I want you to take all your dick," I told her. She said nothing, as if she would comply with my orders. I slipped Skeeter back between her coochee guards and hit that pussy hard. She started whining. It was sort of nice to believe this ho hadn't fucked in a good while. The friction was sensational as heat scoured Henry inch by inch.

My dick began throbbing like it wanted to spit. I had to retreat. Once the penis was all out, I saw a ring of thick honey caught underneath Skeeter's collar.

If I could have I would have sucked my own dick to get at that honey. Instead, I wiped Skeeter on her pussy and put my face right in the middle of her cunt. I licked and sucked all I could collect. The honey was warm but tasted like Castor Oil. Henry told me, "It ain't sweet." From then on, the pussy belonged to him.

Annette let me pound her pussy like I wanted. It was a beautiful fuck. I was sawing her cunt like I was falling a sequoia. I was dipping dick head into her southern comfort like I was fanning a friend at a funeral. I banged her backside like I was "working on the railroad all the live-long day." She allowed Henry to dominate. I was blown away at how she took that dick.

I got a little rough on her ass. I put her into the buck and pounded dick like a blacksmith's hammer working on an anvil. I went up in that pussy like my dick was a cheap pencil being sharpened. Annette's head was banging against the headboard. She showed fright in her eyes but her expression only encouraged me to further damage that cunt. I was waxing that coochee with long strokes, clawing the sheet with my feet, and shot off on my tip toes.

After a few more fucks, I woke up one morning lying next to Annette's ass with my dick as sturdy as a doorframe. I poked my fingertip slightly into her boodee hole for reconnaissance. She said nothing so I assumed it had open borders. For once, I loved the fact that she said nothing and didn't move. There appeared to be no barrier to gettin' the boodee and hope reigned supreme.

I dipped Skeeter into the pussy to get him wet from the nutt I left in the pussy the previous night. Carefully aiming, I placed my dick head on her ass hole and hunched against it. She allowed Skeeter to make it halfway inside (at least it felt that way) before she said, "Stop." It wasn't a firm "Stop" because there was no exclamation. I continued pushing. I got to the point where just a little more force would have made a difference and Annette moved away. I pulled her hips back into place and tried again. Just as soon as the dick head touched her pooter, she said the worst thing she could ever say to me. She belted out an emphatic, "No, Fenn!"

Whenever I heard "No!" Henry went limp. Even worse, she called my name like she was definite about who she was saying "No!" to. I was upset and Henry was disappointed.

In my own mind, I scolded Annette for having the audacity to tell Fenn, "No!" In my own mind I told her that if she wanted to push me to some other woman that wouldn't say "no" or "stop" then its okay by me! Sex with Annette was never the same after that.

Annette's "No!" is what ended a somewhat serious and definitely county-wide monogamous relationship. At that particular time with that particular person, when my dickhead was one poke away from plugging her pooter, "No!" was something that particularly didn't need to be presented.

After she told me, "No!" she started being used. Only when I needed a quickie or felt like I wanted to go 12 inches deep did I search for Annette. After she sputtered that "No!" our relationship was like "Last Sunday."

CHAPTER 3

FRISKED FOREIGNERS

CASABLANCA

T HERE ARE MANY reasons people immigrate to America. The country's reputation for opportunity has been widely reported as awesome. Many come to take advantage of business and educational advantages and never leave. Others infiltrated our borders to fill jobs that new generations of Americans have ceased doing or are intellectually unable to perform. Also, foreigners have supported our government during wars and the nation allows them shelter and citizenship as reward for their support.

Our nation's foreign military contacts are extensive and near Army bases you run up on pussy from all over the world. Many soldiers are a long ways from home when their dicks harden and for some of them a hard dick means it's time for marriage. In many instances, a foreigner will stay married to a soldier only long enough to get citizenship.

It wouldn't be that way with me. I was a member of the "Four F Club." To me, a hard dick meant find 'em, fool 'em, fuck 'em, and forget 'em. As a member of the United States Armed Forces, I took it as a part of my job to scrutinize foreigners. I went on libidinous missions to make sure immigrants were not conspiring against my country.

In the name of national security, the first foreigner I frisked was a native German. She was "circus fat" huge. We were in a 7-Eleven store around 11 p.m. when she gave me the eye of a spy. Wearing enough cloth to cover a Fleetwood Cadillac, she was fidgeting with certain items on the shelves. I figured, big as she was, she was looking for a laxative.

I just politely smiled, got whatever I was buying, and left the store.

Before I could close the door on my car she had waddled outside and, with a noticeable accent, blatantly asked me if I would follow her to her house. Regardless of her accent, to me she was a White girl and they were definitely off limits. I told her fat ass, "No; I don't think I better." She didn't give up. "I like you people," she said.

After her "you people" explanation, we exchanged names and such. Then, she got around to what she really wanted. "How long are you? Let me see," she asked. I graduated from a private high school. I was able to infer she was talking about my dick.

Common sense should have told her that I wasn't going to pull my dick out in the parking lot of a 7-Eleven. But when a fat ass White woman asks a young Black male to show his dick, common sense usually isn't around. I unzipped my pants, pulled on Henry a few times, and told her, "This is all I got." She followed with some words that I always, one way or another, told females and never thought I'd hear from any woman. She said, point-blank, "I want to fuck you."

I was young, dumb, and full of cum back then and would have had sex with anything not nailed down. So, I followed that big ass ho to her house. I had heard through the grapevine German women liked Black dick. Maybe she was stalking the store looking for national treasures and I just happened to come along. Her motive was suspect so I looked at our meeting like it was an investigation; like I was FBI.

This ho was almost as tall as me and two times wider. As she wobbled into her house I noticed she had to turn sideways to get past the doorframe. Once inside she turned to me, looking like Jabba The Hut, and whispered that we had to be quiet because her son was sleeping. Except for the slap of my groin against her space shuttle-sized ass, we fucked without much noise. She insisted on keeping the bedroom light on. I liked that.

I had heard about creepy Caucasians who used whips, chains, and spank benches during sex and I was waiting for her to pull out some handcuffs. She began by rubbing on Henry while he was still in my pants. She told me, with a musical tone, "You've got a hard-on", then yanked Henry out and began milking him like he was a teat on a cow. I rubbed the back of her head as she orally worked Henry from medium to extra-large.

That ho could suck a dick, engulfing Henry like a bunker does a golf ball. If she was trying to impress me she did. The longer Henry got, the more of him she took in. It was an amazing thing to see. Inch by inch, the airspace between my balls and the bottom of her chin was reduced as if her throat had a landing plan.

I love women with accents. Hers sounded brutish yet somehow sexy. "Cock good. Cock getting longer. Cock big," she would describe in-between sucking voraciously.

She was blond but had black hair everywhere else. I mean everywhere; above her top lip; on her forearms; in her armpits; on her shins; on foot and hand; and on her back. I didn't see any evidence that she shaved, like stubble on her face, and was really relieved when she didn't pull out a dick.

Once Henry was long enough, she yanked off that car cover. There were two large folds, like lava flows, of fat below heavy titties and bread rolls on her thighs. She didn't have knees and that blew my mind. She was as pale as a Canadian snowbird.

As she trucked her big ass around for me to fuck her from behind those big ol' thighs were scrubbing each other. She split her legs and pounds of pussy were hanging like a bull's scrotum. With a heavy voice, looking straight ahead, she gave instructions. "You fuck me like this. Cum in mouth, not in cunt." Her accent and ghostly golf umbrella of an ass moved Henry. Unassisted, he lifted and pointed in the direction of Europe.

It took muscle to split her battalions of fat where her "rear guard" was vulnerable to my "Western Front." Eventually I put my "Hogan's Hero" where the German wanted him. Henry became a POW on his first dip into her stalag. He went so deep, I couldn't see my balls any more than "Colonel Klink" saw an escape. It must have looked like I was fucking an albino elephant. Henry was lost all up in there. I heard him calling me and relayed to him the same thing "Sgt. Schultz" always used to say, "I know nothing." The bottom of that pussy seemed a continent away so I blistered its borders.

Thank goodness I had had a conversation with my older brother, a short time after Louisville, that effected my fucking technique. At first, I wished my brother hadn't told me what he told me but found it to be valuable with this ho.

He watched his child being born and while we were talking about that experience he schooled me. "You know how you are getting some pussy and think you're hittin' bottom?" he asked, then answered. "There ain't no bottom."

Before that conversation with my big bro, I hadn't even considered that every man's intention was to hit bottom. After that conversation, I changed my technique. I specifically told Skeeter he was to no longer prioritize penetration to China. I told Henry to emphasize banging the walls of a coochee; to relax its panels.

All that knowledge didn't make much difference with this German ho though. I couldn't dream of having enough dick for this one. I stopped fucking and pulled Henry out to look at him. He looked like he had gotten beat-up after school; like a victim of violence; like he had been disrespected. I could feel him whining. Henry looked like "Bubba" in the Forrest Gump movie when he said, "I wanna go home."

The German looked back as if something was wrong. I went back into battle searching for a better angle, pounding fat flesh as best I could. Just about the time I got tired of pushing all that cock-blocking fat away, she said, "Stop! I suck your cock now."

Her tone sounded like that of a fight crowd where I hadn't delivered enough of a fight and the people wanted their money back. I removed Henry and he drooped like a punchy pugilist. That big ho turned around, moving like "she was comin' 'round the mountain," and told me to lie down. I did.

That elephant ass, pale, bleached-hair, freak, German, ho, with more rolls than the Michelin Man, got on top of me into the 69 position. I couldn't see anything but a big, wide, pale, building. It was like I was facing the rear of The White House. I was somewhere I wasn't supposed to be and knew it.

It was a shame when her ass collided with my face. Anybody seeing that picture would have said, "That's a shame." Her boulder butt was pressed against my face like she was on a mule cart going from East to West Berlin.

I lost my sense of sight because I could get my eyes opened, and my sense of hearing because her blubber covered my ears. Unable to notify the United Nations, I called on Jesus.

Nature is a weird thing. How my dick could be hard at the same time I needed CPR, I just don't know. She was an experienced face-sitter and knew, thank goodness, every now and then she would have to lift off my mugg. Every time she deep-throated Henry, her "Casa blanca" ass lifted off my face.

Searching for sugar, I parted her Central Park-sized thighs, saw her reddening pussy, took a deep breath, and sucked that. Mistakenly I grabbed and hugged her hips and she pressed her pussy on my mouth for so long I was again hurting for air in an emergency manner. I be damn if I didn't enjoy that but had to pound on her back for air before she lifted off.

Moving in slow motion, she climbed off and told me, "I fuck you now." She squatted over my waist and eased her pussy down on Henry. That's the only reason she didn't break both my legs. She rose up and down my dick with her hands on my chest. I could have used those chest compressions when her blubber butt 'bout butchered my breath.

Her big ass dropped heavily on my legs and her tits trapped my throat as she had the nerve to lean over and kiss me. She had a good bed; it didn't make a sound.

She was fucking me like she said she wanted to do. Henry was being jacked by pure pussy. I didn't have to do anything. That fuck was between her and Henry and I just happened to be in the room. She had dick deep, quietly repeating "Cock good! Cock good!" At one point she quaked. It was like the Earth was bustin' a nutt. After a number of facial distortions, she crawled off and went back to sucking my dick.

She told me, "You cum now." She no longer deep-throated but concentrated on Skeeter and, at times, nuzzled her nose against my nuts. I shot jolts of hot skeet directly onto her tongue. The German let her mouth fill with stud syrup and swallowed with loud gulps. That ho said, "More; I want more" and gnawed on Skeeter again. She milked the dick for fluid until it was flat-lined. "You go now," she said.

I told her to let me rest a minute and then I would go. In the meantime, I wanted to play with her body. She had an apron of fat covering her pelvis so I got behind her where I could rodeo her cloud of ass, wondering if I could get all of it in my arms. I couldn't.

There was boodee spilling all over my forearms. I scuba-dived my face into her ass and sucked her boodee hole until my neck got a crick in it.

I got out of there just in time to see the clerk from the 7-Eleven arriving.

Frisked Foreigners

BREAKING AND ENTERING

BEFORE JOINING THE Army in 1972, I hadn't realized to what extent I had been socially raised non-inclusive. For example, back home Black males were stopped and interrogated by the police if we crossed Orange Avenue after sundown. Before school desegregation, Brothers were barred by common law from scooping anything besides Colored pussy.

There were very few Mexicans and no Haitians. Caucasians, who have issues with our planet's nearness to the sun, were considered aliens whose monogamous Race environmentally destroyed the planet Mars and then resettled on Earth.

We were so culturally isolated we thought Oriental women had pussies that stretched sideways like their eyes. After having frisked a Vietnamese girl, I know that's false. She was such an itty bitty thing. Her coochee was tiny but as perpendicular as any other pussy.

Girlfriend Annette was taking classes at the community college and one particular day I had to drop her off there. She was the one that insisted I "be a gentleman" and walk her to class. As we were walking, she stopped and talked to the girl. Before I could get away, Annette asked me to give the Vietnamese girl a ride home. No big deal I thought.

It wasn't until we had reached the car that I asked her what part of Fayetteville she was going. Because of the language barrier, it took time to pinpoint just where she wanted to go. As it turned out, she lived way out by 71st High School on Raeford Road.

I had to take a priority-changing dump. When it's time for the bowels to move, nothing is more important. I had no intention of doing anything in the next few minutes but dropping a few pounds. On the way to taking her to where she wanted to go, I found it convenient to stop at my place to do number two.

I parked, leaving the girl in the car, and both of my housemates were immediately curious. They asked me how I had scooped a White girl. I told them she was one of Annette's friends that I had to take home. While I was contributing fertilizer to local tobacco farmers my roommates came up with other ideas of what to do with the girl.

My most immediate business completed, I stayed in the house more than momentarily talking with them while the girl waited outside. One of my roommates was trying to convince me that we should run a train on the girl. My other roommate was just grinning.

I wasn't about that. If I fucked a girl I wanted to be able to fuck her again and that wouldn't happen if we ran a train on her.

During our deliberations she knocked at the door. I answered and she asked, "You take me home now?" I told her I had to something to do "right quick" and that I would take her home "in a minute." I asked if she wanted to come in. She shook her head "no" and got back into the car. That's when one roommate noticed she was a foreigner, although that's not what he called her. He became more insistent that everybody get the pussy.

While "he" was discussing what "we" should do with her, she came back to the front door. "You take me home now?" she repeated with much accent. I told her to come in and wait until I had finished doing what I had to do and then I would take her home. This time she came inside. She entered the trailer and sat on the couch in the front room. The guys left us alone. It was quiet in that trailer, one of the very few times music wasn't playing. I was sitting at the kitchen table trying to decide what I was going to do.

There were three reasons I decided against us runnin' a train. First, the girl weighed only as much as a windbreaker. Second, while my roommate was talking he referred to the girl as a "Tight-eye." Because he said that, I was concerned as to how he would treat her. Regardless of what happened I was going to get some pussy.

Pointing to my bedroom, I told her I wanted to talk to her "back there." During a few seconds of hesitation that itty bitty thing turned her head three or four times from me towards the front door and back to me. She looked around with "what have I gotten myself into" eyes and said, "Okay. I go with you." Why she consented; why she didn't raise a fuss; or why she didn't just leave, I didn't ask why.

We sat on the bed and I pretty much told her, in an experienced manner, I wanted to fuck her. Looking shameful, as if she was facing deportation, she said nothing.

The best language is a picture so I gave her a snapshot of what was about to "cum." I stood up in front of her, dropped my zipper, and pulled my dick out. Her eyes loosened and she stared at Henry like he was an ICE agent. I rubbed my dick and grabbed her hand, telling her, "Do that." Hesitant at first, she squeezed its growing firmness. While that small hand was clutching my crisp cock, Henry's eye was staring straight at her.

That ho said, "It long. It hard." I 'bout busted a nutt right there. "That's long, stiff dick," I said. "Long, stiff dick is good for you. Don't it feel good? She slightly nodded agreement. I straight-out asked her, "You want long, stiff dick?" She told me, "I a virgin."

I 'bout busted a nutt right there.

Three things entered my mind at that point. I had to get the pussy and it was obviously going to be the best fuck she ever had. Also, at that moment in time, I was the luckiest motherfucker on the planet. I felt exalted.

I tried to comfort any thoughts she may have had about Henry. "Put it in your mouth and see how it fits," I suggested, as I bounced my dick head off her lips. She dropped her jaws and I slipped Skeeter between. When she clamped down, I could have skeeted the liquid capacity of Niagara Falls.

I was so anxious to bust that cherry I didn't care about teaching her how to suck my dick and retrieved Henry from her face. She was hypnotized by Henry, following him with her eyes like somebody was showing her how to get back and forth from New York to Los Angeles on a map of the USA. I guided her off the bed to slip off her clothes. Her doorknob-sized titties, with cotton candy puffiness and hardly any areola, pointed towards the person who was going to be first to lay pipe in her pussy.

She was a virgin but it really turned me on that my dick was almost as wide as her wrist. In a situation where three Black men were ready to fuck the shit out of her, I was her savior from a train. Figuring I should be paid like a mercenary was reasoning to do what I was doing.

I put her on her back, spread open her legs, and smelled the pussy. It smelled like vegetables cooking but I deemed it okay. I was amazed at the size of it. That thing showed just a miniature split; no flaps; no obvious clit cover; no fat to suck on at all.

The cunt lips didn't glisten like I loved lips to do. Her pubic hair looked like an oil slick.

Hunting for her clit, I opened her snatch with my pinch fingers. Her pee hole popped into view and it was large, about the diameter of an ear hole. I tried to reassure the pussy and her, with lenient licks and kisses, that although my long, stiff dick might be a challenge I had nothing to do with evitable hurt.

Talking to the pussy I said something like, "I want you to open up for me (kiss). The more you relax, the less it will hurt (kiss). Take the dick (kiss) like a good little girl." I didn't know if the pussy understood English and it didn't matter.

I got off on her watching me sniff her veggie vagina as intensely as Customs' dogs hopefully had checked her carry-on. As the pussy got hotter, Henry got harder. I wanted to make sure she had a hole down there so I opened the cunt wide. A circle of virginity was the only guard between Skeeter and her throat. I blew over the guardian like it was a lighted match. I briefly stopped to turn the radio louder so my neighbors wouldn't hear her inevitable scream.

I punched prick into that pussy and she responded by lifting her feet, curling her toes, and screaming something that sounded like, "Yatzee!" I instinctively pulled out and all kinds of fluid came rolling out. I gave her time to recover when I pulled off my draws and wiped her broken seal. Fluid was escaping onto the crack of her ass and I also used my underwear to shovel it. I left some fluid down there to prevent my dick from getting skint.

I hovered tall above her and looked directly into those Vietnamese green eyes as I merged into her "Ho Chi Minh Trail." With Skeeter just inside her snatch she took a deep breath and I drilled.

It's a good thing I had had all the practice I had had withholding nutts. I could have "Run Forrest Run" with skeet and launched a "Platoon" of sperms way before I wanted to. I wanted to save the nutt for delivery into the basement of her "Hanoi Hilton." The cunt was gripping Henry as if it was holding the Oscar for "The Deer Hunter." I couldn't help but give her a kiss on the jaw to tell her, "Good Morning Vietnam!" as my "drill sergeant" marched into that ho.

Each time I pushed, she responded with a noise that resembled a muscle man lifting a tractor tire, "Uggh," and would then turn her head from one side to the other. Each time, I told her, "Good girl!" Her legs were working like the doors at Wal-Mart, opening and closing automatically. She had her eyes closed and that was good for me. I didn't want to see stress from her because she had to take the dick whether she wanted to or not. I gave her a pillow to hold as I dove deeper into her "Gulf of Tonkin."

I had jammed only four or five inches of dick into her cunt when that ho told me," It hurt. It hurt bad." I just kept on pushing dick into that miniature muff. I wanted a good stretch of Henry's main vein in that girl when I shot off. Two inches later, she came from behind the pillow and told me, "Long, stiff dick hurt. Big cock. It hurt. It hurt bad." After that, she kept saying "Big cock!" after every thrust as I maintained my drilling operation.

After feeling a little sympathetic towards her taking big dick on her first fuck, I began to slowly pull out. She tighten her grip on the pillow as I slid my dick backwards. When Skeeter finally emerged I looked to see if I had skint Henry in any way. He was straight; no cuts underneath. There was a little blood however. It was mixed with her honey and made an ugly cloud along my dick. I wiped Henry and the cunt again with my underwear as clean as I could.

I put that ho in the buck. She had no idea what was going on when I placed her heels next to her ears with her pussy and ass hole sticking up in the air. Just as soon as she saw Henry headed for her hollow, she hollered, "Big cock! Big cock!" I decided to speak her language and told her, "Big cock good. Big cock good!"

Her hollering kind of scared me so I decided to take it easy on the pussy. I only went as deep as I had been before. I guess because I wasn't punching dick as hard she relaxed a little. The more the cunt loosen the deeper I went but I got frustrated that I couldn't get as deep as quickly as I wanted without her saying "Big cock."

I stood at the side of the bed and pulled her up. She probably thought it was all over but I handed her LSD. "You've got to make it calm down," I told her. "I'll stay big until it calms down." She allowed me to guide her to where she could sit on my dick. Her small paws felt good on my legs as she braced herself. That made Henry boil. When I uploaded dick into the cunt, she bent over and I pushed pole deep. That did it. Henry busted his nutt. I couldn't help but hug her while I was injecting fluid into her belly. I peeped her dark brown boodee hole as that ho was trying desperately to get away from my dick.

As I laid back to rest she got off the dick and climbed on my chest. That ho kissed me on the neck and jaw like I was Batman who had just rescued her from two Jokers.

Literally, I had. Her affection, innocence, and certainly smallness sold me on protecting her from the wolves outside my room door. We quickly passed by my roommates waiting on their turns as we left.

We had limited conversation on my way taking her home. As I described how good the fuck was, her repeated response was, "Big cock good." Basically, I was attempting to build her self-esteem. I wanted her to know she had something to offer Black America. I felt good about fucking any immigrant. They owed me, according to my ancestral guidance counselor.

I hadn't taught her how to suck a dick; hadn't gotten all my dick in her; and I still wanted to explore her really dark ass hole. I told her I wanted some more pussy. She told me, in her broken English, what her situation was. I understood I couldn't call her but she would call me whenever she was able. I figured she wasn't going to tell anybody anything.

Sure enough about 10 days later she called and we met often enough. On weeknights we messed in my car in a parking lot near her home. On weekends, it was at my place.

She liked sucking dick and told me my skeet tasted like chicken. She slobbered on Henry and took all my nutts in the mouth because I told her it was a Green Card requirement to prevent pregnancy.

She became Americanized, competitive. She tried to take all the dick. With her sitting on my lap (her favorite position), she twerked her twat with a twitch trying her best to get all of Henry in. Afraid LSD would rip her apart and she'd end-up in the ER, I never did get all my dick in the pussy. Her ass hole, wide-eyed as it was, wasn't a safe option either.

Our clandestine relationship ended after Annette ordered me to stop fucking her. She used only a four-word statement ending with "Fenn" and delivered it in the same tone she used when she told me, "No!"

BROKEN ARROW

NO WEAPON; NO SERVICE. That was the case when I frisked another international transplant who I mistook as a "lady." I met Perla in Spring Lake, a community next to Bragg where Pope AFB is located. I was getting air shocks installed at an auto repair shop when she, one of the finest looking women I've ever met, pushed my button. "Is that your car?" she asked. I proudly answered yes and she spoke, to me, again. "I love that shade of blue," she told me.

She didn't have much of an accent so I thought she was a home girl, ready to do whatever she could for the home team. I talked to her like she was a Sister. I came out with, "Damn girl, you juicy as hell! You must be from Georgia," I told her. She showed her pearly whites and asked, "Why you say that?" "'Cause it looks like that peach ready to be picked," I answered, as I directed my eyesight at her hips. That ho had the nerve to ask a pervert, "You like juicy, huh?" and then turn her hips towards me as she walked off.

Her brilliant smile and full lips optically said to me, "Stick dick here," but I figured this ho wouldn't swallow sperms. This girl classy, she's a lady, I mistakenly assessed.

She wasn't going to let me shoot off in her mouth. Even if I did she would probably complain about the taste and then brush and gargle afterwards. I hated when a ho did that.

As she moved away her coital course showed a curriculum of classes for me to consider. She had a gap between her legs, especially noticeable in the tights she was wearing. The coochee was coved; her hips howled; and her thighs thundered as she glided off. Even her feet were pretty. My eyes were like truck mirrors in the middle lane as I gazed that ho up and down. That ass was jiggling like jello!

I wanted to petition a poot, right there, in that store next to the mufflers. I wanted my oral post to do calisthenics on any personal partition of her body. I had to make it known I had a penchant for freaky foreplay. I eased up on her and in her ear asked her, "Do the words lickity split mean anything to you?"

We exchanged phone numbers and near noon we were on the phone. That's when I found out Perla was from Panama. She invited me to her place that evening but I wanted her hips ASAP. She went for it. She told me what she liked to drink and I knew then I was in. Liquor and language can turn into lickin' into lovin'.

The bad news was that on two consecutive nights Annette guzzled big nutts out of me!

Annette believed that if she drained my balls I wouldn't have the ability to fuck anybody else. I figured just having oral sex with Perla would be enough, if it came to that. That Panamanian could have just tossed a titty and I would have been happy. Heck, I wouldah parted with a pint to suck her toes.

Before I got out of my car to go inside her trailer, I unfurled Henry out of my draws and placed him alongside my leg. As we had talk and drinks on her living room couch Henry got hard from anticipation. Perla noticed a "billy club" imprint in my pants alongside my thigh and asked, "What's that?" as she reached over and tapped my dick. "That's yours," I said. "Let me see what you got for me," she told me.

I unzipped and pulled Henry out. Her eyes got wide but her legs and lips stayed closed.

Left hands on Henry are unconventional; unconventional is kryptonite. Hers held Henry.

Perla knew what she was doing. She kept her thumb under my dick head while she tickled Skeeter with her fingers like she was untying a bow.

That Panamanian jacked my dick like a machine throughout three slow drinks and then compared my dick's rigidity to bamboo because it wouldn't bend. Occasionally she would stop and take a moment to admire American LSD. When Henry was twice as dense as oak Perla asked, "This is large and hard enough to be a weapon. You got a permit for this thing?" Skeet showed up on Skeeter and I tried to get her to lick it off. That ho wiped it off with her fingers.

Surprisingly she took off her top and bra, got on her knees, and rubbed the dick between her gorgeous tits. Topper was tapping her throat. I should have shot off on her chin because she wouldn't suck my dick for nothing. "Kiss that for me," I told her. She ignored me. I stood up and waved my dick in her face. "Suck that," I said. That ho wouldn't do it. Henry was more than disappointed. I hate when you meet hoes who look meticulously fine and think they're too good for fellatio.

She instead offered her bedroom. It was like Panama between her legs - hot down there. She had a plump pussy with a halo of bushy soft hair from her navel to her ass hole.

I started mowing with my face in her front yard, moved to the insides of her thighs, and clipped her backyard using just lips. This is what I had been practicing for. It was my oral Super Bowl and what a field to play on!

She moaned.

Her hairy hips were perfectly round, perfectly colored, and the boodee hole showed a "Y" shaped crack nicely nasty for my nature.

I hummed the Star Spangled Banner in that pussy, waiting on Henry to rise to the occasion. Regardless of what I did, Henry didn't get hard. This was a first for me. The ho had teased him too much; Annette had sucked me dry; or Henry was being mean.

Regardless, I felt like somebody who couldn't pass a driver's test.

"What's the matter?" she asked. I don't know why women ask that question and rhetorical considerations weren't going to solve the problem. And, what problem did she want to discuss; Annette sucking me dry; her teasing me; or Henry being vindictive. I tried to get around the question by asking for another drink. "That's why you can't get a hard-own," she told me. "You've had too much to drink."

Time had run out for my dick to get hard when that Panamanian pulled a knife on me.

It must have come from under one of the six pillows she had on the bed. Sounding like a Sister from the 'hood with an attitude, Perla said, "I ought to stab yo' ass." Then she told me, "Git it up or I ah cut it off." She wont no lady and definitely wasn't a Sister. No lady would have a knife in the bed and no Sister would cut off a dick.

I replied, "Okay," to her ultimatum. I tried to get hard; honestly I did. But there was just something not connecting. I looked up from between her legs to see if she had her hand under a pillow. That's when I noticed her nipples were very erect, standing like the cross during The Crusades. This ho had a hairy pussy, parentheses thighs, a luscious butt, and deep light brown skin, all that I ever wanted; and I couldn't get hard.

Perla was holding my dick for ransom so I had to activate Plan B. I gently pushed open that pussy with my nose like I was in an egg rolling contest. I put much tongue in that wet hole and loved that coochee with long strokes, starting at the bottom with the base of my tongue to where my laps bristled her clit. I ate that pussy good.

There was no warning when she grabbed the back of my head with both hands, slapped her thighs against my ears into her gorgeous groin and repeatedly squeezed.

While she was busting that nutt she turned us over on our sides. There, she continued to hold my head on her leaking cunt. Her legs trembled. I must have been slurping honey for at least 45 seconds. Damn that ho was wet.

I wondered if all Panamanians cummed that heavy and were that tasty. I wanted to visit her village, record the cuisine, and write a book on a diet that caused a copious amount of smothering, seasoned honey to flow during orgasm. They eat fried bananas down there; maybe that helps.

After the nutt she pushed me away from her tantalizing thighs. She delicately said with an accent, "You need to leave now." Ain't that cold? Because of her moans and nutt busting, Henry seemed like he wanted to come alive just before she spoke that sentence.

Being forced to eat pussy by knifepoint was another first for me. It was great. From that day on, subconsciously I wished another ho would pull a weapon on me and force me to eat her pussy until she came. I told Perla that if she ever wanted me to do "that" again to just call me. She never did.

Frisked Foreigners

TEQUILA SUNRISE

SHE CROSSED THE border; she wasn't native. I was forced to frisk a senorita. It was destiny that brought me and that hot tamale together. I didn't have to wait until immigration reform or Taco Bell to sample Aztec cuisine. We synchronized our mutual curiosity and business into "caliente" activity.

A Mexican soldier wanted to buy my Javelin and that's how I ended-up sampling his sister, Rosa. While he was cruising around his trailer park test driving and showing off my ride to a car-load of family,

Rosa and I were left behind. She was unaware I was obliged to frisk female foreigners.

I took Spanish in school but all I remembered from Mr. Cassanova's class was how to count to 15; say "kiss my ass" and ""I don't know"; and ask "what's happening" and "what time is it." During our limited conversation, Rosa communicated mostly with smiles and a "Si" every now and then. Come to find out, she understood English, she was just "playin' ignant." She knew what was happening when I gave her my phone number.

Her brother wanted me to allow him to drive the car while he made six monthly payments. I had couple of other guys interested in buying the car so I wasn't in a hurry to make a deal. The Mexican called me the following day and I told him I still hadn't made up my mind. Rosa called the next day and, in good English, talked me into allowing her to persuade me into selling the car to her brother.

Rosa and I closed the deal at a friend of mine's trailer. I had my own place but for security reasons reserved time elsewhere. Back then there were hardly any chubby Mexicans and this girl was no exception to that trend. Rosa was as thin as could be. When she took off her clothes she looked like the skeletal model of a human we had in science class. Whenever the teacher wasn't looking guys would hold their hand to its mouth to pretend a "runway model" was giving head. Still, I was excited about having pure, nonfat, hot Latin pussy at my disposal.

Her attitude I didn't like, at first. She seemed to be there only to seal the deal and because of her mental disposition the fuck was frustrating. I scooped my dick out and put Henry directly in front of her nose. "Here, do this," I said. "I don't never do that before," she told me. "You got to do this. Pretend it's a Tootsie Roll pop," I told her. She reluctantly opened her mouth and I lodged Henry inside. It wasn't a pro suck because she was tender and slow, like she was nibbling on an infant's toe. I told her, again, to suck my dick like it was a tootsie pop. She did.

To see what I was working with I split her forested cunt open and sniffed for honey.

The coochee smelled jalapeno. I liked spicy. I wanted to hit the bottom of that pussy on the first dip but she had sadness in her eyes. I flipped her over to where she was facing away from me with her hands and knees on the bed.

Her cunt reflected her manner. I pushed Skeeter in and he went nowhere. She wasn't even damp down there. The pussy needed moisture so I spit on it. The glob of saliva looked good against all that hair, like a cum shot, and made me want to spread it with my tongue. That's when I ran into another road block.

Her ass hole was unusually close to her pussy and had, upon closer examination, what looked to be shit crust around it. My finger inadvertently cracked the crust and some dropped off. The hair around her pussy caught it. I cleared the area by brushing the crust away and continued what I was about to do. Her ass hole smelled unpleasantly cured but my dick was hard and I wasn't going to give my first Mexican meal amnesty because of some discrepancy with a side dish.

I spit on the cunt again, pushed two fingers into her hole, and gave the dick a test run.

The pussy didn't feel tight, just dry. It took two or three strokes before I made measurable progress. That ho started whining but with every dip of Henry she was getting creamier. I knew I was getting somewhere when Rosa straightened out her back, lifted her head, and shook her noggin like she was taking a big dick. She was.

Rosa looked back at me with surrendering eyes. Her look induced my dick to hit another gear and Skeeter slammed against a wall. Rosa dropped from her hands to her elbows on the bed and looked back at me again. This time her eyes were water-filled.

Henry made a bitch boo-hoo. Her look of hurt made me nutt and I drained every drop of cum I could muster into that ho.

Next day, I told the Mexican dude he could buy the car. We met at the NCO Club near Division Headquarters so he wouldn't know where I lived. Rosa was with him and kept her eyes looking downward as if she didn't even know who I was. I should have said something.

Days later Rosa called me at work. It took a while for her to get around to asking for a fuck, too shy to ask straight out for LSD. This time when I got her to another friend's place, I noticed a shit stain in her panties. I didn't want a repeat of avoiding her Latina ass hole because of do-do crust.

Before we showered she had to pee and I made her do it right there in front of me. I watched what was happening between her legs, my head almost in the toilet. I saw Inca gold piss spraying out of nappy Latina hair. Awesome! If she didn't know I was freaky, she should have been assured of that when I insisted on wiping her pissy cunt. That nasty- ass ho pissed on my finger after cleaning and laughed about it.

Following our shower, we fondled opposite anatomy like two kids. She liked playing with my dick and I liked twisting the straight strands covering her cunt. I gave her hairy underarm some head. "Stop," she told me while giggling. "I don't want to laugh." I wanted to do something I was sure she wouldn't laugh about, like put my tongue in her ass hole. We did the 69.

When she put her hip bones in my face, her ass hole and pussy showed to be the fattest parts of her body. That boodee hole, wrinkled to the max and brown, was crying out, "Me first!" but I parted her thick cunt hair to clear the area I wanted to face farm. I found the pussy pretty, real pretty. The cunt's outer lips were thin and lower lips were darker in color and not long enough to cover her cunt hole. The clit was fully covered but stood out. I went over that pussy like a migrant clearing a cabbage crop while Rosa nibbled on my dick head like it was a tootsie pop.

Her ass hole kept saying, "Me! Me! Me!" I attacked that boodee hole with the suction of a Hoover. She pushed my head away but I fought back and vacuumed that circle more.

I pierced her pooter with my tongue and Rosa said, "Carumba!" That's what I was looking for. I wasn't going to try and get the boodee hole right then. I figured I had at least six months to work towards laying pipe between her left and right hip bones.

Once Henry was Paul Bunyan big, I wanted her to sit on my dick. She wanted to jack and suck Henry, hoping he would shoot off and we wouldn't fuck. I sat on the side of the bed and demanded she sit on my dick. When she finally directed her bones towards my lap Skeeter bounced off her anus and Rosa jumped forward. "Wrong hole!" she said.

Smartly, and hurriedly, that ho grabbed Henry and jammed him into her other pocket. I punched in and she collapsed forward, bending over like she had spotted a quarter on the floor. I followed that pussy, stickin' dick, while she was confirming if it was a coin.

This ho turned orange as she took 12 inches of dick. I saw Henry stretched alongside her spine. I lifted her and reached around in front to rub her clit and my balls were hanging below her like they were hers. When I pulled her up from her lean she, again, showed tears. She was a "cry baby" that probably boo-hooed when she left her village in Mexico.

I was worried about the change in her skin color, pulled out, and hugged her in a consolatory way. She wiped her tears just before I picked her up and fucked that lightweight ho standing with her legs wrapped around my waist.

I offered her a view after we began to fuck in the buck. "Look at all that dick you takin'," I told her. She looked for a moment then went back to taking the dick with her eyes closed. Every time I hit that pussy hard, her toes would scrape across my ears. That's what made me nutt. I put a big toe in my mouth and shot skeet deep.

She was glad to get that big dick out of her cunt and exhaled a sign of relief when I climbed off. She quickly closed her legs as if she didn't want to fuck anymore. I laid next to her and told her, "Rub the dick." She pulled on Henry until it got hard again and I ended-up shooting off on one of her hairy underarms.

As time went on Rosa reluctantly took the dick and always showed fright before and during our fucks. She was verbally adamant about my not sticking my dick into her butt. I could have taken it but I didn't. She got better at blowjobs and eventually preferred for me to shoot off into her mouth. By the time I was finished with Rosa, that ho would squeeze out cum over her lips and followed that with a smile.

CHAPTER 4

COOCHEES OF CUMBERLAND COUNTY

AMERICAN PIE

BEFORE PRESIDENT TRUMAN'S racial integration of the Armed Forces, the military mirrored the institutionalized segregation and "Jim Crow" attitudes prevalent in civilian society. After Truman's politically forced dictatorial order, the military advanced a positive social model for the nation and the world.

Many cultural exchanges have happened since. I tolerated a White boy blasting Charlie Pride in the barracks. He tolerated me blasting James Brown. Because of Presidential Executive Order 9981 it soon became the first time a bunch of us African-American soldiers heard country music. Also, since soldiers have a common mission to save the world, housing patterns on and around military bases required families and people to learn and deliver tolerance.

When I moved out of the barracks at Fort Bragg and into Fayetteville I was nearly 20 years old and it was the first time in my life I lived within the habitat of peckerwoods.

I moved on Shaw Mill Road into an apartment complex which consisted of 15, one- bedroom apartments that formed a semi-circle edging a swimming pool. I was the only Black living there. Almost everyday after work, instead of taking a shower, I felt "free" to join the Caucasians at the waterhole.

There was a female peckerwood always pulling up her bikini bottom every time she walked past my up-skirt view of her from the water. What I noticed about her, moreso than any other thing, was the hair sticking out from her bikini crotch. No doubt; I loved a hairy cunt and our racial difference did not dismay my lust nor the fact that she was mated. She was good looking and fine - period. My mother used to always say, "Leave well enough alone," so I tolerated her tease.

Give me credit. I was cool although this particular peckerwood had lively, tight tits, a baseline belly, taught yet tender-looking thighs, cheerleader curved calves, and was a little bowed between the legs like she was the "O" in the cheer line that spelled "Score!"

Her bubbled butt fought the back of her swimsuit for property rights. Compared to female competitors at the pool, this bird was flamboyant; hot. Only her husband's call for her to come into their nest halted her show.

Lo and behold, early one morning that specimen knocked at my back door. I lived about four apartments from her and it was easy for her to slip down the rear of the complex to my place. When I opened the door she flashed open a long coat showing only how she was hatched. I understood then why they call those things headlights.

"My name's Katie. You like?" she asked, with the accent of a bible toting, white lightin' drinking, chaw-chewing, NASCAR watching, and Second Amendment rights radical. Before I could respond she had one foot inside the door. "I like," I told her.

She checked security before going any further, asking, "Anybody else here?" while at the same time headed straight into the bedroom. I "headed" straight for that hairy box between her legs to check out the roots of her coochee curls. I was grinning in front of that pussy like I was inspecting brushed teeth in a mirror. She stopped me before I could put my nose into her crotch.

This ho didn't want head; she wanted LSD. I should have known that a female peckerwood wouldn't invade my nest so she could be eaten. She told me, "No! Don't!" I looked up, trying to figure out what the problem was. She told me, "Sometimes my husband fucks me before he goes to work." I must have still looked confused. "I ain't clean," she added. I stupidly said, "Oh!"

This bird was "fast." I liked "fast." Without hesitation she began working my dick like it was a fresh stick of Doublemint gum. She hurried Henry into her mouth and plucked Skeeter with her lips like she was craving cock. "I could tell you had a big cock," she told me, after unlocking her jaws to make room for speech. "I saw you staring at me like you wanted to fuck the shit out of me. That's why I'm here."

She really got off on looking at the mirrors alongside my bed, already there when I moved into the apartment. "Damn, this IS a big ass cock," she said, admiring Henry from different angles like a hawk standing over its kill. After watching herself stuff my standard into her cunt, she asked if I had a condom. I didn't. Katie continued to crowd her cunt anyway.

"There's no way I can take all of this," she told me, as she slowly worked the penis past her husband's primary point of penetration and paused. "Damn, this fucker's big as hell!" she said. That ho measured Henry, gauging his ground with grips. "Fucking cock is big!" she hollered.

That girl snatched my dick out the cunt, wiped it with the sheet, and jammed Skeeter down her throat. She gagged and it made her eyes water. I was laid back, like I was on vacation with a local from a different climate. She worked like a bird at a feeder.

"I'mma fuck this son-of-a-bitch," she said as she return to her mount. This ho was serious. She moved her ass in all kinds of directions and alternated looking at the mirrors and the real thing. I asked her, "You like them mirrors don't you?" She answered gleefully, saying, "It's like watching a fuckin' porno!"

She told me, "I'm on the pill. You can cum in me if you want to." I didn't want my skeet mixed with her husband's and told her I wanted to shoot off into her mouth. Katie immediately clamped her jaws down on Henry and rolled her tongue underneath Skeeter.

I told her how I wanted my mayonnaise spread. "Cover and grab that dick head with your lips," I instructed. She held my dick head lightly with her lips and confirmed that's what I wanted. "Yes," I said. "But first, I want you to kiss it. Kiss my dick." After four or five tender lip touches on swollen Skeeter, Henry was loaded for bear.

I took my dick out of her hand, skinned it back where Skeeter shined like jewelry, and busted a huge nutt on her precious, perky, pouty lips. I had eleven hard-owns with my toes and dick each pointing north when I shot that load. I lathered Katie's lips and skeet rolled down to her chin. Decades later, I remember that nutt.

I was weak and wanted to skip work. The problem was that in the Army you have to have a better reason for missing work than being lethargic from draining your lizard. I was slow at work all day. My supervisor got on my case in the early afternoon. "You need to get more rest," he said, before adding, "You can't be standing on your dick all night."

The very next morning, real early, here comes Katie. "I'm going to take all of it this time," she told me. To tolerate the dick, she began to talk.

Come to find out she was a hillbilly. I sort of expected that much, if not because of the twang in her voice because of the "Daisy Dukes" she mostly wore. She moved to Carolina with her high school sweetheart, now a soldier, from a coal mining area of West Virginia. Our sunrise rendezvous reminded me of Charlie Pride's big hit, "Kiss An Angel Good Morning." She had just turned 18 and her boldness reflected her Hatfield-McCoy heritage. Either she liked a good libidinous feud or was just straight-up a whore.

The mirrors provided a focal point where we didn't have to constantly look at each other. We experimented as if we were in a laboratory trying to isolate the human gene involved in interracial sexual attraction. One time she slammed her cunt down on the dick and asked me to feel where it had reached near her navel. While she was impressed with herself, I wondered her brain's cell count. "There's more to go," I told her.

One morning she was sucking my dick and that ho announced, "You can eat me out if you want." I didn't know what in the hell "eat out" meant. She explained, "My ol' man didn't fuck me this morning. I gave him a blowjob. You can eat my pussy if you want."

I wanted. We began to do 69 and it took rubbing my face into a Caucasian cunt to learn why they call that thing a pussy. Her pubic hair was softer than White Cloud. It felt like my nose was nuzzling a baby kitty.

While the freakiness of our contrasting skin colors expired rather quickly, her pussy became a curiosity. It changed colors like a chameleon. It wasn't all that sweet so I figured "mountain dew" was an acquired taste. My senses were able to detect when Katie's vagina switched from a cunt into a coochee into a sperm collector and back again.

69 was great and we did that a lot. It blew my mind how red that ho's anus could get.

It was a nice boodee hole. It loosened instead of tightening. I expected some verbal slur from it but that rascal never muttered any message.

To spice up our fucks this girl would, from time to time, show up at my door wearing something other than just her birthday suit. One time she modeled sexy lingerie, stockings, heels, garter belt, and all. She had on make-up and sure enough she looked different in the face. Her hairy, color-changing pussy, clit, and red boodee hole all looked the same however. I pasted her mouth with skeet like I was trying to glue her lips together.

She liked jacking my dick with her feet as we talked or took a break. I liked it too. She asked me very politely not to shoot off while she was doing that, as if she knew that might happen. (It was a waste of cum she said). One time I couldn't help myself and ended-up shooting off all over her feet. Katie walked to the bathroom like she had cuts on her toes because cum was all over her cuticles.

It was pretty much by accident the first time we did anal sex. It was cold outside and our difference in body temperatures put my hot balls on her cool hips to chill. Henry climbed her back like a vine on the outfield wall at Wrigley Field. He got as hard as a lightpole and she moved him between her butt cheeks with Skeeter on her boodee hole.

She recognized that I was punching dick head against her ass hole and her turd cutter pinched my dick head. That caused me to automatically lurch forward forcefully. Without hesitation, Katie reached back and pulled my dick out of the crack of her butt. I thought that ho was about to say "No!" and lecture me about how too big my dick was.

Instead, Katie spit on some fingers, lathered saliva over her ass hole, jacked my dick a couple of times, and then mashed my dick head into her anus. Surprisingly, Skeeter plopped into the boodee hole relatively easily. She gave out a "Whew!" and the muscle of her anus tighten its grip and squeezed what had gotten inside.

Skeeter shrank from the pressure. I could feel the blood rush back towards my groin. She moved her hand and I just let my dick head soak up the feeling of being in a warm, wanting ass hole for the first time. She reached back, felt the connection, and slapped on more saliva.

She grunted as slow penetration occurred. As the volume of the grunts hushed, Henry hardened and buried deeper. Once again, she lathered my dick with spit. When I had a good length of LSD in her butt hole she put a hand on my belly for me to stop. "I want to see," she said. "Get on top." I pulled the covers back, rolled over, and both of us looked at the mirrors to see how my big black dick looked standing down in her soft, bubbled, pale butt. "You got more to go," I told her.

She laughed and said, "No fuckin' way. That bastard's in far enough." I felt her laughs all the way down my dick and it felt good. I didn't stroke the boodee hole because of the possibility of breaking some skin. I just kept digging and she let me. Now and then she would reach back to guide Henry away from her spine and more towards her intestine. As more dick penetrated, Katie would shake her head from side to side, as if she was answering a hillbilly friend's inquiry as to whether she had ever fucked a Black guy.

Intermittent grips by her anus muscle, the small amount of lubrication, and the heat deep in her butt left me helpless. It felt like my whole body had crawled up in that girl's ass. Katie took that dick. She was shaking her head violently as I busted that nutt deep.

Decades later, I remember that.

Easing out of that tight hole was as much an event as stickin' the dick in. Henry didn't want out. Katie was the one who pulled him out of heaven. Afterwards, that hillbilly warned me against shootin' off in a boodee hole. "That's nasty," she said.

I hated it when she and her husband moved. He must have noticed her holes didn't fit his dick. They fit mine fine.

Coochees of Cumberland County

HOCUS POCUS

TRAINING IS CRITICAL in protecting personnel. However, the value of such training is not fully appreciated by recruits until confronted while on mission. For example, one component of that training was preparation for a chemical attack. One would think that being stationed stateside an attack of that nature would be highly unlikely. However, biological agents are everywhere and I was glad I learned to hold my breath for an extended period of time until I could don a gas mask.

I remember the day just as well as I can recall how I got this burn scar on my arm. I picked-up a girl walking on the shoulder of Shaw Mill Road. Her name was Belinda.

She was brown skin, short, wide and moving quickly. Her flip-flops were crushing innocent weeds on the shoulder of the road. Her knees were bumping together as if she didn't know if she wanted to go left or right. Bra-less whale-sized titties flopped around like fish fresh out of water. Her arms were swinging like she was picking stake tomatoes from an adjacent row. Her hair was so nappy, a fire would start if she used a comb.

Like any road agent, Belinda scouted her environment. "You live he ah by yo'self?" she asked. I told her I did. She requested more clarification. "Ain't nobody else he ah?" she inquired. I told her we were alone. She asked a question to learn my mission objective. "You wonna fuck don't cha?" I gave more than my name and serial number. I answered, "Yes."

Belinda beat me to the bedroom, pulling off her T-shirt before kicking off her flip- flops and dropping her shorts. She didn't even mention the mirrors on the wall. She got right to business. "I know you wont to play with dees," she said as she uncovered her tits.

"Dat's prob lee Y you pick me up." I got her straight. "I ain't no tittie man," I told her. "I like pussy and ass."

Hearing that, she dropped her big draws, laid down, and spread her legs. A big dose of "rotten" fumed the air. It was a chemical attack. The pussy made the air heavy enough to cloud up the glass next to the bed. It was an odor that adequately described violence. It was a "Whew!, Goddamnnn!, Flush dat!" kind of odor. That funk was vulgar and actually made me cough - and I didn't have my military gas mask.

I made no assumptions about the attack. I asked, "Damn girl! How long you been walking?" She was nonchalant as she explained why she smelled so awful. "Some guys ran a train on me and put me out foe I could take a baff," she told me.

All of a sudden Belinda began digging between her legs and pulled a condom out the pussy like a magician snatches a rabbit out the hat. "He ah," she said. "Put dis in dah toilet." I was so shocked I did it.

Her cunt lips caught my attention just as much as the funk and her wizardry. Those rascals were long as socks and, no doubt, when she took a pee she had to part them. I asked her why they were that long and she claimed it was because "Niggas like eatin' pussy." She may have been right but I believe she stretched them by playing with herself.

Those things looked like dachshund ears.

"How many guys was in the train?" I asked her. "I don't know," Belinda said, before going into a too-long explanation. Come to find out, she fucked a pair of roommates who later invited the whole neighborhood to come over and get some pussy. "I was drunk,"

Belinda told me, before adding, "Dey couldah toll me dey was gonna run a train on me. I ah nympho. I wouldah done it."

That pussy's odor was "three" strong so I cut the conversation and told her to take a shower. Before she hit the shower she asked me to go to the store and buy her a bottle of Massengill. I wasn't going into any store and walk out with a feminine product. "Well den," she said, "Git me a Coca-cola. Make sho it a 16-ounce." I definitely wanted to see how those cunt lips would feel in my mouth. I fancied parting her pussy like I would turn the page of a book. So, I went to the store.

When I got back she was still in the shower. I sniffed her panties, at an arm's distance, while sitting on the couch. She hollered out of the bathroom for the cola. I told her I put the soda in the freezer, thinking she wanted it cold when she got out the shower. Belinda was somewhat obstinate when she said, "Nigga, is you crazy? Bring it he ah."

That girl took the bottle, squatted in the tub, and parted her cunt lips like she was Secret Service clearing a way for the President to pass through. With her hand over the top, she shook up and then stuck the bottle into the chamber between her legs. Damn if that girl didn't squirt Coca-cola out the coochee. That pussy farted as if it was clearing its throat and its long lips flapped like Old Glory at The Washington Monument in March.

It was an astonishing thing to see and hear. They call that thing a pussy but it didn't purr. Some call it a coochee but it didn't coo. It made a noise like a car rolling on a flat tire. She meticulously wiped her cunt and patted it dry. I paid attention like I was in NASA Mission Control during the moon landing.

Once she laid down, she offered another service communication. "Eat my pussy firss," she told me, as she spread her legs. This time her coochee and I were allies. She let me have all the time I wanted on her dog-eared cunt, to search for fleas and such, while she smoked another joint. Once I declared it critter free I pulled one flap of her cunt lips over one jaw and one over my other. I was masked like I was gonna rob somebody. I gnawed on them; balled them in my mouth; and rubbed my face with them for a long time.

I hummed the Star Spangled Banner while I was muff diving. When I got to the "bombs bursting in air" part, she busted a business-like nutt. That pussy farted on my face, spreading Smucker-thick honey all over my mugg. "Dat was good," she said. "I needed dat. I kant git no nutt on no train." I told her I had plenty of songs to hum if she would make her pussy fart again. Belinda said, "Naw. Let's fuck."

I told her, "Suck my dick den." That girl told me, "I geh good head. I ah make you cum quick. I ain't ready for you to cum. I wanna be fucked." Belinda then asked a question she shouldn't have needed to ask. "You got a rubber?" I told her I didn't have any condoms. "You needs a rubber," she told me. All dem niggas fucked me; I don't know high many it was. I don't know if all dem woe a rubber."

She went into the back pocket of her pants and pulled out two packets. One of the packets was a condom and the other was some sort of lubricant. "At lease you ain't got no lil' dick," she said, as she ripped the tops with her teeth and jacked Henry for fit. "I hate a nigga wit' a lil' dick." She lathered Henry with both hands, to the point where it didn't even feel like I had a condom on. My dick got hard as hell.

Belinda put my penis into her pussy like she was putting in a tampon. I was careful to pummel that pussy with short strokes whereby my dick wouldn't easily come out because we'd have to stop fucking to maneuver Skeeter back between those lips. I hit her cunt walls hard and when Henry struck a nerve she whimpered.

She stayed still as I banged, not running from the dick at all. There were times when I was ready to bust a nutt and she interrupted the fuck by asking questions like "You got a girlfriend?" and "You wont a roommate?" which took my mind off skeetin'.

With all my dick in her pussy, she looked me dead in my eyes with the seriousness of a school principal giving ten days suspension. Like a Home Depot store clerk instructing me how to pressure clean, Belinda told me, "Buss a nutt." I hit that pussy like I was trying to scrape graffiti off her ovaries. She grabbed my balls and massaged them.

Henry started coughing up cum and wouldn't stop until her hand released my family jewels. Belinda hurriedly pushed me off so the condom wouldn't come off in her cunt.

She told me that. "You ah be surprise at what kin git loss in dare," she said.

I retrieved her funky underwear from the couch where, from an arm's distance, I had been sniffing them. "I'll give you a joint to take with you if you let me keep these," I told her. "Let's smoke one nigh and gimme one to go," she answered.

While we got high again, Henry got hard again. I told Belinda, "Since you suck a dick so good, I'll geh yah another joint if you geh me some head." She said, "Bet." I sniffed her draws, from an arm's distance, while she sucked my dick.

This girl had skills. After my first shot of skeet Belinda capped my pee hole with her tongue and blocked the following bolts of brimstone with her lips tight around the base of my dick head. She gulped the remaining spunk while I was up on my heels, braking like a cartoon character trying to stop.

Swallowing skeet was just as natural for Belinda as drinking water. She licked her lips and changed the subject by asking why I wanted to keep her draws. "Don't be puttin' no Roots on me," she said. I told her I didn't believe in Roots and that I just wanted something to remind me of her. I sniffed those panties, from an arm's distance, for days.

Coochees of Cumberland County

28 DAYS

A COMMANDING OFFICER can be the difference between harmony and discord in a military unit. One of the most uncertain times comes when there is a change in the CO.

When a soldier is on a libidinous mission, pussy is the commanding officer. That's why females gravitate to military bases. There's no famous roller coaster on Fort Bragg. It ain't no major tourist attraction. What attracts females to the area is the plethora of penis to command. That was confirmed when I met Miranda. She was from Savannah visiting a dick, I figured, at Fort Bragg.

Being a native of where the Girl Scout organization originated, she was innately mission oriented. For her, fucking and selling cookies was alike and fucking was felicity.

Like a girl scout moving from door to door, not one time did we stay in one position very long during sex. Miranda would seal her sell with a grunt, moan, or fingernails in my back at exactly the right time. She earned her merit badge.

This ho was dark-skinned, petite, and bow legged. Her hips were so well-defined her ass hole was exposed. And, she had a beautiful black boodee hole. It was puffy, uniquely shaped, and lined with five lines exploding from its chocolate Cheerio center. I was back there so much, I called her boodee hole my "Oval Office."

The pussy was fat too. It was one of those black cunts that hung like a hornet nest when her back was turned. I loved watching her pick up things off the floor when she was naked. I'd throw stuff down, usually money. During sex that coochee liked me to chase it.

Miranda would moved like she was trying to get away and then surrendered when I caught up. Every now and then we ended up on the floor, halfway off the bed, or into some position where we both were trying to figure how to get the dick back in.

She took command without even knowing how much dick there would be to manage. I didn't know about her puckered pooter then. She flipped over on the bed so I could hit it from the back and her boodee hole caught my eye like big money found. Her exposed ass hole, placed like a catcher's mitt in a narrow strike zone, challenged me to decide whether I wanted more her sugar or spice.

Our first fuck turned out to be a change of command ceremony. While we were doing it, the phone rang and I answered. That's right, I answered the phone while I was fathoms deep in pussy. We didn't have caller ID back then so I was curious who was calling me during my usual after-work-to-get-ready-for-the-night nap.

It was Annette. She was my steady pussy and oral nutt receptor and I couldn't quickly cut off a conversation with her. Miranda stopped moving and my dick, harder than a bicycle frame, was just sittin' in her pussy.

It must have been obvious to Miranda that I was talking to a female but she remained quiet. Maybe she got off on the fact that I was talking on the phone to another ho while I had dick in her. I know I did. Maybe she just couldn't give a damn because she needed a place to stay. Regardless, I slowly stroked her pussy and dusted my "Oval Office" with a finger as I talked on the phone.

"I need to suck my dick," Annette blatantly told me. That was one of Annette's favorite tricks to get me to come and rescue her from whatever boredom she was ever in.

"It's nap time for me," I told her. "I'm going to take that nutt in my mouth," she responded. "I know that," I said. The moment, a time of decision, evolved. "Come and get me and let me suck my dick. You told me it was my dick to take care of and I wanna suck my dick," she continued. Miranda urged me to hang up by removing my finger off of her attractive ass hole. "I gotta go," I told Annette. "Okay, be that way," she said, and then hung up.

Miranda had been quiet and respectful. I enjoyed thanking her for that. I used every sexual lesson I had learned to do it. I kissed her thighs, blew light breezes across her coochee, and roughly licked, kissed, and sucked the pussy. I flipped that ho over like she was a pancake and poked my tongue as deep as I could into her butt hole. I put my full mouth over her anus and vacuumed my "Oval Office."

We went missionary and I pounded that pussy like I was a blacksmith repairing a bent horseshoe. As my meteor crashed to expand her crater, she uplifted her hips and wrapped her legs around my back. It wasn't long after her putting her legs around me and fingernails in my back that I exploded into mind blowing, nutt blasting non-equilibrium.

Spent. That's what I was. Spent after sex is the closest physical feeling that is comparable to being out of gas halfway between distant exits on the Interstate. Later that night, Miranda got more bounty when she gave me a blowjob. Although I didn't tell her, truthfully that ho whipped me.

The next day when I got home from work she had luggage in my house, still unpacked.

I asked her, "You moving in?" She answered, "You want me to leave?" I didn't.

That Georgia plum stayed and our relationship deepened. I started having feelings for her because she was taking long dick before sleep, accepting quickies early in the morning, and slobbering all over Henry in between. Her allowing me to hunch her hips until I fell asleep was crucial in my growing affection. It seemed all I had to do was have have a hard dick and she would give me somewhere to put it. I was satisfied.

She asked if she could use my car to look for a job. She should have needed to pass her anal sex test before I made a commitment like that. I said yes, however, with one stipulation. I told her, "Don't drive on Bragg Boulevard during rush hour." Sure enough, Miranda was involved in an accident that same day on Bragg Boulevard during rush hour.

She was not at fault but my insurance company didn't care. Injured enough to where she had to stay in the hospital I went up there. She looked at me with sorrowful eyes so I didn't berate or criticize her. Besides, her face was swollen from hitting the steering wheel, which broke her jaw, and she was ugly. That was punishment enough.

After she got out of the hospital, I had a girl in my bed who couldn't suck dick.

Annette regained command. I spent the first few nights of Miranda's home recovery away from home. Once Miranda got the message that I preferred sleeping somewhere else, she made it a point for us to start fucking again.

With her mouth still wired shut, she asked, "It's been more than a week since we fucked. Don't you need some pussy?" I told her I thought she was too injured to take the dick. "I broke my jaw, not my stuff," she said. She peeled off her clothes and bent over, exposing her boodee hole. Her anus looked like Monday morning to a workaholic.

Miranda was conducting a coup. She told me, "I like yo' lips on my ass hole. Kiss my ass." That was it! I bussed her boodee hole heartedly and rubbed my dick on it. "Is that what you want?" she asked me. "I've always wanted it," I told her.

Miranda jacked my dick like it was a part of her physical therapy. I was ready to fuck after that and rubbed Skeeter on her saliva laden, tight anus. On my way in Miranda said, "Don't hurt me." I responded with a lie. I told her, "I promise it won't hurt." After I got the entire dick head in she told me something I already knew. "You got a big dick," she said. Miranda changed her mind and asked me, politely, to wait until later. I didn't want to take the boodee. I wanted her to give it to me, so I did.

Later that night I had my dick against her ass hole and Miranda pulled out a jar of Vaseline. "Here," she said, "use this." I rubbed Vaseline on my lips and wiped them on her ass hole. That was nice. Then I greased a finger and went two knuckles deep into her butt as a test run.

She was lying flat on her belly when I pushed my dick into her ass and there was no inhibition by her as it went in. We laid there for awhile, my dick wallowing in her warm ass, before I began stroking that boodee like it was a pussy. I was sliding in and out that rent like I had a little dick, determined to have my balls bounce off her pussy.

That girl took much dick; not all, only much. She didn't holler or move from my pushing nor tell me to slow down or stop. Her anus loosened enough for me to hit her rectum from different angles. That boodee hole felt so good I made frying sounds, "Ssssss, Ssssss," as Henry went wall to wall, deep and shallow, and slow and fast.

Miranda was taking the dick like a sex doll.

She was responding to anal sex as if she wasn't feeling a thing. Henry wasn't accustomed to that. He - no we - wanted to hear this ho holla. I pulled out, got up off the bed, and cut the room light on. The ass hole was gaped open, wide as a silver dollar where I could see inside. It was beautiful already but the gap made it awesome. I told her I wanted her to sit on the dick.

On the side of the bed she repeatedly slid her boodee hole over my dick. That ho was twerking with LSD all up in her ass. Ready to nutt, I lifted her off the dick and used a washcloth to wipe Henry so I could shoot off on her lips. She didn't want ass-to-mouth even if it didn't touch her lips. "Go wash your dick," she said. Henry wanted a nutt then. I put the dick back into her ass and nutted.

Just before she was scheduled to have her jaws unwired, she put up a fight when I fucked her in the ass and wouldn't let me fuck like I wanted. Something just wasn't right.

I put two and two together and came up an answer. She was able to take the dick in the ass so well the first time because she had taken a pain killer and muscle relaxer.

We had to have a conversation about anal sex after that. I told her she would have to let me fuck the boodee like I wanted to fuck the boodee. She told me I "fucked too hard. You might hurt something back there. And," she added, "it's nasty to shoot off in my ass." She told me she would be willing to let me fuck her in the ass if I didn't try to put all my dick in her and didn't nutt in her butt.

The very next day at work, just before the end of the day, Annette called and ordered me to "bring my ass" to see her, "E-mediately!" She jumped all over my case about avoiding her. She sounded like Patton at the beginning of the movie. Because of the timing I wondered if she had found out about the great sex I was having without her.

Being specific, Annette verified what I wondered.

"Yo' dick too big to be puttin' in my ass, Fenn," Annette said from out of the blue.

Calling me by my last name always made her sound like a commander. She continued her rant. "Ain't it enough I let you fuck me in my pussy how you wont and suck yo' dick like you wont?" she reasoned. "I love you Fenn, but you ask too much of me."

Who knows why Annette threw the anal sex thing at me. She had plenty of other stuff to curse me out about. She went on and on about what she did for me but yet had to run me down for time. "I don't want you to give my dick to nobody else. That's my dick," she argued.

I had to make a decision about Miranda. Annette wouldn't give me any boodee but she was nutt dependable and I had been with her for a long time. Bottom line, I had to let Miranda go. Living with her cramped my bachelor lifestyle anyway. Miranda and I talked breaking up and her finding somewhere else to go. Her inability to find a job helped her decision to return home to Savannah.

Coochees of Cumberland County

RUSH HOUR

ANY OCCUPATION WHERE loaded weapons are carried the workplace is a precarious place.

The close proximity of loaded firearms is the reason police departments established what they call "The Blue Line." That's why law enforcement workers only get a "slap on the wrist" for demeaning their "protect and serve" oath of service. Being around people in possession of firearms is hazardous, period. In any gun-toting family, "Chance" is the middle child.

I took a chance one time, when I was disrespectful to a peer I had to go to the rifle range with. I thought I had good reason. He had a "mama's boy" upbringing and weak "ho hunt" skills. I called myself cultivating him during Wolf Patrol, trying to school him on handling hoes. I caused a rift between us yet never felt the need to apologize.

This new guy scooped a ho who wasn't even all-that. She and I ended-up fucking or I wouldn't be telling this. There was no previous meeting of our eyes, sly remarks, or body bumps between us that I can remember. She had a pussy so a little panting by me and slobbering from Henry was natural. While on Wolf Patrol alone I stopped at her trailer whereas a true friend would have passed by. Being a dogg, I didn't. Sure enough she was home alone.

She plugged into my attention right away when she answered my inquiry as to where my friend was by telling me that she and he had broken up. A light bulb appeared above my crotch as Henry requested and received more head room in my pants. My blood flow startled me down there like the power coming back on after a storm.

I had a noble reason to fuck her. I heard her talk down to my friend, an airborne soldier and my "pupil", like he was a child. She had the new guy pussy-whipped so bad he had to knock on her front door to get in. She was one of those dominate types but she couldn't pull that "good pussy" shit on me. On my first libidinous mission a big, black mama farted in my face. There wasn't anything this ho could do to make me lame brain for her.

What she needed was for Henry to parachute into the "drop zone" of her butt. This ho was really dark skinned and my being partial to probing black holes I was curious if her anus was pronounced or subdued, oval or round, luscious or limp. I wanted to collide with this ho's confidence. Her ass hole was where it was located.

Apparently I showed at the right time. We both recognized we wanted to fuck. In the bedroom I "headed" straight for her cunt, pushing her legs back to where her pussy sprang up like a pop-up book page. The boodee hole was dark chocolate. I liked dark chocolate.

That prompted me to stick my nose in her coochee and lap that ass hole with my tongue. She quietly gave me an "Ummmm!"

Because I had my face all in her cunt and hips for so long, she thought I was primarily oral. I was working on her mind. In between slopping my face in her trough of delight, anytime I made a different move on the cunt or boodee hole I'd say something. I pulled my tongue out of the pussy and told her, "When I do dat, please squeeze." I sucked her ass hole and said, "Gimme dat!" I flicked her tingler with my tongue and asked her, "Why yo' clit so long?"

That ho asked me, "What you wanna do, talk or fuck?"

I teased her more. Intermittent with my kisses on that pussy were very gracious greetings of tongue and nose scrapes over her anus at the most sensuous moment. Her boodee hole pulsated. I licked that breakskin wet and then lightly blew air over it as if I was tending to a child's minor injury. I hoped her pooter would curse me, loudly, for tapping it with my tongue.

Her clit was beige colored and with a pointed tip looked like a typing eraser. It's cover went way back and the antenna was thick at its bottom like one of those fat pencils Kindergarten's use. It looked weird. My face ran among a winking boodee hole, stretched clit, and dewy cunt like a child on a playground. A glob of honey gathered at the entrance of that pu-nanny and that coochee looked like a chocolate cup cake with icing. I licked a tongue tip of honey and sucked it off with a sound like I was responding to someone saying something crazy. I let her know I was enjoying my meal.

Henry took over and long, stiff, determined dick went deep into that ho. Henry hurt her too. "Oh, shit," she yelled more than once. Then she came out with, "Yo' dick too big! Get off me. Yo' dick too big." After more forced strokes in the buck she pressured down her legs and we ended up in the missionary position. After a few complimentary strokes that way, she pushed me off. "I can't take that," she admitted. "You hurtin' my stomach."

That seemed bogus to me. I thought she was the dominate one. I thought she was going to fuck me so good and get my nose so wide open I would fight my apprentice for the rights to the pussy. I knew a big dick would knock her down a few notches.

"Here, suck the dick," I said. She still tried to show she was in charge, saying, "You like to eat pussy. Do that!" That was okay with me because I wanted to continue to lubricate her ass hole for an anal fuck. "Let's 69," I said. She told me to lie near the edge of the bed. I did. She put one knee on the bed and a foot on the floor and squatted over my face, putting her shiny black ass directly in front of my mugg.

Her bending over to put her pussy on my mouth caused her boodee hole to speak. It actually said, "Poot!" It blew my mind how innocently she farted. "Oh!, excuse me," she told me. Her apology told me that I was correct in grading her as not being all-that. A real ho wouldn't have apologized. A real ho would have giggled and asked me if I wanted another. Right then and there I decided my friend could have this ho.

As I felt the poot hit and bounce off my forehead I automatically began to suck that ho's boodee hole like I was trying to get water out of a cactus. I kissed it too. I kissed it as she rubbed her beautiful black anus all over my cigarette holder. I wanted to be gassed again but dared not ask for it because she might put my freakiness in the street.

Between me lathering her pussy and slurping her ass hole and her giving Henry head, it was all good. She could suck a dick. Apparently it was how she was able to rule a nigga. I decided to get a quickie and shoot off in her mouth before she got tired of the 69.

The sweet honey coming out of that black pussy, the sight of her succulent shitter, and her washing Skeeter almost had me whipped enough to change my mind about her.

That ho skint my dick back, wagged my dick, and gobbled like a goblin like she was asking for it. So, I shot off. Just as I did, we both heard a car door slam loudly. She removed her head and boodee hole and looked out the window. Her supposed-to-be ex was slowly moving into the yard. She didn't have time to spit the nutt out. That's how I know she swallowed. I was still skeetin' while I was putting my draws on.

Her ex was slowly moving towards the front door. Thank goodness he didn't have a key - or we were at the rifle range! By the time the guy got to the front door I was closing the door behind me with my sneakers still untied. I did say, "What's up" to him and was safely in my car as he knocked on the door.

Coochees of Cumberland County

BASIC INSTINCT

ALTHOUGH EACH HAS familiar objectives and players, not every mission commences, is conducted, or concludes in the same manner except libidinous ones. Therefore, American soldiers must be able to adapt to whatever type of battle is presented.

On one mission I was tested with an unusual set of circumstances. I preferred women with enough ass to where if I were to toss a quarter onto their ass cheeks, I'd have to conduct a search for the coin. On one particular mission I ran up on a big black mama where if I tossed a quarter on her butt, it would have bounced to Bermuda.

I was introduced to her via chaos. She had four kids ranging in age five and three months. Three of those crumbsnatchers were as wild as the Oklahoma Territory before the Sooners and Tombstone before Wyatt Earp. Their wild west show got my attention before I even considered they had a mama somewhere and then wondered where in the hell she was.

This happened at the wash house. All except the baby were running around like legal civil anarchy had been announced on CNN and as unsupervised as Benjamin Franklin in France. While her kids were out of control their mama was paying attention to the pigs feet she was eating. Her interest in them was telling when she stared at the bone.

She was a big gurl and her entire body looked as solid as Mount Rushmore. Even in a tank top each gallon-large tittie hardly moved. She wasn't fat, just big and imposing. Her head was covered with what looked like a cloth dinner napkin and, like a baby in church, the BB's on the back of her neck were crying out for removal. Her wide feet had punished some thin-soled sandals that seemed to be pleased for a pause.

I took over the dryer she previously used and that's how we first started talking. There happened to be a pair of her panties among my finished clothes. I separated them out and read the graphic "road sign" message "Dangerous Curves" on them. "Dem" draws stretched almost from one of my shoulders to the other. She saw me inspecting her bloomers and came over.

"Dems mines," she said, after she noticed I was holding them up and her knees had knocked her over to where I was. "I musta leff dem in dah dry ya when I took my cloze out." I figured I could get away with anything I wanted to say. "How I know these yours?" I asked. "Red don't fit you. You'd look better in Carolina blue."

I knew right-away this ho didn't have a job because there was no evidence of her having a dental plan. As her cheeks heightened when she smiled a sexy dimple formed on the right side of her face. That dimple looked to be the softest thing on her body and she had only one. "I got some dat color at home," she told me about her unmentionables.

"You geeh me a ride home and I ah show you what dey say. You ah like dem."

I was interested in more than reading her draws. I wanted to try this ho. I wanted to see if she could pop my skull like a pimple with those linebacker legs she had. I wanted to see if I could get her to put my head in a scissor lock and make me say "Uncle" while she was busting a nutt in my mouth. I was curious to see if she could put me in the "sleeper" with her thighs. I wondered if I could stick dick into concrete.

Her oldest came running up to her and started tapping her on the butt. Only because he was tapping, he didn't break his hand. The baby in the child seat was beginning to cry.

Giving myself time to consider her proposal, I turned my attention to the little boy. He spoke right up as we greeted each other with a slap of our palms.

Although she looked grizzly, she went by the delicate name of Lilly. She lived in a fairly large, old house with plenty rooms. Before we got all the clothes out of the car the kids scattered, leaving me and "Young Mother Hubbard" alone.

What I found out was that Lilly didn't have a man; didn't have a clue about child care; and didn't have any inhibitions. The more she moved, the more I was amazed at her physical presence. I figured I could run faster than her so I found the nerve to ask her if she ever thought about being a female wrestler. She said, "I ain't funny. I likes mens."

She told me plenty. She quit school when she had her first baby at 14 years of age. Out of the four kids, she had three baby daddies. It was weird what she told me about their birthdates. "All dem burf day in April," she explained. "Dem two, in dah middle, got dah same daddy but dah other ones got diff rent daddies."

Being that all her kids were born in April, big girl must have been producing eggs big- time in late summer. When she went to get some Kool-Aid she offered, I counted back nine months from April to measure the timing of our meeting. It was mid-July and she was probably hot.

The five-year old, Billy, came in followed by both of his back-ups. "What yo' name is?" Billy asked. I told him who and what I was and that he should address me as "Mister" first. "My name Billy," he told me. "I call Lil' Billy."

Billy explained why he bothered to speak to me in the first place. "Can you fix my bike?" he asked. I told him that it was according to what was wrong with it. His mama spoke up. "Ain't nuttin but dah chain done come off," she said. "I ain't got no wrench tah fix it."

I went to my car and pulled out a wrench. I let Billy tighten the nut while I pulled the chain. On my way back into the house Billy and the crew ran ahead of me and Billy told his mama, "I fix my bike. Mister

Man show me how tah fix it and I fix it." Then he ran back outside and the rest of the crew followed.

"I'm ready to read what's on dem draws you said you had," I told my host. Lilly looked at me like I was a stranger and said, "I thought you was juss be in nice. You wont to see me wit dem on?" I told her, "Yes, ma' am!" emphatically. I played with the three- month old little girl while she went into her bedroom and changed. She walked out of the room with nothing on but baby blue bloomers and that tank-top.

She lifted her top and turned around to show the message on the panties. It showed a sign like you'd see at a fast-food joint or bank. It said, "Drive Thru Only." I wanted to smile but I noticed Lilly had the most lop-sided hips the Lord ever designed. One cheek was higher than the other and even in her panties she didn't have any bounce back there.

Her hips looked to be too hard and tight for me to split. I figured I would need the "Jaws of Life" to get them apart.

I gave a compliment commenting on the lace border of the panties. "Yeah, dey nice," she said. "Dey was a burf day present." My assumption was that the gift came from the man she had two babies from. He probably got the pussy the night of her birthday and made a second crumbsnatcher. Honestly, after looking at her grill and poorly designed hips, I deciphered that this girl had only fucked four times.

Here comes the gang! All big gurl did was pull the shirt down and calmly walk into her room, leaving the door open. Billy sat next to me while his "Two-Live Crew" ran back to wherever their dungeon was located. "You gonna be my new daddy," Billy asked.

"I kind of laughed and asked, "Do you want me to be your new daddy?" Billy answered, "Yeah." Lilly heard us and yelled at Billy. "William Brent, Jr., git yo' ass way from dat man. He ain't come he ah to see you."

I already had something set up for that evening and requested a fucking rain check even though it was difficult to leave "easy." I asked her for a phone number. "I ain't got no phone," she said. "Anyways, yo' wife don't wont me callin' ya'll house." I told her I wasn't married and didn't have a steady girlfriend because I traveled a lot on the weekends. "I need somebody in Fayetteville," I said. It told her I'd be back then to see her later in the week.

During the week, I thought about Billy and that precious, black and beautiful three- month old more than big gurl herself. Before heading home after work on Friday, I headed to Lilly's house to see how the riot was progressing. Billy noticed all the patches I had on my military uniform. "What dat say?' he asked, and I told him. Then, he went on a rampage. "What dat say? What dat say?" His mama saved me. "Billy, lee dat man 'lone."

I told her I liked the way Billy was always asking questions and added that I wanted to get to know her and her "gang" better. "I done toll you 'bout us," she said. "Ain't but one 'nother way you kin git to know me bed dah."

Ignorance is relative. This girl knew exactly what she was talking about when she mentioned "one 'nother way." She scooped up the baby and said, "Com moan." We went into her bedroom and she set the baby in her carseat prison on the floor on the far side of the bed. It surprised me that she directed me to the side of the bed where the baby was.

"I wanna suck yo' dick," she told me. When she said "dick" that one dimple showed up. That girl - no, that woman - unzipped my pants, fumbled through my draws, and pulled out a happy Henry. Right in front of the baby Lilly extricated my balls and handled them like a stripper picking up dollars and then jacked Henry like she was fixing a flat tire in a dangerous neighborhood.

I wanted to shoot off on that dimple but first I had to sit down. She pulled my dick a few more times then treated Henry like he was a genie and her mouth was a bottle. This ho didn't have any teeth in the rear of her mouth on the side where she had the dimple.

While the baby sucked a bottle eyes wide open, Lilly sucked a penis just like that.

One of the kids knocked on the locked door and big gurl never came off the dick. Her non-answer blew my mind. What if the house was on fire? What if "Chester The Molester" had gotten into the crib? It wasn't my problem. I just let big girl do her thing.

Lilly loved sucking dick. I loved hearing her grunt like a bear while she was doing it.

I busted a nutt in her mouth and she swallowed like it was oyster. After siphoning every drop she showed me that one dimple when she asked, "Was dat good?" I told big gurl, "I love you." She laughed with a big smile showing few teeth.

I hated getting the nutt and leaving but she had to feed the kids. She offered me some dinner but when she told me that they were having pork-n-beans I knew it was time to go.

I intentionally returned late, figuring the kids would be fed, bathed, and in bed by 10 o'clock. On the contrary, Billy and the oldest girl were running through the house in hyper mode. "Candy make dem like dat," big gurl said.

Little did I know Lilly was just as anxious to give me more head as I was to receive more. "I like yo' dick big," she told me. I told her, "I like you ain't got no teeth on one side." She laughed and confessed, "Yeah, mens like when I bite dey dick ovah dare," then added, "Tell me when you 'bout to shoot off and I ah put yo' dick on dat side."

Lilly was anxious. On the couch in the front room that ho pulled Henry out and laid her head in my lap and covered-up with the baby's blanket. She sucked my dick like she was trying to get the bean taste out of her mouth.

Every now and then Billy would dash through the area. Big gurl kept her head in my lap and never stopped sucking or grunting. Billy stopped to wonder why his mama never lifted her head. Billy said, "Sit up mama." From under the cover, big gurl said, "Go tah bed Billy." Instead of following orders, one time Billy just stood there.

That girl was jaw-locked on my dick, growling and grunting like a wild bear, right front of her child. I tried to get Billy's attention away from what his mama was doing but he was determined to make sure she was okay under there. I nutted in his mama's mouth with him looking right at me.

The next night, real late, big gurl told me, "I wont tah fuck." We eased into her bedroom and she didn't even bother to cut the light on. She quickly stripped and laid down on the small bed. This ho was solid. There were dents in the mattress where her thighs usually laid. I cut the lamp on. She asked why. "I wanna see," I explained. She halfway sat up and said, "Ain't nuttin wrong wit' me. I ain't got no disease."

I had to explain my explanation. "I just want to look at you," I told her. Big gurl spread her legs, putting a knee up to each big tittie. "He ah! Look all you wont," she said. The first thing that came to my mind was that was the way she must have looked when she was giving birth. I didn't need that picture.

Damn if she didn't have a rough looking, used, jet-black pussy. It was a nappy dugout that had lips folded all over each other and hanging all over the place. I could have eaten on that thing for days. Her pubic area was sparsely covered with patches of hair that looked like tumbleweeds and felt as rough as pine cones. I rubbed with the back of my hand and it felt like I cut myself. I figured that if I ate that pussy I probably get abrasions all over my face.

I must have stared too long. Big gurl asked me, "You like what you see?" I went lowered and took a sniff. She said, "My pussy don't stank." I opened its lips with my fingers and stuck a finger in. Big gurl told me, "Eat it." I lifted her legs to prop the pussy away from her pubic hair so I could suck-up her worn cunt without worry of being the victim of a slasher.

The clit was hiding like the final chapter of a long, difficult book. I skinned it back and her tingler rose like a nuclear missile out of a silo. After I sucked it, Lilly said, "Dat feel good. Do dat ghen." I did. Then I stuck my nose in Lillie's coochee like a puppy who had pooped on the floor one too many times. Carefully, I pushed my tongue into the cunt.

"Dat feel good," she said. "Do dat ghen." My head was right in the middle of her rock hard thighs. I was stretching my tongue like I was a lizard, just to keep my head above torture. That ho said, "Keep yo' tongue in dare whey it at."

I pressed her heavy, vise-grip legs to each side of my head and she caught my signal that I wanted her legs pressed against my ears. Lilly locked me down and not much later that ho started squeezing my head and nutted. The skeet was very fluid, like big gurl was pissing. Honey filled my mouth and was all up in my nose. I couldn't swallow because I couldn't move my jaws. I had to wrestle my head from between her legs and escaped only when she was finished. I had a headache for two days.

The next time I was over there, Lilly told me, "I wonna fuck." Henry wasn't ready for that. We were both worried. I was concerned about her pubic hair puncturing my balls and bleeding. It passed though Henry's mind that Lilly was ripe for pregnancy and any subsequent child would have bad teeth. Bottom line - "we" didn't want to bust a nutt in Lilly, in the mutual interest of offspring survival based on natural selection.

It was early afternoon and the kids were running in and out the house slamming the screen door, like they were alone at the county fair with free ride tickets. She pulled me into her bedroom and jacked Henry hard. While I was trying to convince her I preferred her head more than I wanted to fuck, the kids started banging on the bedroom door.

The most recent baby daddy was outside wanting to see Lilly and their crumbsnatcher.

Big gurl took the baby and they sat in his car talking for a good while. I watched how Billy reacted to him. Passing the car's driver side on his bike multiple times, they didn't even speak.

Lilly figured she had some explaining to do. "He say he wonted tah see dah baby but den axed me to suck hiss dick in dah car. I wont goh do dat in dah public. I told him I had comp knee," she revealed. From then on, I restrained myself from getting too attached to her, Billy, and the baby.

Lilly still tried to give me the pussy but amazingly Henry didn't want the pussy. He drooped whenever I "headed" him that way. In the end, during our brief relationship big gurl only gave me migraines and blowjobs.

Coochees of Cumberland County

ANIMAL HOUSE

UNMARRIED SOLDIERS CAN become as unbalanced at handling finances as pursuing libidinous missions. Paying rent and chasing coochee often becomes burdensome tasks. I had to readjust my spending because runnin' hoes was a religion. So, I decided to move back into the barracks, on base, where a roof and meals were free.

An option developed when I met an older woman, Cynthia, while standing in line at the cleaners. "You high ain't cha'?" she asked. I looked at her like she was asking too much. Then she bragged that she had "the bomb" reefer. "You a good lookin' man, you married?" she inevitably asked. "No," I answered. "I'm just a squirrel tryin' to get a nut."

Cynthia didn't look that bad for a granny wearing glasses. Her invitation to smoke some weed at her home intrigued me to where stickin' dick actually passed through my mind. That's why I accepted her invitation. She was dark-skinned and kind of thick. I could see myself jumpin' them bones. Besides, she was just asking for "it."

I thought we would be alone and I could, at least, get some head while we smoked dope. Instead, at Cynthia's house I was introduced to her seven year-old son, named Marvin, and a slim redbone named Denise, who Cynthia claimed was her teenage daughter but yet was smoking dope with us. Including Cynthia's little white dog, "Cracker", it was crowded.

Cynthia got into my personal business and brought up the idea of me renting a room at her place. I was non-committal, at first, but behind more drinks and weed Cynthia and I reached an agreement. Under-the-influence Henry made my decision for me. There were two coochees at Cynt's house, he told me, two birds and one long, stiff stone.

Securing privacy in that house was impossible. It just never dawned upon me I would have that problem. Apparently the little boy was slow (mentally challenged) and Cynthia had all the door locks taken off. Not even Cynthia's bedroom door was secure. I didn't have any valuables, just clothes, so I just brushed it off. Then, "Cracker" shitted in my sneaker the first day I was gone. Having an unsecured bedroom door turned out to be the smallest of matters in that house.

One morning Denise crawled into bed with me. I didn't say anything. What she was up to didn't get hard quickly enough because she eventually turned and reached inside my draws. Henry stretched, like Rip Van Winkle, as she jacked him out of his sleep.

"You a little girl and that's a big dick," I told her, as she yanked and then massaged my mass with meaningful compressions. She said nothing; just kept on pulling and squeezing. Hardening Henry suggested to her that we fuck. "Wait a minute," she said, and then pulled off her panties. When she resettled, I asked her, "Are you old enough to be in here?" She urged me on top and spread her legs. I fucked the hell out that ho.

Hoping to deter her from bothering me again, I punched Skeeter into the crack of her ass. The boodee hole was tight and dry and I could only try to get in it. Henry must have enjoyed probing because he creamed her pooter. With skeet smothering her ass hole, she put on her draws and left the room.

One day after work, before I could get away, Cynthia and I were alone when she asked me to come into her room. Cynthia didn't waste any time getting to the point. "Denise say you and huh fucked. She say you got a big dick and you hurt huh." A lot of things went through my mind when Cynt put "Denise" and "fucked" in the same sentence.

"Denise ain't nothin' but 16 years old. If you wont some pussy, you needs to fuck me," she said, as she began peeling off clothes. My body's blood flowing southward somehow made her attractive and by the time Cynt was down to her bra and panties I had my dick out. If I had to dust off this ho's pussy, I figured I may as well have fun doing it. I bounced Henry a couple of times against her mouth and the little dog barked. "Shut up, Cracker!" Cynt hollered.

Before I gave her LSD, I asked Cynt, "Are you sure your heart can handle this?" Cynt took hold of Henry and answered. "I ain't got no heart problems," she said. "I got a wont some of dis dick problem." Cynt sucked Henry until he filled snugly between her jaws.

"Cracker" watched in the posture of a pimp, as if he was waiting on his money.

I was undecided about eating Cynt's cunt. I wanted to just fuck, at first. Her pussy was ugly. It's loose lips folded all over the hole that wasn't pink. Between her legs looked like a gorilla in a forested cover but somehow its stubby grey hair and jet black color made it exciting - an adventure. Black cunt lips always turned me on and this pussy had a freaky, fetish ugliness. I felt a connection between myself and my ancestors.

Her floppy, shiny pussy lips seduced my carnal playfulness. I pulled back the coochee's raven clit jacket, expecting to find a huge hominid underneath. She didn't even have a big clit. It was tiny as hell. I could only hope the taste of her pussy would make it worthwhile my being down there. I stuck my tongue deep into her box and it tasted like leftovers, bland.

I needed to work up a good sample of her honey. That's why I dove dick into the deep end on my first dive, stabbing that coochee hard. Cynt grunted and the dog began barking.

"Shut up, Cracker!" Cynt yelled. After a couple of more thrusts into her gut, I pulled out and went downtown to taste what Henry excavated. The honey was thick and not too bad tasting - tolerable. I began to like those liberated, lickable, lush lips though. They were a mouthful of suckable yum.

I tried my best to remodel that "old house" but it was as worn as grave digger gloves. Henry rammed like a riveter while Skeeter clawed at its walls like the back of a hammer.

My dick damaged a corner in that coochee and Cynt screamed, "Oh, shit!"

The dog jumped into the bed like it was going to do something. He was a pimp without a gun so I didn't feel threatened. I ignored the mutt, at first, and just kept stroking that pussy. But then that little bastard hugged my lower leg and started hunching it. He was loaded to kill. I grabbed his head and threw his ass off the bed. "Don't hurt him,"

Cynt told me. "He smell sex." Cynt told the dog, "Sit, Cracker, sit."

Cynt's loud grunting, the dog barking, Henry sloshing around in sloppy pussy and Cynt's jet black cunt farting was too much for me. It sounded like that pussy was saying "Deeper!" every time I hit it. I nutted up in there; deep, too. Cynt said, "Dat was good," three times before I pulled out.

Looking for a creampie to admire, I found Cynt had the ugliest boodee hole I'd ever see. It had what looked like a hemorrhoid on it. That turned me off. Whatever it was, it looked like a prune. That boodee hole shook me off like a pitcher not wanting to throw a curve. I quickly put her legs down.

We shared a joint and Cynthia started talking. "Dat's too much dick for Denise," she told me. "You gonna hurt dat girl and she ah haf tah go the doctor. I ain't got no money fah no doctor. When you wont some pussy, you kin fuck me for 20 dollars." I told that ho, "How about you pay me 20 dollars?" Cynt said, "I kin do wit'out dick. Dat big dick kant do wit'out some pussy."

Two days later, here comes Denise looking for some dick. I told her, "Cynt told me not to fuck you 'cause you 16 and you told her I hurt you." Denise's response shocked me. "Fuck what Cynt say. She ain't my mama. I ain't no 16. I'mma grown ass woman juss like huh," she charged. I slowed her drama by asking how Cynt wasn't her mama.

She wouldn't say. "I'll tell you about it one day but not right now," she answered.

There were issues I needed to find out about. I decided to get Denise away from Cynt where she would tell all. A couple of days later I used a friend's trailer for us to fuck. I planned to stick dick in each of Denise's holes regardless of who her mama was.

Denise took her clothes off in a hurry and paraded around buck naked, loud talkin'. "I know my body better than Cynt's. Did you fuck that old woman? You musta been hard up. Did you pay huh for some pussy?" she exhorted. That was the most conversation I'd ever had with Denise so something was surely different. The way she opened up I realized I was living with strangers. It was petty to compare her body to Cynt's and she knew Cynt was prostituting. Maybe Denise was also.

To get answers, I began to "whip" her. I massaged her back and used my lips as a facilitator as I kissed on her boodee hole. I said, "Talk to me (kiss). Tell me what's going on (suck). I can't be with you like I want to (kiss) unless I know what's going on (licks)."

Her ass hole pulsated and Denise started to confess.

Come to find out not only was Denise not Cynt's daughter but the little boy, Marvin, was her grandson who Cynt was keeping because Cynt's real daughter was in prison. The house we all lived in wasn't Cynt's house; she was just renting. On top of all that Cynthia was an ex con. Come to find out Denise was 19, not underage like Cynthia was saying. Denise said Cynthia took her in after they met at the bus station when Denise had run out of bus fare. Also, Denise suggested that Cynt liked women more than men. When Denise implied that, I automatically figured those two had done lesbian stuff.

Transitioning from emotional testimony to fucking would have been easier if my rocket ship was fueled but it wasn't ready for launch. Henry wanted "out of Dodge."

However, Denise had been honest with me, or so I thought, and I wanted to be honest somehow with her. I decided to reveal something private about myself.

After planting a good suck on her ass hole, I asked Denise for a fart. She lifted her head and said, "What?" I said, "I want to you to try and fart." "In yo' face?! Nigga, you nasty," she said. I tried to cover up a freakishness by explaining that I asked for the fart only so I could watch her ass hole move in and out.

That changed the subject all right. The cute little brown-eyed hole between her hips began moving back and forth. I sucked and licked that boodee hole, desperately wanting it to poot. When it finally did exhale a little "Burrp!" Denise asked, "You like dat nigga?"

I said, "Yeah." It got Henry erect in anticipation of corking her cornhole. I put my dick head on her ass hole and Denise told me, straight out, that was mission impossible. I pounded that pussy in the buck and we left.

Back at the house, Cynt became bold and would blatantly offer her services to me in front of Denise, like I was a trick. Denise would get upset about Cynt's advances. One time Denise walked in on Cynt jacking my dick, trying to get me to spend 20 dollars. That caused Denise and I to have another problem. She wouldn't give me head because she believed I was fucking Cynt without a condom when she wasn't around. Denise wanted exclusive rights to Henry.

Denise and I had to flirt discretely. One day, that ho waited until Cynthia was deep into an afternoon nap with Marvin to sneak a fuck. She came into my room with hugs and kisses, like I was Prince Charming, instead of her usual dick grab.

Denise was the one that shoved Henry into her cunt. She was the one riding my dick like she was on a toy horse in front of a department store. The fuck was rousing because there were conditions to our fucking with Cynt in the next room. It was like I was sneaking skeet. It was like she was an innocent intern alone with the President.

I was dipping and shifting LSD in that cunt trying to nutt quickly. I hopped up on my feet to hit it from the back. I was in the middle of an outstroke, in the middle of a recoil that would bust guts and nutt, when Marvin came through the door like he was the police.

He caught us when I had at least 10 inches of dutiful dick displayed. "Get outta here Marvin!" Denise ordered. The kid didn't move. "Get outta here!" she said again. Marvin still didn't move. Cynt heard the ruckus, came into the room, and manhandled Marvin out. "Cracker" stood there with a smirk on his face.

The situation at Cynt's house digressed big time after one of my baby mamas showed up unexpectedly at the house. She was six months pregnant and that sent a message to Denise that she was on the outside looking in. She and Denise got into it. Denise expressed her dissatisfaction of me to me by cutting up my car's driver seat. She moved into a trailer down the street from Cynt's house with some guy. No doubt she had been fucking he and I.

Once Denise was out, Cynt would constantly get my dick hard and then demand 20 dollars to fuck. Thank goodness I knew Annette. However, living in that house became so intolerable I informed Cynt I was planning to move out at the end that month. To get Cynt off my case, I told her I'd give her 20 dollars if she let me fuck her in the ass. She told me she had had an operation "back there" and anal sex was not possible. I told her "back there" looked like it needed more surgery.

Just before I was to move out, Cynt and Denise told me they wanted to give me a good send-off, "So we can part as friends," Cynt said. I should have known better but I welcomed armistice. Cynt offered to cook me a meal but I was leery of eating anything coming from somebody I was getting the hell away from.

My final evening with Cynt and Denise was, now no surprise, deviously planned.

Marvin wasn't anywhere around and Cynt began with us smoking weed and drinking wine in her living room. The higher we got the more Cynt acted like a prostitute. She rubbed my dick and tried me with, "I wont tah git some of dat dick one more time foe you leave." I told her, "I ain't got 20 dollars."

I decided to mess with her for a change. I pulled my dick out and played with it in front of her. Sure enough, Cynt leaned over on the couch and sucked the dick like fellatio was a condition of her parole. "Cracker" was watching like an overseer in an early 19th Century Mississippi cotton field.

Just as soon as I was ready to bust a nutt, here comes Denise entering without knocking. "Cynt, you ain't right," Denise yelled, as she caught Cynthia trying to hide 12 inches of swollen cock with both hands. "That's why me and you kant get along."

Denise turned her ire towards me. "That man don't need you to suck his dick," she said. "The son-of-a-bitch got a girlfriend." Cynt didn't say anything as Denise continued to open-up on both of us. "Ain't neither one of ya'll niggas 'bout shit." I had hoped for a threesome but that went out the window with that last statement.

Then, Denise flipped her script. She told me she had something special for me. "Here, get comfortable," she said, "and hurry up," she added, as she arranged me prone on the couch. "I got something for you," she said, as she showed she didn't have any draws on.

"Close your eyes," she told me. I thought maybe she was about to sit on my dick.

Instead, she placed her bony butt on my mouth and set off the loudest series of farts I had ever heard. "Bruuurp! Pop! Swoosh! P-yaw!" is how her horn blew. The movement of air bounced off my lips hard enough to make them flap. It sounded like her ass said, "Bon voyage bitch!" The farts smelled like as soon as you take the cap off Boones Farm Strawberry Hill wine.

"Cracker" snorted like any mutt smelling another dog's doo-doo and Cynt laughed.

"That shit stank," she managed to get out. Denise couldn't help but laugh along with the both of them. "He like fah it to stank!" Denise explained. Then she turned her remarks to me. "There's plenty more where that came from nigga. I ought to shit on yo' no good ass.

Here, take another one." Before I could decide whether I wanted to turn away, she perfectly placed her ass on my mouth and lifted off with another blast. It was a two- syllable fart I interpreted saying, "Take this!"

Denise jacked my dick to where Henry was harder than she had ever seen him then just dropped the dick, like a rapper with a microphone, and walked out the door.

Cynt showed sympathy by grabbing my true heart via sucking my dick like it would be the last time she would see a 12-inch dick. She took the nutt in her mouth with both hands wrapped around the base of my dick like she was holding an umbrella during Hurricane Katrina. Afterwards, she asked me for ten dollars. "Cracker" barked when I refused to pay her.

As fate would have it, around 25 years later "Denise" was visiting South Florida, remembered where I was from, and we hooked-up. This time she was using her real name.

CHAPTER 5

HOES ON TOBACCO ROADS

DO THE RIGHT THING

MILITARY BASES ARE filled with hard working, physical people who welcome any opportunity to relieve the descending weight of the oath-taken responsibility of protecting the nation. In warfare, the United States flag is what gets a grunt's dick hard. In peacetime, it's pussy. Either way, somebody gets screwed.

Defending the nation often requires hand-to-hand combat. Therefore, the military trained soldiers how to use their extremities as well as a fixed bayonet. That training came in handy when a female attempted to subvert my service to my country and I was forced to demonstrate my combat expertise.

I met her at a local club, trying to entertain four females at one table. I was game. I knew if you buy one a drink that invites you over to buy everybody a drink. I didn't mind. I figured I would get the pick of the litter. Instead, one of the litter picked me.

This ho danced so nasty in "hindsight" I figured she liked her dick from the back. When we did the "bump" she bounced her boodee against my groin like she wanted dick in her ass. After we "slow dragged" she turned and pressed her ass against my groin.

"Gimme dat," I whispered in her ear. I had a handful of her ass when she asked me to take her home. Either she was into anal action or she liked it doggy style. I was into both.

I had problems wit' this ho. That's why I remember her so well. Come to find out she was from Durham, a city over an hour away. I wanted to take her to my place locally but she insisted on getting back to Durham because she had to go to work early the next day.

Yeah, she was probably lying about work but it was her hips telling the lie.

I expected two good fucks, vaginal and anal. That's why I drove her to Durham and didn't flinch when I saw she stayed in a shack of a house. Her domicile was just the first clue this wasn't going to turn out a middle-class encounter.

It wasn't too long after we got inside her place I really began to wonder what I had gotten myself into. When I grabbed her ass or rubbed between her legs she would say, "Not yet." I felt like I was sitting on a tarmac, during a delayed flight, after having paid to "get there" on time. I wasn't in control, so I said nothing. Plastic, like that of a cold storage area, hung from her bedroom doorframe. She kept going through it and moving things around. Every now and then the ho peeped out a window.

Sure enough, as soon as one o'clock struck she invited me into her bedroom. We jumped into a small bed, rubbing and feeling all over each other as if we were explorers just rescued from a tribe of cannibals.

Undressed, her titties hung like socks on a clothesline; ass had bumps on it; pubic hair and armpits were crew cut; knees defined sharp; and her feet were considerably crusty. No wonder she was so quick to separate herself from her friends. She had a soft ass. That's about the best I can say about her body.

When I went downtown to recon and sensed heat as I took a good snort of her flat coochee. I peeled back the cover of her clit, licked it, and that girl started to "act a fool."

She slammed my face into her pussy and massaged it between her legs with both hands. The scratchiness of her fresh cut down there, somehow, appealed to me. Maybe subconsciously I challenged myself to torture training.

This ho was directing our movements, like she was a "fucking" traffic cop, repeating instructions as if I was in driver's ed. "Eat dat pussy muthafucka! Eat dat pussy!" she told me, like a trainer scolding a new driver who didn't look both ways. She gave me directions every time she gave me a chance to breathe. "Lick it!, Lick it, bitch" or "Suck dat pussy, suck it!" Hoping to park Henry in her butt, I followed instructions.

She continued giving orders but messed up when she hollered, "Fuck me! Fuck me muthafucka!" My bayonet was pointed and on the ready.

I thought Henry was going to pile drive her pie. Instead, heavy Henry wanted some head.

I bounced my stretched dick off her face for some oral attention. "This (slap) is (slap) Henry (slap)," I told her, poking my dick head between her lips occasionally. "Suck (slap) that (slap) muthafucka (slap) (poke)." Wrinkles formed on her forehead. I thought she was trying to figure out how to put all that dick between her jaws.

That girl looked at me as if I was at the wrong place at the wrong time. "How you call yo' dick Henry?" she asked. "Dat's my daddy name." I laid my dick on her lips and she held them tightly closed as if penis was a vegetable she didn't care for. She snatched her head to the side and told me, "I ain't gonna suck yo' dick."

I didn't want "oral argument." Henry wanted some head. "You gonna suck my dick just like I ate your pussy," I forcefully told her. "No I ain't," she replied. Her refusal took over my thought process so I had to take a break. Instead of me forcing the fellatio issue, Henry needed immediate attention and "we" settled on just fucking.

"Turn yo' ass over," I ordered, because "we" didn't even want to look at her face anymore. I helped her flip over onto her belly and guided her ass straight up in the air.

Henry dove into that ho's pussy like a bowling ball into a pool. She was quiet when that happened. After a few bangs into her gut she started ordering me around again. "Fuck dat pussy! Gimme dat big dick!" she yelled, giving orders again.

Looking at how she took that dick, like it was regular, Henry came up with a plan to set this ho straight about what he was. A thought popped into my head. I pulled out and ate the pussy from behind with my mouth lathering spit and honey from the coochee onto her boodee hole. I moistened her anus good. She liked me licking and sucking back there.

"Umm," she cooed. "Lick my ass! Suck my ass!" she ordered.

Her boodee hole was relaxed enough to take the first knuckle of my thumb before she slapped my finger out. That slap pissed Henry off, for real. I vacuumed the boodee hole and then supplied saliva to her pooter. "Suck dat ass! Suck dat ass nigga!" she ordered.

I split her hips with my hands like I was going to "suck that ass" and Henry jumped from the coochee into the boodee hole and was no way supple about it. I got Skeeter and an inch completely in. She collapsed and rocked from side to side like she was trying to wake from a bad dream. "Oh, shit!" she hollered, "Dat dick too big. Dat dick too big!"

I could feel Henry chuckle as he broke ground. The more her ass hole tightened the deeper he delved into her digestion. She twerked her torso as we both wrestled. Skeeter finally became more comfortable in her poot chute. Eventually she slowed her squirming but didn't completely give up moving her butt for acclimation to his size. "Take the dick like a good girl," I whispered in her ear. "See high deep it can go," I told her.

She began squeezing her asshole, I suspect to relieve pain. I took those squeezes as responses of enjoyment and put an exclamation on our exercise by pulling Henry almost all the way out then inch-doubling dick down.

Before too much longer that girl was exorcised. "Fuck dah ass. Fuck it!" she ordered.

She liked the way I was stroking and I liked the way she surrendered. She told me, "Fuck me in dah ass daddy. Oh daddy, daddy, daddy fuck me in my ass." I didn't care about the "daddy" reference and kept plowing that boodee hole. Again, I slowly inched out so she could get an idea of just how much dick she was taking then jumped back down in it.

As I was stroking I was trying to determine just what I was going to do with the nutt. I didn't want to skeet in the boodee hole. She had too many bumps on her butt. I didn't want to force my dick into her mouth. She may have bitten me. I optioned to jack off on her face. I sat on her back and held her head down with one hand. With the other, I jacked Henry and sent hot sperm all over her left eye. I put the remainder into that ho's ear.

Hoes on Tobacco Roads

A RIVER RUNS THROUGH IT

WHEN SOLDIERS ARE on patrol there is usually one trooper in front. He is called the point-man. Soldiers take pride in being the point-man because they are recognized as having the skills to watch out for everybody.

On one libidinous mission, my point man was a runnin' partner named Matt. He had planned a two-couples weekend with one of his lady friends with the three of us treking to visit one of her female friends in some hick town in South Carolina. When we picked up Matt's lady friend, however, she brought along her local runnin' partner. Matt nor I expected that.

Don't get me wrong, the extra female was a thick, high-yella red bone and looked good enough to eat. She was built like Annette and I bowed to big hips. However, when we got to where we were going, almost three hours away from Bragg, I found I could have done well enough without the "spare." The girl we went to visit was printer ink black, thick, and had a load of ass that needed wheel barrow support.

On the way there I wanted to eat the red bone's pussy and once we got there I wanted the black girl to sit on my face. We all played off whether I would choose which pussy I wanted, which pussy would choose me, or have a threesome. I was in the rocking chair but I wasn't comfortable. I was never good at measuring triangles.

Before long it was late enough to where everybody was ready for bed. Matt and his lady went into one room and I was left with "Salt and Pepper" in the two bedroom trailer. "Pepper" got up and went into the other bedroom and soon thereafter "Salt" followed her.

I was alone on the couch.

Not too much later, the red bone came out of the room and started rubbing my dick, eventually pulling Henry out. "Damn," she asked, "how much longer is this thing going to get?" I was hoping she would take me into the bedroom and show Pepper my prick. I had never initiated a threesome before and didn't know how to potential one.

She directed me to lie on the floor and the next thing I knew her bare yella' ass was headed straight for my face into the 69 position. It wasn't long before we were conducting oral sex like a couple of porn stars in the middle of the living room. I heard a couple of "Umms" from her and that's the only clue I was either doing something correctly or Henry felt good to her mouth. Her blowjob and phat yella ass in my face made me nutt quick. She took the shots in her mouth and spit them out in the kitchen sink.

I had got my nutt and was sitting on the couch to see what was next. What was next was her putting me back down on the floor. "Let me get mine," she told me, and guided me back on the floor. The red bone squatted over my face, recovered my head with her gown, then began rubbing her cunt on my face. I reinserted my tongue into her pussy and sucked the coochee, wanting her to also get off quick, so we wouldn't get caught. I was working. While I was reciprocating pleasure, she gave no response of "Umm, Oooh," or anything. She was real quiet about the purposeful play I put on her pussy.

From time to time she produced a wet I had never before felt on my lips nor tasted on my tongue. It had a different flavor, more fluid than honey, and came in small squirts. I thought she was busting pre-mee nutts. All of a sudden, a gush of more liquid over- powered my mouth. That woman was pissing. I turned my head to spit out what I could and that nasty ho shot urine on my ear.

I was shocked and didn't know what to do. I just laid there as she dumped her bladder.

This ho was bold. She pulled her gown up in the front, looked at me from between her legs, and shot a long squirt of hot piss in my face. The heated water rolled off me onto the floor.

I blew water out my nose and hopped up quick. We stood next to the wet spot on the linoleum as I waited for an explanation. She looked up at me like my midget fourth grade teacher used to do at the chalkboard. The red bone told me why she did what she did. She said that if I told anybody what we did to make sure her pissing in my mouth was included. That ho didn't even have the decency to ask me if I liked it.

She cut on lights and made noisy commotion trying to find something to clean up the mess she made on the floor. That commotion caused our host to come out of her room.

"What are you looking for?" Pepper asked Salt. "I need something to clean this water off the floor," she answered. "How you get water on the floor?" The red bone pointed at me.

My wet shirt explained. "Ya'll ought to be ashamed," Pepper said, laughing on the way to where she had paper towels. "I hope ya'll didn't get my couch wet."

I passed both women on my way to the bathroom to clean up. Feeling like an outhouse, I returned to face the music. "The floor is wet, so you will have to come back here," Pepper said, directing me towards her room at the back of the trailer.

The red bone and I sat on the edge of the bed as Pepper cleared space next to it, moving rugs and such. "I'll get something to put under his head," she said before leaving the room. "Oh shoot!" I thought, "We fixin' to have a threesome." I figured they had decided to make-up for the girl pissing on me. I just knew I was about to get some pussy.

While Pepper was gone, the red bone told me point-blank, "You ain't fuckin' neither one of us; so get that out yo' mind. You might hurt somebody wit' that thing 'tween yo' legs. We got to go to work Monday." Right in front of Pepper, Salt jacked Henry vigorously. Pepper spread an armful of towels on the floor then watched Salt make Henry grow. "Look at this thing," Salt told Pepper.

Those hoes used Cherokee wind talker code I didn't understand, at first. Salt asked Pepper, "You gotta go yet?" Pepper answered, "I'm working on it. I'll be ready in a minute."

Salt directed me to lie on floor with my head on those towels, kneeled between my legs, and began sucking my dick. Pepper climbed over my head, lifted her gown, and sat her big, black, beautiful boodee on my forehead. I put my hands under her hips to keep her from breaking my face. I split her cheeks and sucked her boodee hole, trying to pull out a fart. As she watched Salt suck the dick Pepper revealed to the red bone, "This man sucking on my ass hole." Salt told her, "Piss on his ass."

Pepper lifted her anus off my lips, put her pussy there, and peed a pound. Hers came in a strong, powerful stream and lasted forever. I had to let her fill my mouth to keep from drowning. I didn't know what else to do with her hot water so I spit it back at Pepper's pussy. "Oooh!," she hollered. Salt asked, "What he do?" Pepper said, "Let him show you." I stayed on the floor, like a CPR dummy, while those two hoes switched-up.

Henry's hardness had me partially paralyzed. I couldn't, maybe didn't want to, move.

Out of gas on any intervention, the only thing I could do besides being a toilet was get a feel of their hips, suck a boodee hole, and eat cunt. The red bone smashed her fat cat on my mouth and I put my nose into her ass hole. She jumped off my snout like she had just been saved. "Get outta there," she told me. Pepper asked her what I had done. "He stuck his nose in my ass," she told Pepper. Pepper said, "Piss on his ass."

Salt's water flowed slowly and I was able to manage her drainage and enjoy Pepper performing on my prick. I skeeted into Pepper's mouth while Salt was leaking and rubbing her pissy pussy on my mouth. For a long time after the nutt, Pepper didn't come off the dick and Salt wouldn't stop what she was doing. I spew the piss I collected back on the red bone's coochee. "Oh, yeah. I like how he spit it back out," She told Pepper.

Those hoes emptied their vagina pails on my face and put me out the room. After analyzing how I had been used like a commode, I found I liked it.

In the morning Matt and I took off early, hunted some hoes at a nearby college, and didn't return until near dark. When we got back our suitcases were in the yard. We didn't even attempt to go inside.

Hoes on Tobacco Roads

FRIENDLY FIRE

IN SOUTHERN FLORIDA the heat is called "The Bear" because it jumps on the back of people and knocks them to ground. When I joined the Army in January I was out of my element at Fort Knox, Kentucky. There, I had to learn to contend with "The Hawk." Now, cold weather always reminds me of a certain libidinous mission.

It was winter and it was the weekend. Those were big barriers to my wanting to get from under cover, out of bed. A bulging bladder became my prompt. I felt like a sniper in the bushes and a large snake was testing my patience. I needed more incentive to vacate my cover so I promised myself a joint. Unfortunately, I was out of reefer. Since I was forced to get up and out the door to payday my head, I decided to make a major move.

I invented a trip to Salisbury, NC where one of my more infrequent runnin' partners, Reggie, had gone home for the weekend. I had been to his hometown once and knew where his mother's house was.

When I got there, it crossed my mind to return to Bragg because people acted like they didn't want to answer my knock. I guess it was because it was so cold outside. Those old wooden houses were drafty and moving from one room to another was like exiting a plane from Florida onto a tarmac in Siberia. Reggie wasn't there. Some female other than his mother directed me to some house where she thought he may have spent the night.

I went to the other place and some guy came to the door. He turned out to be Reggie's brother. I explained what I was doing in Salisbury and he seemed surprised that Reggie wasn't at their mother's place. "He wont dare?" he asked. "Well, he might uh spent dah night at hiss uncle house." I have to give the Brother some props; he invited me inside.

Where he directed me I had to maneuver inches of snow on a dirt road to get there. The only reason I didn't immediately turn around is because there were fresh tracks in the snow where a car had recently driven.

I knocked on the door and a hooded ho answered the door. She had on a big coat as if there wasn't any heat in the house. I told her I was looking for Reggie. "Dat's my brother," she told me, as she guided me in so she could close the door. "He left a little while ago wit' hiss girlfriend and I don't know where dey went or when dey ah be back," she said.

The house felt colder than outside and she hurriedly invited me into another room.

That's where Reggie's sister, Jennifer, had camped out. She had blankets and pillows on the floor in front of a small fireplace and it was blasting enough heat to keep the relatively small room livable. "Have a seat," she said, as she closed sliding doors behind her. "You git high?" she asked and then paused before continuing, "Because I was juss 'bout to smoke a joint." I laughed before responding to her question with, "If your brother gets high, then I get high."

Jennifer was talkative and that helped relax us both. She was asking questions as if I was "new meat." I told her that her brother and I had the same sense of humor and that encouraged our friendship from the first time we met.

Reggie's verbal descriptions of reality were weird until you got to know him. For example, it was like pulling teeth to get him to chip-in on herb or wine. "Ain't you got a job nigga?" a buddy confronted him with. Reggie's excuse was, "My mama ain't got no legs," he would always answer. I met his mother; she had legs. That statement was a metaphor he used to explain that his mother didn't have a job and he helped her out financially.

As Jennifer and I passed the joint, the more she came out layers of clothes. She was nowhere as thick as she first appeared. As it turned out, she was a slim jim. By the time we lit up the third joint she had nothing on but pajama shorts and a loose tank top, looking like a wire hanger with a track uniform on it.

She had just enough tittie to show she was a girl and when she leaned over to roll a joint I peeped pointed nipples. I liked her color. She was a nice light brown but I could see that her areolas were jet black. That perked my interest in the color of her ass hole. I first imagined her boodee hole being brilliant brown but now expected it to be real dark.

She had long, thin fingers and I suspected her coochee lips to be the same.

She was nice enough not to say anything when she caught me staring at what little tittie she had, as they jiggled independently. "Dare some wine leff from lass night. You wont some?" she asked. "Sure," I said. She brought out an unfinished half-gallon of Thunderbird and a pint of Wild Irish Rose. "What yo' pleasure?" she asked. I looked at that girl, dead in her face, and said, "Right about now, you." She laughed then stared.

If the joint and fireplace wasn't enough, the Thunderbird got me warm. It must have gotten us both warm because she forgot about tending her caveman heater. I continued to size her up for a fuck.

She was nappy haired but what Black woman ain't early in the morning. I expected her pubic hair to be just as nappy. The full lips on her face made me change my mind about her pussy. I now hoped her cunt lips were just as thick. That ho's mouth was so wide it looked like she could suck three dicks at once. I watched her bend to stir the fire and imagined I could get much dick into her small ass.

I must have shown the countenance of a pervert. "You keep lookin' at me. You like what you see?" she asked, and caused me to grin. I responded with, "You the one who gave me the reefer and the wine. What you expect me to look at?" That girl told me to mine my manners. "It's impolite to stare," she said. I told her point-blank, "You look good enough to eat." Jennifer didn't even look my way when she said, "Dat's dat wine and reefer talkin'. Who is you? I don't know you." I told her, "I'm just a squirrel, tryin' to get a nut."

"I'mma tell my brother," she said came back with. Her smirk told me she was kidding.

Her brother would automatically assume, if he found out we spent time together, I cracked on his sister for some pussy. He might also assume she sucked my dick. That's why she told me, "If the squirrel git a nut, you beddah not tell nobody." There was no reason for me to say anything else.

We didn't waste time after that. Jennifer got off the floor and sat next to me. "I like to do sex when I'm high," she said. We had that in common. I pulled her closer and squeezed what was only anatomically a thigh. She put her hand on my dick and when she felt solid growth, she said, "Dat don't fee like no squirrel. Dat feel like a big snake." She didn't stop there. Jennifer told me she wanted to see my dick and brashly pulled Henry out. She smelled it like she was at the meat market. "When dah lass time you had some pussy?" she asked. "In a few minutes," I answered.

She made her move. "You ain't gonna tell nobody is you?" she asked. "What we do ain't nobody's business except ours." I answered. I must have responded like she wanted because she completely opened up. Jennifer said, "I'm gonna suck yo' dick and you beddah not bust no nutt in my mouff." Being a carnal sniper on a mission, I was patient.

Somebody or somebodies must have told Jennifer she gave good head or else she just liked sucking dick. She wiped my dickhead off on her shirt and went to work. I could tell she was enjoying what she was doing. Every now and then she would look up at me and smile. She reminded me of a child walking away from the ice cream truck.

Slurping her cream bar, hittin' the joint, and sipping wine, Jennifer still found time to talk. "You gotta fat dick head. I like high I kin grab it wit' my mouff," she told me. Once she got Henry fully stretched out, she commented. "You got a big dick. I don't know if I kin let you fuck me." I told her, "Take the opportunity to see how much you can take."

She got up, pulled off her bottoms, and got on the floor with her lower limbs spread.

Her exposed pussy looked like an abandoned bird's nest in a dead tree. I hovered over her and she stopped me right there. "Eat my pussy firss," she told me. I intentionally tried to respond like a kindergartener on the first day of school. "I ain't good at it," I said. "I ain't done it that much before. Most of the time I just fuck." Jennifer said, "I'mma geh you some pussy but I wont you to eat my pussy firss."

That ho pulled pubic hairs to separate her cunt lips and slapped her hand between her legs. "Put yo' face right he ah and see how far you kin git yo' tongue in dare." I did just that. I nestled my nose against her nest, opened the cunt with my tongue, then sucked that rascal with long, stiff tongue in the middle of it. I moved my mouth like I was doing speech therapy exercises. "Suck dat pussy, baby" she instructed. I went up and down that cunt, tweaking much twat. Her pussy tasted like sour grass. I liked sour grass.

She had her knees bent back to her chest when she told me, "I'mma buss a nutt in yo' mouth nigga! I'mma buss a nutt!" I didn't want her to "buss" a nutt so I stopped. "Did I do good?" I asked. "Why you stop? Don't play wit' me," she ordered.

Jennifer dug through her bush, like she was clearing forest for a highway, and exposed her lengthy clit while arching her back. Amongst all that hair, that thing looked like a cattail in the Everglades; like "The Tower of Babel" in the Amazon; or The Leaning Tower of Pisa on the Great Plain.

"Suck dat," she said, "and don't stop." I put my lips around Jennifer's bowling pin shaped clit and pulled on it. "You ain't doin' it right," she told me." That ho told me, the best cunniliguser on the planet, that I "need more practice" eating pussy.

"I wouldah kept doin' you but you was 'bout to nutt in my mouth," I told her. Jennifer gave me a cunnilingus lesson. "When I tell you I'm fixin' to cum, don't stop," she said, "Eat dah pussy, nigga. It protein. It good fah ya."

What immediately followed I didn't understand, at first. She put me on my back and rubbed her pussy over my dick head then began poking Skeeter into her pussy. She would pull my dick out and suck off the honey glossing my dick head. "My pussy taste good," she said, after a few tongue swipes on Skeeter. She didn't get that opinion from her taste buds. Some nigga in Salisbury told her that.

Jennifer moved her pussy just above my face. "He ah," she said, as she peeled back her clit where it stuck out just above my nose. "Suck my dick," she ordered, as she lowered her groin. I gave her clit another lip-lock. "Suck dat dick nigga!" she told me. I pulled her clit like I was trying to yank it off. "Nigh, eat dah pussy. Eat dat pussy nigga!"

I went pro on that pussy. Jennifer said, "Oh, shit!" and nutted.

She leaked heavily and told me, "Git dat. Lick it out." I went over the pussy with my mouth and Jennifer was defeated. "You kin fuck me nigh," she quietly said.

I was more than happy to finally stick dick. I lifted her legs to fuck her in the buck and punched hard to get to the bottom of that cunt. I did a touch-and-go with her lowest rib.

"You hurtin' me," she calmly said. I didn't think once I pulled out she'd let me back in. That's why I continued trying to get all up in there and hit that pussy harder. Cool as a cucumber, Jennifer told me, "Stop. Take it out." She was the sister of a friend so I did.

"You got a big dick. You gots to be mo' careful," she told me. Then she noticed how Henry was standing straight out without any support, like a number line, defying gravity.

"You need some pussy, don't you?" she asked. She turned her ass towards me and said, "Git it like dis but don't fuck me hard like you was doin'." Henry led from behind.

Her pooter was dark brown. The sight of the hair circling that tight hole made me want to stick dick in the boodee hole. I rubbed Henry up and down her crack, as if I was trying to find the pussy. I punched the dick head onto her asshole. "Wrong hole," she told me. I pushed again in the same spot. "Not dare!" she yelled, and then moved away.

She must have felt like I was a rookie and needed instructions. Or, she knew I was trying to stick my dick in her ass for real. Either way, she got away from me.

"Let me sit on it," she told me. Her clit was peeking out from her weedy pubic hair like a rodent in tall grass hiding from a hawk. With one hand holding my dick she controlled my dick's depth while facing me. She had a choke hold on Henry and I couldn't get a nutt like that. She could. That ho busted a nutt with her anus throbbing on my pinkie. She liked something in her ass. She just feared it being my dick.

As we smoked a joint, I spoke up. "Since we gonna be quiet about this," I told her, "I want you to do something I've always wanted to try, to see if I liked it, but never met the right person to try it with. Jennifer gave me a "What you talkin' 'bout Willis?" look.

"I want you to pee pee on me," I said. After an initial contemplation of disbelief, Jennifer told me, "It a wonder you wont me to do dat. I needs to take a piss anyway." That ho anxiously squatted over me. "Naw," I told her. "I want it in my face." Jennifer said, "Freaky!", moved up to my head, and opened the cunt with her hand. A strong stream of warm urine splashed my face like it was aftershave. I actually saw its exit. That was cool.

Jennifer took off her top and dried me off. "I ain't finish. I'mma git a towel," she said.

That girl was looking serious, focused when her bony ass returned naked as a jaybird from the cold part of the house. This time she squatted where she was more comfortable.

She told me what to do. "Open yo' mouth," she said." I did. She rubbed her pussy on my mouth until she found a spot to her liking. "Right dare," she said, "Don't move."

After inhaling herb that ho pissed, filling my mouth with accuracy a short shot of hot water. I spit it out, spread it over her asshole and cunt, and licked each of them. "Damn, dat shit was good," she said, as she finally exhaled. "I liked dat. Do dat ghen." I did.

We finished with her giving me a blowjob. I nutted, filling her mouth, and she spit in the ashtray. I told her she was wasting protein.

"I kant do dis wit' you no mo," she said. "Why?" I asked. "If I be wit' you aghen, I ah fall in love." I wanted to get into her head so I told her, "You supposed to be teachin' me how to eat pussy. You wont somebody else to show me?"

That wasn't the last time I hooked-up with Jennifer. More than once she called to confirm that I had a hold on her. "Come and git it," she would tell me. I did.

SCARY MOVIE

LIKE IN REAL war, libidinous missions can include mind games where people strategize how to outmaneuver people. In the real world, it's called "runnin' game." World leaders have used "game" to promulgate policy, with quotes such as: "We have nothing to fear but fear itself" (FDR); "Ask not what your country can do for you, ask what you can do for your country" (JFK); and "I Have a Dream" (MLK). One key to social self- preservation is recognizing when someone is "running game."

I thought I had attained expert status in recognizing "game" until a female set me straight. That ho sucked my dick for a whole hour-plus, working hard for me to bust a nutt. I was runnin' game on her by holding off so I could get more. A few days later I confronted her about a loan I made to her. "You got yo' money when I sucked yo' dick," she explained. She ran "game."

That was a wake-up call. So, when it came time for me to run game I tried to "kill them all and let God sort 'em out." As a matter of fact, one time I purposely ran game on Willie D, one of my regular runnin' partners. He and I were easing down Highway 74 West on the way from Bragg to Charlotte one Friday afternoon and I ran game on him.

While passing through a town I better not name, for fear of a lawsuit, Willie and I noticed a girl's name and phone number spray painted on the wall of a car wash. We stopped, I called the number, and asked for that particular person. She got on the phone and I explained to her that Willie and I were passing through town and saw her number at the car wash. She invited us over. I couldn't believe it!

A number of things could explain the invitation because I had seen this type of "Craigslist" behavior before. One reason for her cordiality may have been that I told her we were soldiers (were employed). Another could have been because we were just passing through. A third reason, and probably the real reason, she invited us over appeared once we got to "The Last House on the Left" on Elm Street.

The girl whose personal information was scrawled on the wall of the car wash was eye candy - beautiful and super fine. That red bone had a nice big, round ass way-larger than her waist with healthy, settin' on the table tits. She was straight-up porno material, a "brick house" with a provincial porch out front and a hellavah deck in back. Her face, tits, and ass constantly scrambled a man's beams. Like a rose among all flowers, her body was created to example perfection. She was destined to be some man's expensive trophy.

Bad as I wanted the beauty queen's pussy, pee, poots, and politeness, I concluded she wouldn't appreciate my sexual probes. Her body was bangin' by itself.

Her sister was totally opposite. She was a sore-eye without one obvious sexual feature. That girl was ugg-lee, like wrong-colored shit. First impression would question who would want to fuck that? I looked at that ho and whispered to Willie, "It's Alive!"

Willie said, "Jeepers Creepers." She looked like the lovechild of "Carrie" and "Pumpkinhead."

Usually on patrol, whoever was driving got the pick of any pussy litter. Willie wasn't driving but I ran "game" and told him to scoop the beauty queen. In a hick town where I didn't know anybody, I didn't want any local dickslinger in my rearview mirror. I figured no one in that town would be upset about me fucking the ugg-lee ho. Don't get me wrong; I knew I still had to be careful. I was living proof that no matter how ugly a girl is, somebody is fucking 'em.

It seemed like "Friday the 13th" and "Halloween" on the same day. Before our foursome divided I asked Willie if I made a "Wrong Turn" because I felt "Tremors" when I approached that "Side Show" because she had "Faults." That "Scarecrow" looked like one of "Them!"; like she had been "Unearthed" just before we arrived; or wandered away from "The People Under the Stairs" or some "Crawlspace."

Willie happily went to beg for some pussy from the libido magnet in one room and the "Bad Seed" entertained me in another. I kissed "Freddy Kruger." I did it; I'll admit it. It was like being the first victim in the "Texas Chainsaw Massacre." We only had time for "Visiting Hours." Their "Mommie Dearest" was due home and we only managed to get through introductions.

It was late Sunday night on our "Return to Haunted Hill." Before our "Knock, Knock" I asked Willie, "Are You Scared 2" because I had had "Bad Dreams" about "Monsters" and a "Dungeon Girl" who wanted to perform an "Autopsy" on me. Ugg-lee poked her head out the door and Willie gave out a "Scream." She told us her mama was out and that the beauty queen didn't care for company. Willie had to wait in the car. He ran there.

My "Tales from The Crypt" host whorishly whipped out my dick and began her "Creepshow." That gargoyle got "What Lies Beneath" hardened and was taken aback by the size of "King Kong." I told her "Don't Be Afraid" as I checked her neck for 666. "The Thing" hurried her "Jaws" on my dick like it was a "Feast." Her head worked like a famished walker from "The Walking Dead." My dick was "Fresh Flesh" to her.

The blowjob and coochee were so good I wondered if this was a "Trick 'R Treat."

"The Awakening" happened in a chair and her pussy covered Henry like it was "The Blob." We were "Alone in the Dark" and could "See No Evil" as she held onto a closet door and had a "Joy Ride" on my lap. I made sure to wear a condom because, as ugg-lee as she was, I didn't want to have to visit "Horrible Doc Bones" with "The Burning."

The fuck became a "Blair Witch Project" because ugg-lee wanted her sister to hear us screwing. Every time we fucked in the house "The Bone Eater" would loudly "Holla" how my dick was too little. When I fucked that "Nightcrawler" in my car, she was runnin' from "Hard Candy." I didn't realize it at our first fuck but ugg-lee was "runnin' game" on her sister. She was "Scared" her new dick would be "Taken." "The Bride of Frankenstein" didn't want the beauty queen to know she was fucking a "Frankenrod."

That ho "Of Unknown Origin" had some good, sloppy "Zombeaver." I held on to her waist as her coochee "Skinned Alive" what it was pole-sliding on. I felt "The Mist" of honey on my pubic hair when she busted a nutt as I skeeted "Grave Dancers" into Henry's slicker.

A week later I drove 150 miles just to fuck "Rosemary's Baby." I had logged into "Fear Dot Com" and wanted her to "Let Me In" again. Her mom was home and ugg-lee couldn't get her "Midnight Meat" at home. We took a "Dark Ride" on "The Road of the Dead" to where "The Hills Have Eyes" to fuck. "The Seed of Chucky" knew a spot near "Lake Dead" where Lizzie Borden once lived. She kneeled on my reclined front seat against the steering wheel and hopped on my dick like a bear scratching its back.

"The Haunting" ended when that "Troll" made it impossible for us to continue seeing each other. With "Eyes of a Stranger" that "Monkey's Paw" told me her "Ouija" told her not to give me anymore pussy unless I entered the "Twilight Zone" by marrying her.

People tend to make bad decisions in scary movies. The main rule is "Don't Blink." I didn't. I knew marrying an "Alien" is a "Dead End."

"The Thaw" began as I hatched a "game" plan to become "The Terminator" of our relationship. I gave her an ultimatum. I told her "The Funhouse" was closing unless she let me fuck her in the ass.

Twice I had tried to get up in that "Rest Stop." I told her if we got married she would have get used to me fucking her in the ass to prevent pregnancy. I figured she would find "No Way Out" and the "Psycho" agreed to give me a "Thriller." A "Species" will do whatever it takes to survive.

I found a "Bates Motel" so she would feel at home in a "House of Dark Shadows." It was the only time she and I got into a bed to fuck. I expected to see "The Frighteners" between her legs and an "Alien

Outpost" between her hips. Come to find out, her coochee was better looking than her and the boodee hole was beautiful. I liked beautiful.

I took time to look for "Critters" and "Gremlins" then made a "Mark of the Vampire" between her legs. A poke into her buttt confirmed the boodee hole was tight. As Henry eased into "The Shining" talk was used as a distraction to expected "Drive Thru" pain. I kept telling her to take the dick but she told me to stop talking and "get it over with."

I acted like the "The Body Snatcher" and put all my dick into that "Predator." That "Trog" lifted her head and looked "Petrified" back at me like "Dracula" rising out of his coffin. As I fucked her she had to take a break and went into the bathroom, walking like "The Living Dead."

When she returned I greased her ass hole and jumped back in it. That horror ho took most all that dick, wiped it with the sheet, and sucked a nutt out of it while I was smelling her pussy. Her ass-to-mouth confirmed my belief that she was "Horrible."

After the "Nightmare on Elm Street" we didn't see each other for weeks. I got a craving for some of that boodee and went looking for her. When I popped-up at her mama's house I found she needed "The Exorcist" not me. That ho was pregnant.

THE BIG KAHUNA

THE RAP GROUP Houdini made the song, "The Freaks Come Out at Night." It was a hit mostly because of the beat yet it carried the message that people are more real after dark.

It also revealed that people tend not to pay peak attention after the sun goes down.

Throughout history many nations have faltered due to a lackadaisical attitude towards what happens during "o-dark thirty" hours. The British didn't believe American colonists had the nerve after nine. Germany was able to rebuild after World War I via its creepy crawling just before the crack of dawn. The White House was nonchalant, in America's darkest hours, just before Pearl Harbor and 9-11. Check out movies, what happens in the dark always comes to light.

It was "last call for alcohol" in a club when my runnin' partner Willie D met Lois. A married woman, she was visiting Fayetteville from a nearby hick town. Willie topped off her drunk at our table and somehow brought up the subject of blowjobs. Touting her expertise on the subject, Lois offered both of us some head. Willie and I looked at each other, laughed, and said together, "The freaks come out at night."

I wasn't desperate for her attention but apparently Willie was. He took the freak out to the parking lot and she gave him some head in my car. Willie was just-a grinning when I caught her with the car door opened spitting out skeet. She stared me down like she was saying, "Next?" I turned my head to let her know, "Thanks but no thanks." No disrespect to my partner but this ho was less particular than me about what she put her mouth on.

She was destined to hook up with somebody, anybody. It just happened to be with Willie.

Those two had been talking for about two or three weeks when Willie convinced me to drive him to a small town called Spivey's Corner, where she lived. According to Willie, her husband was a truck driver and out of town on a run. All I knew was that Willie was going to fuck this ho at a working man's house. I insisted that I not be anywhere around.

Lois found somebody to baby sit me. She was married too.

Her name was Bernice and when I saw her I was reminded of a line in Houdini's song which said that "Freaks come in all colors, shapes, and sizes." On the recording, I thought Houdini was rapping about Black Republicans.

The song described Bernice to a tee. This ho had a weird body. She was thick as an elephant from her chins down. Her head may have been regular sized but I couldn't tell. It looked small.

This ho was obese; I mean "O"bese. Come to find out, her husband was also a truck driver on a run. The bottom line was that both husbands were away making money and their wives had scrupulous dicks at the crib they were working to pay for.

We avoided direct eye contact, like a taxi driver to a Black man in New York. She offered me food and drink and we conversed. She did catch me looking at her when she turned, like a aircraft carrier, to go into the kitchen. I couldn't help but wonder how she could move at all since her husband had the truck.

Honestly, I wasn't in the mind to approach that huge ho for sex, at first. I was in as much danger with Bernice as I would have been at Willie's girlfriend house. I wanted to make sure that if her husband came home he would find me in the front room and not the bedroom. I had to trust Bernice to baby sit me in safety because Willie had my car.

I won't use the excuse of being high for eventually admiring her. Some people figure Bernice had a perfect body for a female. She looked comforting, like a comforter, from her neck down. Also, the lighter colored a person is the more there is a perception of "clean." Bernice was high yella.

I ain't stupid! Of course I asked her, "When yo' husband supposed to be back?" She answered that he had just left for Virginia that morning and wouldn't be back for two days. After the husband question, she really loosened up. She excused herself and went into a bedroom and came back out after changing clothes. Instead of the wide shorts and really loose top, she came out wearing only a football jersey large enough for Refrigerator Perry and Vince Wolfork to fit into together. Even then, as she moved around her fat fidgeted in that shirt like clowns in a car.

I began to weigh the pros and cons of stickin' dick into this big ass ho. As we talked, she gave her opinion about her married friend cheating with Willie. "Truck drivers can find somebody to be with wherever they go," she explained. "I don't blame her for cheating on him because he probably cheating on her." I asked her what she thought about people cheating on each other. "She prophetically said, "Ain't nothing wrong with taking a coffee break." I asked her if she ever took a coffee break and she answered, "No, I never have. I like hot chocklat."

We were teasing each other. "I prefer my coffee with lots of cream and sugar," I told her, and then asked, "You keep any of that around?" She replied, "I got plenty of both. Do you like big cups or little cups? For some men "big cups" is too much." I smartly told her, "I got no problem with having "more."" Bernice said, "Follow me. I'll show you what "more" looks like."

She waddled into the bedroom and removed the jersey she was wearing. "More" was right. I was startled by her boldness and her body. She modeled for me, turning all the way around so I could count the flabs of fat from her necks to her ankles. I was bowled over as I stared at the blubbery on her body.

This ho had humongous saddlebags, looking like decent-sized watermelons, lumbered down the sides of something. Her ass spilled, like water over a dam, out of her bloomers and her calves hung down over her ankles. Her thighs were wider than my waist and one of her calves was the size of both my legs. I know; she wanted to see if lumpish left me limp. Just the idea of being in the middle of all that got Henry interested. I wasn't as sure.

I had to take a minute so I went outside and smoked a joint. Henry and I decided to try this ho although it had been a long time since The Louisiana Purchase. I had much country to conquer but took the challenge. The only thing I would have to be on guard for would be her sitting on my face, something libidinous men like big hoes to do. I told myself I wasn't going to let her do that.

When I got back to the room, she was topless on her hands and knees with her campground-sized ass turned towards my entrance. I wanted to pull her draws down and put my face in her butt to see how deep I had to dig to get to the earth's core. When I yanked on her panties, she rolled, I mean rolled, over.

Her titties really got my attention. They had a large area of dark brown encircling the nipples that looked like controlled-burns on the face of identical mountains. "These are beautiful," I said, as I did nipple pinches on both. "Let me see what else you got." I helped her slip her draws over her wide rock crusher feet and surveyed her acres of lard. What I saw was a lot, a whole lot. Everything was huge, including her bed, except for that ho's head.

I was pushing the heavy fat of her thighs all sorts of ways, wanting to see how a coochee survived without air. I told her, "I can't see what you got." She looked at me like I had never seen between a female's legs. "What you want? To see my stuff?" she asked.

"Yeah, I want to see the pussy," I answered. She wallowed her big butt backwards, right and left, right and left, right and left, and spread her legs. Bernice split her thighs apart and there was jet black, matted pubic hair and a dark brown, honeycomb-like fat cunt with curvy, thick lips loitering.

"That pussy fat," I told her. Unintentionally using the word "fat" I tried to clean-up my comment by telling her, "I could suck on that thing for days." There was moisture at the bottom of her colossal cunt I just had to do something with it. "Hold that for me," I told her, as I released some fat I was helping her hold back. I smelled the gargantuan gopher and kissed it. Moisture landed on my bottom lip. "It's wet," I stupidly announced. "The fatter the berry, the sweeter the juice," she answered.

"Let me see what you got," she said. I dropped my drawers and showed her curled Henry. Her fingers did a quick inspection and Bernice astounded me when she said, "This ain't enough?" Like a involuntary reflex muscle, I told her, "The harder it gets, the larger it gets." She rolled over on her side like a boat, no - like the Titanic going under, to put her head in front of my groin and dropped her jaw like she was about to swoop a spoonful of Chunky Soup. "I need a long dick 'cause my legs so big," she said.

Once my dick got hard, I told her, "I'mma hafta hit this from behind." She said, "You so bad. You want to fuck me doggy style." It's a turn-on to flip a ho like they are a rag doll. That wasn't going to happen here.

She had divots on her bulky butt that looked like an archipelago. Really, it looked like Tiger Woods had practiced his golf swing on her ass. I parted her cheeks and found Bernice, somehow, had a tiny ass hole. I parted her rear cleavage and touched her anus with my lips after my nose sniffed the boodee hole. She jumped forward and the fat of her buttocks flopped closed.

I wasn't deterred and drilled my face right back into battle. She responded with "Yes!" and pushed back. Although I enjoyed my face in the crack of her ass, soon enough my neck grew tired of the strengthening exercises it took to keep her cheeks apart. On a final dip, I jammed my nose into her ass and raked my tongue across her coochee and held it there. Bernice said, "Oooh, wee!"

My face was in "Hog Heaven" when the phone rang. "Minuteman" Willie had done his deed and was ready to head back. Before I could put my dick back into my draws I had to force my dick out of Bernice's mouth. "Wait a minute," she said each time I tried to get my dick back. She put a lip-lock on Henry and sucked the dick like it was her last supper before Lent.

Lois left her husband and began living with Willie in Fayetteville. Since Willie didn't have much reason to go to Spivey's Corner I didn't either. It must have been three weeks before I saw Bernice again. Lois needed to collect some belongings from her husband's house and that's what got me and Bernice back together.

When we got there, Bernice's old man was out on a trip just like Lois' estranged husband. I asked to be dropped off at Bernice's, "Just to say hello" as they went to pack the car with Lois' stuff. Although Lois and Willie never mentioned Bernice to me, they knew I was going over there to fuck because they stayed away for a good while.

Bernice and I didn't waste anytime getting in the bed because we both were anxious to finish what we started almost a month earlier. Before we even got into the bedroom she told me she wanted my nose in her ass hole. My dick was hardening and I wanted some of her good head. She figured the best thing to do was the 69 and insisted she be on top.

My horny ass allowed it.

Bernice knew what she was doing. She arranged pillows on the sides of my head, climbed above my torso, and positioned her knees on the pillows. I was under her groin like a mechanic under a car. My only concern was that she might "drop it while it's hot" and I would get smothered by her "Ponderosa" pussy. I sucked on all kinds of fat while I was changing her oil.

After we got out of the 69 I got into the reserved section of her stadium of fat and stroked that pussy. Bernice locked down her arms on my back, enveloped me among her titties, and we nutted together. Ain't nothing in the world like creaming into a tub of lard.

Hoes on Tobacco Roads

DELIVERANCE

ONE OF THE personal security benefits of the military, besides parental-type care, is the opportunity to wear the uniform. In towns near military bases Army work uniforms, called fatigues, aren't regarded as "unique" clothing. They blend in with regular civilians.

However, away from military installations fatigues drew favorable attention.

On one road trip to Charlotte wearing my work uniform came in handy - I mean real handy. It was a payday Friday and I had to work late, getting off well-after all my road partners had initiated Wolf Patrols and began their weekends. In such a hurry to catch up with anybody, I didn't even take the time to change from my fatigues into civilian clothes.

It must have been around midnight when, alone, I decided to get on Highway 74 West and go to Charlotte.

On the way I ran into car trouble. I had a flat tire and for some reason no tire iron. The flat tire blew my high and put me into depression. I could only cuss the wind for which of my partners had taken the spinner out of my trunk. It turned out to be Willie trying to help patrol prey. That's what friends cost.

It was a blur previously passing through this stretch of road because I had never even considered stopping. Just before the flat tire, the only landmark I remember seeing was a sign proudly announcing that a town called Marshville was the home of country and western music singer Randy Travis. Only that gave me some idea of my location and environment.

A little hole-in-the-wall bar called "Two Turtles" was where I eased off the road to change the tire. It was nearly one-thirty in the morning and there were three vehicles in the unpaved parking lot, including a wrecker. Going inside that red neck bar was my best option. If I hadn't been in uniform and had not seen the wrecker, I would have slept in my car until daylight.

A bar just before closing time is scary. That's when ugly usually happens. I kept my eyes forward and headed straight for the bartender. She was an older tar heel with blond hair that had black roots. I noticed a large black mole just above the left side of her lip.

The Dolly Parton look-alike, I figured, came straight out of 'dem dare hills.

Out of everything, it was that mole which distracted me most. I had never seen anything like that on a human. It looked like an animal dropping. The sick bastard in me wondered if I shot off on that mole whether it would get pregnant.

A soldier can get accustomed to not giving his name because it's on your shirt. Without properly introducing myself I told the bartender straight up, "I got a problem." She smiled and replied, "I'll bet you do" before adding, "Specialist Fenn" with emphasis.

I told her my car was in her parking lot with a flat tire and my tire iron was missing.

"You from Bragg?" she asked. "I responded with a simple nod. She went on and on about her having a son at Bragg. She recognized the patch on the left shoulder of my shirt. He's in the 82nd just like you. He's in the 321st Infantry. He's in the field all time and only gets home on some weekends. Thank goodness he went in. I bet your mama glad you're in the Army." As she talked, I was still distracted by that mole but managed to reply every now and then with an emphatic "Oh, yeah!" or "Is that right?"

I started feeling better about her greeting because I remember once before being in the Army helped me avoid a potentially volatile situation. A country cop stopped Willie and I late one night. He visually searched the car (the weed and papers were in Willie's underwear) and found only a half-filled bottle of wine. It could have easily gotten ugly.

The cop let us go, I believe, because of two main factors. We showed him our military ID and all soldiers have lawyers.

On this trip I was alone. The only thing in my favor was that my fatigues gave these particular red necks a warning that if you lynch me the United States government will be on your ass. Yet I was still leery because some hillbillies think just having their hick town on the red neck news for conducting a lynching is a positive thing.

"I'm Lynnette," the bartender said as she continued talking. That's all I needed, I thought to myself. Here I am near the boyhood home of a well-known "twanger" with a bartender who was a cross between Minnie Pearl and Tammy Wynette. The bleached blond behind the bar told me, "My other boy over there. He can help you."

Over where she was pointing was a stringy haired White boy with a Jack Daniels ball cap, a "The South Will Rise Again" t-shirt, cowboy boots, and a chain from his belt loop to his tall wallet in his back pocket spitting into a cup. He was among five patrons in the bar and the driver of the wrecker. "Jimmy," she called to one of the peckerwoods sitting in a booth, "Come and help this solider." He and I went into the parking lot and he did most of the work changing the tire.

Before Jimmy was halfway done everybody exited the bar. Lynette left in one car with somebody and a couple sped away in another, leaving me with Jimmy and his lady. His woman sat in the truck and whatever direction that was, I didn't look that way. Jimmy hurried to get the job done and I was glad. As that couple disappeared down the highway I took the time alone to roll and begin smoking a joint.

Lynettes scared me as she reentered the parking lot. I tapped the joint in the ashtray, 'bout to lose another high, and she stopped her car next to mine. Before I put my car into gear, hoping to reverse the anxiety I was experiencing, she began interrogating me.

"Where you goin', when you gotta be there, what's in Charlotte?" she asked. The inquisition included a critique about the times of morning her son gets home from Bragg and that he always wanted her to cook. "You wont somethin' to eat?" she asked.

I declined her invitation of food but she kept urging, telling me that she lived right behind the bar, alone, and it wouldn't be much of a bother to "fix some sausage and grits." I thought the whole episode was strange including how she kept calling me by the name on my fatigue shirt. It sounded weird coming from a red neck accent.

I thought Lynette was looking at me like a son, at first, but in reality she only knew me as an unknown solder in her son's large unit. I got egotistical and thought about collecting any benefit I could from my service. Maybe Lynette was a patriot, a true patriot I told myself. I didn't want to bust her red, white and blue bubble. All that thought hit me as quickly as that fat girl's fresh fart in Louisville. That's why after her constant urging I agreed to allow Lynette to cook me a meal. She said, "Follow me," and both cars went behind the bar to a residence attached to the business.

Inside, I declined the Jack Daniels she offered. I wanted to maintain an ability to run, in a direct manner, while looking out for White folks in hoods and robes.

Besides the trashiness of her place the thing that grabbed my attention was her cat. She let her pet out and told the feline not to bother crying at the door because she wasn't going to let it back in. I caught the signal that she didn't want to be interrupted.

As Lynnette prepared some grits and sausage, I went outside and smoked a joint while looking for a cross on fire. I had an appetite when she placed my plate on a table in front of the cluttered couch I was sitting on. She sat there and watched me eat, like she was in a sperm bank waiting room. When I was just about finished eating, Lynette went into a room and came back with a videotape.

"I've got something I want to show you," she said, then slid a tape into the VCR machine on top of the TV. It was a porno movie this ho didn't even have to cue up. On the screen was a Black guy slapping a White girl in the face with a horse-sized dick.

It took only one minute of viewing before Lynette asked for Henry. "That shit makes me hot," she said. "I'mma be honest with you. I want to be slapped like that by a black cock. I never expected one to walk into my bar."

She wanted my dick specifically because it was black. It wasn't because she was patriotic; Henry wasn't red, white, and blue. It wasn't because my dick was large; she didn't know that. Henry was a simply a symbol.

"Don't let me stop you," I answered. "Take it out," she ordered. I leaned back and pulled Henry out. Lynette slapped herself across the face then shook him like she was at a military parade and she was showing her patriotism. Henry got hard and I skinned my dick back and reached for her lips with it.

I hadn't even gotten to the last bite of my meal when she began slurping hers. "Whoa, Jesus. It's gettin' bigger," she said, as she began having trouble stretching her jaws enough. She stopped, pulled the table away, and got down on her knees. She admired my dick like it was a harvest moon. I asked if that was what she wanted. Lynette said, "Yes; a beautiful, long, black, hard cock."

This ho's blow was serious. She slobbered heavily and was jerking her head back like she was repeatedly swallowing aspirins. The cat's meow to watch irritated her. When she stopped to let the cat in I stood to stretch and Henry, much closer to Charlotte than I was, looked as if he had been out in the rain.

I was paranoid about being there and hurried the nutt. I hit her in the forehead on the second shot but followed by jamming my dick back into her mouth with more for her tongue. I wiped skeet on that mole. "God that was good," she said, after she gargled and returned. "When can I get the pussy?" I asked before I left. "Take my phone number instead," she told me.

Lynette did only oral on me the next two times we hooked-up. I pressed her for pussy.

She gave in. The first time we fucked her cat made it a threesome. Each time I recoiled her cat would smell my ass hole. I must have bumped into that feline's nose four or five times before it jumped off the bed. Talk about freaky! I liked it; I liked it a lot.

CHAPTER 6

FREAKS NEAR CAPE FEAR

OPPORTUNITY KNOCKS

I N WAR, WHERE the shooting battle is located is called "The Front." Further back, where planning for the battle takes place, is called "The Rear." Considering that killings are occurring at "The Front," staple pullers like I was are more comfortable at "The Rear."

That's why after leaving "Animal House" I was inclined to move back on quiet Shaw Mill Road. This was a different group of apartments, more secluded than where I lived previously on that desolate road. Unlike most others in the complex, my apartment was bi-level with the living room and kitchen upstairs and two bedrooms and bath downstairs.

My crib was perfectly located near the entrance for sneaking skanks home and I pummeled plenty pussy in that pad.

A female neighbor living two doors down took it upon herself to be the complex's welcome wagon. She was an older, small-framed White woman with long blond hair accentuated by pinkish frosting. Her tits stood out, like attachments, on her petite frame. I was washing my car, minding my own business, and here she comes with questions. I gave her neighborly but cautious attention.

Among many distractions, an immediate one was solicited by her nipples. They protruded impressively in her tank top which showed big time cleavage. She had a deep tan as if she hated to be pale. I noticed her small feet were manicured as they peeked out from her miniature high heels.

She threw out a binder of information about herself. Her name was Dottie and from my count she was about 12 to 15 years older than me. She was recently divorced and her ex-husband was active duty military who trained soldiers in Special Forces techniques.

Here's the kicker: Her ex-husband lived in the apartment between us. Come to find out, her husband had left her for a man. When it dawned upon me that the two guys, living next door to me, were gay I stopped washing the car and just listened.

I could have gone for the rest of my life without knowing the apartment connected to mine housed guys that were funny. I wondered why Dottie offered that kind of information. I thought that maybe she informed me about next door to see if I had "sugar in my shit" or "pooped paisley."

I also felt like she was being a snitch. I wondered what was wrong with Dottie, not her ex. She didn't look bad so maybe she was a bitch to live with. Maybe she was the type to tell her husband, "No!" Why would a man give up those titties and a tailored, carefully crafted coochee to care for a dick? I was confused.

In these exact words I asked Dottie, "You a good looking woman. What's wrong wit' him?" Her answer gave insight to how a man could "switch out" in the middle of life.

Dottie told me, "He say he tired of pussy. He say he tired of big breasts. That son-of-a- bitch rather suck a dick than suck a clit. He'd rather fuck a man in the ass than fuck me." I told Dottie point-blank, "That don't make no sense to me." She said, "Me neither."

I invited Dottie inside and while I sipped cold Thunderbird (she didn't want any) she expanded on her life story. She was a stripper when she and her ex met in Texas. "You must-a-been a hellafied stripper," I said. "I didn't have these tits then," Dottie responded.

"Wait a minute," she added, "I'll be right back," then hurried out the door. She returned with pictures. "This is how I looked when I worked," she told me.

Dottie wasn't nude in the pictures but what she showed was close to that. Like most White girls in their teens and early twenties, those were Dottie's best years cosmetically.

Peckerwoods, especially the females, have a "false positive" beauty. Her backside carried the usual Caucasian curse of flatness but at one time Dottie looked good enough to toss dollars at. Her "little girl" stature and act with pony tails on stage was enough to prickle a pervert. It caught my eye. She hinted that she had something much more magnificent to offer patrons than knockers.

I told her I had one more question about her ex and that would be the last time I mentioned him. "Go ahead and ask," she exhorted me. "I ain't got no feelings for his punk ass." I asked her, "How you know what he doing with that guy. They may be just good friends. What make you think they fucking?" Dottie graphically explained what she was talking about wasn't theory. "I caught 'em," she told me, and then continued. "I walked-in on my husband screwin' a man. They didn't even stop. I hear them now, next door, fussin' about fuckin'. Don't you hear them arguing?"

She was right about the noise coming from next door. Their wall connected to my apartment and often there were squabbles, upstairs and downstairs. Every now and then I would hear one of them holler, "Stop Dick!" or "Leave me alone Dick." At first I thought one of the occupants had a woman in the crib but Dottie bluntly told me, "My husband's name is Richard but his "girlfriend" calls him Dick. If you hear somebody that sounds like a woman, that's his roommate Paul. You wanna know how sick those bastards are?

Richard calls him Paula!"

Like when a pregnant woman's water suddenly breaks, Dottie changed the subject. "You got a girlfriend?" I told her I had a girlfriend but that she wouldn't be at my house unless I brought her. "What she like?" she asked. "She got a big ass but I hate she tells me "No" sometimes," I answered. I wanted to tell Dottie everything about me and Annette.

I wanted to tell her that Annette loved pleasing me but wouldn't have anal sex with me. That was just too much to confess until I was ready to prompt her pooter.

Dottie regained being the topic of conversation by boosting her breasts with her hands.

"You like these?" she asked. "They ain't real but they're firm. Go ahead, take a feel." She lifted her tank top, allowing me to scrutinize fake tits. "They feel weird, at first, but you get used to them," she told me. When it comes to tits and ass, inflated can be as functional as flat so I didn't mind feeling her chest.

As I contributed conservative clutches to her bosom, she continued to berate her former husband and chronicled more of their history. "Richard said he'd pay for them if I married him, so I did," she revealed. "Now he tired of tits and cunt. All he wants is anal sex and blowjobs. It's because I could never get pregnant. He always held that against me.

I should have never allowed him to fuck me in the ass. Anal sex and blowjobs kant make no baby. We couldah kept trying."

Then Dottie just up and left. "I got to go right now but I'll be back later," she said. "You got any plans for tonight?" she asked, as she bolted towards the door. I had plans alright. I had plans to stick dick in every hole she made available, but I answered, "No."

I wanted to be ready for Dottie. The last nutt I busted was a couple of days earlier when Annette vacuumed skeet out of Henry like a Hoover does dust. Exercise helps produce sperm so I took a walk down Shaw Mill Road to my former apartment complex to see who was freaking off those mirrors on the bedroom wall.

Acting like I was interested in renting it because of the mirrors, I found the occupants were a Black couple who couldn't even get along during the little time I spent meeting them. The woman was in the Army and she had her lip turned up when she said her ol' man didn't leave that apartment except to get the mail. But that's another story.

I figured washing my car and taking that walk would insure my readiness for Dottie.

She didn't even show up. It wasn't the first time pussy stood me up.

I didn't want to leave the house that next day for fear of runnin up on some ho and nuttin' in her mouth. It was early evening when Dottie returned. "Hey girl," I said. "I thought you were coming over last night." She shot straight from the door over to the couch. "I had to cook last night and I was tired afterwards," she told me. "I got a friend with a sick husband and was at her house all day," she went on to explain. "But I ain't tired now. I'm curious. Give me some of that wine." She drank some T-bird and got real.

"I wanna see what your cock looks like," she said, before adding, "I want to know if if it was worth meeting you. I'm used to a lot of meat. Pull it out it out and let me see." I leaned back and pulled my dick through the sides of my draws and shorts. Dottie reached over, like she had seen a Black dick before, and commented on what she had a handle on.

"I expect that's gonna get bigger," she said, as she began to claw at my dick.

It didn't take too long for stiff dick to show up because Dottie's hand was as potent as pickle pulp. I didn't have to tell her anything. She jacked it, shook it, pulled it, and skinned it back until my dick pointed, without support, the same direction of a space shuttle at liftoff. Dottie made a comment after Henry's growth spurts like that of a mother shopping with a teenager. She told me, "That looks nice on you." She was impressed when Henry hardened to maximum density and showed unusual nerve when she hollered, "Goddam nigga!"

She looked at me timidly after she said that and asked, "You don't mind me calling you that, do you? My Black friends overlook it when I get that comfortable with them."

Henry showed no ill towards the term she used. My dick was in Dottie's hand, hunting her mouth, and hoping to explode in it. "It ain't no skin off my dick," I told her.

I asked her about giving up the pussy as I wiggled my shorts down. "We shouldn't fuck so soon," she told me. "I don't want Richard throwing that up in my face." I asked her, "What you gonna do with the dick you done got hard?" "I'll just give you a blowjob right now," she answered, "and fuck this thing later."

Dottie liked to talk while, even while giving head. Her lips tickled when she worked words with LSD on her tongue. "Whew!" she exclaimed. "How long can this thing last before shooting off?" she asked. I responded by telling her I was ready to nutt. "Right now?" she asked. "Right now," I said. "Right now isn't a good time," she told me.

My dick was taller than the Empire State Building and pre-mee sperms were jumping off committing suicide. "Stand up and let me see what yo' cock looks like," she asked. I stood and that ho yanked my standard into different angles before dunking my dick halfway down her throat. "I dreamed you cumming in my mouth," Dottie admitted.

"Now, after seeing this thing, I'd rather you shoot off on my face."

She brewed a nutt and amazingly knew just when to pull the dick out and face rapid fire. Henry soiled her make-up with a thick line of skeet on her jaw but most of it landed between her nose and lips. I milked my dick onto her bottom lip. Dottie wiped off some cum with a finger and put it into her mouth, sucking her finger on its way out. It sounded like she was eating Sugar Smacks. "Not too bad," she said. Next time, I'll let you shoot off in my mouth and blow some cum bubbles for you."

This ho was a pro.

I had plenty left for her when I got home from work that next day. We had to run two miles on Mondays and, no doubt, I built my sperm count back up. I was anticipating getting to know Dottie's fake titties and real pussy, but it didn't happen. Because love don't love nobody, I spent the night home alone.

Real early, before my usual wake time, that next morning Dottie knocked at my downstairs back door. After my wake-up piss, I found her buck naked brandishing pale breasts above the cover. She went straight for my dick and balls and I had to give Dottie a proper introduction to both Henry and Skeeter. "How in the hell you come up with those names?" she asked. I told her they just popped into my head. "Well," Dottie said, as she boosted her titties up towards me, "these are my favorite flowers, Rose and Violet."

I remembered a lesson I learned. Dottie hadn't come over to a Black man's crib at four o'clock in the morning for some head. I climbed over to lay pipe and she stopped me right there. "I don't want it that way," she told me. She turned and put her flat ass up. "I like it like this," she said. Pale lines from her thong bikini were easily visible on her backside and even with the light out I saw the butterfly tattoo on her lower back.

I poked Skeeter in and out of the pussy to prompt lubrication. After getting a couple of inches deep, I jammed. "Take it easy," she said. "It's been a while." As I recoiled, that cunt grabbed Henry and squeezed him like he was a long, lost friend. I concentrated on bumping into and loosening the walls in that coochee. Every time I clobbered a confine, Dottie looked back at me trying to gauge whether I cared to take it easy.

To get to the chapter in her book I really wanted to read, I pulled out the pussy and sucked her boodee hole like it was Halle Berry's mouth. As I vacuumed her butt, Dottie said, "Ooh! Ooh!" She raised her hips each time my tongue poked into her anus, which wanted to be stabbed.

Henry got my mind off the boodee. He had become bulged like a balloon and the anticipation of nuttin' into a White ho made him indefatigable as diamond. I drove back into her cunt like I was speeding and no cops were around. Dottie looked over her shoulder at me and said, "Fuck me you son-of-a-bitch."

The way she did it, calling me derogatory names seemed to be a fetish of Dottie's.

She liked being hurt by a dick. In her mind, name calling helped make that happen. A few times she hollered at Henry, "Fuck me nigga!" Another time she called Henry a "black motherfucker." The racial monikers may have been to alert Richard, next door, of what was happening. He had to hear it. She was loud enough.

"Pull my hair," she told me. I grabbed her head and yanked on it like I was cropping corn. "Oh, shit!" she hollered. "Fuck me nigga. Fuck me harder." Henry was so in-tuned with her fucking advice that he got used to her yelps. Henry wanted to hurt that pussy.

To take a break, I flipped her over into the buck position and directed my face between her legs. She lifted her hips and her pussy and my mouth met her muff in mid-air. My taste buds tapped her twat and Dottie worked it. I caught a glimpse of something odd looking just above my nose. It was shadowy in the room and I couldn't confirm what looked like some sort of an attachment. I thought, maybe, her clit was pierced.

Further discovery was delayed because Dottie flipped over and sat on my face. That ho did it without losing our connection. She was fucking proficient. After pressing and rubbing her cunt on my face a few times she backed off, turned, and put us into the 69. It seemed this ho had come to my house with fucking battle plans.

Dottie slid her best parts down my face and sat on my dick facing away from me. Once Henry was comfortably in the pussy, she encouraged me with verbal challenges to bust a nutt. I lurched and twisted dick in that pussy like I was having a heroin withdrawal episode. No matter which way I moved she stayed on top. Henry erupted like a volcano.

As I regained my composure, Dottie rubbed between her legs. Later I realized she mixed her honey with my creampie skeet onto her boodee hole. She turned her back to me and massaged my dick head all over that wet spot and wormed re-filled Skeeter into her butt hole. She took the whole dick head into her anus and squeezed the swell out of my dick before easing Henry out her ass. "I haven't done that in a while," she said. "We'll have to work on that. Right now, it hurts." Dottie washed my dick with soap and water, like it was her dildo, then sucked out a nutt.

I was dragging ass getting ready for work that morning. Richard gave me the evil eye as we ended-up leaving at the same time. I wondered if he heard me and his ex-wife fucking. I also wondered if he had gotten some boodee too.

That very afternoon Dottie called me to come over to her place. "You left me horny this morning. I need a nutt. I want you to suck my clit. Do you mind?" That girl didn't even have to ask me that. "You can leave your pants on because I don't want to fuck," she told me. "I'm still sore in both places from what we did this morning."

The first thing she took off was the first thing she always took off, her top. "Ain't no clit on yo' tits," I told her. She laughed. "I have to be comfortable. Rose and Violet have to blossom." Exposing her breasts afforded me the opportunity to really fondle her flowers. I treated her nipples like nachos while she was propped up on pillows permitting a vibrator to hum her hick.

Tired of the titties, I put my head between her legs to get a closer look at what was happening downtown. That's when I saw, clear as danger, Dottie had a dick. I kissed her thighs to make it seem as though I wasn't startled. She had a digit that stuck out at the bottom of her pelvis like a bicycle's kickstand. When she had that vibrator on it, it looked like she was trying to light a candle. Dottie had the longest clit with the fattest head I had ever seen. No wonder Richard revered rigid.

I commented, "Damn girl, you got a big clit." Dottie cut off the vibrator, lifted up my chin, and directed my face up to hers and asked, "Do you like it? It's not too much is it?"

I told Dottie, "That thing like a dick." Dottie sounded apologetic when she responded to my observation. "Don't be scared of it," she told me. "Most men like it. When I stripped, it was my money maker. Please play with it." This ho asked me, Prince Pervert, to play with her extra long, fat-headed, hard, reddening, uncovered sex utensil. I did.

First, I had to do some research. "Is it gonna skeet?" I asked her. Dottie laughed. "No, silly. I cum the same place any other woman does. It's just big." The more I pulled on that thing the more rigid and fat it got, just like Henry. I put that rascal between my lips and easily flicked it with my tongue. I sucked the hell out that fixed freak.

She turned to set her cunt on my face with her honey pistol in my mouth, hunched, and nutted. I could feel her clit throbbing on my tongue, probably trying to shoot off.

"That was good," she said, as she rested. "Wait a minute," I told her, as I faced the pussy again. "I want that juice." "Be careful," she told me. "I'm still sore down there."

My tongue carefully scooped as much of her honey as I could. Some of it was thick as tartar sauce while heat had changed some into juice.

Both brands lathered my tongue. I kissed the cunt and that cunt kissed back as it squeezed more honey out.

I would visit Dottie but never spent the night there, especially after she told me that Richard had a key. We became such good friends I was content with her allowance of me putting only nine inches, Richard's maximum, in her rear.

GREAT DAY IN THE MORNING

ARGUABLY THE WORST casualties of a combat mission can be those missing in action.

When specific facts from any operation, especially where a solider is MIA, are left unknown it can cause a family to never attain complete closure. Inevitably, questions are asked. Some questions are unable to be answered and a fitting finish is unobtainable.

Therefore, it took a lot of patience and understanding on my part to help a widow let her recent loss go. However, I was happy to help her attain closure. It's funny - well, maybe not funny but surely odd - how easily the name of the family member lost was more notable than the name of the "suffering" widow.

I had been on a weekend visit to Washington, D.C. with Dottie but that's another story. It must have been at least 10 days before Dottie and I hooked-up afterwards. That in itself was unusual. On my way to work one day, I saw her in the parking lot of our apartment complex and she tried to explain why she hadn't been over. "A friend lost her husband and I've been spending a lot of time at her house," she said. "The funeral is Saturday." I just said okay and went on about my business.

Come that Saturday night Dottie calls and tells me she was bringing somebody over to meet me. She showed up with the woman who had just buried her husband. The petite woman was dark-skinned, had a short, blond afro hair style, and wore thick glasses. She had a big ass nose. It looked like one of those attachments you'd put on a Mr. Potato Head. The only sexual attractions I noticed were her lips, dark skin, and petite frame.

"You got anything to drink?" Dottie asked, as she busted into my place. The other woman followed and sat on the couch as Dottie raided the kitchen. The widow told Dottie, "I really don't want anything to drink." Dottie thought otherwise and grabbed wine out my box and glasses from my kitchen cabinet - liked she lived there.

I attempted to get acquainted with the new widow with small talk and Dottie must have thought introductions were over. "I need to use your bathroom," was the next thing Dottie insisted on. She headed downstairs and called me to join her. "Watch me take a piss?" she whispered, with a gleam in her eye. "I don't want to see you pee," I retorted. "Well, watch anyway because I need to talk to you," she told me.

Dottie gave me the 411 on the woman who had just buried her husband that same day.

"He was sick for a long time, so she ain't all that hurt about him being gone. But she don't need to be by herself. I asked her to spend the night with me," Dottie said, "but I got to thinking that maybe what's in your pants will get the funeral off her mind. I want you to be nice to her. I'll be home. Call if you need me."

I couldn't believe Dottie planned to leave me alone with a brand new widow. If this woman started crying or something, it would be like calling an ambulance for a corpse.

I tried to find something to talk to the woman about other than the most recent significant event in her life. I started rattling off about where I was from. "Have you ever been to Florida," I asked. She said, "No." "Do you like the beach?" I asked. She said, "No." I kept trying. "The weather is always warm in Florida, or do you like having four seasons?" I queried. She said, "No." I offered her a drink and she shook her head "No." I offered her a nicely rolled joint and she shook her head "No."

After all that, I was ready for Thelma to leave. The only thing I hadn't tried was being real. I decided to let her know I was a "sick bastard." I moved closer to her, grabbed her hand, and put it on my dick. That got her attention. She snatched her hand back but the deed had been done. I told her, "I want you to pretend there is nobody else in the world right now but me and you. Do you think you can do that?" She said, "No." Since she didn't get up and run out the door, anything was possible. You feel me?

Once I was high enough, I wanted to lie down and really didn't care if she got up and left. That gave me license to pull out my dick. "Here's something to help get your mind off what happened today," I told her, as I grabbed her hand, again, and put it on my dick. I held it down this time. She wouldn't even look at what she had her hand on. As a matter of fact Thelma turned her head to demonstrate she didn't prefer anything in that direction.

I fitted Henry into her palm, squeezed her hand on the dick, and told her, "Rub that for me." She wouldn't do it. But still, she didn't get up and leave.

Out of nowhere, Thelma asked me to pour her some T-bird. After I did, she squeezed Henry like she was feeling fruit in the produce department at Food Lion. I didn't want to be crude in asking her the last time she fucked. I went the same place in another direction.

"I bet you tight," I told her. "It's not good to be too tight. It can keep you from being able to rest. Relax, girl," I added. Thelma looked me sternly in the face, looked down at my "proud as a peacock" prick, and said, "Ain't nobody called me girl in a long time." It was tough getting my dick fully hard because Henry wasn't sure he was going to get some pussy.

It took gulps of T-bird but Thelma finally started talking. "Dottie set this up so I wouldn't feel bad about today," she said, while looking inside her cup after taking a big gulp. "I'm glad he's gone," she continued, as she examined my bag of herb like she knew one brand from another. "I didn't even bother to get out of the car when they put him in his new home. That son-of-a-bitch didn't do nothin' but make me feel bad about myself."

Okay. Now I understood what I was up against. "Some man" abused her and she was leery about showing "appreciation" for dick. She didn't even want to look at a new one.

Here I was, acting like an opportunistic dyke, trying to take advantage of her.

It flashed in my mind that Dottie got me into this mess. I started to call her ass up but sensitive me apologized to the widow. "We don't have to do nothin'," I said. She came back with, "We ain't gonna do nothing." I responded with, "Dottie just thought it would be nice to direct your attention away from what happened today."

A few seconds later Thelma looked down at what her left hand had been bothering and gave a look as if she had a problem. That ho said, "You got a big dick." I didn't respond because there was nothing more to add on that issue. She was correct; her glasses were working properly.

Then she comes out with, "I been rubbing this thing for a while and it ain't even all the way hard. What's wrong wit' you?" I told her, "You got to handle him with passion." I put her hand back on the dick, guided her to yank like we were loading a shotgun, and then helped her shake it so she would feel its weight. As Henry began stretching I told Thelma, "Look how swole it's gettin'. That's once in a lifetime dick, girl."

Thelma gulped down her remaining wine and demonstrably set the cup down like she had made her mind up about something. She turned towards me, reached over with her other hand, and began pulling my dick head with the fingers of her other hand like she was plucking a chicken.

Without any move to insert my penis into her mouth, I realized she was too content doing what she was doing. I acted like I was going to put Henry back into my pants. "You got my attention," she said. "Leave it where it at." I told her that if all she was going to do was tease the dick, "We'd be more comfortable downstairs." She popped right up off the couch like she was going on holiday.

She sat in the "fuck chair" across from my bed and I realized just how small she was.

"How you gonna rub me sitting over there," I said. That got her out the chair and we laid down with all our clothes on with my dick hanging out my shorts. "Who in the world let you put all of this in them?" she asked, as she continued to tease my dick head with one hand and choke it with the other. I chose not to answer.

She finally relented and stripped to her white bra and old lady panties. I spread her legs. "This is what I want," I told her, while stroking her crotch with the back of my hand.

"I ain't had a man in a long time," she said. "Just relax and let me do everything," I said. I moved to expose her cunt. "Let me see what this thing look like," I told her.

"I rather just rub you," she said, as she signaled for me to stop yanking on her underwear. I realized I was supposed to be there for her; not her there for me. I got up and took my pants off, leaving my underwear on. She began pulling on my dick like she was trying to start a lawn mower. The longer my dick got the more she stared at it. At one point she gave a glance like it was an antagonist, like it was bothering her.

I just had to say something. "That's Henry you're holding," I told her. "Henry?" she asked, responding as if a doctor announced she had cancer. I said, "Yeah, that's what I call it." She asked me, "Where you get the name Henry?" I told her my dick looked like a Henry. "That's my husband's name," she told me. Fortunately, I had a quick reply, "Does it look anything like him?" She said, "It don't look like him but it's what he was."

I played my blunder off by trying to seem reasonable. "Giving my dick a name makes asking somebody to put it in their mouth much easier," I told her. "Suck my dick can be such a non-musical phrase. Give Henry some head sounds much better." She laughed at my explanation and even told me my reasoning made sense but told me, "It still don't mean I'm gonna suck yo' dick."

Thelma choked Henry and shook him like she had an enemy by the neck. Then that ho began to talk directly to my dick like she wanted to continue an argument. "I ain't done this in a long time but I'mma give you what you want," she said, while looking directly at Henry. "Don't get mad at me if I don't do it right," she suggested. ·

"Give Henry a kiss," I told her. Thelma smiled then puckered her big lips like she was offering a sensual separation. That got good to her and she continued to tap her big lips on Skeeter. She was compassionate, touching tenderly those black, soft, trademark African lips against something that was hard as hell. Henry's ring size grew greatly.

Her memory of how to suck a dick came back to her. She gripped her lips at the base of my dick head like she was removing the last bit of new recipe off a spoon. A bead of skeet popped up. "You leaking," she said. "You did it," I told her. "See what it taste like."

That ho wiped the cum drop off with fingers then jumped her jaws back on my dick like flavoring was falling off a fruit.

Occasionally stopping and staring, sometimes Thelma would stare at my dick like it was a Picasso she was trying to understand. As she continued to work on that dick I began to believe she was psychologically giving her husband one last good time. She was also restraining herself from getting too happy. I just laid back and let her give "Henry" all the attention she wanted him to have.

The only thing that interrupted us was my need to go back upstairs to get more wine.

For somebody who preferred red (Wild Irish Rose) she sure didn't mind sucking up my white (T-bird). Upon my return she was sitting on the side of the bed with a "What's next?" look, still with her underwear on. "I'm tired of watching you have all the fun," I told her and talked her into the 69 position.

She kept her draws on and because she was petite her ass ended-up a ways from my face. I did something to take my mind off my disappointment that she wasn't ready to fuck. I pulled her panties to the side in the crotch and looked. Her short-haired twat lips were thin and couldn't cover her coochee's door knocker clit that was peering out. I rubbed her pussy with my mouth like I was taking the wrapper off a Starburst. I tried to imagine how a creampie would look on her awesome anus. Pudding with icing, I figured.

We were real quiet, except for the sound of her working my dick head in and out her face. She never asked me to turn out the light so I figured she liked looking at what she was wolfing down. I wanted her to acknowledge that I was playing with her pussy although I really wanted her to take off those draws. "How many children this thing done had?" I asked. "I don't have any children," she answered.

Her coochee's hole looked like it hadn't had dick in a long time, compared to some of the young girls I had looked inside of. Her boodee hole, dark chocolate as it was, looked worn but yet tight. Innocent is how I would describe it. I liked innocent boodee holes.

Her ass and pussy seemed a good distance apart so I took a measurement. I used my fingers to see how my nose and tongue matched the distance between her clit and anus. I didn't have anything else to do while I was back there.

She had to be uncomfortable with me pulling on her draws but that ol' ho just wouldn't take them off. She was having such a good time on my dick I didn't want to interrupt her obsession by asking her, again, to fuck. Other than a sniff and kiss every now and then, I just looked at pure pussy and boodee hole as each looked back at me.

Thelma also absolutely refused to taste the beads of skeet that popped up. Every now and then I felt her pinching the tip of my dick to get them off. I messed up by asking her, "What you want me to do if I haff to nutt?" "Don't do it," she said. "You working on that dick good and pretty soon I'm gonna shoot off," I told her with a strain in my voice.

She shocked me when she said, "I better stop," and then did.

I had fucked up with words again. I should have just nutted in her mouth. But I hated it when a ho pulled away while I was shootin' off. It's the same feeling of non-satisfaction one gets from pulling out to keep a girl from getting pregnant. It's like forgetting, for one blessed moment, that you're terminally ill and then a TV commercial reminds you.

As she began to crawl off me, I pulled her small hips to my face and slammed my nose against her ass hole with my tongue on her pussy. She tried to remove my plastered face from between her hips but I held on. She fell over on her side with her hand pushing my head away as if she was lifting off a sunken seat. I got a good grip on her cunt with my mouth and pulled. "No, no!" she hollered and I stopped.

I turned away and she felt the need to console me. "I don't think it's right to have sex tonight," she said. I thought that was bullshit. "Turn the light off and let's go to sleep," she added. I sacrificed the remainder of my evening "In Remembrance" of a "Henry" I didn't know. I put my dick alongside the back of Thelma's thighs and Skeeter ended-up poking against her cloth-covered boodee hole. I was content with something to hunch until I fell off to sleep.

Before sunlight Thelma woke up a different person. She was buck naked and telling me, "Get me wet." She put my hand on her clit and guided my rub until she got up and placed her pussy on my face in the 69. Her coochee was on my mouth and her boodee hole was on the bridge of my sniffer. Once the cunt was wet enough, Thelma snatched the pussy off my mouth like it didn't belong there.

She reached over to my nightstand, put her bifocals on, grabbed my dick, and squatted over my dick like she was about to start a campfire. It was my first fuck while my partner had extra eyes. I found I liked fucking a ho wearing glasses. I pretended she was my fifth grade, fresh out of college, teacher Ms. Easter. I had been wanting that pussy ever since I was ten years old.

That ho was facing me with an intense look, like Ms. Easter was introducing a math method, while her coochee was sliding up and down my dick. She jammed Henry into her cunt like she was putting too much pork into a link. The little light coming through the curtains shined up and down her glasses on our movements. That ho said "Oh, Henry!" after every thrust downward and every inch deeper the dick went. "Oh, Henry!" was what she was saying when I blasted her cunt with a gang of sperms headed for death row.

Thelma pulled my penis out of her sperm grave, looked down at my dick, and sent a shot of hot piss on Henry and all over my balls. You could tell it was a deliberate, purposeful pee designed to push out everything because the coochee farted. I didn't say a word because it was freaky. I liked freaky. I cut on the light and noticed cum still exiting her cunt like the last spectators leaving a stadium. "Stop looking and wipe me," she said.

As I wiped her, she tried to push more out and the pussy produced another bass sounding cunt fart that said, "Booooooo!" like somebody had sung badly at The Apollo. I interpreted it as her dead ol man's opinion of our fuck. I had to test Thelma's willingness to be fucked in the ass. She did get off on my dick pressing against her anus. No doubt her dead Henry had done at least that, probably more.

She laughed when I couldn't get in. We had a freaky conversation while I was trying my damnest to get dick into her butt. "Git it!" that ho told me, knowing she blocking brick.

Thelma promised to come back whenever she missed Henry. "It'll be difficult but I will," she told me. My friendship with Dottie, her consolation being away from "Henry", and/or my freakiness must have been too much for her cougar ass. I never saw her again.

Freaks Near Cape Fear

WHEN NATURE CALLS

THE FIRST IMMIGRANTS to the Western Hemisphere, specifically the United States, were made up of fanatical religious groups, economic losers, convicts, occupiers, and slavers.

It was a "melting pot" comprised of the genes and norms of low-lifes and extremists.

Those kindred spirits were in addition to slaves whose vintage was a village culture and non-Christian beliefs. The result of that "copulative soup" of peoples now permeates our society in the midst of concurrent natural selection.

The most reliable method for survival among groups has been to have a numbers dominance. To account for changing numbers, "civilized" humans developed strategies such as democracy. Uncivilized people argue that removal or reduction in numbers via violence, incarceration, and institutionalized discrimination insure survival. Apocalyptic believers propose there's no middle ground and that compromise is impossible.

Survival of my genes and norms - no doubt about it - is what led me to pick up Judy.

I was coming out of a grocery store and saw her butt "breaking bad" at the back of her sun dress. Her heavy hips were moving up and down like a pair of inhaling and exhaling elephant lungs. As I naturally watched this woman's ass wobble wobble my dick got hard in the middle of pedestrian traffic. Her boodee was lighting a lamp, quivering and it wasn't even cold. Her backside reminded me of a song called, "Good Golly Miss Molly."

Her caboose lifted up and dropped back down all the way to where she parked her love train on a bench in front of another store. Bouncing breasts, awesome ass, thumping thighs, smooth skin, minus make-up, head full of combed hair, and luscious lips on her face; this caravan had it all. Did I mention harkening hips? I kept my eye that-a-way as best I could while I was putting groceries into my car.

She had more cargo. In addition to hauling the hiney of a champion heifer, she had a baby in one arm, a suitcase in one hand, and was being followed by another crumb-snatcher. This Black woman was takin' care of hers but seemed to be out of steam.

Naturally, I went over there. "Are you lost or something?" I asked. "We ain't got no ride," she said. When I heard that, even I had to sit down. How was it a fine, full-bowl butt female having any problem? Niggas gone crazy, I thought.

"How you ain't got no ride?" I asked her, trying to mimic how she sounded like a three-year old lost in a mall. "My boyfriend put us out dah cah," she answered. "I needs to git to my mama house in Dunn but ain't got no way to git dare." Her speech gave me a clue as to why she may be having a problem. Her drawl reminded me of those old 1932 movies where stereotypical Black folks spoke "Negro."

I felt sorry for her. I felt sorry for the kids. I wanted to check out them hips. Having mercy and passing a favor forward, I told her she could come home with me until I found time to take her home. That girl didn't even hesitate to follow me. She didn't ask if I was a promising pedophile, convicted creep, married maggot, a descendant of America's first free settlers, or worse. I'm glad she didn't ask. I may have had to tell a lie.

"Dah baby needs some Pampers," she told me after we all piled into the car. She hadn't even given her name and already she was weighing on my resources. The fact that the diapers were for the baby girl made me feel okay about going back into the store.

"My name Judy," she said, before not even saying "thank you" when I returned. "People call me big boodee Judy." "No, doubt," I whispered just before I told her my name, that I lived just a short distance away, and I'd take her to Dunn when I had a chance.

At my place she came out with, "Dah baby needs some milk and I needs some douche." I told her, "I don't have any milk and I ain't buying no feminine product. Ya'll ah have to come to the store wit' me."

I was getting perturbed about all the things I was doing for her and hers and had yet gotten my nose into the crack of her ass. I began to wonder which of us was "slow."

Imagining my sniffer in the middle of all that probably peach-colored boodee did the trick. The main thing that kept me going was the way her ass jiggled in that sun dress.

Back at my place she mostly stayed down stairs as I watched TV upstairs. The baby girl would whine a little but the little boy was super quiet. He followed his mama like he was physically attached to her and showed much disinterest in me. I still wondered how the kids' father(s) or mother's boyfriend(s) could kick this fine ass girl to the curb.

I heard Judy taking a shower and figured both kids were asleep because that little boy wasn't going to let her out of his sight. Getting high delayed me so by the time I got downstairs Judy was asleep in my small extra bed with the kids. She had on a short nightgown and her butt cheeks were hanging off the mattress like hams in a smokehouse.

I looked at her and the kids at peace and figured I'd leave her alone.

Before sun-up the next morning Dottie, my "fucking" neighbor, loudly knocked on my downstairs outside door. She offered me sex so I invited her in and showed her Judy and the kids in the extra bedroom. "How long they gonna be here?" Dottie wondered. All I could tell her is that they had to be gone by the time I went to work on Monday.

Dottie left and no sooner than when the door closed Judy came out of the extra room.

"Dat yo' girlfriend?" she asked. I explained who Dottie was and that I didn't have a girlfriend. "You live he ah by yo'self?" she asked. "Yes I live here by myself," I answered. Then Judy asked me something that told

125

me she wasn't as dumb as her drawl implied. She asked, "Is you gonna fuck me?"

"Yes I am," I answered as I closed the room door. I helped her pull off her night gown.

Her titties had complimentary dark brown areas around big dark brown nipples against tanned yella skin. Her headlights were like neon signs flashing "Adults Only." She had on some draws, colored boundary black, that stretched to make it look like she was carrying a personal suitcase below her back.

Other findings made me salivate. Judy is the softest thick woman I ever squeezed. My hands sunk into her flesh like fingers holding a marshmallow. This ho had a Botswana bush of jet black hair from her pelvis to inside her darkened thick thighs. Her belly was relatively flat and attractive just as her hips were "asstounding!" Most of all, the crown of her butt was curved, sloping downwards. Her rear was in low gear.

Judy's butt hung so low that the line between her thighs and boodee was covered with soft, pliable, succulent flesh. In other words, one would have to lift her butt to see where her ass ended and her legs began. My nature turned her around to put those butt cheeks directly in front of my face.

"You gonna fuck me dis way?" she asked. "I don't think we should fuck right now," I told her. "The kids might wake up and I'll have to stop. I just want to see what you got look like," I explained to her.

An ass like hers had always been my theoretic goal of final libidinous destination for my face. I opened up the heavy gates to her anus and found a chocolate-colored goddess among an aura of Sahara dust color highlighting its throne. I immediately wanted to kiss her boodee hole, just for being allowed to witness its presence. However, there were guardians at the gate. "You got some long hair back here," I told her. "I know," she answered. "I kant har-lee clean myself. It need cut."

We went into the bathroom so I could remove some of the angel locks draping her ass hole. I usually liked a little friction for my lips around a boodee hole but not a mess of mane. Suckling her anus would have been like eating shag carpeting. That girl had so much ass she had to do a toe-touch for me to adequately get under all that ass and divide her cheeks. Even then ass was in the way. Using a dull shaving razor, I got the job done.

Back in the room I gave her ass hole area time to recover from the dry shave by putting her on her back and inspecting her cunt. She had her head on pillows watching me as I first took a comb and straightened out her bushy pubic bangs. When I smelled her pussy she told me, "It clean. You know I douche yestiddy." The outer lips of that pussy were thick and its inner lips were blooming over the outer ones. It gave the cunt a flowered look. That pussy was fat. Succulent is how I would describe it. I liked succulent.

Judy expected, wanted, and preferred dick. After I punched that pussy a few times with my tongue and sucked her pussy, she asked, "When you gonna fuck me?" "Not right now," I said, again. She seemed surprised, confused, or disappointed I was spearing tongue instead of stickin' dick. She stared at me as I breakfasted her coochee. "Why you ain't tryin' to fuck me?" she asked. "Not right now," I said. Sure enough, while I was flicking tongue against her anus we heard the little boy climbing the stairs.

All day, I sneaked feels or kisses on her ass when the kids weren't around. I caught her in the bedroom while they were upstairs, put my head under her dress, pulled down her draws, bent her over, and put my face in the middle of all that ass. She let me suck her boodee hole like it was pay for pampers. I would have married that girl - kids, speech problem, and all - if only she had farted while I was doing that.

Judy let me do anything I wanted to do. If I were the captor type, like the nation's first immigrants, she would have made a great belly warmer.

By Saturday night I still hadn't taken her to Dunn and we still hadn't fucked. I got her drunk on T-bird (she liked it straight) before she retired into the room to put the kids to bed. "Let me know when you have to use the bathroom," I told her. Sure enough tinkle time came just as the kids fell asleep.

I pulled out some towels and spread them on the floor. "Why we gonna do it on the flo'? she asked. "We not gonna fuck on the floor. I want you to pee pee on me," I answered. She looked at me like she didn't know what "pee pee on me" meant. "Squat yo' big ass over my face," I said, as I directed her chunky to where I wanted it. After getting her pussy directly over my mouth, I told the coochee, "Nigh, pee pee on me."

After a few seconds the cunt squirted out a warm, short shot of piss. Judy stood up to see what her coochee had done. Wet mouth and all I told her, "That's what I want. Do that again and let it all out."

I shouldn't have put it that way because that girl squatted back down and hosed my head at full tilt. Water emerged from three sections of the pussy. My face became soaking wet and urine went up my nose. I said, "Stop!" and she cut off the water like her coochee was a faucet. I blew out what went into my nose like I had a cold.

"Okay," I said. "Gimme the rest of it but do it slow." She carefully put her big hips and hairy pussy back into position. Before she let go, I found time to split her ass, find her piss-wet boodee hole, and kiss it preciously, repeatedly. "Stop," she told me. "I kant piss why you do dat." I ate that pussy while Judy was pissing. As she pushed to get out the last drops, I was able to watch her boodee hole wink wantonly.

Judy still had that dress on without draws on, lying on her side asleep when I got back into the room after I washed. She wasn't just asleep. She was knocked out. The wine, reefer, and empty bladder had done their job. She remained quiet and motionless as I pushed my face between her ass cheeks and sucked that boodee hole again. I tested how deep in sleep she was by voraciously vacuuming her pooter. She still didn't stir. I poked my finger deep into her anus and she didn't move a muscle.

She had too much ass for optimum anal sex but I got the boodee as Judy laid there like a magazine in a doctor's office as I conducted my business. Still, I enjoyed the bit of dick I had in her. I hunched in that hole until I busted a nutt.

The next morning that ho woke me up. "You been messin'," she said, "'cause my butt hurt," she offered as circumstantial evidence. I told her the truth. "You went to sleep foe we got a chance to fuck," I offered as a defense. "I was hunching yo' hips and my dick found a hole." Judy called me a name. "You a boodee bandit," she labeled me.

"When you gonna fuck me for real?" she asked. "Right now," I said. She sucked and jacked the dick hard and didn't seem impressed at all with how much dick I had. I could have had a 20-inch dick. It wouldn't have mattered to her.

I pounded that pussy missionary. Judy handled Henry like he was a poodle instead of the pit bull he had the rep for being. I pushed her knees back and damn if that ho didn't take mo' dick. That ho absorbed the assault without a whimper.

The coochee made a "swoosh" sound each time I reached a new depth. Judy looked at me occasionally as if she was saying, "Go ahead, bust a nutt and make a baby." I got off on that look. Following a sound like a vacuum release from the pussy, sperms rioted out my shaft into deep space.

After breakfast I took her home to her mother's house in Dunn, only a short 30 or so miles from Fayetteville up I-95. I wasn't finished with Judy. Henry wanted a rematch.

Freaks Near Cape Fear

SOUL FOOD

IT'S HIGHLY UNLIKELY a soldier remains with the same buddies throughout a tenure in the military. Change in personnel is a common occurrence and sometimes a relationship is more easily recognized than a face and name. Soldiers constantly forge new friends.

That's why I was prepared when a libidinous cohort confronted me early one morning.

It was shortly after 1 a.m., following a drive up I-95 returning from a Thanksgiving meal at Matt's mama's house in Dillon, South Carolina. Because of the reefer and angel dust collaboration I sucked-up during the trip home, I could only attempt to find the key hole in my front door. That's when a cunt showed up, probing.

"Where you takin' yo' fine ass?" I heard from a stopped car. I looked back and replied, "I'm taking my fine ass in my house to get some sleep." The voice replied. "Who yo' fine ass gonna sleep wit'?" "I'm gonna sleep with me, myself, and I," I answered.

"We gonna have a threesome." The driver laughed and said, "I gots to find out who yo' fine ass is," and then parked.

I had to check this loud-ass ho out. I peered through an opened window and she looked huge in that little car. She was crunched so close to the steering wheel, it looked like she was trying to get to where she was going before the car. When I lowered my head into the passenger window, the odor of alcohol hit me as hard as the scent of a dead cat. The junk she was driving needed a muffler and she needed not to be driving. I'd like to think I saved that woman's life that night or at least her from arrest.

Sure enough she was a big girl but not the usual kind of big girl. When she emerged from her car I easily noticed she was shaped like a triangle in slacks and blouse. She was broad in the shoulders with big titties but narrow from there down. Tall for a girl, with straight, long legs, I figured I'd have to climb this ho. Her feet looked to be longer than her reach. When she stepped onto my stoop, height-wise I only had her about an inch. It was understandable why she wasn't wearing heels.

"You ah have to excuse me, I don't usually yell at men from my car. Hi!, I'm Lenora," she told me as we shook hands. "I was at Yolanda's house for Thanksgiving," she explained, pointing to one of the cribs in the middle of the complex. "You couldn't help yo'self for hollerin'," I replied. "I'm just that fine." She laughed as she came inside.

"I see you sometimes when I come over here to visit Londa. Dat's why I felt brave enough to yell at cha." I asked Lenora why she hadn't stopped before. "Londa say you fucking some White woman." I told her that didn't keep her from yelling at me this time.

"I'm drunk," she admitted, as she pulled the blouse out of her pants. "Oh, yeah?" I asked. "That means I can take advantage of you."

Her spread legs caught my eye but she thought I was looking at her big titties - or at least that's where she wanted the conversation headed. "You like 'em huh?" she asked in slurred speech, eyes half shut, and while pushing up her bra with both hands. I used reverse psychology by asking her, "Those real?" She told me, "Yeah dey real, unlike some other people." I gave her two credits. One credit was for having a nice set of tits.

The other credit was for directing my attention that-away. "Go ahead, feel 'em," she challenged. I did.

"We can stay up here and talk or we can go downstairs to my bedroom and do it," I eventually got around to. "Do what?" she asked. "The same thing we doing up here, talking," I answered. She neither turned down a joint I offered nor the invitation. "You know you don't want to just talk," she said as she took a hit. "I'mma go but don't let me have to whip yo' ass tonight. I just need to lay my head down for a while foe I go."

She laid hands on my shoulders to help brace herself as I led her down the stairs. That ho still almost tripped trying to lift those longships she used as feet. She saw the bathroom and asked to use it. I heard her fart and it sounded like it said, "Holiday." I cut the music on in the room to make it seem like I didn't hear it. Lenora came out of the bathroom with her blouse off. "My stomach hurt. I got gas. My head hurt too. Cut that music and light off," she told me.

This girl had gas. I felt like I had won a Pot Luck prize. It wasn't the lottery because she didn't have much ass, only gas, titties, and long toes. I planned to skeet on those feet.

She undressed as if she knew what we were in the bedroom for.

Her breasts were huge. She was a "juggzilla" with nipples that, if I weren't careful, would give me a black eye. I surveyed her body in the dark headed for her pooter.

I rubbed her back and ass to start off and then got busy. My sniffer bumped her ass hole and acted as a fart button. That ho cut a two-syllable fart which sounded like it said, "turkey," and was stink. "You better be careful where you put your face," she advised me.

"I told you. I got gas and it hurts my stomach if I don't let it out." I told Lenora, "Wherever you may be, let your fart fly free."

"Let's fuck and get this over with so I can go to sleep," she said, as she turned over on her back. I replied honestly, "I ain't finished doing what I want to do." "You ain't no freak are you?" she asked. I said, "Yeah! - and?" I got up and turned the light back on. "I like to see," I said, as I lowered my face towards her crotch. She spread her legs far apart.

"He ah," she told me, "eat all dah pussy yo' freaky ass wont." Instead, I flipped her over to reward her ass hole for the fart.

Her pooter continued to replicate Hollywood sound tracts and to tell me what Lenora had for dinner. Each fart had the power of a leaf blower.

Just as I put my mouth on her ass hole Lenora set it off with flatulence that exited with the rapid sound of shots in a drive-by. She must have felt the fart coming because she reached back to direct my head away from danger. I fought to get my head back to where the explosion would occur. I had my lips on the boodee hole when that girl came out with a long, four-syllable blast that sounded like it said, "tater salad." When I didn't recoil, she held my head against her anus to make sure I savored her meal's remnants. Her boodee hole vibrated and trembled on my lips like it was scared. It had reason to be.

That ho told me what I already knew, "You a freaky motherfucka."

I got her up on her knees and turned her ass towards the side of the bed. "Oh!" she said, as I raised her into the doggy position, "you wont it like dat." She thought I was going to stick dick doggy style. Instead, I got on my knees to suck where the farts came from. I stuck as much tongue in her boodee hole as her anus would stretch.

"Oooh, shit!" was her verbal response. She scooted her knees closer to the edge of the bed as I jabbed her butt hole with my oral lance. As soon as my tongue exited, her trumpet cut another series of farts. "Bruup! Swoosh! Pop! PeeeeYew!" Her ass sounded like it said, "macaroni and cheese." I rewarded that snitch with plenty pecks of pleasure.

As I trenched her ass hole with my tongue, her anus started opening and closing, as if it was trying to get some air. Another long winded fart came out. This time the boodee hole sounded grumpy, producing a "Grrr" sound that seemed to say, "gravy." Her gabby butt hole deserved a suck and I gave it a good long one. Lenora was trying so hard to keep her ass against my mouth her knee slipped off the edge of the bed.

"I wont dat dick," was what she said to get me to stop slobbering back there. I cut the light off and put Vaseline on my lips. She thought I was mouthing her ass hole but I was greasing her boodee hole. I did that twice, trying to get as much lubrication on her crack without her knowing what I was doing or preparing her for.

I shoved dick into her pussy and a finger into her ass hole. "Get yo' finger out my ass!" she demanded. I did. It was a good fuck for her because I poled Henry just enough for her to be comfortable. I kept feeling like I was about to shoot off but wanted to save the nutt for her ass hole. To keep from cumming too soon, I told her I wanted some head.

"Gimme dat dick," she ordered. I wiped Henry off with a towel and climbed over to her face. "Goddamn nigga!" she said when she held how much dick she was in the bed with. "You was fuckin' me wit' dis?" she asked.

That ho kissed from my balls to my dickhead and showed me she had jaws as strong as the odor from her farts. Lenora asked me a rhetorical question that the only answer to is yes, like she was trying to make a point. "I suck dick good, don't it?" she asked. I knew from the jump I wasn't expected to answer. She continued, "I'mma ghee you a nutt but right nigh I wont you tah fuck me wit' dis big dick sum mo'. And dis time be real wit it."

We went missionary. Henry was handling his business by bumping borders burly.

Calmly, Lenora tells me, "You hurtin' me." Henry appreciated knowing that. On his next dive he hit deeper and something "new." Monica lifted her knees in the air and started shaking. She didn't say anything aloud; her body told it all. She was nuttin'. She went limp as Henry dunked down another inch or two.

I moved to attain minimal depth in her greased boodee hole. As I did, she sprayed a fart which caused pause. It made a multi-syllable sound like her boodee hole was saying, "sweet potato!" It had so much force Skeeter shot out from between her cheeks.

I put Topper back on her anus and slowly hunched the dick head in. Little by little Henry eased into her boodee hole. This ho wasn't drunk enough. "You tryin' aghen?" she asked. "I'm just trying to get comfortable," I said. "Wait a minute," she said, as she reached back and pulled Henry out. Then, all of a sudden that that ho farted again. My dick was blasted, literally, from between her cheeks up to against my belly. I be damn if her ass hole didn't sound like it said "dark meat." I told Lenora, "I'mma plug dat." She said, "You kin try but I don't think it gonna stay."

Skeeter eased into her anus, needing one good shove. I rubbed the clit and she instinctively moved her hips towards me. That ushered Skeeter completely into her ass and it was gripped by her anus muscle. "Umm," I moaned. "You like that?" she asked. "Yeah," I answered. "Be careful," she told me.

I got greedy. I drilled into her butt like it was a hole in my mattress. When she finally realized how deep into her butt I was, she asked me, again, to care. "That's far enough," she said and used her hand on my groin as a stop sign. I pushed her hand off my upper thigh, cracked her hips wider, and bowed my back to get more inches in.

My hand-on-clit, dick-in-boodee hole clockwork produced tremendous action and we busted tremendous nutts together. I laid there, weak, with my dick in her ass for a minute or two. That ho shit my dick out and farted. Clear as day, I heard her boodee hole say, "pound cake." She put a tittie in my mouth and we went to sleep like that.

When I woke up, she was dressed and ready to leave. "I kin get used to what we did lass night," she told me, "but you fuckin' dat White woman. If I keep seein' you, you might break my heart. I kant be dat." I asked her about her decision to just walk away from a big dick. That ho said, It was nice meetin' it. Bye."

Freaks Near Cape Fear

THE GRADUATE

B ACK IN THE early 1970's the Army was NOT an all-volunteer institution as it is now.

Unfortunately, most citizens are reluctant to insurant risk to their physical being willingly for uncertain benefits once the fight is over. There are too many examples in the hood where "it ain't that kind of party."

Having tested The White Man's system of things in both the civilian and military environments I found it rewarding, serendipitously, only in the military to go beyond the call of duty. For example, against the advice of peers I volunteered to get my military driver's license. As I drove the equipment truck to training sites, advisors who told me not to go beyond my standard contract of following orders marched miles while I rode.

I hoped for that same time of positive, unintended outcome when I volunteered my service to Dottie for one libidinous mission in particular. Her petition turned out to be priceless as Dottie asked me to fuck her niece. The niece hadn't had sex but one time and Dottie wanted her niece to experience mutual sex. Dottie wanted to show the niece how to "handle" a dick, including oral sex. She expected the niece at her apartment in a few days and pleaded for me to save semen.

"I ain't even gonna give yo' ass none," she told me. "I wont you to be horny as hell." I was listening intently with amazement and glee but was pessimistic this thing would jump off. Henry asked me to ask Dottie if she would be around. With my dick head on her lips, Dottie told Henry, "Yes. I don't want her to be scared of your size 'cause sometimes you can get too happy." Henry told me to tell Dottie, "True dat." I did.

Dottie explained that the girl was her school's top academic graduate and was coming to Carolina the next week to visit Duke University. Supposedly, she lost her virginity on her prom night and Dottie was the only person she told about it. "She needs to orgasm. I need your dick to bring it. I want her to know what fucking is all about before she starts going down on girls," Dottie rationalized. In her initial outline, Dottie failed to mention that the niece was Richard's, her ex- husband, sister's daughter. I immediately wanted to know if Richard might cock-block Dottie's plan. Her explanation was that Richard will be home only two days while the niece was in town. "He's on temporary duty and won't see her except for her first day and last night here," she said. My observation was the mission was timed well.

I didn't even bother to ask Dottie what the girl looked like. Come to find out, Tammy wasn't ugly but this girl was too fat for a teenager. Whoever jumped her plump either just wanted to bust a cherry or win a bet. She wore large, black-framed glasses and was pale as hell. She had fat, white fingers. That was a plus.

Dottie also failed to mention that Henry was a graduation gift to her niece. "You brought me all the way over here to give me my gift? You could have hid it in your house somewhere." Dottie told her, "I don't think so." That was my only clue as to how Dottie got the girl so close to a big black dick.

Once cordiality was over, the time came to give Tammy her present. "Okay," she said, in a teenager kind of way, "I'm ready for my gift!" Dottie looked at me and I looked at Tammy. Tammy looked at me and then looked back at Dottie. Tammy said, "No. I don't believe it!" Dottie responded with, "I told you. You need a good fuck. He's going to give it to you and I'll be there so he won't force you to do anything you don't want to do."

Regardless of the influence of her aunt, Tammy had a "big" decision to make. Dottie grabbed Tammy's hand and squeezed it. Tammy glanced at me and Dottie then said, "I'm amenable. I wouldn't ever turn down a gift from my auntie." Dottie got up off the couch, pulled Tammy up with her, and they hugged.

Dottie got the thing going by laying down the law. "We have to be quiet," she said. "I don't want Paul (Richard's roommate) next door to get any of this back to Richard."

Tammy gave a reflection of caution towards Dottie and said, "I concur." We went to my bedroom and Dottie pointed to a wall, telling Tammy it wasn't totally soundproof.

"Take your clothes off and get in the bed," Dottie told Tammy. "We'll be right back."

Dottie took my hand and guided me into the bathroom. While she was leaking she began instructing me on what to do with Tammy. "Eat her out first," she said. "Be easy with her.

I want her to like sex. Ain't nobody ate her out before so don't be rough. She should be ready because we've been watching porn."

Dottie tore off some paper and said, "Here, wipe me, front to back, like I showed you."

When we got back to Tammy I pulled the covers back and a fat, Icelandic-pale, teenager was waiting on a stiff tongue and an improbable prick. I spread her legs and lifted them at the knees to unfold the pussy. I stuck my nose down there, sniffed, and planted a kiss right where her cunt lips ended. I sucked the pussy from bottom to top.

From my fuck chair, Dottie asked her, "You like that?" Tammy, with her glasses still on, must have answered with a nod. "He gives good head," Dottie reassured Tammy.

Honey began to collect on the dewy coochee and I went after it voraciously. "Don't let him do all the work," Dottie told her quietly. "Hold his head. Hold his head and lift your cunt up to his mouth." We both went into attack mode. "Eat it," Dottie whispered. "Eat it out. That's it. Smother his ass. Make him eat all of it," Dottie ordered.

I had Tammy's coochee in my mouth and that pussy was red as a beet. She lifted her hips, up and down, up and down, pushing more pussy onto my face. As we got a rhythm going Tammy took off her glasses. I closed her thighs tightly against my ears and, shaking like a paint mixer, she said, "Oh, God!" loudly and lifted her butt off the bed. All of a sudden that pussy started drooling heavily. I slurped like I was trying to catch the overspill that came from a shaken pop. Dottie put all the evidence together and said, "She got an orgasm. Thank you Jesus."

I was hatin' my tongue wasn't large enough to catch all the flow as Tammy just laid there trembling. "Ya'll got me horny," Dottie said. "I got to get me some of that." Dottie undressed below her waist, pushed Tammy over, and skinned back her clit dick. It was the first time I had seen her half-naked.

I went to work on her. Once Tammy recovered from her orgasm, she sat up and watched. With Dottie's "Long Ranger" rubbing against my tongue, for a good minute I forgot this was supposed to be a lesson for Tammy. Dottie didn't. She guided my head up and down, talking to Tammy at the same time. "See," she said. "Wipe his face between your legs. His whole face ought to be wet when he finishes." Out the corner of my eye, I saw Tammy's observation was intense.

"I hate we ain't got all night," Dottie told us. She directed me to pull off my draws and Tammy stared at my dick like it was a college entrance exam. Dottie began pulling on the dick. "Jack it," she told Tammy.

Dottie handed the dick over to Tammy and her soft, fat paw felt good. "He named is dick Henry," Dottie told her niece. "We gonna give Henry some head."

Dottie climbed over me into the 69, blocking with her flat-screen ass my view of Tammy clucking on my dick head. This was what I was worried about. A just-turned 18-year old White girl was ready to dunk my dick into her throat and I was unable to see because of Dottie's old-ass boodee. I could only rub that creamy flat ass and tease her ass hole with a finger because her dick-clit kept moving away.

"It's getting longer," Tammy noticed, "and it's volume is increasing expeditiously."

"If you keep jacking it, it's gonna cum," Dottie told her. "Suck that son-of-a-bitch." I felt Tammy put her lips on the dick head, hardly touching it at first, then engulfing as much of Henry as she could. The dick hit her tonsils and she gagged, coughed, and almost threw up. "Go down on it and like you saw in the porno," Dottie said. "I thought I did," Tammy replied. "Like this," Dottie said, as she put Skeeter in her mouth, gripped, and yanked.

Tammy clamped down on Henry like my dick was a toothbrush and held it. "Suck it,"

Dottie told her. "Suck that black dick." Tammy pulled hard, like my penis was a cartoon character, but it felt just as good as it hurt. "Now pull with your lips as you slide it out of your mouth," Dottie directed. Tammy did just that, slurping Skeeter with her lips like she was removing venom from a snake-bite victim.

Tammy's touch was fresh. I wanted to bust a nutt the next time her lips touched dick head. I told Dottie, "I'm going to skeet if you don't give me something to do." Dottie said, "Here, and be quiet," as she scooted back and planted her ass right onto my face.

She didn't aim her cunt or ass hole carefully. She sat down on my mugg like anywhere back there was a good place. It was.

Skeet on the tip of Topper gave academic Tammy a research project. "What's that?"

Tammy asked Dottie. "Is he cumming?" "That's a pre-mee," Dottie said. "Lick it off."

Tammy follow her instruction, smacking her lips like she was testing a new recipe. It was while she was scrapping her tongue across the apex of my dick, that I had to stick my nose in Dottie's waste bucket to keep from busting a nutt. Dottie leaned back and wiggled my snout deeper.

"What's he doing back there," Tammy asked. "He's got his nose in my ass. Don't worry about that," Dottie said. "You can sit your ass on his face later. Right now, you better take the cum off that cock or I'm going to." Tammy licked the tip of my dick every time Dottie primed my pump and sperms showed up.

"He ain't had no pussy in a while," she told her niece. "It looks like he's ready to shoot off. Let's switch places." They moved to where Tammy's ass was now in my face. I had boodee duty with a bigger, fatter, younger, whiter ass in my face and was four times happier. I marked my territory with "Rose Bud" red hickeys and noticed there was a difference between having a wide white ass and a wider white ass in your face.

Dottie continued with her lessons. "When you really want to please a man, suck his dick like this," Dottie said as she continued to give Tammy FYI. Dottie bobbed her head up and down, jacking my dick with her mouth. Tammy's blizzard of a butt had my attention. I forgot all about them having sex education class between my legs.

To get Tammy's snow blanket butt closer to my face, I sucked that ass hole like it was a cough drop and jammed my nose into it like it was an oxygen mask. "My God!" she said. I vacuumed her reddening boodee hole and that ho said, "Jesus!", nearly hollering loudly. "Now do you see what he was doing to me?" Dottie asked. Tammy said, "That's stimulating. That's very stimulating."

Dottie reached under my mattress and pulled out a condom. Tammy scooted her ass away from my face to place her pussy on my dick as Dottie instructed her. "Go down easy," Dottie warned, as Henry slid into Tammy's once invaded hollow. "It's large," Tammy said. "It's protracting my pussy."

Dottie was boosting her, saying, "Get down on it. Just a little bit more. Just a little bit more. That's it." As for me, I couldn't help it. Tammy's cunt was tubular and tight and soft and sultry and wet and withering and good and gushy. Dottie said, "That's it" once too many times and I busted a huge nutt. Tammy looked at Dottie, like somebody was putting a hand up her skirt, and was confident when she told her aunt, "He's ejaculating!"

The novice felt the throbs of my dick exploding and rolled off me like a beachgoer falling off an inner tube. "Oh, Jesus, Jesus!" she called as she rolled. Dottie must have thought I was hurting her, because I was still trying to stick dick. She pushed me away from Tammy.

Dottie snatched the condom off and massaged Henry with a towel like she was trying to work out a muscle cramp. "Come on," said Dottie. "It's almost one o'clock and Richard will be calling to see what time we got home." Tammy wanted more dick. She asked Dottie for another lesson. Dottie said, "No!" I told Dottie, "Leave her here and you go home." "We both gotta get out of here," Dottie said.

I found a way for Tammy to get extra credit with Henry. The next day she sneaked over and sucked the dick. Like Dottie, she liked to talk while giving head. "Dottie's scared I might not like White boys with small dicks and big money," Tammy told me, while her mouth was pole dancing. I told Tammy she wouldn't ever have to settle for sexual incompetence as long as we kept in contact." I gave her my phone number before Dottie "policed" her back home.

I didn't see her again until....

Freaks Near Cape Fear

CLEAN SLATE

OUL BROTHER NO. 1 James Brown wrote a movie sound track called "The Big Payback." The movie and song centered around revenge. It was motivational music much like the theme song to the movie "Rocky." Either one of those sound tracks can be played just before going into war. That was the type of music I heard after I got involved in an unexpected libidinous battle.

My battle began via the breaking of a trust. In a little store a woman walked up on me and asked a favor. "If you're going to pay for that with cash will you let me pay for it with stamps and you give me the cash?" she asked. "I have to pay my phone bill and I don't have the money," she added after my frown. "I can do that," I answered.

That's how Johnnie rolled up on me. Horse-mane wig and all, she was dressed-to-kill but in distress. After she committed fraud, out in the parking lot she asked if I would give her a ride to the phone company. As we traveled to Ma Bell's office I was tapped again for a third favor.

Johnnie was still 25 dollars short on the phone bill and had the nerve to ask for the amount she lacked.

I loaned her the money and she was really happy when she came out of the phone company's office. I was ready to get that way. "When am I going to get the 25 dollars back?" I asked. "You know I ain't got no money," she threw back at me. "What you wont, some pussy?" You wont me to suck yo' dick or somethin'? What you wont?" I straight out told that ho, "I wont sum thin!" Johnnie told me, "We goh settle dis right nigh. I don't like owe in people. Take me to my house!"

I didn't appreciate this ho offering sex so bluntly, like I was a trick. She probably didn't appreciate me hassling her for immediate payment, like I was Ma Bell.

Johnnie's phone was ringing as we entered her trailer. She answered the caller with a "Hey bitch!" while pointing for me to have a seat. That girl fumbled with my zipper and motioned for me to pull my dick out. As she worked the phone, she rubbed Henry. Once my dick got half as hard and long as a crowbar, Johnnie hollered. "Got damn!" and had to explain, with a lie, to the "bitch" she was talking why she said it.

That ho put her hand over the phone, looked at me, and said, "Dis foe dah money."

She tickled Skeeter with her lips while the receiver was on her ear. She was able to mumble to the caller, "Uh, huh," with her jaws locked down on dick. Whoever she was talking to must have confronted Johnnie about the sounds coming over the phone.

Johnnie had to lie again. "I ain't suckin' no dick," she said.

Once Henry reached stadium light standard stature, she hung up the phone. "You got a big ass dick," she told me. "You need to hurry up and buss a nutt. I got things to do." I told Johnnie, "You had the time to ask me for 25 dollars and take you where you wanted to go. Make time to fuck this dick." Johnnie came back with, "Fucking me goh coss you mo' dan 25 dollars," she propositioned. I told her, "If you count the favor I did, the cash I gave, the ride I offered, and the time you required, you owe me more than 25 dollars."

That broke her down and Johnnie began to set "fucking" ground rules. "We kin fuck but don't try and put all that in me," she expressed. "I'mma put 25 dollars worth in," I told her. That ho told me I was a trip. "How in the hell you gonna figgah how much is 25 dollars worth?" she asked.

Once we got into her bedroom, she snatched off her attire and dropped her draws like this was all business. Below her waist was exceptional. She had rounded thighs over-built for her mediocre butt. There was a gap just below her coochee that, when she turned towards an open curtain, made it look as if she was holding a penlight between her legs.

I came across bad pubic hair. I went to put a finger in the coochee and it was like reaching for a cat in a rose bush. There wasn't much of a scruff but what she had could have been used to remove grout. I turned her and kissed her on the hips. "Leave my ass alone and git the pussy nigga," she told me.

As I carefully sniffed and nuzzled the coochee with my nose the phone rang. As she answered, I peeled back her clit cover and flicked it with my tongue. Immediately Johnnie said, "I gotta go," and hung up the phone. I found it less threatening to lick her clit than eat her pussy but she pushed my head lower. The phone rang again and she was upset this time. "Y in the fuck you keep callin' me," she told the caller before she realized it was some guy. As I was measuring to see how deep my tongue could get into her coochee without putting my face on her cunt, Johnnie flirted on the phone talking graphic sex with the guy. She told him she was rubbing her pussy and thinking about him.

She described how she wanted him to perform cunnilingus on her while, at the same time, telling me what to do. I played along. "I wont yo whole mouth on the pussy.

"Suck it," she told both of us. "Nigh, lick it a lil' bit. Lick it!," she demanded. "Nigh eat that pussy for me baby," she moaned. As she talked, she lightly rubbed my head like she was rewarding me for being a quiet, good little boy.

I challenged myself to make her hang up the phone by flipping her over and sucking her ass hole like I was trying to retrieve the last thing she ate. She told the guy, "Wait a minute," and looked back at me like I was a blood sucker. I stuck my nose in her wet, slippery boodee hole and Johnnie said, "Oh, shit!" and again she lied. She told the caller she had nutted.

"You a freaky motherfucker aren't you?" she asked us both. She kept looking back and smiling like she was getting a thrill from two men at once. Henry wanted in on the action. I rubbed my dick head on her boodee hole and that ho moved quicker than an accident to get her ass hole away from my dick. She told the caller she'd call him right back and slammed the phone down, then quickly flipped and told me, "Oh, hell naw!"

We got in the buck after she made sure we were both protected. Henry's first dive was deep because she was wetter than an Amazon amphibian. It was slutty, sloppy slide. As I hit it, that pussy made sounds like water draining out of a tub. It was one of the most serviced snatches I'd ever been in. That cunt didn't have any mulish tendency.

I went wall-to-wall, front door to back in that pussy, attempting to get way more than 25 dollars worth. Henry was pulverizing that pu-nanny and that ho started backing away, trying to get from under me. She was wiggling and hollering, "Dat's enough!" I, in-turn, locked her down in the buck where her cunt was directly in front of my belly button. She looked like she was in a gym class learning how to tumble.

I felt a nutt coming and pulled completely out to hold it off. On my way back in Henry bounced off her boodee hole. Johnnie hollered, "No!! No!" and I hadn't even penetrated.

After escaping that, she allowed Henry in the pussy as deep as he wanted to go. I got all 12 inches in that ho and shot off with my knees and her waist lifted off the bed.

Johnnie called me at the office about three days later and got right to the point. "I wont to be wit you ghen but you wont to fuck a bitch in the ass," she told me. "It ah coss you 50 dollars to do dat," she offered. Just to see how bad she wanted 50 dollars, I went ahead and planned to get much dick in her ass hole. I agreed to give her 50 dollars that I didn't have. After we finished I was going to ask her to let me owe her, like she did me.

I got lucky. That ho gave up the boodee without taking the money first. If she was a prostitute she wasn't being professional. Helped by a condom and lubricant, my dick slipped into darkness easily. Only her combat maneuvers prevented Henry from reaching her throat. "Dat's enough!" she insisted, while kicking like a dog covering poo.

Her movement of crawling to get from under me, while my dick was pounding her butt, made me nutt. I made my escape to pay while she was sitting on the toilet.

USUAL SUSPECTS

SOLDIERS ARE LIKE anyone else; they have "ruthers." The common paratrooper would "ruther" parachute out of a helicopter than a jet and a jet "ruther" than an airplane. Most soldiers would "ruther" work for the General's Staff than be a grunt in an infantry platoon. Most soldiers "ruther" not be in the military when the nation is involved in war.

When I ran up on identical twins Shay and May I couldn't immediately determine a "ruther." Both were wide "ruther" than slim; roughneck "ruther" than chic; and wigged "ruther" than natural. Both had big butts boxed in hot pants and hefty hooters hanging out of halters. I didn't notice any difference.

To better ascertain a "ruther" required me to use some sort of incentive to get them to reveal a difference. "Sugar will melt" was one line used to urge them out of the parking lot's heat. I also mentioned that my nearby apartment stocked reefer and wine. Shay kept her eyes on me while May looked around like she wanted else. Both expressed that whatever jumped off they would jump off together.

As they followed me home, no doubt, Shay and May schemed how they would run game on me by smoking all my reefer and leave without giving up some ass. I was confident it would be well-worth letting them suck up my herb and chilled Thunderbird.

Squeezing Shay's big boodee as she walked into my apartment was my first move. Without any drama, she let her sister know. "He feelin' on my ass," she told May. "Don't be telling' me what that man doin'. You dah one who wonted to ware dees outfits. Half yo' ass out hanging out dem pants like it a part of yo' leg," May responded with.

After those hoes got high, I dropped a libidinous bomb. I asked, "Which one of ya'll gonna let me smell dey pussy?" Both ladies laughed. "I'm serious," I said. "I got two fine women up in here suckin' up my herb and drinking my wine. I need, at least, to smell somebody's coochee." May said, "I kant believe dis man talkin' 'bout see in what somebody smell like tween dey legs."

Shay verified which was the boldest twin and that's how I initially distinguished them.

"You kin smell mines," she said, as she choked on an inhale after a giggle. While she was coughing May told her, "You SO fast!." May was being conservative. I don't "ruther" a conservative hoe. To me, if you're going to be a ho be a ho like the airborne stanchion - "ALL THE WAY."

I "ruther" a curious ho and it was Shay's curiosity that eventually moved us into the bedroom. May flew over to sit in my fuck chair as Shay began wiggling out of her shorts.

My anticipation was hyped as if someone at a knife fight was pulling out a gun.

Unembarrassed, Shay probed her really hairy, black pussy with a finger and stuck it up to her nose. "It smell alright," she reported and then gave a giggle.

As I leaned over and stuck my nose between Shay's legs, May said, "He serious!" I sniffed the coochee and told both hoes, "That pussy hot." Shay giggled again and asked, "What it smell like?" "No fish, no fowl. It alright," I answered. I pushed her legs back and her boodee hole was rough looking, like an extinct volcano with a cracked crater.

May hopped off the chair and began to pull her hot pants down. "Smell mines," she told me. She scooted and spread her legs to where her pussy was over the edge of the seat.

Unlike her sister May's pussy was shaved and it showed a wide and fat clit that looked like a sumo wrestler. That thing stuck out like a mountaintop observatory. I wanted to take that tentacle's temperature with my tongue.

"Go ahead, smell huhs," Shay told me, to snap me out of my stare. I got my head between May's thick thighs and sniffed. "Ummm," I smell honey. That thing need some attention," I told her. "Do me firss," Shay said. May instead leaped on the bed. "He wont to do me," she told her sister. Shay watched me eat May and got hot doing it. "Let me see yo' dick," she asked. I lifted my head from May's groin and May pushed it back down and locked her oak-hard thighs on my ears.

I was grabbed onto that coochee and sucked it. Jerking left to right like she was on a amusement ride, May busted a nutt. Her honey was sweet. I "ruther" sweet. The nutt came with a wave of heat, like when you remove the cover of a barbeque pit and it blasts your face. Immediately, Henry stretched as if somebody had ironed him. He looked like he was directing traffic and there was only one car.

Those hoes began to "tap out" like a tag team without even touching hands. Shay said, "Do me nigh!" and quick as a blink placed her pussy in front of my face. While I was orally mugging her, May sat in the chair smoking reefer, sipping wine, and rubbing herself. After a while of that, May let us know, "I'm hot again." All that time, Shay had only prepared my face for a shave. I was happy as hell to take a break from her.

A whole new chapter began when those girls realized I was holding LSD. Shay just had to say something first. "Dat nigga got a big ass dick'," she expressed. May told her sister, "Naw. That muthafucka got three legs," and both girls laughed. "Geh him credit," Shay said, "Dat's a big ass dick." May put her arm out to see how far up Henry stretched and shook her head in disbelief.

Those hoes double-teamed Henry, collaborating on the cock. While Skeeter was swollen and firm one was pulling my dick while the other was mashing my meat like she was measuring the tenderness of a pork chop at a butcher's shop. Every now and then Shay would slap hard Henry and watch him recoil. She liked doing that. Henry was long, too. If I had been standing at a sink, my dick would have reached the wall behind it.

Shay was first to put her mouth on it. Quickly, May had her to refocus. "Let him get on the bed," May told Shay to get her to pause. Shay stopped sucking on my knob long enough for me to get all three of us right. I hurriedly grabbed some towels and laid them under my head as I stretched out on the bed. Meanwhile, May watched as my dick waved from my knees to my navel and Shay grabbed my pennant and put it back into her mouth.

"You dah one ain't got a nutt yet," I told Shay. "Gimme that pussy," I said, as I directed her to 69 her ass over my face. "After you bust that nutt, put some piss wit' it so I ah know you got it." After those instructions Shay stopped giving Henry head. For a few seconds, both faces expressed a team opinion that they had wandered into a porno video. Shay hurried her hips towards my face as May remained stunned.

Shay couldn't wait to do what I asked. She scrubbed her cunt over my mouth, like a brake pad slowing a Ferrari, and busted a hurried, maybe pretended, nutt. Then she watered me with pee pee. I thought she was going to squirt. But nooo! Shay lifted her groin off my face and let loose like she was putting out a campfire.

Shay and I must have looked to May like a dumb and dumber skit. Shay sprayed urine from all areas of her pussy, leaking like she hadn't pissed in days. I was concerned the water would miss the towels or soak them too much. I was trying to pull her ass closer to hold down the splash. She was lifting her hips, trying to watch what she was doing. We fought. I blew piss out my nose and she still wouldn't stop.

May stopped sucking my dick to watch what Shay was doing. She may as well been holding a bucket of popcorn as I managed to glimpse both while in battle. I had hoped to bust a nutt in May's mouth while Shay was leaking but that didn't happen because of Shay's downpour and May's stoppage. May even told her sister, "You goh drown dat man." Shay didn't answer. She just kept on pissing.

My mouth kept being refilled and I couldn't say anything like "Stop" or "Wait a minute." Finally, after what seemed an eternity Shay ended her watering abruptly. I thought she had finished and here came another shot; then another. I sprayed her body's burn out I had collected on her boodee hole and coochee and sucked it off. That ho said, "Ummm," as if she had just taken a good dump.

I didn't even get time to take a break. As soon as Shay got off May got on. "Let me," that ho said. On her ass' way down to my face I noticed May's succulent looking boodee hole. It was creased with less wrinkles than her sister's crater. Shining from perspiration that thing was pretty. I got a quick suck on it before May moved her cunt onto my mouth.

"Lick it," she told me. I lapped that course like a roadrunner over road. I stretched my tongue as far as I could into May's cunt and wiggled it. May quickly and quietly busted another nutt. As she recovered while I was digging out honey with "Ummm."

May told Shay to watch as that ho began to pee pee on me. While leaking steady but lightly, May told her sister, "He wont it on his mouth, not all over his face, his head, and the bed." This ho was talking and peeing on me at the same time. As May was leaking, Shay snatched Henry like he was hers and sucked. By the time May finished frothing my face, I had shot off on Shay's molars.

Those hoes started talking about Henry like he wasn't in the room. Shay sounded sincere when she told her sister, "His dick still hard. I wanna fuck." May told her sister, "You SO fast. Dat's a manaconda, girl. It ah damage yo' ovaries and you wont be able to have no chullan," she warned.

Those hoes were fully dressed and getting high when I came out the shower. Shay started pulling on my fresh dick and told me, "My sister ready to leave." I told May to let Shay play with the dick. May said, "Ain't no sense in gettin' it hard aghen. You ain't gettin' no pussy." I told May,

"See how long and hard she can get it while I get my head back right. Don't ya'll wont to see it shoot off?"

May watched intensely Shay sucking and jacking my dick. She couldn't even concentrate and dropped the joint as I passed it to her. She sounded impatient when she told me to "Hurry up and get a nutt." I needed for Henry to calm down because I didn't want those hoes to leave. I told Shay I had something special I wanted to do.

I got behind Shay, split open her tight butt cheeks, and raked my tongue over her ass hole like I was sealing an envelope. She had hair around her boode hole. You know I liked that. I turned back towards May sitting in the chair, exposed and pointed to her sister's anus, and said, "I'mma stick my tongue right dare."

May turned her head, refusing to continue looking at her sister's boodee hole, and didn't respond. I got my face back between Shay's butt cheeks and sang, "Row, row, row your boat gently down the stream" then dove into it using my tongue. I followed-up with a nose-dive into that boodee hole. May hollered, "Oooh, lord!"

"Do me," May said, and then got undressed. She bent over on the bed and I put little pecks of pleasure on May's ass hole, at first, just to fuck wit' her mind. Then, with my lips lying against her ass hole, I said, "Peter Piper picked a peck of peppers" just before I sucked her anus as if I was trying to remove her sphincter. I hurt my neck trying to get my tongue so deep in her butt it would come out brown. May said, "Mercy! Damn, dat shit good." On top of that, that ho didn't know what to do when I vacuumed her anus.

In the meantime, Shay had been pulling my dick between my legs, jacking Henry vigorously. As soon as May seemed satisfied with what I had done to her, Shay found the opportunity to direct me on the bed on my back. That's when Shay climbed across my legs and began sliding Henry in and out her pussy. Meanwhile, May still wanted her ass hole on my mouth.

May sat on my face and those hoes took turns sucking my dick. My face was on boodee hole so I don't know which had Henry in their mouth when I exploded. May caught me while I was weak and rubbed her boodee hole across my mouth then pissed on my neck. During that, I busted a nutt. Now spent, I was ready for those hoes to leave.

Two weeks later the twins showed up while I already had company. Shay tried to get my guest to leave, saying she wanted me to "smell huh pussy again." That remark didn't faze my guest. Shay even told the lady at my house that she wanted me to sing while I was sucking her ass hole. May joined-in with her desire to again piss in my mouth "like I did the last time," she proudly announced.

I was proud of my female friend. She got all up in both girls' faces and, looking both up and down like she wanted to whip both asses, loudly asked, "Is that all he did?! Did he eat a fart? If you didn't fart in his mouth, you bitches got left out." Those twins didn't have a comeback for that except to leave. Dottie had responded perfectly.

Freaks Near Cape Fear

TRADING PLACES

DEFENDING A NATION can result in mental fatigue. Back in the day, like a football coach who frowned on water breaks, officers expected a regular G.I. to just "walk it off." As a result, creative and horny soldiers invented a myriad of remedies to boost morale so a "gung ho" attitude could return.

One method of rejuvenating the call of duty, in Vietnam for example, was when a soldier was able to "relieve his rocks" into a resident of a raided village. That would heighten the motivation for the next mission into a rural settlement. A letter from home boosted morale. A favored combat ration could put a pep into a soldier's step.

An incentive to get a trooper back on track boiled down to allowing different strokes for different folks. It included what the Navy called "Shore Leave." In the military that is the only time where improvisation and inventive chaos is tolerated with legal protection.

On occasion I experienced libidinous doldrums and needed a morale boost. I didn't know what was required to reclaim mission motivation. What's one to do when wanting a snack but unable to decide what kind? One particular time I didn't want intercourse; didn't want fellatio; and somehow didn't crave cunnilingus.

Eventually, I realized my desire was to be splashed by a ho's vaginal fountain. I wanted to watch water come out a pussy; have the water bounce off my face; seep heavily into my mouth; spit that piss back onto the cunt and anus; and then lick it all off. A fart in my face anytime that was happening would have been icing on the cake.

Someone who may have been sympathetic to my perverse condition, I figured, would be Teresa, a fellow soldier, who had moved into my old apartment down the street. Her long legs would allow her to squat over my face and have her pee hole visible. That's exactly what I needed. It was worth a try. A "sick bastard" will do anything to get a fix.

She had seemed to be an unhappy, disgruntled wife when I met her and her ol' man months earlier. Those type people tend to break-up and I reckoned she had dumped her unemployed, labeled lazy, ball-and-chain of a husband. I reckoned right. Teresa's husband was permanently postponed back to where he had come from.

I played off my surprise visit as if I was seeking permission to get into the pool at the apartment complex there. We talked military affairs and discussed our most previous visit to our respective hometowns before I inserted sex into our conversation.

"How you gonna take advantage of those mirrors in the bedroom now that yo' ol' man gone, Tee?" was how I introduced my main idea. She responded directly to the topic sentence. "Those mirrors don't do nothing for me," she said. I gave supporting evidence for the premise of my inquiry. It wasn't going to hurt me to toss out what was on my mind. All Teresa could do was throw me out and let another ho pee on me.

"That's smart not to depend on sexual aids," I told her. "When I was living here sometimes I didn't even want to have sex unless it was in front of those mirrors. That kind of stuff can develop into a fetish. You know what a fetish is, Tee?" I asked. Teresa told me she had heard of such a thing but wasn't exactly sure what it was.

Offering an example to support my facts, I told her, "One time I was giving oral sex and the pussy pissed. Later when I had time to think about it, I realized I liked it because it was warm and wet. Sex is good anytime it's warm and wet. Ever since then I've tried to find another woman that would do that. Just like seeing myself in those mirrors, I developed a fetish."

Let me get this straight," Teresa calmly replied. "You liked it when somebody pissed in your mouth?" "That's the gist of it," I answered. "Would you do that for me?" I asked, as a concluding statement.

Teresa cocked her head to the side and looked at me like a person not understanding why a key didn't fit a lock. She could have deduced why I had two towels and that I had this planned. Maybe I was so outlandish no thought other than "freaky" came to mind.

Suddenly, Teresa looked at me like I was a welcomed superhero appearing from nowhere. She responded with, "Maybe we can do that," before she included two conditions. She didn't want to fuck nor did she want me to even touch her.

Teresa asked that I return in an hour after she had a beer and more time to think about "it." Leaving the towels was a good move. If she changed her mind they would possibly get me past the door to beg more. If she was still game, the towels would already be there.

High as hell, I knocked on her door 45 minutes later. As she let me in, Tee told me she had two beers and was ready to tinkle. "You're just in time," she told me. "I gotta go."

I looked that ho dead in the face, like a person facing his brother who voted for Dubya Bush twice, and described just how liberal I was. I scripted to her how I wanted "it." I told her, "Put on your military clothes, boots, and combat helmet and act like you're in war, in the woods, and gotta take a leak." Tee said, "You got a freaky fetish!" Although she was ready to tinkle Teresa took the time to get into her gear. When she came out of her bedroom, I was on her living room floor with those towels under my head.

That ho should have won an Oscar. She played her character as well as Diana Ross played Billie Holiday in "Lady Sings the Blues" and I played mine as well as Denzel Washington in "Devil in a Blue Dress." Neither gained that accolade for that role because White just ain't right.

Teresa moved her butt above my head and looked around as if she wanted to make sure she was alone. She loosened her belt and pulled out her shirt as she moved towards a window. She crouched to look out and at the same time lowered her pants to the bottom of her hips, showing all draws. I was grinning, showing teeth like Kunta Kinte to Fiddler.

She moved towards her kitchen and peeped around the corner as if making sure no one was around. On her way back to me, Tee slid her draws halfway down her slim thighs and stopped where she squatted her bare butt just above my head. I was smiling big time.

Tee teased more. She raised up, paused, and looked around like she had heard something. The way she was in character, I thought she did. She shuffled over to a house plant and peered through it like she was in the woods. Finally, she backed up to me and squatted her ass over my face with one knee on the floor like she was about to draw hopscotch lines on a sidewalk.

She was showing me all that and I noticed all kinds of things between her legs. She was mulatto and her slim pussy lips were near-white with dark edge. Her cunt lips were firm, as if her husband hadn't been eating that coochee right or enough. There was peach fuzz from her pelvis to her ass hole. I liked fuzz on my pussy and boodee hole. The coochee's hole was gaped open like she had just finished working a dildo and the clit was prominent. Their was a jagged line from her cunt to her anus like welder's work.

Her ass hole was a gorgeous dark brown. I liked dark brown boodee holes on high yella hoes. It looked tight and luscious and was caved by surrounding smooth, beige butt cheeks. Her anus had one crack and it was down the middle, like that ass hole had one purpose. Somehow the words, "A fart; a fart; my kingdom for a fart," came to mind because historically the English know just what to say.

She didn't look down. Teresa maintained her character, looking around to make sure nobody was watching. I was waiting, like a villain at the end of a movie about to get his head blown off and getting impatient. I wanted to part her pu-nanny so I could see exactly where the pee would be coming from but I didn't dare. "I can't see the pee hole," I told her. Tee reached down and opened her coochee for me, for me. It was like a ho saying "Yes" or "Fuck Me" or "Eat Me" or "Kiss my ass," or "Lick it" or "Git it!."

That pussy squirted before I could stop smiling. Every time I hear the song, "Whoop! There it is!" I'm reminded of pee pee exiting that particular pu-nanny at that particular time. That pussy was pretty when it pissed.

I sucked my bottom lip and licked the top one to get a taste. Teresa knew I was serious after she watch me do that and really got into what we were doing. I caught the next one.

A stream of warm water hit my tongue and I caressed it like I was melting a mint in my mouth. When she saw what I had mis-collected in my mouth drool down the sides of my face, Tee cut her fountain off. I spit that mouthful of warm, dirty water back on the pussy. That ho filled my face again. From then on, Teresa made sure I caught every molecule. Watered-down Budweiser; that's what it tasted like.

Piss began to drip like drops of rain falling off a roof. I couldn't wait on each drop to reach my lips from her pussy and wet ass hole. I put my mouth on the coochee and that ho hollered, "Don't touch me!" I hadn't forgotten I wasn't supposed to touch. I thought she meant with my hands or dick.

Teresa quickly moved away and wiped the coochee with toilet paper she had in her pants. I asked her if I could have the paper. She looked at me like I was a "sick bastard" and put me and my towels out of her house.

It was the very next weekend Teresa stopped by my apartment to ask if I wanted to "go swimming again." She was looking as serious as I did when I asked her to pee on me.

"My pleasure," I told her. My dick was as hopeful as my mouth and my libidinous taste buds couldn't wait. I even forgot my towels.

You just never know about people. When I got inside Teresa's place that girl was wearing a lingerie outfit that had a large opening in the crotch of red panties, red stockings, and red high heels with a red leather garter. As she closed the door loudly, Tee told me, "We played your fetish game last time. This time we're going to play mine."

Sounding and looking like a dominatrix, I knew what was up. She pointed to newspaper on the floor and ordered me to take my shirt off and get my "dogg ass" on my hands and knees on it. She told me I better be that way when she returned.

From the jump, I didn't like this set-up but what was I supposed to do? The pee was in the pussy. She wasn't dispensing it over the counter.

I did as ordered and when Teresa returned she had on a black half-mask and carried a short black stick in her hand. I didn't see any cause for either. That ho hit me on my butt with that stick. I sat back on my heels and told her, "Oh, hell naw!" Teresa popped me upside the head with it and said, "Get your punk ass back down bitch!" I did.

That ho faced me, put a foot on some furniture, yanked my head towards the crotch of her outfit, and squirted piss at me like her coochee was a water bottle. I didn't know a ho could piss while standing until I was victimized. "That's what you get when you play right," she said. "This is what you'll get if you don't." As soon as she finished the word "don't" Tee whacked me twice upside my short haircut. "I'mma play along," I cried.

After her carrot and stick resolution, Tee pushed backwards my forehead and pissed on my mouth again. "Drink it bitch," she told me, as she spurted urine out. I tried to catch the water from the fountain by putting my lips closer to her cunt but went too far. "Don't touch me!" she hollered, as she stopped pissing and popped me upside the head again.

"Ow!," I yelled. "Stick out your tongue," she ordered. I put my tongue out like I was mimicking a kid with a tongue on a frozen flag pole. Teresa pissed again.

I thought she had pissed out and would let me go home to check my wounds. I thought wrong. "Crawl your ass into the room," she told me. I headed that way but just inside the door frame she stopped, lifted my face up by my chin, and bumped her cunt against my nose. I got a "whack!" on the top of the head. "That's not fair," I pleaded.

"You can't help putting your mouth on this pussy, can you?" she asked, as she began a series of rhetorical questions. "You want to fuck this pussy, don't you? You'd like to make a baby in this pussy, wouldn't you? This pussy isn't yours. All you can do is lick it bitch. Lick it as much as you want because you're not going to fuck it." I did.

I wont no punk but damn if I didn't feel like one. As for Henry? He was missing in action, curled between my legs. His scary ass didn't want to get hit. I was mad at him.

"Crawl your freaky black ass over there and put the back of your head on those towels," she told me. On all fours I hustled over to her bed and placed my back against it and laid my head on the towels she had laid out. Facing the mirrors, Teresa mounted my face. "Gimme that tongue," she said. I must was slow in my movement or maybe my tongue wasn't long enough because that ho spanked me across my arm. "Lick that pussy bitch!" she said. I put more tongue out, saying "Ahhh," like I was at the doctor's office.

That ho didn't show any concern for a comrade she was nearly sitting on. As I licked, She put what seemed like her entire weight on my nose and chin while hunching her smooth ass up and down, as if it hadn't saddled a face in a long time. She began to breathe like she was taking a stress test and busted a nutt, belting out an "Oh, shit!" like a wounded warrior. I slurped whatever honey I could catch. It tasted so-so.

I grabbed her ass and managed to get my nose into her boodee hole. She was scurrying to get off but I held on. It took her to whack me with that stick before I let go.

Teresa wasn't finished. She put a foot on the floor, slammed my head back down, aimed her coochee at my nose and began leaking urine like she had saved a bladder. That ho said, "Drink it or drown bitch." I saw her looking at the bedside mirrors as she let all out what she had left. I coughed on the cunt and that ho still wouldn't stop.

To keep from drowning I had to catch the urine in my mouth. I had one eye open when I spit a mouthful of piss onto Tee's beautiful boodee hole. I had to see that. She responded with the sound of a wounded warrior getting morphine. "Hmmm!" she hummed. As I went back-and-forth sucking the piss off her ass hole and pussy Teresa flopped over onto the bed towards the mirrors. I took advantage of her wounded status by turning around and pulling her hips to the edge of the bed. I stuck much tongue dead into the middle of her anus.

That ho said, "Yo nose. Put yo' nose in it."

There are muscles in a nose. She couldn't handle mine flexing in her ass. She did a female push-up, lifting her hips with my face between her boodee cheeks. I put a vacuum suck on that almond anus, suctioning her pooter like a plunger. Once again, Tee responded with a wounded warrior scream. "Ohhh! Ohhhh!," she hollered. I stopped right there, hoping she had found a new fetish. She stared at me and flicked her stick, without hitting me, as she ordered me to leave her house. I did.

The next weekend I stopped by Teresa's place, wishing I could "go swimming" again.

Before I could knock on the door somebody at the pool told me she had moved out. I felt like a wounded warrior.

DANCES WITH WOLVES

AMONG CIVILIANS, THE word "police" usually serves as a noun. The military, however, commonly used the word "police" as a verb. For example, soldiers were often ordered to "police" the grounds which was the disgusting chore of collecting tossed waste. This was done without gloves and included oral trash like cigarette butts.

I decided to flip the script on the word "police." While on wolf patrol I tried my best to "police" pussy in Cumberland County. Just like cigarette butts, some coochees were more crass than others.

Stephanie was the epitome of crass. She smelled bad and looked worn and less-than. That may have been what drew my practiced attention. She was a ho and proud of it. She said so.

As a member of the United States Armed Forces being paid by the taxpayers to "police" the world, she was another "butt" I was obliged to pick up.

I noticed her bony butt bouncing around in the street in a little skirt like she was warming up for a marathon. The skirt kept flying up and she kept showing ass. I pictured my dick in her butt, wondering how deep it could get in back there, and bet Henry she couldn't take all. Henry bet me she could. We both concluded, "Ain't no harm in tryin'."

Looking like a Pall Mall reject, she was cursing out a husky black woman. People were coming out of their trailers as they heard some flyweight talking smack loudly. The woman being cursed was a boulder compared to Stephanie's pebble-sized butt. Still, Steff didn't back down.

Before I ran up on all this I was on my way to meet Annette so she could give me some head. I was simply amazed how Stephanie was verbally boosting a battle. She intertwined vernacular verbs with noticeable nouns, adverse adjectives, and descriptive directives as well as a rigger packs a parachute. I figured I'd hang until the meat wagon showed up to scoop her off the pavement.

With the crowd gathering, the black woman backed off and Stephanie had the nerve to follow her as she went into the yard of a trailer. Even when she went to open the door, Steff continued her rant. "I ah fuck yo' man aghen if dat motherfucka got dah money, bitch!" I heard her say. I eased my car near Stephanie and offered some advice. "That woman might come out that trailer with a gun," I told her. "Your best bet right about now is to move on."

Stephanie looked into my car. "Who dah fuck is you?" she asked. "I'm just a squirrel trying to get a nut," I replied. That girl started cursing me out. "Whoa! Whoa!" I told her. "Calm you ass down. Look here," I added, then showed her a fat joint. Stephanie leaned further my way, stuck her head in my window, and said, "I don't give a damn 'bout no reefer. High much money you goh spin to git dat nutt?" then plopped her butt into my car.

I told her to fire up the joint, so she could have something to do with her mouth besides cursing. For multiple reasons I sped off quickly. "While you smoke that, rub this," I told her, as I pulled Henry out.

Up close Stephanie looked younger. That's the first thing I noticed even before her odor. It was her language that aged her. "Where in the hell we goin'?" she asked. I talked to her with the tone of a teacher. "First of all," I said, "we are going to my apartment.

Second of all, I went to Catholic school. I was taught by nuns. You need to stop all that cussing." Stephanie said, "Well 'cuse the fuck outta me. Did dem damn nuns teach yo' ass to show a muthafucka yo' dick?"

While continuing to rub and puff, Stephanie told me, "I ain't goh keep jacking yo' dick 'less you got some money." At a stop light I put her on notice. "I ain't paying for no pussy but I will give you 20 dollars if you let me fuck you in yo' ass." Stephanie said, "Let me see dah money." I showed what was in my wallet. That shut her up.

She continued to pull on Henry, making him as stretched as Bragg Boulevard, then started thinking about taking all that dick in her butt. "You got a long ass dick," she told me. "And I wont to put it all in yo' ass," I replied. "I'mma do it but take me to my sister house so it ah be somebody dare wit us." I was okay with that because Annette would be calling my place to find out why Henry wasn't already down her throat.

I asked Stephanie if her sister knew she was selling ass. "My damn sister sell ass," she told me, as if I was new in town. There was no shame in my game even though her sister's trailer was located on the same street where Steff was cursing out that woman. I followed her inside like any person visiting a small business.

Her sister's name was Marissa. She was much better looking and must have been selling more pussy than Steff because she seemed healthier. There were two very young crumbsnatchers of walking age being babysat by cartoons. Marissa questioned Stephanie about me while I was rolling another blunt. Stephanie didn't hesitate at all in telling her sister, in front of the kids, that I had a "long ass dick."

"We waz gonna fuck at hiss place but I wonted somebody else 'round in case if I say stop and he don't," she told Marissa. Steff's sister said, "I wont to see dis dick. Let me see," and all three of us went into the bedroom near the front door. I unzipped my pants and pulled Henry out. He was still plump from Stephanie's foreplay. "Dat muthafucka done went down some," Steff told Marissa. "It was lone gah din dat in dah cah."

Back in the living room, right in front of the kids, Marissa propagandized her pu-nanny. "My pussy beddah dan huhs," she said.

Stephanie jumped right in. "He don't wont no pussy. He wont to fuck me in my ass." Marissa said, "All dat dick in yo' ass?

Bitch you crazy." Stephanie went on to explain her incentive to give up the boodee. "He goh geh me 20 dollars," she told her sister. Marissa said, "Dats all? 20 dollars? Long as dat nigga dick is? And it ain't even all dah way hard. Bitch you crazy."

"Gimme me the money," Steff asked me for. I told her she would get the money only after she completed our deal which was her taking every inch of my dick into her ass. "I kin do dat," she said. I sent her to the bathroom to wash, specifically her ass hole and underarms. "Leave that pussy alone, keep your skirt on, and don't Vaseline yo' butt," I directed. Stephanie just had to say something back. "You ain't tellin' me nuttin I don't know," she stopped to tell me. "I been fucked in the ass be foe."

Marissa directed me to the trailer's back room and surprised me with a condom. She grabbed Henry from my hand and conducted erection maintenance. "My sistah stupid as hell," she said, "letting you fuck huh in huh ass wit dis big dick for 20 dollars. Gimme a joint." I rolled reefer and she continued to peddle her pussy as she jacked then covered Henry.

Stephanie came in and immediately told her sister, "I don't know why you messin'. Dis my trick." Right in front of her sister Stephanie climbed on the bed and got on all fours. I looked to make sure her ass hole was clean then tapped her anus with my lips. "Spit on dat muthafucka. I wont tah git dis shit ovah wit," Steff said. Marissa remarked, "I gotta see dis shit."

I pushed Skeeter into her ass. Marissa gave her sister play-by-play. "Dat muthafucka got a lot to go," she reported. Steff said, "Spit on that muthafucka aghen." This time Marissa splashed mouthfuls of spit on my dick and Steff's rear-end bungalow.

Stephanie was taking the dick nicely, at first. Her ass hole was relaxed, taking dick like a ticket taker takes tickets. I already had much in when I slammed three inches all at once. Stephanie "sold out" and flattened. "You kant take all dat dick," Marissa told her. I hit that boodee with another half inch and Stephanie hollered, "Shit! Shit! Shit! Take dat muthafucka out. You hurtin' my fuckin' stomach."

Marissa pushed me off even though I was already pulling out the boodee. There was a bit of brown shit on the tip of the condom. It looked so nasty I snatched the condom off.

Marissa saw the scat and shook her head in disgust. Steff went to the bathroom.

While Steff was missing (shitting I guessed) Marissa dropped her draws and showed me her hairy cunt. "I got some good ass pussy," she said. "Geh me dat 20 dollars and you kin stick all dat long ass dick in it." I told Marissa to let me smell it. She spread her legs wider and I took a sniff. I was down there a good minute, rubbing my face lightly all in its soft shrubbery. I made a note to come back one day and "git that." Right then, Henry wanted some boodee.

Steff returned, saw me eating her sister's pussy, and demanded 20 dollars. I reminded her of our agreement where she promised to take all the dick. "You got my stomach hurtin'," she said. "You problee wont tah fuck my sister," she wondered aloud. "Why you kant fuck me in dah pussy? What? You gay tah day?"

"Dis nigga got too much damn dick to be fuckin' either one of us in dah ass," Marissa surmised. "I'mma call Lydia. How much money you got?" I reemphasized I wasn't going to pay anything more than 20 dollars whether it was one of them or whoever Lydia was.

Both girls said together, "Dat's my mama." Then Steff added, "Lydia ah let you fuck huh in dah ass but it goh coss mo' dan 20 damn dollars." I decided to compromise. "I might kin give up 25 but that's all," I said, then added, "If I kant get my whole dick in some ass, me and my money needs to leave.

Those hoes didn't want that money walking out the door. Marissa said, "Hold on.

I'mma call mama. I ah be right back." Marissa returned with a big announcement. Lydia suggested I fuck Loretta. "Mama say if he don't wont to fuck Loretta she ah come over and he kin fuck huh in the ass for 25 dollars," Marissa revealed. "Who's Loretta?" I asked. Both girls said together, "Dat's my granny." I told those hoes, "Whatever."

We were all getting high in the living room when in comes Loretta, a much older ho.

I was shocked, at first, for two reasons. She didn't look like a grandmother and was obviously more Caucasian than Steff and Marissa. Each of them sounded and acted Black but had the color of whole milk. The real shock came when I saw how much ass Loretta had. That White ho had a badonkadonk boodee.

Between the waist and knees, Loretta was as wide and as crowned in the rear as any Black woman I had ever seen selling pussy on Hay Street. Her ass was curved and drooped like a Sister's, sitting over the back of her thighs like a mushroom. She must have been a mutant. She looked young enough to deliver a baby but what got most my attention was that a large portion of her hips was still outside when both her feet were in the house.

Loretta took a hit off a joint, looked at me, and then asked, "He dah one wit the big dick?" Both girls answered, "Yeah." Loretta said, "Where dah 25 dollars and witch room we doin' dis in? This was happening as quickly as a collision on a highway. I was nearly comatose from looking at all that ass and it took the issue of money to be revived. I handed Loretta a 20 and a five. Marissa told her granny, "You kin go back dare."

As I followed Loretta to the bedroom I watched her ass. That White woman's hips analogized war drums, going boom, boom, boom! She had a batter of a boodee and I wanted to mash my mugg into her cake. I reckoned her butt cheeks alone would take up half of Henry.

We sat on the bed and Loretta told me, "If you wont more dan to fuck me in my ass, I ah tell you how much it gonna coss." She then proceeded to strip. She didn't do it as a strip tease act, which would have been enjoyed. She did it like we were at Men's Warehouse where I had decided to buy and only needed to determine accessories.

She snatched off her draws and threw them at me. "What dat smell like?" she asked. I took a long sniff of the crotch and said, "Pussy." Loretta spread her legs and pointed at her cunt. "What dat smell like?" she asked. I lowered my noggin between her luscious cotton-colored thighs and took a deeper sniff. "Pussy," I answered. I must have flunked her test because Loretta told me I didn't know the difference between pussy and good pussy. "No wonder you wontin' to fuck ass," she added.

That ho turned away from me, on her hands and knees with her shoulders on the bed and her ass up and thighs apart. She grabbed each cheek of her hips and split them, giving me a view of her coochee hole and a puffy, dark brown, greased anus. "Witch one of dem you wont to stick yo' dick in?" she asked. "Make up yo' mind. I ain't got all day."

I moved to put my face between her hips and tongue into her cunt but when my head touched her thunder butt that ho pushed it away. "You gots to pay for dat," she said.

Damn that pussy was fat. Damn all that ass looked good. I couldn't make up my mind and told her so. "I wont both," I told her. With all that pussy and ass in my face Loretta asked, "You got dah money for bouff?" I asked her, "How much bouff gonna cost?"

Loretta turned back over and said, "If you gotta ask, you ain't got dah money."

She told me that by the time she got my dick hard, like she wanted it, I had better know what I wanted. Loretta started jacking my dick and while she was doing that she stuck her finger in her coochee. She put that finger in my mouth and said, "Taste dat."

That coochee looked, smelled, and tasted damn good and I told her I wanted it. She pulled a purple condom out of her bra and rolled it on my dick. It fit.

Loretta spread her legs for me to fuck her and that gorgeous gulf between her legs looked as exotic as the area between the Yucatan Peninsula and the Florida Panhandle. I told her I liked to knock before entering and asked if I could kiss the pussy. That ho sounded sexy as hell when she answered. "Yes, Mr. Big Dick. You kin kiss my pussy."

My mouth touched down on her coochee like I was a cunt connoisseur; like a rich guy bracing his lips against a glass to sample a fine wine. My lips trembled on that cunt.

On the way putting my dick in, I purposely poked the boodee hole as if my aim was off. That ho knew all the tricks. Loretta reached down, grabbed Henry, and massaged him between her bald, fat, soft, cougar cunt lips.

As I was sliding into that pussy Loretta looked dead into my eyes and told me, "Don't play wit me. Fuck dat." I pushed much penis hard as I could into that ho. The pussy jacked Henry like it was a hand and I busted a nutt quicker than it takes time to change a channel with a remote. I didn't even get a chance to stroke the pussy. I was ashamed.

Loretta pushed me off and hopped up, like shopping was over. I managed to get out a sentence. "Don't you wont to get a nutt?" I asked. Loretta answered with, "If you wont me to get a nutt, it gonna coss you ten dollars to eat my pussy 'til I cum." I still had the honey taste of her vagina on my lips and wanted more. I told her I wanted her to cum but actually just wanted to eat her pussy. I pulled a ten from my wallet and handed it to her.

I was slobbering, big time, in that fat, heated pussy and enjoying it. It was so good I asked Loretta to pee pee. "Mix that honey with some pee," I told her. Loretta didn't respond to my request like I was a "sick bastard."

She handled my request like a pro. "Dat gonna coss you ten mo' dollars," she said. I said okay and had to stop again to reach into my funds.

It was beautiful the way she lifted, with one hand, my face off the cunt and divided her pussy lips with the other just before the coochee started pissing. It was the first time a ho peed at me while lying on her back. I let that water hit the roof of my mouth and flow out over my lips. Her fat cunt was soaked and I helped myself to cleaning it by suction. I hated I didn't have the money for a fart as I tried to lick the pee off her ass hole. It would have been worth ten dollars, even if it turned out to be only a try, just to see her anus pouting and spouting in the middle of all that fine white ass.

The bed was wet but it wasn't my mine to make-up. The condom, loaded with front row sperms, was somewhere on the floor but it wasn't my room to police. Loretta grabbed her clothes, went into the bathroom, and I met her in the living room. Stephanie was back in the street and Loretta told Marissa to give her ten dollars. Loretta gave me her phone number after we exited at the same time. Come to find out, she lived next door.

It turned out to be a good thing to know.

CHAPTER 7

TAR HEEL TARTS

THE AFRICAN QUEEN

THERE ARE MANY justifications why each military branch is uniformed in distinctive dress apparel. Life forms, civilizations, and organizations rely on common images to enhance unity and recognition. Harmony is better achieved when visuals acknowledge common core similarities not their differences.

That's why I was astonished when I met a woman so dark I questioned my clan's relationship with her tribe. Her hue was as extreme as pale but way more beautiful. That ho was so black if she made a move muted at midnight with her glance grudging, no way I would have noticed her.

I met her on a humbug as I was coming out of the NCO club one night. As I held the door for a couple to walk through, I turned my head to look at the entering female's bubbly boodee plop plop and fizz fizz into the lobby as it fought for space in a mini skirt.

Upon releasing the door, I turned and literally bumped into an African-American goddess. "Excuse me girl!" I told her. "As black as you are, I didn't even see you." She gave me a "middle finger" type of stare and verbally pounced on me. "Open dem pop eyes and watch where you going," she threw back at me. I tried to smooth over my calling her a color. "They say the blacker the berry, the sweeter the juice," I offered, as I glanced her up and down. "You won't ever know," she said.

She got me going with her "won't ever know" challenge. I had to come back with something. "I'll die trying," I said. She pounced on me again. "Do that somewhere else. Right now, you needs to get the hell outta my way," she tossed back.

"Whoa," I said. "Don't take the juice inside just yet. I'm going to my car to burn some paper. You want to join me?" That beauty looked directly at my eyes and told me, "You look like you already burned some paper." Everything I threw at her she had a comeback.

Our battle subsided when she agreed to join me in my car. As we weaved through the parking lot I asked her if she was the police. She told me, "If I am, you already busted nigga," and didn't laugh. I didn't think that was funny either.

From her nose to her toes, this ho was dressed to kill. She wasn't going to let a humbug meeting ruin her Saturday night out. She was fine and gorgeous, that was a given. What peaked my interest most was that she was the blackest girl I had ever seen.

There was a more civil conversation in the car; smoking weed will do that. Her name was Jessica and she lived in Lumberton, a town about 40 miles to the south where a lot of people were mixed with Indian. She had long, shiny, beautiful hair like an Indian. Her type welcomed many men buying her drinks before settling on which "hard head" she wanted to eat her pussy. I was lucky to catch her before other wolves did. By the time we finished burning some paper she had my phone number. She wouldn't give me hers.

That following Thursday Jessica called me. "What you wanna talk to me about man?" she asked in a dominant tone. I had heard this kind of attitude, multiple times before.

Punk niggas, spending money on hoes, caused Jessica to believe she was all that. I reminded Jessica we never got around to talking about "juice." She continued her act.

"You got to pay for the juice. I don't give up nothing for free." She pissed me off with that "pay" word. I was blunt with her. "You a prostitute or you a ho?" I asked. "I ain't neither one," she whispered. "Then why a nigga got to pay?" I confronted her with.

"What you wont, man?" she threw back at me. I told her, "Give me five minutes and when I'm finished talking if you don't like what I say, you can hang up and keep your beautiful black ass in Lumberton for all I care." She said, "You got the flo nigga, talk!"

Libidinous missions usually begin with a covert objective. I just blurted mine out.

"You know I want some of that. I love dark-skinned women and you the darkest-skinned woman I've ever met. If you agree to spend some time with me, I promise you'll enjoy yourself." That was the gist of my plea and I got "reasonable doubt" in return.

"Maybe we can do something," she answered. "I was thinking about coming back to Fayetteville on Friday but maybe you can come to Lumberton. Let me think about it."

Friday was payday. Regardless of what people say, a man's payday is a woman's time of the month. To my surprise, before I went to work on Friday, Jessica called. She wanted me to meet her at a motel just off I-95 in Lumberton around 8 p.m.

I instructed her to drink much water all day and use the bathroom as less as possible.

"When you have to go, let out enough just enough to make yourself comfortable. That will make your juice juicier," I explained. I also told her I wanted her to eat something that gave her gas. "It will help make that coochee fart," I had to explain. "I want that thing to talk to me," I told her. She laughed and it was encouraging.

After work, while I was checking out my payday ounce of reefer, Dottie knocked on my front door. "Where you going this weekend?" she asked, as she entered. "I'm going out of town and I don't know if I'm going to be back tonight. Right now, I'm about to take a shower," I told her.

Then Dottie tried me. She tried me. She pulled off her shorts and panties, laid on the couch with her legs spread, and skinned her dick-sized clit. "I'm horny. Suck clitty for me before you go," she said. I did. I sucked that rascal until she busted a nutt. Then she bent over. "Since I'm already wet, here, get yours," she said. Whether she was offering her ass hole or pussy, it didn't matter. "Now right now," I told her.

While I was showering I thought more about sticking dick into that White woman than the opportunity to play with the blackest ass in the world. By the time I got out of the bathroom I wanted to stick dick in Dottie's butt. That woman's boodee hole had that kind of pull because it was fucking good. I had to tell Henry "No!"

The closer I got to Lumberton the more I hoped Jessica would show-up. I stood outside to make sure she knew which room as she circled my car in the parking lot. Once inside she didn't seem to be all that nervous and I was careful not to give her the impression I was some kind of sexual deviant, even though I was. I rolled joints while we relaxed into our second meeting.

Jessica wasn't shy and I followed her lead of stripping as we got high. She felt my dick when it was still in my underwear. "That's juvenile nigga. It got some growing to do," she said. I told Jessica, "Oh it goh grow. When it do, you gonna have a hard time deciding whether to take it or leave it." I expected Henry would want to hurt her for that slur.

I liked the way we went about this. We weren't in there to forge a relationship. We were in a motel to fuck. No game, no pain.

Her tits were awesome but eating her pussy seemed to be the best way to start. "I'm gonna be busy for a little while so let me know when you got to use the bathroom," I said.

Jessica made another one of her brilliant come backs. "I don't know which gonna come out first, something from my pussy or something from my ass," was the way she put it.

She looked absolutely stunning on the white sheets. This ho had two sets of tits. Her regular breasts supported a raised area around her nipples which looked like miniature versions of Hershey Kisses. Everything was jet black and shiny. Stretch marks on the sides of her breasts made it appear her titties were still growing. Before I went downtown, I diverted my mouth to her breasts. She was one of those hoes that liked men to suck the titties. She massaged the back of my head while my mouth was tugging on tit.

As I rose into the missionary position, her legs opened. "Turn out the light," she said. I told Jessica, "No way!" knowing I wouldn't be able to find her if she got off those sheets.

I got my arms under the back of her knees and lifted her hips off the sheet. Her midnight colored cunt I couldn't see, at first. It was shrouded in long black hair so I moved her legs farther back and that pussy popped apart. There was a hot pink color between the fat bit of lip hidden by hair at the bottom of her cunt. I propped her feet on my shoulders and directed my face downtown to get a sniff of her navy blue boodee hole.

On cue, with the touch of my nose against her ass hole, there came an abbreviated but loud, heavy fart. It was so on-time I believed that ho did it on purpose. It sounded like it said, "Black!" No doubt, I said to myself. Aloud, Jessica said, "Excuse me!" I told her she didn't have to say excuse me for something I wanted. "It ain't like you stepped on my toe. Gas is what I wanted. I should thank you for it."

"You want me to pass gas?" she asked to begin a rant. "Are you a freak or something? What you want me to do next, nigga, shit on you?" I told her, "Just be prepared to do some things that you normally don't do. After all that, I felt it was okay then to flip her over to get at her ass hole.

I spread her beautiful, soft, ass cheeks and found my target amongst deep space camouflage. I didn't bother introducing myself to her pooter by kissing it first. I sucked that boodee hole from the get-go. She liked that. She got on her knees and ended-up rising onto the balls of her feet trying to mash her ass against my face. Her ass was so stuck out, she looked like somebody trying to fit their butt into a tire swing.

I didn't want this to be the only time with this girl. Without any thought, it just came out when I asked her what her last name was. Jessica told me, "People laugh when I tell them my last name." "How come?" I asked her. Jessica said, "My last name Black."

In a sneaky way of changing the subject and to stop my laughing, Jessica turned over on her back and asked, "Yo' dick hard yet?" I ignored her question for a moment and spread her legs. I parted the lips on the coochee with my nose and inside the color shade of ripe watermelon appeared. Right there, I named that pussy "Pinky."

I kissed "Pinky" as I answered Jessica's last question. "You don't want (kiss) no dick (kiss)," I told her. "You (kiss) probably scared (kiss) of the dick (kiss)." After all those kisses, I put that whole pussy in my mouth and squished it with my jaws. "Oooh, shit!" she hollered out. "I'mma shoot off in yo' mouth nigga. I'mma nutt," she warned.

I had to raise up because I got a hair on my tongue. Before I could pinch the hair out of my mouth that girl pushed my head back down from whence it came. "Eat that pussy for me baby," she said. "Don't stop. Eat me!" I was practically forced back down but this time I aimed for her clit. "Not there; not that," she told me. "Eat dat pussy. Eat dat pussy." I followed her request by curling my tongue and dipping it into the cunt.

Minutes later Jessica said, "I can't get a nutt. I got to piss." Her need to pee couldn't have come at a better time. "Wait a minute," I told her. I got towels and placed them next to the bed. She watched me like she was learning how to properly parallel park. "I would do this in the bed but I'mma let you to do it down here," I told her.

"Do what?" she asked. When I guided her hips above my face she thought I only wanted her to sit on my face. "You a freaky motherfucker!" she said, as she hopped over me like a gymnastics pro and "backed that thang up" over my grill. I opened her pussy by grabbing her ass cheeks and splitting them. That black coochee, with all that long hair, looked like a Black Santa Claus with his mouth opened saying "Ho! Ho! Ho!"

I began talking to "Pinky." "Give me some pee pee Pinky. I want you to piss all over my face." Speaking for "Pinky", that ho said, "Do what?" Apparently "Pinky" couldn't hear because of its hairy covering so I talked to Jessica.

"Piss on me," I told her. After a glance downward water emerged from Jessica's beautiful, black, hairy, wide opened, lathered with slob pussy. I made sure she heard me smack her first short spurt, as if I had just tasted strong lemonade. "Pinky" stopped leaking, Jessica looked down, and Pinky pissed again. I caught some of the wide stream of urine and shot it back on that forested cunt. That ho said, "Woo!"

Pinky stopped again, Jessica looked down again, and both told me "Open yo' mouth."

I did. Her black, hairy pussy landed squarely on my mouth and while I was tonguing that cunt that girl pushed out more pee pee. She kept Pinky on my mouth, filling my jaws with hot piss. Each time I spurted it back where it came from. I sucked piss off that black pussy and "Darth Vader" boodee hole. She liked that. Me too.

She heard me in the bathroom loudly rinsing out my mouth. "It didn't taste that bad, did it?" she hollered. "No," I told her. "It's just that it's better coming than going."

I felt like I needed a shower. "While I'm in there I want you to think about what we've done so far and tell me what you liked and did not like," I told her. She said, "Okay." I also told her to decide whether she wanted to fuck so I'll know how excited I should get."

She said, "Okay." Her one-word answers told me I had blown this egotistical ho's mind.

I washed her coochee and ass hole with soap like she was a baby. She liked being pampered. Once I understood that, I gave her a complete massage. After that, she was like clay in an artist's hands.

I actually told her I was going to suck her ass hole and stick my tongue in it and she smiled. I also told her to fart when she felt like it. "That ho only said, "Okay." Me and this bitch were going to be a good team, I thought. I gripped each ass cheek with a hand and split them apart. Jessica's pooter popped out like a whack-a-mole. I told her anus, "Gimme gas." The boodee hole followed my order and farted for me with a superb- ending push of air. It sounded like it said, "Pierce" and perfumed pleasingly.

I thought you told me your last name was Black?" I asked her. "My last name is Black," she said. "Then who in the hell is Pierce?" I asked. "Pierce! What you know about Pierce?" she asked. "Your fart sounded like it said Pierce," I told her. "It said Pierce?" she asked. I said, "Yeah. Who is Pierce?" "That's my maiden name," she answered. Really, I didn't care if her ass hole was informing on her. It was talkin' - that's all I cared about.

I massaged her back, neck, and shoulders while we continued to talk. She liked my hands. "That's nice. Everything nice except I ain't got no nutt yet," she told me. "There ain't no guarantee given either one of us gonna do that," I said. "You keep making me feel good, like you are right now, good things will happen," she came back with.

"How many women done pissed in yo' mouth?" Jessica had the nerve to ask me.

Then, with a small laugh, she added on, "I'm sho' glad I didn't kiss you." I started to ask her how many dicks she had sucked and how many sperms she had swallowed. Instead, I told her, "You ain't the first and you probably won't be the last," then requested her opinion. "How you like it?" I asked. "It's kind of messy; kinda freaky," she answered.

She kept asking questions about my libidinous missions and it bothered me to give out classified information. To steer her away from asking mission secrets, I decided to suck another fart out. I rounded my lips like I was trying to whistle and vacuumed her ass hole repeatedly. "Damn nigga," Jessica said. "What you trying to do, blow my mind?" Been there, done that already I figured.

Expecting more info about her via flatulence I told her ass hole to "Gimme gas."

"Hold on," Jessica told me. "It fixin' to say something." I put my nose directly on her ass hole, sniffing to catch every molecule. Jessica said, "Kiss my ass." I did. My lips partially blocked the escaping gas. When the boodee hole let go it sounded like it said, "Precious."

"Okay," I said, "who or what is precious?" Jessica responded as if somebody had put a whoopee cushion under her. She jumped up on her knees, looked back at me, and told me, "I'm scared of you." She moved away further, leaning her back against the head of the bed like she was finished with some task. "What you mean you scared of me?" I asked. "You the Devil," she called me. I laughed.

After a hard stare, like I had just sprouted horns on my head, Jessica announced, "Precious is my daughter's name." I said, "What? You got a kid?" "Yes," she answered, "and her name is Precious Pierce." I asked her, "What you trying to do, blow my mind?"

Jessica repeated what she had said earlier. "You the Devil," and added, "I'm fixin' to go. Fucking you might send me to Hell," she told me. "I knew yo' ass was strange when you wanted me to fart in your face," she explained, as she was getting dressed. "But I didn't mind trying something new," she continued.

Then, Jessica popped rhetorical questions which had already crossed my mind. Jessica asked, "What kinda nigga wants somebody to fart in dey face or piss in dey mouth? How me passing gas tellin' you stuff? You weird nigga. You dah Devil."

As she rolled joints for her black ass to leave with, Jessica threw out another question.

"Foe I pissed in yo' mouth you called me Pinky. Why you call me that?" she asked. "I named my dick Henry, so I figured I'd name yo' pussy Pinky," I answered.

Jessica slowed her roll and looked at me, real hard, like she had just seen the opposite image of the Virgin Mary in a grilled cheese sandwich. Just prior to walking out the door the door she tossed the two joints she had rolled towards me and told me, "Henry is my baby father's name. You kin have these back. I don't wont nuttin' you got to offer."

Tar Heel Tarts

THE UNDERSTUDY

THE UNITED STATES government does a decent job making sure every active duty soldier's basic health and welfare needs are met. When a soldier is jailed, Uncle Sam provides a lawyer. Military doctors corral the clap and wrestle with wisdom teeth. A teamwork attitude is instilled immediately among recruits after taking the oath.

I had that same type of attitude and exampled that same type of teamwork when I went to rescue "Big Boodee Judy." Like a ship at sea about to hit an iceberg, she cast a "May Day" alert for me to get her out of harm's way; poor thing. That girl's butt was too bodacious to be in palpable peril so I answered her summons.

"You needs to come and git me," she said, with her usual drawl. Of course I asked why. Judy went into this whole police story about how her son's father hit her "upside the head" and was subsequently locked up. She figured he was going to get out of jail by week's end and she didn't want to be anywhere around when he was released.

I only hoped her crumbsnatchers weren't a part of the rescue and told her as much. Judy said she would see if she could get somebody to keep her kids but insisted I pick her up on Friday, the assailant's payday.

Judy called back and told me her sister, Connie, would baby sit only Saturday night and wanted to be compensated. I called Connie at a different number and, instead of cash, she and I agreed she could use my car to go out to a club in Fayetteville on Friday night.

I'd return them all to Dunn Saturday morning, so Connie could go to work, and then return that evening to bring only Judy back to Fayetteville. Running up and down Tobacco Road was required if I was to have two nights with Judy's big boodee. I hadn't fucked her liked I wanted; hadn't got a fart; and hadn't 69. We had work to do.

Before I got off the phone I asked Connie if she looked like Judy. "Me and my sister got diff'rent daddies," she began to explain. "I don't look nothing like my sister or my mama. I wear glasses and I'm dark skin. Dey yella in got good eyes. My grandmama got a big ass, my mama got a big ass, and my sister got a big ass. I got a regular ass." There was another difference I noticed. Connie didn't have a drawl like Judy.

Friday evening Judy showed better sense this time by not getting toe-up on wine. Once she got the kids asleep, she was able to climb the stairs to where I was. "Dey gone to sleep. You goh fuck me nigh?" she asked. I was high as hell and only heard the word "fuck." "Suck my dick, first. Then I'mma stick my dick in that big butt you got," I told her. Judy said, "I knowed you was gonna wonna fuck me back dare." I told her, "You knowed right."

I took my dick out and began slapping it into the palm of one hand like it was a strap.

She leaned over and sucked on flaccid Henry like she was fulfilling a contract. "If that's the way you suck yo' baby daddy dick, no wonder he hit you upside the head," I scolded her with. "Slow down on that dick." My hand in her draws gripped her hips like I was trying to pick up a beach ball. A finger probed her anus and her ass hole was squeezing it. "Squeeze dat boodee hole like that when I got all dis dick in all dat ass," I ordered.

Upon inspection, I didn't see or smell do-do on my finger. The hole was clear for entry.

With my cranium mellow, dick hard, and a fine piece of ass available, I bent her over on my bed with her ass hole aimed towards the room's illumination. That wasn't good enough. To angle the pole hole better I put her knees under pillows. Her nose was pointed down like she was a bloodhound on the trail of a coon. I sucked that boodee hole until Henry began bobbing and weaving like a streamer in a windstorm.

That boodee hole charmed Henry like high definition seduces the eyes. As Skeeter entered her slightly greased anus Judy didn't move nor say anything. With only a slight bend at my knees, I got all up in there and humped hard. Her low-rider, large hips cock- blocked more than a couple of inches. "Hold yo' hips apart," I told her. She did and Henry drilled deeper.

I liked it when a ho took it like a man.

One time I had a perfect angle of penetration, yanked her waist backwards, and lodged long dick into that rump. I hit that boodee hard and as she moved to get her knees back onto the pillows her big hips closed around any dick remaining outside her butt. It felt like I had 12 inches of LSD in that ho and Judy acted like all I was doing back there was dancing. I was doing that too.

I wanted to fuck her in the butt until her sister returned. However, one particular moment Judy did what I had told her. She squeezed her anus around the base of my penis and Henry puked on her colon like a college freshman on a drinking binge.

That ho didn't have a complaint about how I tried my best to deconstruct her digestive system. She acted as if all I'd done was get something out of the refrigerator. As a matter of fact, Judy told me she appreciated that I fucked her in the ass with her knowledge. "It beddah like dat," she said.

I let Connie in about 2 a.m. while Judy was knocked out and I was upstairs gettin' high. The first thing she asked was, "Where my sister at?" as if I had murdered Judy and her children or something. She didn't go downstairs to check to see if my answer was valid so I figured she was just making conversation.

Connie's eyes told me she was already high when she grabbed my bag of herb to roll a joint. I tried her. "I appreciate you watching the kids tomorrow," I told her. "Anything special I can do for you?" She looked at me, knowing what I was talking about. "You kant do nothin' for me. You go wit' my sister," she said, as she took a hit off a blunt.

"That's yo' half sister. I want to show appreciation to the other half," I responded.

"What kin you do for me?" Connie asked, as the joint got shorter. "Something that half of you need to keep secret," I answered. Connie told me, "I tell people all the time, don't ask me no questions and I won't tell you no lies."

I jumped up and went to get some towels. When I returned, I got the room dark then arranged myself on the floor with my back to the couch and my head on its seat. "Lift that skirt, drop dem draws, and have a seat right here," I said, pointing to my face. She stared at me for a minute and then pulled her draws off. I directed her to climb over and sit on my face. "Knees on the couch," I said. She caught what I wanted and put a slim thigh on each side of my head facing the wall.

I couldn't see what was on my nose but it was smelly; a good smelly. Just from the sniff Henry got hard as hell. She lowered her coochee and that pussy was moist on my mouth. Her getting a quickie would be the best thing for both of us so I put a fried chicken lickin' on that pussy. She made me eat that coochee for a long time. I just knew Judy would catch us. Finally, Connie mashed my head forcefully with her thighs like she was nuttin' and climbed off before I could finish slurping what she creamed.

"I'm ready to go," she said, as she rolled over. I pushed her down, grabbed an ass cheek in each hand, split her buttocks, and sucked her boodee hole. She lurched forward and bumped her head on the arm of the couch. I sucked, licked, and poked her ass hole with my tongue as diligently as it takes to find a topnotch thesaurus term. "Let's fuck," I told her, after she pushed my head from between her ass cheeks. "I kant do dat. You fuckin' my sister," she said, as she was pulling her panties up. "At least you can water me. That's why I got the towels," I said. "Water you? What you mean water you?" she asked. "I want that pussy to pee pee on me," I replied.

I could see in the dark Connie giving me that "sick bastard" look. I got into position on the floor and all of a sudden she jumped up, dropped her draws below her knees, and squatted over my head like she was a hiker in the forest about to fertilize a fern.

"I got to piss for real," she said, as she looked down between her legs. I told her to turn the other way. "No," she said. "I wont to do it dis way." No doubt, Connie was way different from her sister. Since her aim was a little off I motioned her to where her coochee lined-up with my mouth. "Oh, you wont it on yo' face?" she asked, as if she didn't know how to water a plant. I separated her pussy lips by wiggling my nostrils into her cunt to encourage a direct stream.

It took Connie a long time to start leaking but I enjoyed messing with her boodee hole and coochee while in a "standby" mode. It took so long I thought about going into the kitchen and running some water. She didn't like it when I planted kisses on her pooter.

"Stop kissing my ass," she said. "I kant piss why you doin' dat." Trying hard to pee, Connie farted. It sounded like it said, "Whew!"

Seconds later I got my first shot of her urine. It was noticeably hot and bounced off my bottom lip and drizzle off one side of my face. "Is dat enough?" she asked, as she stood up like she was through. "You ain't done nothing yet," I countered with. Connie squatted back down and when her vagina contacted my lips a downpour of piss erupted. As the pussy precipitated, I had my nose on her ass.

We heard Judy coming up the stairs. Connie stopped pissing like it was the fortieth night of "The Great Flood." I guess holding her down told her to continue. We were still in that position when Judy busted us. My mouth was filled with urine so I couldn't talk to tell Connie to stop or keep going. She leaked more pee and ended with concluding farts.

One sounded like it said, "Get" and the other seemed to say "Up!"

I had a mouthful of her relief when Judy reached the top of the stairs. By the time Judy asked, "What ya'll doing?" I was spitting the muddled malt back on Connie's cunt and ass hole. "Oh, shit!" Connie went ahead and hollered.

Judy cut the light on. There I was on the floor, wet and happy. Judy just stood there and Connie did the explaining while she was pulling up her draws. "He wonted me to piss on him," she told her sister. Judy said, "Ya'll some nasty bitches."

"I'mma piss too," she told us. Judy flipped up her gown, pulled her bloomers below her knees, squatted over me, and squirted quickly. Before I could get her pee hole aimed correctly, she hit my chin and sprayed waste water all over my neck. The torrent was heavy as if she woke up to go to the bathroom.

As Judy raised up, Connie told Judy, "You meet some freaky ass niggas." Simple ass Judy wanted to know, "right nigh" whether Connie and I had fucked. "I wont gonna fuck dat nigga. You see I didn't have my clothes off," Connie reasoned, "He just wanted me to piss on him." Debra looked at me and asked, "Y you ax my sister tah do dat?" I had my reason ready. "You were sleep," I said.

Connie rolled a joint and went downstairs. Judy followed. I did all the cleaning up I could upstairs and went downstairs into the bathroom and the shower. When I got out, Judy was still awake when I snuggled up next to her big hips. "I'm mad at you," she said, as I put my dick between her ass cheeks. I got as much dick as I could into her boodee hole, busted a nutt, and went to sleep.

Connie woke me at sunrise. "Take yo' dick outta my sister and take me home," she told me. Once all of us got to Dunn, Connie was dropped off at the girls' mother's house.

I was forced to take Judy and her kids to the girls' grandmother's place. Judy invited me in so I went in. Connie was right when she said her grandmother had a big ass.

She started talkin' shit to Judy about having her children around "so many" different men. I spoke my mind. "Goll-lee, grandma," I said, "you a healthy young lady." Grandma knew what I was talking about. "All you mens alike," she said. "Ain't nunna ya'll shit."

"Where you get this one from, Fort Bragg?" grandma asked. Judy told her how we met and that I had come to get her away from her baby daddy. I told grandma, "You see, all men ain't alike," I said. Grandma answered. "Yeah, the hell ya'll is," before getting on Judy about depending on "any man." While Judy was in another room, Grandma made a point to switch her butt close to my face. I took it as having purpose.

On my return to Dunn later that day, when I went to first pick up Connie I made it a point to go inside to see the girls' mom's hips. Confirmation occurred. She had a huge ass formed just like Judy's and they were the same light complexion. Judy was shorter so her ass looked larger. Deep brown-skinned Grandma had the largest ass out of three generations of big boodee. I labeled her "Queen Boodee."

On our way to grandma's house to get Judy and for Connie to baby sit, we hadn't even turned the corner when Connie tried me. "Debra say you got a big dick," she just threw out, as if she had seen the image of a penis in a cloud. "She say you fuck hard," Connie added. I said, "True dat. True dat."

That ho wanted me to show her my dick. I told her that if she wanted to see my dick she should have fucked me the night before. "My sister woulddah had a fit if she haddah caught us fucking," she said. I told her to see my dick she would have to fuck it or suck it.

She got quiet then. "What else Debra told you?" I asked. "She say you fuck people in dey butt why dey sleep." I told her fucking women in the ass was my way to see if they were qualified. "You got to be grown to take a dick like this like that," I told her.

Connie reached over and started rubbing Henry. "Why I gotta give you some pussy or put my mouth on you just to see how big yo' dick is?" she asked. "I take my dick out for only three things," I told her, "to piss, wash, or bust a nutt." She removed her hand and got quiet again.

When we pulled up to grandma's house she told me, "Next time you come to Dunn, come and git me," she said. "We kant fuck 'cause you fuckin' my sister but I'll do the other thing for you." I told that ho, "You must be kant keep a secret."

Connie dashed into her grandmother's house, stayed a few minutes, and then got back into the car. "My grandmama won't let her go," she said. "Maw maw say she got to stay home with her chullun." Disappointment went through my mind because I wanted all night Saturday and all day Sunday with Judy without the kids.

"I need to talk to Judy before we go," I told Connie. We went into the house together and she called Judy out of a room. Grandma was talking shit from the kitchen. "She ain't goin' wit' you. Didn't Constance tell you dat? Go find somebody else to be wit'. Judy ain't goin' nowhere." I actually went up to granny and calmly, quietly requested she allow Judy to go to Fayetteville. Granny stared at me and said, "You kin find better. Just look in the right place."

Before I even cranked the car, Connie was staring me down. She had unexpectedly found an avenue to get the dick she had asked for. We headed directly for Fayetteville.

"You are not goin' to get me drunk like you did my sister," she said. "I'm gonna know when you try in fuck me in my ass." I told her I wasn't going to force anything but my dick on her tonsils. She laughed when I told her that. She didn't understand I was talking about reaching her

175

tonsils via her anus. I expected her to be walking real funny by the time she got back home.

She kept feeling on my dick while I was driving, asking for me to pull it out. So I pulled out Henry and let her play with him. "Go ahead, suck the dick," I told her. "How you tellin' me to suck yo' dick. I'm scared of you," she said. "That's what you said you would do, so do it," I told her.

Connie stalled by confessing she didn't think she was good at fellatio. "When I do it with my friend, he always stops me so we can fuck," she explained. "If I'm doing it so good, why does he stop me?" I told Connie that maybe she didn't know how to suck a dick. "Tell me how to do it," she requested. As a servant of the taxpayer, I did.

Connie sucked the dick roughly, like it was business. I hated that. "A nutt coming. Get ready to swallow dat," I told her. Connie took her mouth off the dick and, unlike her sister, told me what to do. "Put it in my hand." I told that ho to get her head out of my lap and leave my dick alone. I made sure she knew I was irritated.

I stopped to get more reefer and some wine on the way home. Connie wanted some beer. I told her I didn't drink beer and she'd have to pay for it if she wanted some. That ho told me beer made her piss and that's why she wanted it. I bought a six pack of tall cans and paid for it.

While I was recording what happened in Dunn in my diary, that ho showered but put the same draws she had worked in back on. I made her take them off and I sniffed her panties while she rubbed and sucked my dick while she was swallowing beer like it was an energy drink. Once she got high enough she got naked below the waist, sat over my lap, and poked Skeeter in and out her cunt. "Git down on that dick," I told her. "See how much you can take." We were passing the joint and giving each other shotguns as she was sliding up and down on Henry. She told me in my ear, "You got a big dick" and nutted.

We went downstairs. I turned the shower water on and her doped ass followed me into the bathroom. "I got to pee," she said. I let her urinate on me in the tub. That ho pissed on my head like she was baptizing me, laughing while she was leaking. She didn't bathe, as if she got into the tub to do one thing.

She was laid back on the bed horny as hell when I got into the room. I knew she wanted to suck the dick so we got into the 69. Underneath her ass, I examined that ho like she was a stalled car engine. I stretched her pussy all kinds of ways and was digging in her ass hole like I was trying to get a bullet out of it. She sucked my dick like when "some is good and more is better." She pee peed while I was back there with scant squirts.

I alternated kisses on the pussy with kisses on her boodee hole. That ho didn't know where my face was going next. I teased her anus with my tongue and nose and she would wiggle off each. "You gotta be still," I told her. "I can't help it," she said. "Yo' nose and tongue ticklin' me. How you know people like dat?" she asked. "Don't ask me no questions and I won't tell you no lies," I answered.

It must have been between three and four three in the morning when we decided to fuck, maybe just so we could go to sleep. I was on top of her in the missionary position, knocking down walls in that pussy. Every time I jammed dick into that cunt she hollered, "Shit!" She must have said "shit" fifty times while she was taking "dicktation." She really liked that we nutted together.

Constance woke me up, repeatedly saying, "I gotta pee." I told her to "Put it in the toilet" before I explained, "Dirt in you accumulates while you're sleep and is in your morning pee. That's why it's usually darker. The clearer the pee the cleaner it is. I don't want no yellow pee," I emphasized. "How you know all that?" she asked.

She played with and sucked my dick most of Sunday as we smoked herb and watched TV. At one point, she announced that she had to use the bathroom. "I wanna shit on you," that ho had the nerve to say. "I'm scared of you," I replied, "Tellin' me you want to shit on me. I'm freaky but I ain't nasty," I told her."

As she went down the stairs I thought about it and realized I had an opportunity to watch somebody else take a shit. In the bathroom, with my head nearly in the toilet, I saw that thin-ass ho slowly drop a torpedo turd into the water. I knew then she could take a big dick in the boodee. She hugged me as she needed support to squeeze out midget mud.

"What I gotta do to be qualified to be wit you?" she asked, while she was still shittin'.

"You gotta swallow the nutt and you got to give up the boodee. That first turd you just dropped was bigger than my dick. You kin take this dick in yo' butt easy," I told her. I added that it wasn't because Judy had a big ass that made her good to be with. I said it was because she gave a man whatever he wanted without any fuss.

Connie told me, "You right. You right. Me and my sister like night and day. My sister let men do whatever dey wont." She thought about what I wanted and said, "I ah let you shoot off in my mouth. I know mens like dat. But yo' dick big and I ain't never done that before." That ho sucked my dick while she was taking a shit and I nutted in her mouth to add to her resume as a note of qualification. "Swallow dat," I ordered. She did.

This girl was getting serious about us. So she wouldn't get too attached, I let her know that I was about to get out of the Army and that I probably would never see her nor her sister again. "That's why I let ya'll pee on me," I said. "Once I leave here I'll be gone forever. I'll just be a memory." "Well then, let me shit on you," she reasoned. "I saved some just in case you let me to do it." I didn't.

Her continuous begging to shit on me got old. I wanted her to leave. She didn't want to go. That's what prompted me to demand anal sex, hoping that would urge her out the door. I thought I greased her ass hole good but when I pushed Henry into her butt, she yelled and grunted like she was having a baby. I stroked that boodee hole while she was wiggling like bait at the end of a line. I fussed at her about my getting shit on my dick.

Once she realized she wasn't as qualified as her sister, she was ready to go home.

Tar Heel Tarts

WHATEVER WORKS

WITH THE RIGHT tool you can do any job. On libidinous missions a soldier's tool box didn't hurt to include some sort of mind-altering substance.

On one operation in particular, reefer from Grenada turned out to be a great resource.

It was one-toke weed people refer to as "dah bomb." Being high-up on neon green- colored Grenadian grass liberated me to take on a ho foe like no other I had engaged before. That herb gave me "the nerve."

I needed nerve. My mission objective was to place my face in the anatomical middle of Judy and Connie's grandmother. I wanted her leg walls to wallop my ears and humongous hips to tremendously trap my jaws. That's all. Any resulting brain damage or lockjaw condition from a lack of oxygen or pressure, I figured, would be worth it.

Big Mama had been on my hit list since I first saw the carry-on luggage below her waist. I equated granny's hips with a C-130, the Hercules of aircraft. Hugging that boodee would be like putting wrestler "Andre the Giant" in the bear hug. Craving her big butt I traveled with all the tools, spunk, sperm, and sanguineness I thought would be necessary to grovel her groundswell of bluffed butt.

I planned it well, showing up at granny's house when she was home alone on an early Saturday afternoon. "Debra ain't he ah," maw maw told me, when I lied about why I was there. Na-nah said she didn't know where Judy was and wasn't going to look for Judy.

She noticed my eyes and accused me of being drunk. "I'm not drunk," I told her. "I'm here to go to Heaven."

I continued to speak bluntly as I stood on her porch talking through her screen door. I told granny, "The last time I was here you told me to look elsewhere. I think it's because that thing dusty and you know it need to be cleaned. If you alone, let me duss it off for you while I'm here." Granny said, "I know what you mean. You got some nerve 'pectin' me to play games wit' a jitterbug."

I pulled out five twenty-dollar bills to gain granny's interest. "Dis how much nerve I got," I told her. Na-nah was busted when she didn't curse and slam the door in my face.

"You gonna need mo' money dan dat," she told me. "Whatever works," I said, then emptied my wallet with 40 dollars more. That did it. Grandma said, "You kin come in."

I hustled over to her couch like any salesman trying to seal a deal made at the door.

She stood over me, collected the cash, and counted it. I felt desperate, awkward, and lecherous while that old woman was counting "my" money. It was like I was starving, had put my last coins in an unreliable vending machine, was waiting for the honey bun I chose, and ready to shake the dispenser if necessary.

"All ya'll mens juss alike," she said, as she went to close some curtains and her back door. "What you wont to do?" she asked. I straight out told her, "I want to put my face right in the middle of yo' butt and dem big thighs you got, grandma," I answered. She responded quickly. "Stop calling me grandma. My name Verna."

"Is you show dat's all you wont to do?" she asked. "Whatever you ah let me get away with," I answered. "Juss open up yo' legs and hips so I ah know what it's gonna be like entering the Pearly Gates. I wont to see how cozy it is up in dare. Let me taste all dat," I added. Verna said, "You ah nasty son-of-a-bitch." I answered, "True dat. True dat."

She was looking at me like I was "Pete the Pervert" but my simple objective hastened her bloomers down. "We gonna do dis out here?" I asked. Verna said, "You kin do what you ask to do right he ah on the settee." Maw maw was wearing some big ass draws.

After she arduously managed to slide them over her feet I snatched and sniffed them. Granny said, "You a sick bastard." I again confronted truth. "True dat. True dat," I said.

Verna lifted her house dress, laid back on the couch, and spread her legs. I don't know how I could have truly imagined how heaven would be without granny's herald.

Her coochee was like the tunnel like a football team runs through onto the field. She had a big, crooked cunt with thick, dark brown lips. The hair, some grey, was spotty, making the coochee look like an old person in a fetal position on their deathbed. Darker inner lips were loitering outside the top of that thing. Her hot pocket look as good as an old cunt could. I lowered my head, Verna widen her legs, and told me, "Eat it iffin you wont to."

I lost my mind.

I nuzzled my nose against her clit and chomped down on her coochee like it was a Big Mac and sucked it like it was a strawberry shake. I held my face down there, between granny's legs, like oxygen was overrated, facetime was funtime, and dusting was my design.

I lifted my face to kamikaze that cunt once more and granny knocked me over with one thigh, like a nose tackle nudging me out the hole. That old ho flipped and put her big butt all in my face. "He ah!" she said. "I know dis what you really wont. Eat dat."

I lost my mind.

I couldn't believe it. What a continent! I said to myself about the first time I saw the size of Africa, my homeland. Right in front of me there was butter!, cheddar!, mustard!, or mayonnaise!; anything that spread came to mind. I split open her cheeks and saw her boodee hole. I stared like I had found a new planet.

I grabbed with my arms and planted kisses on that big ass. Hugging her hips was like hugging the hungry on the planet; I couldn't comfort all of it. Therefore, I dove head first into its canyon with my tongue towards its centerpiece and then poked, drilled, and vacuumed her pooter.

Granny had long hairs around that boodee hole. I grabbed the bangs with my lips and pulled. Big Mama "backed that thang up" and it shoved my head backwards to where it was like I was looking up at the apex of a 50-story building.

She got up. "You got what you paid for," Verna told me. "You kin leave nigh."

Granny was right but I wasn't happy about her stopping me. I told maw maw, "Let me suck that corner sum mo' so I kin git the dust out." Grandma said, "You gots to leave."

Watching her pull up her draws was an unexpected pleasure. Hoes with an ass that big have to squat and shake to get their underwear on. I was in awe as granny twerked right in front of me.

"I'mma give you my phone number for when you need somebody's head between your legs," I told her. "If I do, it wont be you. I know mens," she retorted. She wouldn't take the number so I laid it on a table. She had to swat my hands off her ass as her hips directed me to the door.

That same night, real late, Verna called me. "You gave me the hots, man!" she said. "It been almost 10 years since I had the hots. I kant sleep." I told her, "You need some attention, girl. Let me dust dat." After a little coaxing Verna asked, "Whey in Fayetteville you live?" Mee maw got on I-95 and brought that big ass to me; to me. I must have gone to the window fifty times looking for her.

This time she was the bold one. Granny wouldn't drink any wine but smoked some Grenadian grass. "I ah try it," she blessedly agreed to. She took shotguns and hit the pipe. Once she got over her initial coughing, her giggling told me na-nah was good to go.

In my living room, she stepped out of some fancy turquoise underwear, twirled them on a finger, and asked, "You wanna smell 'em?" I told that ho I wanted to smell the real thing. Granny lifted her dress, split her big thighs apart, and told me, "He ah. Smell it."

I lost my mind.

Her ol' ass wouldn't let me smell the coochee independently. That ho had to help.

She grabbed the back of my head and mashed my face between her legs like it was actually a sample of the after-life. I took deep whiffs of that fat, hot pussy. I sucked the cunt for a good minute and after that she was ready to fuck. "Ain't you got a bed somewhere?" she asked.

I didn't nickname myself "Handsome Devil" without thought of who I was. I wanted to fuck maw maw, right there, on the same couch where her granddaughters and I had sex. Verna motioned to move and I pushed her back down. I got a mouthful of coochee and na-nah told me what to do and then let me handle my business. It was like Connie and Judy were one. I could only imagine Judy's mama managing me.

"Eat dat pussy baby. Suck dat pussy good," she said, like Connie told me. When I came off, I saw Granny's exposed fat, pointed but burly clit like Judy's standing out like a club bouncer with his arms crossed. I carefully skinned it back, lowered my mouth on it, and then sucked. She hollered, "Woo! Woo!," like she was repeatedly touching a hot pot.

I had my head between granny's legs, eating her pussy in my front room with the light on and the curtains open.

After we got downstairs she looked at my fuck chair, knowing her ass was too big for it, and dissed it like it was the wrong-sized shoe. I gave her a moment alone to undress by returning upstairs to get her draws and the herb. Her panties were damp in the crotch. Big Mama must have honeyed them on the way to my place. I sniffed them good.

When I got back Verna had the light off and was lying buck naked under the cover. I stretched Henry to medium size, grabbed her hand, and put my dick in it. I told that ho, "My rod and my staff will comfort thee." Granny said, You ain't nothin' but the devil." I cut the light on and Verna cracked one eye open and looked at my prick pointedly. "It done got hard so I know what you wont me tah do," she said. "I ain't come tah do dat."

"Just lay back and let me mess. You can take the LSD later," I told her. She started giggling. "I heard 'bout dat stuff. I don't do no drugs," she said. I explained that the LSD I was talking about was LONG, STIFF DICK. Verna said, "It long alright."

Granny asked me if I had a rubber. "The only protection you need is how deep I'mma be digging that dust out," I told her. "I knows I needs to be fucked," she answered. "But I don't wont no VD." I told her, "Yeah, I got a rubber."

Verna's breasts got her hyped. While I was eating her pussy she massaged them violently. As big as her ass was, I found it strange she was that particular about her tits. I ate that pussy for a good while, trying to work the dust out that cunt while she mashed her melons. She wiggled like a person being tickled and I thought she forgot how to cum.

"Let me play in that ass," I told her as I tried but couldn't turn her ass towards my face unless she wanted to go that way. I had to guide her over. After I got Grandma over I put a fresh pipe of herb in front of her. "What you trying to do, git me drunk?" she asked. I'm gonna be busy for a while. Smoke dat while I do all ah dis heah," I told her.

I pulled Verna up on her knees and elbows with her ass towards my face. I yanked and her cheeks opened like cellar doors. That yank caused Granny to fart. Her puny pooter peeped, passed gas, and produced a sounded like it said "Poker!" or "Poke her."

I lost my mind.

She knew she had farted because the gale was strong enough for her to feel; the sound loud enough to hear; and stink bad enough to hang around. Yet she was experienced enough not to say anything. What happened was just between me and her anus.

Quickly I put my mouth where the breeze originated, licking that boodee hole for any residue. I let her cheeks flop closed and then pushed them against my head. While I was in there lapping, maw maw squeezed my tongue with her anus then made a break from my face.

Immediately I went head first back into that ass. Verna's boodee closed ranks so I head-butted that boodee. Whenever my lips touched her anus her hips squeezed my head.

I repeatedly had to pull my face out to prevent decapitation. She responded to one of my pullouts with a loud, long, fragmented, fabulous fart that echoed the word "Foot - ball."

Her farts were naming games.

I lost my mind.

This one was so stink it made Verna take more notice after I said, "Damn!" She told me, "I tried to move yo' head away." I opened her cheeks and kissed her boodee hole to thank it for the stinky. Verna must have felt like the fart and funk needed an explanation and blamed it on lima beans. "Let it go girl," I said. "I wont the duss and the fuss."

Granny changed the subject by telling me to fuck her. She didn't want her legs in the air and brought up the condom thing again. "If you want me to wear a rubber, then you put it on," I told her. Grandma didn't hesitate. She ripped the packet like a pro and dressed Henry.

Verna jacked and hand-stroked the dick until it was ready. I wont tah put this big dick in my mouff but my grandchild probably done dat," Verna confessed. I told her, "Not wit' a rubbah on it." Granny said, "I wont it in my mouff" twice more before she finally gripped Skeeter with her jaws. She quickly came off the dick and said, "Excuse me."

When she said that I thought she was about to fart again. But no! Maw maw put her dentures on the night stand.

That meant this ho was 'bout to put a hurtin' on Henry. Her head felt like crushing, wet pliers. Na-nah bit my dick with her side gums like she was gnawing on gristle and nibbled with her front gums on Henry like he was lobster.

I lost my mind.

"If we ain't gonna fuck then I need something to do," I told her. "I'm enjoin' myself," she responded with. "What you wont tah do, dah freaky deaky?" Without provocation, Granny maneuvered her ass over my face and shook "all dat" just above my eyes. It was jelly because jam don't shake like that. I rolled my face into her alley and was compelled to stay long enough where I was 'bout to suffocate. Injury to insult, that ho expelled a double-barrel fart. It said, "Bow - ling!"

I lost my mind.

It was the stinkiest fart ever released and tasted like onion. It made Henry recoil and shoot off a premee. "Don't shoot off," she said. However, the lingering smell of the fart and my licking her ass hole like I was getting cheese off nachos caused more premees.

"Let's fuck nigh," Verna said. I got between her legs, kissed the pussy, and stuck hard, straight-forward, determined to destroy dick in her taut, honey dried, pudgy pussy. Big Mama hollered, "Woo! Woo!" every time I jammed LSD into her.

After only a few strokes maw maw nutted. This ho hadn't been fucked in years and simple strokes broke the time vault. Henry didn't have much resistance after that. He was slippin' and slidin' and banging and battering. We had a good, sloppy fuck. I got all my dick into that ho. Her big hips tickled my balls and I busted a nutt as big as Brazil.

You remind me of my first husband," she told me as we rested. "He like did nasty stuff juss like you." Come to find out, her first husband shot and killed her second husband and was still in prison for it. I told

Verna I had thought about asking her to marry me. "Now that I know about your husbands, forget about it," I remarked. She got the joke.

I disposed of the condom and rolled a joint. She got up on all fours, putting much ass in front of me as I sat in my chair. I had to stop and love her hips. I couldn't help it. I parted her boodee and licked her ass hole and sucked all over her cunt. Granny said, "Roll the stuff. I ah keep back dare open. I know mens like to see dat."

That ho's arms were too short to split all her humongous ass. I had to help her get her cheeks apart. As soon as they parted that boodee hole winked before Verna farted again. The sounded effects vibrated off the valley walls of her hips as granny let out a series of gaudy gusts. Put together they sounded like, "Vol-ley-ball."

I lost my mind.

"You ought to feel better now," I told her. To divert my attention from the funk Verna got real. "You like fah me to pass gas?" I told her I liked everything back there. "I got gas bad," she warned. "Some mo' comin'. Put yo' face in dare when I tell you." Granny rubbed her stomach and clapped her hips, about to cause an earthquake, and told me, "It comin'. Eat it iffin you wont to."

I lost my mind.

I covered her ass hole with my face and granny blew her horn. With my mouth so close to her anus the fart emitted a taste more than a sound. It was brown, dark brown, if you can imagine flavoring a color.

Maybe it was the methane I inhaled that made me just stare at her butt hole like it was a picture in a precious locket. I felt faint as I began thinking about how my dick would fit between all that ass in her tight little boodee hole. She must have heard me thinking.

Verna said, "You kin put yo' dick in dare iffin you wont to. I done done dat be foe."

I lost my mind.

I jumped out of my seat and rubbed Henry on her pooter. I tried to get into that ass, pushing hard, but after failing Henry became limp. That ho just had too much ass. To keep from being embarrassed I told Verna I'd try later. I got up and got some towels.

Yes, I was going to get my 140 dollars worth. "Do what?" she asked. I told her, "Pee pee and pass gas at the same time." Verna didn't look at me like I was a sick bastard. She already knew that. She smiled and then moved relatively swiftly into position. "I ain't neh vah done nothin' like dis be foe," she said. "Me neither," I lied.

I was on the floor under maw maw's brownstone colored, dimple-covered, aged butt again and, again, opened her ass to make room for flatulence. I pecked on her boodee hole while I was waiting on some sort of commerce. "I kant piss why you doin' dat," she said.

A minute later she said, "It comin'." Na-nah farted on my nose and then immediately pissed in my mouth. The fart was nearly silent but swooshed out the word "Sock-errr"; still naming games. Damn that thing was stink. Her watering was wonderful but her fart was too short-lived. It was beautiful as I got both at the same time. I wanted her to try again. Glazed mouth and all, I told granny, "Let everything go. Act like you on the toilet."

Heaven on earth, that's what it was. Three streams of hot water fell from the crumpled lips of her cunt. I tried my best to catch every drop. I was able to keep her hips parted and watch maw maw's ass hole pulse. All I needed to put the cherry on top was one more fart.

Granny gave it up. It sounded like it said, "Base - ball!" and was raunchy as hell.

I lost my mind.

Just as I was about to lick her pooter I saw a turd at the edge of her anus. It looked like a paratrooper at the door, ready to jump out. I smelled it but there was no distinctive aroma that signaled it needed to be avoided. The visual, however, was enough. There's no way to get toothpaste back into the tube. She and I both knew Granny needed to take a shit. "I got to use the baff room," she said, as she hurriedly hopped up. I followed to watch her take a shit like I did her granddaughter.

To my surprise Granny sat on the toilet seat just like I do. I couldn't figured that out. She didn't have to divide her ass at all when it came time to take a dump.

"I told you I got to use the baff room," she said. "Go ahead," I told her. She gave me the "sick bastard" look then covered her face with her hands as she dropped a torpedo turd. It went quietly into the water as if it was evading sonar. The strain on her face told me she had another to be released as Verna rubbed her belly. "Hold me," she requested. I got on my knees in front of her and massaged her lower back as she dropped more heat.

"Woo!" she said, then pushed me away so she could rub her belly again.

Maw-maw sucked my dick while she was taking a shit. I really wanted to nutt in her mouth but the smell got real bad. As a matter of fact, wise old granny told me I would have to "burn some paper" to get rid of the odor.

The dump seemed to kill granny's high. She did allow me to nutt on her titties after she jacked Henry into a corner. Thereafter, she policed her teeth and left.

Tar Heel Tarts

POOTIE TANG

B ENEFITS. THAT'S WHAT serving in the military ends up being about, whether you get out dead or alive. A death benefit of $10,000 quiets widows. Benefits such as a free burial plot, unfettered college tuition, an unbound home loan, and available accolades for having "served" the nation make it arguably worth being demeaned for a relatively short period of time. Military personnel are pets performing for a treat, just like everybody else.

Tammy, who turned out to be a treat, was a benefit of me serving Dottie. The still-teen niece of Dottie's had settled-in at Duke University, had an open weekend, and wanted me to visit. Now far from home, part of survival mode for her fat ass included taking LSD.

On the phone she felt like she needed to explain why she called. "Terribly insufficient sexual intercourse remanded me, unfortunately, highly dissatisfied and unsatisfied," she said, before continuing her confession. "It has resulted in frustration. My concentration in class has wavered. My mistake was to generalized efficiency. He was a Black guy, but not a Soul Brother like you. After conferring with Dottie, we both concluded I need a good fuck. I crave capital cock, that's why I contacted you."

She went on and on for a good while then offered a final plea. "I need YOU. I have challenged myself to get all of Henry in me and MUST have your stimulating, wide nose in my ass again. I need to FUCK," she added. Her blatantly asking for my sniffer to languish in her boodee hole was bold of her. "You need to be with ME," she observed.

I got the message and agreed that I clearly carried the best remedies for her inability to enhance concentration on her studies. As she talked, my dick rose like an evangelist in the pulpit. Giving her an Amen, I told her I'd be there. I advised her to pretend her toughest class was my dick head and gobble it accordingly, until I brought the real thing.

During our conversation the following night, Tammy got all up in my business talking about what Dottie and I do. "I'm aware that you two have anal sex," she revealed. "Dottie says it's wonderfully personal. I want to try it." I warned Tammy that I sometimes get carried away during anal sex. "I want to conquer my inhibitions," her naïve ass said. "I want that and you to cum in my mouth," she insisted.

Saturday afternoon I picked up Tammy up on some corner near campus and we headed to a motel room. We both were uncomfortable at first. Being with a White girl in North Carolina was always a little nerve-racking for me. Tammy literally exuded nervousness.

At one point, the air in the car became stink. I thought it was because of a sewage treatment plant we were passing. Come to find out later, Tammy farted.

As she tried to divert attention from the funk with conversation, I learned that she had "insufficient" sex with a visiting relative of her Black roommate. "He finished in about two minutes," Tammy reported. I asked her if she had tried a White boy. "Oh no!" she cried out, "White guys are creepy."

Once we entered the motel room I did an inspection. "Let me see if you've grown any," I told her. I helped her pull her Duke t-shirt and bra off, revealing her very pale, now larger breasts. "They've gotten bigger," I said. "Make sure to give me a tittie fuck."

To my surprise Tammy was wearing a G-string on her huge white cheddar ass. The string underwear looked on her fat ass like lines drawn for plastic surgery.

TV helped the day. Watching football was something that kept me from nuttin' too quick. I gained an appreciation for time outs, injuries, and punts. Tammy recognized my interest and often had to divert my attention.

Once we were naked, she laid my family jewels in her palm like they were beauties from a bag of marbles. "I like Henry when he's hard headed," she said. "That's your dick today," I told her. "Make him hard headed." Tammy took that and ran with it. I was sitting on the bed, rolling a joint of course, and she pulled me backwards and put my face under her groin. She bounced Henry off various areas of her face before dipping my dick into her mouth. "I love how it expands," she said, as she admired her work.

All of a sudden Tammy popped up and went into the bag she brought and pulled out a camera to take a picture of my dick. "So I won't have to imagine what it looks like," she said. As long as my face wasn't in the picture it didn't bother me. She clicked out three pictures taken from different angles. I took a picture with her holding my dick with both hands "to get a perspective of how extreme it is," she said. Henry looked good on a Polaroid.

I was high, sippin' on some T-bird, with a horny, hairy teenage girl and occasionally peeping around the corner of her fat, wide, Caucasian ass to watch football while gettin' some head and at liberty to bust a nutt any time in her mouth. You couldn't tell me I wasn't livin' "large."

I blew a puff of herb off Tammy's fat ass and her boodee hole blew back at me. That ho farted directly onto my face just as the foot hit the ball on a Demon Deacon punt. The funk flashed like a math card. It's sound effects blurted, "Buffalo!" It was horribly stink.

Tammy asked, "You like that?" I favored the breeze but not what lingered and told her so.

"Dottie says you're partial to scents so I prepared prompt malodorous flatulence. That might be why it offends," she told me. "Offend isn't the word I'd use," I told her. "What in the hell did you eat?" I asked. Tammy laughed. "My roommate suggested cabbage," she answered. "Did yo' roommate tell you to fart in my face?" I asked. "No," Tammy said. "Dottie told me you envisioned any anal decoration produced as an act of grace."

Apparently Dottie didn't tell Tammy "the rest of the story." On our ride back from visiting D.C. I did confess to Dottie that I was partial to poots, but not from White women. No doubt, Tammy decided on her own to cross that line. That fart alone, coming from Tammy, was just as awful as the odor I encountered passing the sewage plant. "Did you cut one in the car on our way here?" I asked. "Yeah; want another one?" she replied.

There were multiple sarcastic repercussions to Tammy's funky flatulence. I would be unable to walk the Duke University campus because

I now had a fart sniffing rep. On campus, I would have to face students looking at me with a grin and an uncomfortable exotic curiosity. Also, Tammy's farts were so uniquely stink I associated hers to every White woman. I still believe all Caucasians hoes naturally have funky farts.

As Tammy blasted bombs unusual for me was that I didn't hope for one, at first. I always held my breath. "God, that's awful," she said after one of them. "Awful farts are awful," I told her. She seemed taken aback by the way I turned my head so I had to encourage her to ferment more farts. "Gas me when you feel like it," I told her. "I always say, wherever you may be let your fart fly free." I was on biological attack alert all day.

"One's coming," Tammy said. "Gimme your face." That girl exhaled a three-syllable fart onto my chin I felt. Although the immediate translation of the fart was that it stank, I heard it say, "Powder Puff." I asked her what "Powder Puff" meant to her. "That's the flag football league I play in," she said. "I'm on the Buffalo Bills."

"There's cum on your cock," Tammy said, before licking it off. "I'm not ready for you to cum. I don't want us to waste time because you have to rest. What you need is a good funky fart." I couldn't believe it when she tried and one didn't come. That ho grunted out loud. I hate a ho grunting out a fart in my face because more than gas is liable to escape.

Tammy was a smart girl. She knew one proven way to keep me from nuttin' was to distract me. One time she stopped fellatio and split the crack of her ass just to show me her anus. It looked like a cherry in vanilla yogurt. "Kiss my ass," she boldly told me. I love it when a ho tells me that but, instead, I inserted my nose. "If you put your nose in it, I can't fart," she explained. I had to comeback with something. "That's what I was hoping for," I told her. "You got me afraid of dying." That got another laugh out of Tammy. She was in a good mood, being the one doing all the farting.

She sat on Henry like she did the first time we were together. She put the dick head in, climbed off, sucked the honey off the dick, and put the dick back in. She repeated that like she was following somebody's instructions. I didn't know when she was going to climb off the dick, jack the dick, suck the dick, how much dick she was going to sit on, nor how long or deep she would sit on it. That ho even farted while she was poking my dick into her pussy.

Like someone had pushed a button, Tammy got out the bed, headed somewhere, and stopped in the middle of a step. "I got one," she said.

She put one foot on the bed while the other was on the floor, pulled my head towards her fat ass, directed my nose to the middle of her butt, and cut loose. It was a big one. It was a long one. My nose was so close to the funk for so long, the stank seemed to turn into a solid.

No way would a person break wind and it have such a lasting malodorous odor unless it was meant to be special. I didn't want to hold my breath anymore. I took it all in.

Tammy said, "Damn, that hurt. That has to be the last of it." No, no I thought; she couldn't be all done. I was reminded of a touchdown cheer in high school and told Tammy, "We want another one just like the other one."

Tammy headed for the bathroom. I thought she was going to take a shit after that last blast. I didn't particularly care for her doing that. That would probably result in green dookie on my dick when I fucked her in the ass. Instead, Tammy came back into the room with towels and the shower mat. What she was doing I surmised was something else Dottie had told her.

Tammy issued an order like a leader. "Get over here." Wont no need in me frontin'.

Tammy squatted over my face, pulled the G-string to the side, and looked down. "How you like it, intermittently or continuously?" she asked. "However you want to do it," I sheepishly said. She didn't respond, as if she knew I would take it "lying down."

She put the pussy over my mouth, bounced her jelly-stack cunt off my lips, and pushed out a quick shot of piss. Tammy stood up to see what she had done. I don't know why women do that. She squatted back down, took the time to line up her pee hole again, and more warm piss came out the pussy. It streamed like water with a finger in the hose.

One time she advertised her utilities like she was a Duke Energy representative. "Tell me when you want water or gas," she said.

Tammy experimented all day and it included something I had never had done to me before. She had me to turn towards the end of the bed on my belly where I could watch the game comfortably on pillows. She pulled my dick between my legs and sucked Henry with my ass in her face. That was new. That was different.

That's not all. Tammy rubbed my ass and back, giving me a massage like I had done her aunt and many other hoes. "Gosh, you're hairy," she said. The next thing I knew Tammy was splitting my ass cheeks open, inspecting my boodee hole. All of a sudden, to me, Tammy kissed my ass hole and stuck her sharp nose into the crack of my ass. I jumped. "Keep still," she ordered. She licked and stuck her wet, slippery tongue in my ass hole over and over. I squeezed my boodee hole and gripped her poker. It all felt good.

I only wish I could have farted. Lord knows I tried.

I tried to act as though what she was doing was no big deal but it was. I felt like a ho.

She sucked my ass like she was siphoning gasoline. I understood, then, what that girl in Lumberton was talking about when she said, "What you trying to do, blow my mind?"

She sucked my dick with her sharp nose in my ass. Henry was bent and twisted like a curly fry. "I'm ready to fuck," she announced as she got up, pulled her G-string off, and bent over the end of the bed. "Fuck me," she said. "Fuck me with that long black cock."

I entered with a hard push and Tammy's heels lifted off the floor. I was tearing that pussy up and talking smack as she appeared to be runnin' while I was hittin' it. I told Tammy, "Take that dick!" On the next down stroke, I said, "Gimme that pussy!" One time when she moved away I told her, "Bring it back heah." I spanked that ass each time she ran and each time she "backed that thang up." I was fucking that ho wit' attitude.

I was deep in that pussy when Henry coughed up cum. Tammy and I remained connected as she collapsed. Henry followed the pussy downward trying to make sure every drop of skeet got to the back of her belly, like he does when he makes a baby.

Between TV games, I went outside and got my travel tube of Vaseline. "I'm going to fuck that ass now and I've got something that will keep it from hurting." Tammy told me, "Regardless, if I say stop, you have to stop." I tried to assure her that I didn't intend to hurt her. Tammy looked serious when she said, "You told me that sometimes you get carried away during anal sex. I don't want any more than the nine inches you and Dottie agreed upon." This ho had analogized her ass as a parking lot with limited space.

I bent Tammy over in the doggy position and greased her ass hole carefully, unlike how I was going to stick dick. "I like your finger," she said. "Just finger me back there." I told her that she needed dick in the boodee and that she, after all, asked me to fuck her in the ass. "I know," she said, "but I miscalculated just how large you are."

After anal preparation, it was right after she pushed out a silent poot, while her boodee hole was puckered, that Skeeter slipped into her anus. She moved forward just a little but otherwise took the initial penetration well. For a while I left the dick head sitting just inside her anus, like it was a stick in mud. She reached back to feel how much dick was into her poot chute. "That's amazing," she said.

Henry looked pretty in her butt hole. The picture included a Black dick and a snow white, tundra-looking ass with a bright red anus encircling LSD. I wished I had her camera. I pulled out to see the gap I had opened in her boodee. Tammy acted like that girl in the movie "The Exorcist" when she looked back at me and said, "Don't take it out."

When I stuck Henry back in, it was much easier than the first time. "I'm ready," she said. "Fuck me back there. Fuck me in my ass." I was just-a stroking and she comes out with, "You must be hitting my bladder. I've got to wee wee." I kept my dick in her ass and told her she would have to piss while we were fucking because I wasn't going to pull out. She did. She wet the edge of the bed and I helped by putting my hand under her to direct the water. I nested a huge nutt in her butt while warm water rolled off my fingers.

We took a shower together and went to sleep. I woke up needing to take a leak. When I came back she put the dick on the boodee hole and started hunching. It wouldn't go in.

"Where's that stuff?" she asked. I got the Vaseline and greased her ass hole good. She took the dick she had been jacking while I was fingering her ass hole and guided it into her butt. When she reached her limit, she said, "Right there. Fuck me slow." All that fat ass; it didn't take long for me to bust a nutt.

The next time I awoke, hard as usual, it was nearly 11 a.m., checkout time. "It's time for us to go," I told her. "Fuck my breasts," she said. I put my dick between her titties as she mashed them against my dick. Henry punched repeatedly in her reddening neck. I wanted to nutt like that but I had to get that pussy "one more ghen." I stuck Henry in the cunt. "All of it," she requested. "I have to take all of it before we leave." We mated at maximum like it was mandatory meeting.

Eyes closed and huffing, Tammy took all the dick. My balls were wallowing in the fat of her pussy. She hollered while we fucked. She kept telling me, "Fuck me!" Each time I followed with a punch into her coochee she would say, "Uggh!" Before I nutted, I was able to pull out. I shot off load after load on Tammy's tongue. Henry painted her taste buds with cum while she was looking me dead in the face. I remember that nutt like I got it this morning.

I thought I'd never hear from her again but she called me a couple of days later. She told me she gave her roommate one of her pictures of my dick. "The one I have of Skeeter is my favorite," she said. "I'll always remember how it jerked on my lips when you shot off into my mouth. That was the best."

BORN YESTERDAY

A NYTHING DONE RECENTLY over a long period of time is routine. Highly skilled soldiers can become unmotivated when routine becomes monotonous. To combat routine turning into oversight, there is something called Temporary Duty (TDY). That's where personnel are assigned routine at a new duty station for a limited period of time.

Embarking on a libidinous mission at a new duty station can enhance motivation even if it's just a "wham-bam-thank-you-mam" or "hit-it-and-quit-it" operation. TDY can sometimes be so good a soldier requests that it become a Permanent Duty Station (PDS).

Permanency crossed my mind during my libidinous TDY mission with Crystal.

She was a fresh assignment with limited carnal knowledge but "in the end" she couldn't handled "it." One thing was for sure, once my TDY with Crystal was over she was definite about what libidinous actions she considered out of bounds.

Like me, she grew up in a small town where hypocrites determined what "normal" was and keeping libidinous desires in the closet was routine. She, like me, didn't want hometown people to even think she would freak. However, like me she had an innate desire to experiment. All she needed was for someone to ring her bell. I did.

I met her on my way to Charlotte at a Hardee's in Wadesboro. I was dressed like a routine soldier and she kept looking over at my table and it got my attention. She looked to be jail bait therefore a careful approach was my first move. On my way out the door I went over to her and said something like, "If you like what you see, I'd be glad to show you more." She replied very nicely, "Excuse me for staring. I've been thinking about joining the Army and wondered if you were from Fort Bragg."

I could only hope for TDY because I really didn't think much would come of our meeting. She was a routinely built girl with nothing to drool over except my imagining her big lips slurping on Skeeter. She showed some interest and some interest is all it took for me to act out. We exchanged phone numbers and I got back on the road.

On the way back from Charlotte, I made a stop to check out any likely TDY orders she would offer. When she answered the phone I felt her "why you calling me three o'clock in the morning" voice and told her, "I'll catch you on the rebound."

I was encouraged that next evening when she called me at home. Come to find out she was a very recent high school graduate. She had a car, a job at her family's business, her own place, and a boyfriend. However, she wanted to leave town "in the worst way."

She felt like me when I was 18. She told me, "I'm tired of school and books," as she explained why she was considering joining the military. I let her know how it was in the real world. "I know how you feel. I joined the Army because I was tired of school. Then, the first thing the Army gave me after my oath was a book."

We talked every night that week, eventually getting on the subject of her love life.

"What love life?" she asked me. "My boyfriend is in college in Atlanta so ain't nothing going on here." That's where she opened the door. It was just a small opening but I put my foot down so she wouldn't close it.

"You sound like you need some attention girl," I told her. "What you mean I need attention?" she asked. I really wanted to say she needed some dick but went about getting into her personal business carefully. "Everybody got needs," I said. "If you don't take care of those needs then you're liable to start unraveling like a ball of string." She didn't know I was also a practicing psychiatrist. She asked me, "What kind of needs?" as if she was interested in some of what I was selling. So, I went ahead and explained how she was holding honey that needed to be released.

I dug too deep. She didn't respond to that amateur assessment until the following evening to get clarification of what "honey" was. After

I presentyed more opinion and analysis of her previously unknown problem, we got into a deep conversation about sex.

My military training was clerical so when she described how she and her boyfriend fucked I filed her evaluation in the same manner I did the attractiveness of former First Lady Eleanor Roosevelt, under "Pathetic."

It was missionary position and she had never seen "him." I was like Sigmund Freud, bluntly drilling for issues. "That means you ain't never jacked his dick for him and he's never put his head between your legs?" I asked." She laughed then admitted she had never touched her boyfriend in that way. At first, I wondered how could the boyfriend call himself gettin' some pussy without either one of them first preparing the tools? Then I remembered my years of adolescent fucking. It was just like that.

Crystal's sex life had been in black and white with a Puritan director, an "Ozzie and Harriet" script, and silent movie props in her "Pre-Golden Age" of talkies experience. I had all kinds of thoughts about how to introduce her to "Disney's Wonderful World of Color." I felt like Henry was Quentin Tarantino. All I had to do was to get her into a theater and show her his work.

It was a saving grace she wasn't a virgin waiting on marriage to take part in a porno.

What, I think, sealed the deal was when I told her, "The Lord moves in mysterious ways."

I told her that our meeting was destiny allowing her to be enlightened. My diagnosis was enough to get her to come to Fayetteville to see me. I think partly she visited just to see if I was telling her the truth about living alone and that I had no "real" girlfriend because I traveled a lot. The other part of the circle was curiosity.

She was a nerd. Once she was seated I asked her, "What's the word?" expecting her to say "Thunderbird and herb" or "Rose and reefer." Instead, she gave me the look of a teen who had just found out what hot dogs were made from.

I was already high and horny when she arrived but was able to keep my lust on the down-low. She told me she could handle The Bird. "Okay," I said, "but the bedrooms are downstairs. When your head gets heavy, you don't need to be trying to walk down those stairs to find a place where you can lay down. Let's go downstairs now." She stared at me, grinned, and then lifted her victim vagina off the couch.

The signal to make my move came when her speech speeded and her eyes, bright and white as they once were, became bloodshot. I stood her up and grabbed all the African-American ass I could get between my hands and squeezed. There was no inhibition on her part. Her body was relaxed and that told me she was ready for Big Dick 101 instruction.

"All you have to do is say "No" and I'll stop," I told her as I kissed her on the neck. "I want this. That's why I came. I won't say no," she said.

A ho told me, "I won't say "No.""

Untouched, my zipper loosened as Henry almost jumped out of my pants. He became "fully" aware that Crystal had driven, round-trip totaling over a hundred miles, expecting to give him some pussy.

I unhooked her bra and fondled her breasts from behind. This girl didn't have titties. Crystal had firm knockers with perfect nipples. They distracted my attention like someone peeping in my window. "Let me see what you got in here," I said, as I unfastened her jeans. "You know what's in there," she said. "I'll bet you've been with a lot of girls."

The "been with a lot of girls" comment is a trap. I slipped past it by keeping my mouth shut until I was ready to gormandize her cunt. Crystal was wearing "Saturday" panties. I couldn't believe it. I had never seen "Saturday" panties on an actual ass before.

"Let me see what Saturday is like," I said, and then directed my nose towards sundown.

She seemed anxious for me to put my head between her legs. She spread them real wide, like I had a big head or she had taken to heart my advice that her man should put his face down there. Brushing my nose against her coochee while it was still covered was enough to get her to moan. I pulled off her panties and saw this girl had more hair on her pelvis than I had on my head. Immediately I began telling lies about my need for somebody permanent.

She didn't know I was like a croc on a coochee, attacking prey whenever one wandered my way. I handled that thing like it was a bad child needing a tongue lashing.

I wanted to do it right. I wanted her to be comfortable but also wanted to get my tongue deep in her slit. I didn't want her watching me. I wanted what I would be doing to be told by her sense of feel rather than sight. She kicked off her draws like they were uncomfortable shoes. That was unfortunate for me. I wanted her to see me sniff her panties to show just how freaky I was.

She had minimal ass so maximum tongue depth would be better realized by plowing her cunt from behind. Plus, I wanted to check out that boodee hole. Once I turned her over I kissed her black butt, two or three times, softly. I lifted her by the waist to put her on her knees and that coochee crackled when it opened like it was a new book.

Without even knowing what I was about to do, she told me, "Take it easy." Only one half of her request would be fulfilled. I was going to take it but it wasn't going to be easy.

I surveyed her property back there and found she had a bold boodee hole. Everything was buttoned-down, tight and neat. I looked new. It was beautiful. Her pubic hair was thick, soft, and shiny and thin bristles of it accentuated her ass hole, reaching the top of her butt. Her anus cracked a smile, as if it were saying "Hi!", like a familiar associate at a neighborhood store.

I told Crystal, "What I want is smiling at me." She asked me "What is it that you want?" I kissed her pussy and then her ass hole. "I wont all this," I told her. "I just don't know where to start." All of a sudden the boodee hole puffed up, like a body builder, reaching for my lips. Right then! Right then I wanted her anus to poot on my pucker.

I figure, if a nigga, wit' a hard dick doesn't want some pussy after a girl farted on his mouth, he didn't want any pussy in the first place. An unsolicited poot would have told me a lot about this girl's "natural" libidinous inclination. She didn't fart and that was the first sign that this was likely to be only a TDY assignment.

Crystal's boodee hole was a teaser. It flirted with me, snapping at my nose, winking occasionally, and just-a grinning. I was shocked, shocked at her anus' arrogance! All that reminded me, somehow, what my mother used to say when I told her I wanted something.

"Ain't no harm in wontin'. A wont leads to work," she always told me.

Humbled by an ass hole, I turned my attention to the coochee. It was hidden behind all that hair. I pulled apart its sides and that cunt hole widened, looking like the entrance to an underground chamber.

My mouth was like a raiding party looking to ravage. The clit lips were firm, protruding, narrow, and textbook quality. From hole to clit, I wolfed that pussy like it was expensive ice cream that dropped into my lover's lap in the bedroom. Crystal said, "Hmmm!" and pushed backwards. When I sucked it, I tried my best to crumple that cunt.

When I licked it, I tried my best to scrape any secrete. When I poked my tongue in it, I tried my best to get my tongue into the middle of her torso.

Crystal responded to my head by pushing back harder. I wish I could have studied her face but my nose was in her ass while my tongue was trenching her twat. She made huffing sounds, as if she was trying to fly. I felt her ass cheeks dancing on the sides of my eyes. With my nose plugging her boodee, I guess that pussy had to do something so it pissed. It wasn't a squirt. Fluid meandered out like a leak as she screamed, "Stop!"

Once I had her licked out she wanted to rest but I wouldn't let her. "That was good," I said, as I flipped her on her back and spread her legs. That pussy, hair, and boodee hole looked like a cultural exhibit of African cunts. I wanted to take-in all its festivities and began by peeling back her clit. That thing jumped onto my tongue like it had legs.

As I ate that pussy and sucked her clit, Crystal looked menacingly at me and began convulsing like she was having a seizure. "Eagle! Eagle!" she hollered. That ho was cumming. She had scored a second run and for the second time was putting out piss.

Although I thought I had her twat totally tongued, I couldn't catch it all. Excess juice jaunted off my chin and I must have sounded like a ho gagging on a dick trying to vacuum cream and water out of all that hair.

"You alright?" she asked. "I'm wondering about you," I told her, and then asked what in the hell an endangered species had to do with her cumming. She explained. "Eagle is something we were taught to say, rather than cursing, to relieve stress." Because she didn't apologize or even mention it, I don't think this ho even realized she pissed.

My oral sex fixation was rudely interrupted when Henry made me uncomfortable.

"Okay Henry," I told him, as I removed him from my draws. "You got choices but get the pussy first. Save the boodee hole for later." I challenged Henry to make Crystal holler out, "LSD, LSD," another endangered species."

Henry was about eight inches strong when I laid next to Crystal and began using him as a lecturer's prop. I did a "This is a dick and this is what you do with it," lesson while she listened. Poor thing, Crystal had no idea Henry was only at 75 percent. She probably figured that was as large as he would get. I put her hand around my teaching aid and told her how to grip it, shake it, and jack it.

"You want me to put my mouth on it, don't you?" she asked. "Only if you want to," I answered. "Ain't nobody in this room but me and you. Go ahead and have a good time — experiment," I advised. Crystal stared at my dick like she was being shown her assigned seat on the first day of kindergarten. "Kiss it. That way it will know you mean it no harm and it won't spit at you," I told her. "It'll spit?" Crystal asked. "Like a cobra," I answered.

"No wonder it looks like a big snake," she reasoned.

She put her lips tenderly on my dick head and Henry responded by jumping out of her hand. "Oooh!" a surprised Crystal let out. She held it tighter and then kissed the same spot, hoping to make it jump again. It did.

"Shake it," I told her. She gave a description of the dick after she did that. "It's like one of those corn dogs on a stick you get at the fair," she said. "The difference is that this dog will hunt," I told her. Maybe she remembered, her next time at the county fairgrounds, that clamping down on a tubular object in public gives perverts ammunition.

She didn't suck it, at first, and I didn't want to tell her to suck it. I was going to leave that up to nature. "It's a pickle sausage," I told her. "Do what you do with one of those."

Crystal locked her jaws down and slightly bit my dick. It was mostly Henry's fault because he swelled into her teeth. "Putting it into my mouth makes it larger," she told me.

She got the hang of it. She became so proficient so quickly that I was ready to move on to the next lesson. But Crystal's mouth wouldn't let go. When Henry gained full strength Crystal said, "It's a large snake!"

"That dick good, ain't it?" I asked her. She didn't want to remove the dick from her mouth so she just nodded. I told her, "Kiss that dick when you want it to know it's good.

Bounce that thing off your mouth when you want it harder. Grab that dick head with yo' lips and pull it when you want to give it a reward." Crystal did all that. When a drop of skeet formed, I told her to lick it off. "Get that girl," I insisted. Crystal licked the skeet pearl and tapped her tongue against the roof of her mouth. That ho said, "Dick is good."

She worked on Henry like she was researching her heritage. I was ready to bust a nutt.

"It's about to spit," I told her. She stared at the dick's pee hole, like she wanted to see it spit, and got scared. That ho handed Henry to me. "Here, do something with it," she said.

I should have shot off in her eye.

I hate it when people blow my high. I lifted Crystal's legs to put her in the buck and she stopped me right there. "Aren't you forgetting something?" she asked. I rubbed my dick head on the pussy, trying to make her as nonchalant as I was. She gave me a look that forced me to reach under my mattress and pull out a rubber. "You want it, you put it on," I said. This girl was absolutely excited to put a raincap on Henry. She did it carefully like she was preparing a concussion science experiment.

Dressed like it was a bad weather game, about four inches of Henry went into her coochee and stopped. I figured that was about how deep her boyfriend had gotten. I went to a spread offense, targeting my dick head from sideline to sideline, attacking with dinks and dunks of dick. Inch by inch Henry moved downfield, matriculating in her tight cunt.

As her cunt lathered LSD with honey, Crystal stared at my strokes like someone videotaping a police officer choking a citizen. No doubt, I was banging dem guts. At one point, she seemed to be trying to escape my dick's demolition by wiggling away. She was just-a huffing. Piss was wetting my dick and balls. Crystal kissed me dead in the mouth as our nutts dropped together. She may have been kissing me to keep from screaming, "Eagle! Eagle!" or "Manatee, Manatee!" or "Spotted owl, Spotted owl!"

Crystal didn't like anal sex and that's what prevented me from making our relationship permanent duty. I thought she was ready to commit to Henry and that meant giving up the boodee hole. Things were all discombobulated when Topper decided to play putt putt with her pooter. She squirmed a lot. When I did manage to get Topper in she quickly ordered his retreat.

After that, Crystal was scared to let my dick anywhere near her ass hole. That included fucking her pussy from behind. Also, she learned that my sucking her butt hole was a preliminary to my sticking dick in her butt hole. She loved sucking the dick and tasting sperms and got to the point where that ho would spit my skeet in her hand and lick it out.

"That's nasty," I told her. "I like it because it's salty," she said.

Eventually it became routine for Crystal to tell me she was "busy", "sleepy", "tired", "on her way somewhere" or "had company." I knew then TDY was over.

Tar Hell Tarts

ARRESTED DEVELOPMENT

EVERYBODY'S IGNORANT; NOBODY knows everything. For instance, come to find out Willie, my riding partner's married girlfriend had been up to criminal mischief. I found out about all this only after Willie asked me to take him to Raleigh so he could visit the lawbreaker at the women's prison.

It was summertime and terribly hot sitting in that parking lot while Willie took at least an hour to get in and an hour to visit. I must have made that trip at least three times, for a fellow airborne trooper, before I told him that something had to change. I suggested his girlfriend, Lois, find an inmate for me to visit. She did. It would have been more exciting if she had been a murderer. Thank goodness she wasn't.

Lois set me up with a girl named Veronica but, of course, everybody called her Ronnie. She was locked-up for the same thing Willie's girlfriend was in for - forged checks. It took weeks for me to see Ronnie because I had to be cleared for visitation. In the meantime, I was writing her.

The only thing I knew about her was that she was a convict, something I didn't want to bring up in the letters. She had been "detained" for about three months and, according to prison movies, hadn't had any dick. I thought I was doing a good deed by writing something she could masturbate off on. After about my third letter she wrote back that the guards read my letters before giving them to her. Ronnie said that my blunt brag and descriptive narrative of how I used my penis as a power tool was embarrassing, for her.

Soon afterwards, a uniformed guard approached me in the parking lot of the prison.

That blew my high. "Are you here to see Ronnie?" she asked. I told her yes, thinking she was bringing me my visitation approval. "You write a good letter," she told me. "Can you back up what you write?" I wasn't embarrassed. "I'm just a squirrel trying to get a nut," I answered. She told me, "You ain't got to wait on Ronnie. You can get one right here."

I had forgotten exactly what I wrote in those letters. I couldn't remember if I told Ronnie I wanted to suck her boodee hole or not. I couldn't confirm whether I suggested she pee pee on me. For the life of me, I couldn't recall if I ever mentioned farts. I definitely remembered harping on honey. Maybe just the fact I wrote that I was "packin"

was enough to get the guard interested. Regardless, there was a rump in Raleigh requesting LSD and I was a pusher.

The guard's name was Jackie and she gave me her phone number, address, and work schedule. As she walked away I evaluated nuttin' in that but I noticed her backside didn't have any jiggle. I thought maybe she had a girdle on. She didn't. When Willie came out I didn't tell him about the guard coming to meet me because I didn't want it to get back to Ronnie. That same Sunday night I called Jackie and we had "get to know" conversation. I drove back to Raleigh on Monday to get the pussy.

Jackie was a prison guard, not a Miss America. She was horny though. Before my butt hit her couch she said, "We talked enough last night. I'm red to fuck." Jackie was in a hurry to see, for herself, if my LSD was as advertised.

My prick had a little plumpness when I dropped my draws. "His name Henry," I said.

Jackie replied, "Oh, yeah." She yanked my dick and began checking its flexibility. She bent my brand like it was one of those glow sticks and worked her fingers over Skeeter like she was revolving a combination lock. As soon as she felt firmness, she grabbed my dick with her mouth and pulled her head upwards like she was coming out from under a bed. Henry reached eight inches, easy, before she paused.

Holding my dick like it was a sawed-off shotgun, Jackie asked me, "Where's the rest of it?" There's supposed to be more," she added. "I ain't comfortable," I told her. "You still have clothes on and I ain't touched nothing of yours." Jackie pretty much admitted she wasn't voluptuous. "I ain't got nothing special but if you want me to take my clothes off, I can do that." She only pulled her blouse and pants off. The little bit of skin I saw was enough for Henry. He grew. Jackie went back down and sucked more dick.

Once she got Topper "standing at the top" I lifted Jackie's head off my dick and stood up. Henry was arrowed towards Chapel Hill. "Are we going to do this in here and with clothes on?", I asked. Jackie reshaped her jaws to answer. Staring at my dick she ordered me like I was an inmate. "Bring that thing in here," she told me, as she guided me to her bedroom.

She got into the bed with her bra and panties still on. "How we gonna fuck wit' your clothes on?" I asked. "I'm enjoying what I'm doing," she said, and then added, "We gonna fuck. Don't be in such a rush." She went back to suffocating Henry. I'd seen her type before. She only wanted to suck the dick.

Then again, I thought, maybe she was waiting on the remaining daylight to extinguish before really getting busy. That made me concerned about what was on her body. Maybe she had a rash between her legs. Maybe her pussy was poor or, worst yet, tasteless.

Maybe she had one of those things that looked like a prune on her boodee hole. All kinds of things ran through my mind just because I was the only one with genitals exposed.

I kept pulling on her panties, hinting that I wanted her to pull them off. She repeatedly moved my hand. I laid there thinking about my gas money spent to be with this woman who had a brick butt and only wanted to use Henry as a peppermint stick. That girl slobbered on my dick and played with my balls until the sun went down.

Finally we undressed and I saw this ho had a bad body. Her titties hung like socks on a clothesline. Jackie bent over to remove her panties from her feet and come to find out one tittie, the left one, was collapsed. She didn't even offer a reason for her handicap.

Henry ignored the pancake tittie and reached for her throat via her mouth.

Trying to make her believe I hadn't seen the dead knocker, I told her, "I love ass. Put yours in my face." Jackie climbed on top of me into the 69 and put her butt right where I wanted it. I tried to open her cheeks to nudge at her anus with my nose and couldn't find any handles. Her boodee hole was like those people where she worked, on lock down. I wondered how in the world how she took a shit. I figured I would need a crowbar or a file in a cake to get her cheeks apart.

I didn't know which was tighter, her ass cheeks or labia. How in the hell piss got out, I wondered. The hair between her legs was rough and cropped close with sharp bristles.

When I mashed my face between her legs it felt like I was smooching a porcupine. The niggas she had been with must not have spent any time eating the pussy, and for good reason. That ho had steel-toed cunt lips with a Brillo border.

When I put my mouth on her pussy it seemed to surprise her. She stopped sucking the dick and looked back at me like she had caught me breaking into her car. In her effort to get right for cunnilingus, she pushed her ass further back and moved her legs. I was touched by Jackie's feet and they were soft as hell. I turned my head and put my nose on her arches and, sho' nuff, her gait mates were lovely. The toes were perfect; not too large and not sitting on top of each other. Even her heels were soft.

It took an airborne effort to get her ass cheeks to separate and my nose bumrushed Jackie's boodee hole like someone trying to get into a crowded elevator. You could tell she wasn't accustomed to getting her coochee kissed. She whimpered like a child who didn't get their face painted like all the others. When I dipped tongue into that coochee, she raised her head and made a sound like a pirate, "Arrgh!"

I flipped Jackie over into the buck just so her feet could rub against my face while I was stickin' dick. Getting into that pussy was like fitting a half-inch bolt into a quarter- inch slot. Henry bent a couple of times.

Jackie harassed Henry's hustle. "I ain't on birff control," she said. I kept pushing.

"Don't shoot off in me," she mentioned every deep dip. At times she would say, "You fuckin' me too hard." After that, she came out with, "I kant take all dat dick." That pussy was good-n-tight. In a tug-of-war between that cunt and Henry, I jammed much dick into that ho. Not all but much. When I was ready to nutt, I jacked my dick with her feet and cum rocketed towards her shins. Final shots were wiped on her toes, arches, and heels.

"You eat pussy good," Jackie awarded me with. "Do that som mo'." That pussy needed it but I was already concerned about how I would look with band aids on my lips.

As I waited for Henry to get back up after that tremendous nutt, I went downtown to carefully clean out what he had pulled out the pussy.

Afterwards I went back into the living room to smoke a joint. As soon as she entered the room, she hijacked my high. "What you gonna to do about Ronnie?" she asked. "I'm hoping to be with Ronnie," I said. "High you goh be fuckin' bouff ah us?" she asked. "I'll cross that bridge when I come to it," I answered.

For the next three months Jackie took nutts in her mouth, ass, or between her toes to avoid pregnancy. A month before Ronnie was expected to be released, Jackie claimed she she had begun taking birth control so I dropped armies of sperms into that bogus cunt.

Tar Heel Tarts

THE WRONG MAN

I COULDN'T WAIT. Whenever I watched Ronnie walk out of the visitation area, I envisioned how my dick would look climbing her back via her cunt. She was nice looking, statuesque, light-skinned, with long legs. She could have been a model. For a jailbird, her skin didn't show a blemish. She had a nice bump of butt and imagination told me I could get my tongue easily into the crack between the cheeks of her ass.

Visitation at the prison went on until Ronnie was scheduled for release to a halfway house. On her second day there, I picked her up and we went to a motel. During the ride, not a word was spoken. We both knew what was up.

We got into the bed without any conversation or amorous activity. She didn't have to get me hard. Knowing she hadn't had dick in nine months, Henry saluted the opening of her legs as if her coochee was the Star Spangled Banner. He had the bombs to burst and put that ho on notice from the get-go. The first thing on my body to touch her body was swollen, solid dick head.

Damn she was tight. She pushed me in the chest and told me, "Get me wet first." I didn't want lubrication. I wanted stubborn. I ignored her and penetrated, feeling the walls of her resistant yet yielding cunt collapsing. Henry was sliding into that coochee like somebody working their way through a fraternity hazing.

When I had enough in, for her, Ronnie looked at me for mercy. There's no mercy rule in the "big" leagues so I widen her legs and dove in harder. Ronnie pulled me down towards her, grunted, and dug her fingernails into my back. That was all she wrote.

I busted a huge nutt, like four Mason jars worth, that I happily wiped out the pussy.

Henry headed back in. "I see you ain't finished," she told me. "I gotta get it loose," I said. "It hurts," she retorted. "Take it out." I eased out and Ronnie pulled my dick from between my legs like she was taking a clarinet out its case and went face to face with Henry. "You got a big dick," she told me, as she took a "long" look at my penis. "You've got to be careful wit this thing."

His name Henry I told her. She wiped then kissed my dick and said, "Hi Henry." That along with the warmth of her mouth on my dick head made him feel welcomed. I was impressed with her fellatio as Ronnie knew what to do when my legs stiffened. That ho skint my dick back with two hands, wrapped her lips tightly around Skeeter with her tongue wiggling underneath, and let Henry ejaculate into her mouth like I was filling a cup. After I recovered, Ronnie went down on Henry again.

The day I picked Ronnie up to come and live with me I didn't know I had the upper hand in this relationship. I was her get-out-of-jail-early card and she was required to live with me as a condition of her parole.

At home, it didn't take long for me to begin inspecting my goods. I knew she had a hairy pussy settled snugly between her legs. Her clit was well hidden, prompting me to treasure hunt. I liked treasure hunting. I lifted her legs and the boodee hole appeared. I love it when an ass hole does that.

I asked her, "How you get a nutt?" Ronnie said, "Wait a minute." She got up and sat on my mugg facing me, exactly how Dottie liked to do, hunching her horn against my grill. It took a while but she finally nutted. After she rolled off I put my nose into her ass, tongue into her cunt, and licked all that out. She just laid there and let me.

Looking at her tight, fresh boodee hole got Henry harder than the rock used to build the Lincoln Memorial. "Leave my ass alone and loosen this pussy," she told me. I jumped into the coochee and before our fuck was over we worked about four different positions. I wiped creampie off and out the cunt like it was excess glue on an arts and craft project.

I got the boodee hole the very next morning but the beauty of it was how we nutted together. I got my dick head wet in the coochee and then put it in her ass. Skeeter made it just inside her muscle when Ronnie said, "That's far enough." I rubbed her clit and she started wiggling her butt and that got Henry deeper. Our nutts were announced only by our bodies and we both exploded at the same time.

This girl seemed to be a dream come true. She knew how to handle our business and pleasure. She allowed me to come and go as I pleased without issue. Affection and sexual intercourse was timely. Henry was unloading skeet with lava flows into which ever hole I desired. I didn't realize I had fallen in love until it was too late.

I continued to take Willie to Raleigh to see Lois but winter was nearing. Lois offered to introduce me to another inmate but there was nothing I could do with another woman with Ronnie around. I told Willie I wasn't going to sit in that prison parking lot anymore.

That's when he came out with much background information on Ronnie.

According to him, via Lois, Ronnie was convicted for forging her employer's checks for a boyfriend. That boyfriend was a soldier at Fort Bragg. That meant that Ronnie knew somebody at Bragg who she was once so in love with she committed a felonious crime.

Who knew what she and he may have been doing while I was taking Willie to Raleigh, at work, or out of town. I also wondered if the ex-boyfriend had been writing to her in prison and picked her up from the halfway house in Raleigh like I did.

I kept Willie's breaking news to myself until one day Ronnie brought up her old boyfriend. We were on the couch watching TV and she told me, "My last boyfriend liked for me to suck on him while we watched TV." I asked her what else she did for her ex- boyfriend but she didn't want to talk about forging checks for the nigga. I let her suck the dick though.

After that, I wasn't in the mood to have "concerned" sex with Ronnie anymore. In addition, I was getting pressure from Dottie who didn't appreciate my having a woman living with me. Annette was a bother, wanting to suck "huh dick" even though we were "off again." My baby mama in Charlotte didn't like a woman answering my phone and wouldn't give me any.

During our time together, I knew Ronnie had been talking on the phone with one of her ex-guards who lived in Raleigh. At the time I didn't know it was Jackie. I only found out which guard it was when I asked Ronnie for a "break." She made arrangements to spend some time in Raleigh with her former guard.

On the way taking her there, I told Ronnie that I wanted her to never come back. She said, "If I have to leave you, I don't want to live," and opened the car door and threatened to jump out. I told her, "Go ahead, you're the one that's going to get hurt." Thank goodness she didn't jump because she could have told the police anything.

Ronnie directed me to Jackie's house. I dropped her off at the curb and quickly pushed off, never seeing Jackie. That should have been the end of me and Ronnie but I had feelings for that girl.

I was craving her and ended-up driving to Raleigh for her affection. We couldn't fuck where she lived so she took me to some house that didn't have any power. It must have been below 32 degrees in that place when we climbed into bed under plenty of covers.

We snuggled up and my dick got hard. "I need Longer Stiffer Dick from you tonight," she told me at the top of a speech. "I want you to fuck the shit out of me. You've given me something special and I want to make sure I remember where it came from. I want you to make love to me like you've never done anyone before." Ronnie and I had the most passionate sex we ever had. She kept telling me, "Don't cum." I did.

The next morning Ronnie stuffed Skeeter into her anus and sat her ass over my dick where it could stretch. I couldn't see, only feel, because of the darkness and the cover. I felt her pelvis rubbing against mine while my big dick was in her boodee hole. I nutted with at least 10 inches of dick in her and it felt like our world's apocalyptic consequences.

A few weeks later I was back in Raleigh again looking for Ronnie. This time, she was obviously pregnant. She explained that she and the woman she was living with were going to raise the baby. I didn't ask her who the baby's father was. According to my up- bringing, that's a question a man should not have to ask.

Tar Heel Tarts

WEEKEND AT BERNIE'S

L OGISTICAL PROBLEMS AND scanty resources can cause bottlenecks in the successful completion of any mission. That's why fire hydrants were invented. Likewise, libidinous missions require critical components for "putting out fires." Therefore, it is necessary to know "hydrant" hoes.

On one occasion Bernice, the "Shamu" sized woman who cheated on her truck driver husband with me, was my fireplug. I was surprised at her call because previously she was afraid her thinner-half would see my number on their phone bill.

"What's up girl?" I asked, glad to hear from anybody at such a penniless time. "What up wit' you?" was her greeting to me. Then I got into her business. "Yo' husband gonna beat your ass for calling me," I told her. Bernice sounded like a child on Christmas morning when she told me, "I ain't married no mo'. My divorce was final yesterday."

She asked me for some LSD. "Come and see me," she said. Thanks a lot, I thought to myself. Here's a three to four hundred-pound woman, just divorced, and probably ain't busted a nutt since the last full eclipse. "I got gas to get there but I'mma need more once I get there," I told her. "You come and see me and I'll take care of all that," she offered.

I hadn't picked-up anything heavier than a spoon since the time I forklift Bernice's leg to get at her pussy. The ride to Spivey's Corner gave me time to figure out how best to "harpoon" a whale.

However, a more relevant thought popped into my head. I had a short time remaining in the Army and needed a back-up plan as to what I was going to do after terminating my service. I imagined that Bernice could be a step-ladder to my future by providing a temporary domicile. Like a poacher, I'd hustle an elephant if my future depended on it.

Bernice greeted me with the hug of a spinster aunt who had been waiting since the last family reunion to cop a squeeze. It was a huggy bear embrace. It was exactly what teammates would do if I batted with a runner on third in the bottom of the ninth in a scoreless, two-way no-hitter, seventh game of the World Series and laid down a perfect bunt. She was squeezing the shit out of me.

"I got some weed," she said, with the volume of someone talking as if a police officer was in the next room. "Since when you smoke dope?" I asked. "Ever since Lois been back," she answered. "Lois? Lois out?" I wondered aloud.

"Yeah, I'm out. How long you thought dey was gonna keep me?" was what Lois threw at me as she entered the room. "Hey, girl," I greeted her with, along with a hug.

"Where my dogg Willie at?" I asked. Lois and Willie stopped seeing each other while Lois was still locked up. Apparently his scanty resources prevented him from servicing her with visits after I plucked Ronnie from the "doll house."

"If it wont for me you in Bernice would dah never met," Lois broke a moment of silence with, as Bernice filled into her kitchen. "I always wanted to fuck you but I was fuckin' yo' friend. I ain't fuckin' him now." Upon her return, Bernice ratted out Lois.

"I knowed you was gonna wonna fuck him," she told Lois. "That ho a hooker. She sell ass," Bernice announced. I responded by saying, "People gotta do what people gotta do."

Lois said, "See, it don't bother him. Now let the man relax. He juss got off the highway." I told both of them, "Yeah, but I ain't that tired," and pulled my dick out.

Bernice snatched the dick like it was a sandwich. Lois responded as if she knew me well. "He ah freak," Lois said. "I heard how you got a big dick in fuck people in dey ass."

Playtime commenced. I predict that as soon as all 50 states legalize marijuana pollsters will find having a mate play with your dick while you're getting high to be America's favorite pastime. It'll reduce divorce rates. It's the only way televised soccer will catch on. Better is having two hoes playing "Pick-up Stix" with your penis.

Henry became stretched for success. "That dick long enough for bouff of us," Lois told Bernice. She used that as a "can I play with it too" request and both women were fondling Henry. "Who goh suck that?" I asked. "Move yo' hand," Lois told Bernice. "Move yo' hand," Bernice replied. "You know damn well you kant ben over to geh dat man no head," Lois told Bernice. Then Lois got on the floor on her knees in front of my lap.

Minutes later, Bernice told Lois, "You hurtin' him," because Lois was going to town on Henry. It was just a way for Bernice to get Lois to pause. "Come on, let's go in my room," Bernice told me. As she completed the puzzling process of getting her big ass off the couch, Bernice started pulling off the bed spread she was wearing. Her huge backside dominated my view. "I wont dat," I told her, as I squeezed her wall-sized boodee. Bernice said, "It wont you."

I was delayed when Lois quickly grabbed my dick and continued her blowjob. She did manage to get out a sentence. "She ready to fuck nigh. When you fuck her, don't shoot off," she whispered, as Bernice finally got around the corner. "I'mma let you shoot off in my mouff. You like that, don't cha? Don't worry, you ain't got to pay me." Again Lois was mentioning she knew something about what I liked.

When I walked into the bedroom Bernice was buck-naked on the bed with her legs spread. She definitely looked like she had gained weight.

I distinctly remember she had three rolls of fat between her chins and waists. Now, as she laid on the bed in front of me, I counted at least four bundles. I did remember how good it felt when I busted my nutt among all that lard. I undressed and aimed Henry into her Hoover Dam.

"Fuck me harder," she moaned. Easier said than done. I pushed and somewhere down there my dick head stopped. It was like her pussy had a LSD checkpoint. I did a bench-lift with her thighs, hit that pussy again, and must have struck a nerve because she hollered.

Fat was beginning to slip off my hands and I needed her legs as wide as could be. I decided to get Lois involved. "Lois," I called. "Com'meer." I gave Lois one leg and I held the other and it helped split the fat. Her belly was like a bounce house. I told Bernice, "Hold that for me." "Oh, shit!" Bernice cried out again when I hit it.

I noticed honey on Henry's neck and head. "I wont some of that honey," I told her. "Fuck me," she said. "He gonna geh you some head," Lois told her. "He like to eat pussy. Let him eat yo' pussy, Bernice." For whatever reason, Bernice didn't want head. She said, "I wonna fuck!"

How in the hell her obese ass was doing any fucking, I couldn't tell. I was doing all the work. I told her, "Calm down for a minute. I want to see what you taste like." I sopped up as much honey as my tongue could scoop. Bernice's honey was heavy as mayonnaise and tasted burnt. I got one more taste of it to be sure. I was right the first time.

Lois got wet from rubbing her cunt and watching Bernice take dick and couldn't resist wanting to fuck. "You niggas got me hot," she said, before dropping Bernice's trunk of a leg. It was a blessing when Bernice said, "I'm tired anyway." Lois took that statement and ran with it. She dropped her draws, and crabbed over Bernice's lightpole- size ankles. "Fuck me," Lois demanded.

I got behind Lois' charcoal colored hips and dipped my tongue into that pussy. This ho was sweet. She was also wet as hell. Henry went up in there faster than a race car at the checkered flag at Rockingham Speedway. That ho said, "Wooo weee!" when I lowered her ass and hit that pussy hard. It was a perfect shot, like hitting all-net from half-court.

I dug so deep in that cooochee Lois ran from the dick like she was an escaping prisoner. She scooted across Bernice's legs and exited on the other side of the bed.

Bernice laughed and told everybody, "Dat hooker kant take dat big dick." Lois looked at her and quietly said, "I don't wont him to shoot off in me," and left the room.

Bernice and I made "love." The reason I say we made "love" was because Bernice showed me, without telling me specifically, the way she and her husband must have fucked. Lying on her side and facing me, she raised a leg, lifted her bellies, and put Henry somewhere down there and started hunching. My dick was like a pig in a blanket. Now she was fucking! At one precious, wonderful, thank goodness moment she told me, "I'm gonna cum." I made it two orders of skeet and busted a nutt.

I went back into the living room, in my underwear, to roll a joint and Lois didn't say a word. Feeling my power, I began to verbally mess with her. "The dick good, ain't it?" I asked. She looked at me like she didn't want to give Henry any credit. "I'm scared of you.

You needs to put on a rubber," she said.

Later, Lois' fellatio got the dick back up while she was "toe up" from wine and reefer.

I reminded her that she owed me a nutt. She told me, "Com' on nigga. Let's fuck." We went into Lois' room and that ho bent over doggy style on the bed. I told Lois, "I know good and well you don't want this dick like that again." Lois said, "I know you like it like dis, nigga. Just don't nutt in me. You already got two people pregnant." I was stunned by her remark. "What you talkin' 'bout?" I asked. "Never mine," she answered. "Juss don't shoot off in me," she said.

Her boodee hole was looking so good. Playing with it, I measured to see how deep she would let my finger get in without lubrication. She responded by sounding like a snake, "Siss!" as I got the second knuckle in. "That's what you really wont, ain't nah?" she asked. "Not right now," I said. "Not right now."

I was buck naked on my knees, pulling on my dick, eating pussy, and sucking asshole when Bernice waddled into the room. I ignored her presence and kept right on doing what I was doing. I flipped Lois over on her back and put her feet in the air. That pussy was exposed like a houseplant outside in December.

Bernice held Lois' feet while I was eatin' Lois' pussy. Lois' boodee hole was going crazy, twerking on my chin. Lois started kicking her legs and Bernice told her to be still.

"He suckin' my ass," she told her. Lois moved my head to put her pussy against my face.

When she was about to nutt; I don't know how she knew it; Bernice told Lois, "Bust that nutt! Bust that nutt!" Lois did. I licked the honey out the pussy until all dat was gone.

"Ya'll done got me hot," Bernice said. "Come on, let's go in my room." In there, Bernice told me, "Do me. Suck my ass." I did.

She arranged me under her blob of a butt in the 69, just like we had done on an earlier visit. I know what an egg feels like under a fat hen. I saw her blotter of butt coming and took a deep breath. I stuck my tongue in her pooter and vacuumed her anus. She was saying something but I couldn't hear.

Lois may have saved my life when she came into the room and started laughing at how we looked with Bernice sitting on my face. With Lois' laughter, Bernice paused and I took advantage of the moment to escape. I guided her over on her side and went to sleep with my dick somewhere stretched-out within the Prime Meridian of her heavy hips.

I woke up on the edge of the bed, nearly off it. I got my travel tube of Vaseline out of my pants pocket but Henry couldn't find the exact spot between Bernice's universal ass. I went into Lois' room. She was lying naked on her side with her legs partially split. I divided her ass cheeks, exposing her boodee hole to my tongue. When I sucked her anus, Lois responded with "Ummm" and began wiggling.

I cut a lamp on. "You like to look at it, don't you?" she asked. I didn't say anything. I put Vaseline on a finger and rubbed the tight crack in her butt. "Sssss," she said. "Why you like fuckin' people in dey ass?" she asked. "It's tight and I can shoot off in there wit'out causing problems," I answered.

Lying on my side, I put my dick head on her boodee hole, rubbed Skeeter up and down, slightly in and out, and pressed. "It gonna hurt," she said. "It's already in there," I told her. "The hurt is over." That must have relaxed her. I punched in the ass hole deeper and Lois started shaking like she was freezing. In a whisper, Lois said, "You got a big dick." She sounded like she was in discomfort yet sexy.

To keep myself from busting a nutt, I put something else on my mind. I asked her how she knew so much about how I liked to fuck and what "two people" I had pregnant. While I was stroking her boodee, Lois told me that both Jackie and Ronnie were pregnant from me. "You know

214

they live together, don't you?" she asked. "Jackie due to have huh baby foe Ronnie, post to be, but they don't know who gonna be first."

Thinking about what Ronnie said to me the last time we fucked, my mind went elsewhere, my dick softened, and Lois was able to shit Henry out. I had to take a break after that.

I went across the hallway to the bathroom. Bernice was snoring loudly. I got back into the bed with Lois and got Henry back up. Taking advantage of the lubrication still on her ass hole, I slipped my dick back into darkness. "Buss a nutt so I kin go back to sleep," she said. I did.

Henry was "woe out." After breakfast I gave Lois some great head. She busted two nutts in ten minutes. While she rested I licked her ass hole with long strokes. "Try to fart," I told her. "Lois said, "What?" I repeated my request. "I like to see your ass hole moving but you better not fart in my face girl," I told her. Lois' anus began exercising on my tongue. "Pinch it," I told her. "Pinch my tongue with that boodee hole." She did.

Bernice was watching like she was flipping the channels and stumbled upon a National Geographic documentary on the copulation habits of homosexual hyenas.

Printed in the United States
By Bookmasters